THE SISTERHOOD

G000067009

Also by Sara Fraser

In the Tildy series:

TILDY

POORHOUSE WOMAN

NURSING WOMAN

POINTING WOMAN

RADICAL WOMAN

GANG WOMAN

WIDOW WOMAN

INVINCIBLE WOMAN

THE BITTER DAWNING

THE HARSH NOONTIDE

THE SUMMER OF THE FANCY MAN

SARA FRASER

The Sisterhood

WARNER BOOKS

A *Warner* Book

First published in Great Britain
by Little, Brown in 1994
This edition published by Warner in 1995

Copyright © Roy Clews 1994

The moral right of the author has been asserted.

A CIP catalogue record for this book is
available from the British Library.

ISBN 0 7515 1136 6

Printed in England by Clays Ltd, St Ives plc

Warner Books
A Division of
Little, Brown and Company (UK)
Brettenham House
Lancaster Place
London WC2E 7EN

Introduction

In the England of 1906 women were treated as an inferior breed. Many docilely accepted such treatment as their fated lot in life. But there were other women who fought against that fated lot, and demanded justice and equality with men.

These women who fought came from widely diverse backgrounds, and their battle for equality took very different forms, yet essentially they were one sisterhood.

Chapter One

Redditch, Worcestershire. Late June, 1906.

The lengthening rays of the late afternoon sun shone dazzlingly on the closed casement windows of the opulent house. On the roadway in front of the building swathes of straw had been spread thickly to deaden the sounds of horses' hooves and iron-rimmed cartwheels, and passers-by knew when they came to that makeshift carpeting that within the walls of that house a human life was approaching its end.

In the large drawing-room that fronted the roadway several well-dressed men and women were gathered, sitting stiffly, facing inwards upon an arranged circle of ornate chairs in a muted atmosphere of strained expectancy. Before the window on a chair, set as if in deliberate withdrawal from that circle, an elegantly-gowned young woman of startling physical beauty sat half-turned away from her companions, her gaze fixed upon the outside world beyond the drawn net curtains. Within the circle hostile eyes continually glanced towards her then roamed and met each other in brief meaningful exchange; and then abruptly broke away from that exchange as if their owners were afraid of being detected in their unspoken condemnation.

The door of the room opened and an elderly, frock-coated man entered. His entrance created a rustle of movement and intakes of sharply drawn breaths among those already within the room. With a grave expression the elderly man approached the young woman seated near to the window and said quietly, 'It is with profound regret

3

that I have to tell you, Mrs Josceleyne, that your husband's end is very near. He has indicated that he wishes to speak with you.'

Her face betrayed no expression, but as her black eyes fixed upon the man he experienced a sense of shock, as for a fleeting moment he thought he detected a gleam of exultation in their shimmering depths.

'Thank you, Doctor Pierce, I'll come up directly.'

As Emma Josceleyne rose to her feet and shook out her long skirts a hugely fat woman erupted into noisy sobs, and one of the men present declaimed sonorously: 'It is a most tragic loss! Tragic!'

Emma Josceleyne directed a contemptuous look at the speaker and followed the doctor towards the door.

Another of the women questioned: 'Has not Hector asked for anyone else, Doctor?'

The doctor shook his head. 'No, Mrs Fleming, he asks only to see Mrs Josceleyne.'

The woman's hatchet features frowned and she sniffed indignantly. 'Well I declare! Whatever is this world coming to!' She nodded her head angrily, causing the long plume of feathers upon her large hat to bounce in furious motion. 'Hector must be under some form of duress to behave so. I find it impossible to believe that he has not asked for his own flesh and blood to be with him in his final moments.'

Emma Josceleyne paused and told the woman scornfully, 'Hector couldn't abide you when he was feeling well, Aggie Fleming, so I'm not surprised that the old bugger doon't want you near him when he's drawing his last breaths.'

A concerted exclamation of shocked outrage erupted from her listeners, and with a hint of a smile quirking the corners of her full shapely lips Emma Josceleyne swept from the room in a frothy swirl of silken-laced petticoats.

At the foot of the staircase in the large hallway, a fat middle-aged woman wearing the voluminous white apron and antique mobcap of a cook stood flanked by two young pert-featured maidservants, smart in long-streamered lace caps, high-bibbed aprons and black dresses.

4

Emma Josceleyne smiled gaily at the older woman as she passed and told her, 'You'd best send one of the girls to fetch your old man, Mrs Elwood. He'll be needed shortly.' She winked broadly, and added in a lower tone, 'And you can get the bottles and glasses out ready as well.'

Mounting the stairs ahead of her the medical man overheard the words and frowned with disapproval at the light-hearted manner of the soon-to-be widowed Mrs Josceleyne. Although he might well understand the reasons for the young woman's attitude, nevertheless he considered that the correct proprieties should be observed in the presence of imminent bereavement.

Hector Josceleyne was laying on his back, his skull-like, waxen-skinned bald head propped up on pillows. He breathed stertorously through his gaping toothless mouth, and though his sunken eyes were closed his shrivelled, claw-like hands moved restlessly over the top of the counterpane, plucking at the thick material as if it were the strings of an instrument.

Emma's puckish sense of gallows humour irresistibly impelled her to think, 'Just look at him! The old sod's practising playing his harp already.'

The doctor moved to the side of the bed and bending low spoke into Hector Josceleyne's hairy ear.

'Mr Hector, your wife is here.'

There was no sign of any reaction to the words from the dying man, and the doctor repeated himself in a louder voice.

'Mr Hector, your wife is here.'

Although Emma Josceleyne was young in years, she was old in the ways of death and could recognise its onset. When the doctor once more tried to rouse her husband she intervened.

'Leave him be, Doctor Pierce. Let him go in peace.'

The medical man regarded her ambiguously, and there was irony in his voice as he accepted her command. 'Very well, Mrs Josceleyne. No doubt it would be kinder to let him be. Perhaps he deserves peace in his last moments.'

The young woman's shrewdness detected the veiled gibe, and her dark eyes sparkled with quick resentment.

5

'Does you expect me to act the hypocrite like those buggers downstairs, Doctor?' she flared. 'Well that's the last thing I'll bloody well do.' She pointed one shapely, beringed hand at the dying man. 'He was a bad old bastard when he was living, and just because he's dying it doon't alter that fact.'

'There is the question of due propriety to be observed, Mrs Josceleyne: if only to show a decent respect for his surviving kinfolk,' the doctor pointed out acidly.

'You knows what you can do with your due propriety, doon't you. You can shove it wheer the monkey shoves his nuts!' Emma retorted scathingly. 'And as for his surviving kinfolk, there aren't one on 'um who doon't hate the old sod, and God only knows he give 'um good cause to do just that.' As her anger fuelled upon itself, the young woman's speech became an increasingly strident betrayal of her lowly origins.

Suddenly the dying man cried out and his rheumed eyes opened and fixed upon the flushed face of his wife. 'Take your clothes off and come to bed you damned prick teaser,' he ordered in a strong clear voice, then his eyes rolled upwards, his head lolled to one side, and his life left him in a drawn out gurgling of breath.

Doctor Pierce placed his ear against the shrunken chest, then felt for the carotid artery at the sides of the wattled neck. He shrugged and shook his head.

'It is over.'

He closed the lids over the dead eyes, arranged the arms across the chest, straightened the lolling head upon the pillows and gently drew the sheet up and over the lifeless features.

'I'll send the death certificate to you this evening, Mrs Josceleyne.' His professional instincts reasserted their hold upon him. 'Now, if you are in need of anything to enable you to bear your grievous loss,' he offered in unconscious irony, 'I can prescribe something to help soothe you in this hour of tragic bereavement.'

It was Emma Josceleyne's turn to smile ironically at her companion. 'No thank you, Doctor. I have everything I need right here in this house. I shall bear my loss well enough.'

'Then I'll bid you good-day, Mrs Josceleyne,' he told her stiffly.

She nodded absently. 'Good-day, Doctor.'

After he had left the room she moved forwards to pull the covering sheet from her husband's face. To her own amazement a fleeting sense of loss struck through her. In a perverse way she had been quite fond of this wicked old man. On impulse she bent and briefly touched her lips to the waxen forehead.

'Tarraa you bad old bugger,' she whispered, then smiled and patted the withered cheek. 'I'll bet you'm already trying to get your hand up somebody's skirts wherever you am right now.'

Mrs Elwood came into the room. 'He's gone then, has he?' She pursed her lips as she regarded the dead man and declared with heartfelt feeling: 'Good riddance to bad rubbish!'

Emma smiled wryly as she rearranged the sheet over Hector Josceleyne's head, and reproved half-jokingly, 'Now, now, Mrs Elwood, it doon't do to speak ill of the dead!'

'Phooo!' The fat woman expelled a noisy gust of derision. 'How could I ever find anything good to say about the evil old sod!'

Emma straightened and grinned at her companion. 'Well, to start with, theer's a couple of bottles of finest gin that he paid for, that you, me and the girls are going to be getting stuck into in very short order. You can thank him for that, at least.'

'All right then.' The fat woman chuckled hoarsely and told the shrouded head: 'Taa very much, Hector Josceleyne. And when I'm drinking the gin that you'se provided I'll wish you good health and good luck.' She paused and grinned ruefully. 'Mind you, it's a wee bit late to be doing that, aren't it.'

The two women returned downstairs and while the cook went into her kitchen to lay out the bottles of gin and glasses, Emma went back into the drawing-room.

Doctor Pierce had already told the gathering of Hector Josceleyne's death, and they had reacted to the news as

7

propriety demanded. Emma found the women crying noisily, and their menfolk wearing well-assumed expressions of grief being bravely borne.

'And how will poor dear Miriam and poor dear Franklin bear up when they receive this dreadful news?' Agatha Fleming was loudly bewailing, referring to the dead man's adult children who had both moved away from the town to live in other parts of the country.

'Very easily I should think!' Emma snapped tartly. Then as all eyes swung to her she ordered: 'I want you all to leave my house immediately. You're not welcome here. Any of you.' She called to the wide-eyed maidservant who was hovering in the hallway: 'Becca, bring the gentlemen their hats and gloves will you. They're leaving directly.'

At first the sheer shock of this dismissal engendered silence, then Agatha Fleming's hatchet features reddened with rage. 'How dare you?' she challenged indignantly, and a rumble of support sounded around the circle. 'Who do you think you are talking to?'

Emma grinned broadly at her challenger. 'Oh I know very well who I'm talking to, Aggie Fleming. I'm talking to a load of bloody hypocrites and mean-souled, cadging bastards, whom only here to see what they can get out on it for themselves.' A hiss of menace entered her voice. 'Now bugger off, afore I puts you out wi' my boot up your arse.'

Her bold black eyes traversed the faces of the others. 'And that goes for any one on you. For theer's not a man among you who can match me if I loses me rag.' Her voice rose to a strident shout. 'Now gerrout, all on you, and doon't you come near this house agen!'

With glares and mutterings of pure hatred the gathering trooped from the room and out of the house. Doctor Pierce was the last to leave and at the outer door he turned to ask Emma with an air of puzzlement: 'Why have you so wantonly created so many new enemies for yourself, Mrs Josceleyne?'

Hot colour burned in her cheeks and her eyes were fiery, but she replied in even tones. 'They'm not new enemies I've created, Doctor Pierce, they'm all very old enemies o' mine . . . and I doon't include you in with that

8

bloody lot. You'se always been a good decent man.'

Still puzzled he shook his head. 'I do not understand what you mean. Old enemies? How can that be? I doubt that you have even met some of them before this day?'

'I doon't have to have met 'um before to know that they'm old enemies o' mine,' she stated firmly.

'That is nonsense!' he exclaimed irritably.

'Oh no, it's not a nonsense!' she declared emphatically. 'It's not a nonsense if you was born and bred in Silver Street like I was. A kid brought up in Silver Street soon comes to know who its enemies am, old or new.'

Comprehension dawned in the man's eyes, but still he argued. 'I appreciate what you are saying, Mrs Josceleyne, and I accept that Silver Street is a truly vile slum. But you are no longer living there, are you. You are now a woman possessing considerable wealth, and you could attain high social position in this district should you so desire. You have left your lowly origins far behind you now, Mrs Josceleyne. You have left the Silver Street and all that it stands for.'

'Oh no, Doctor Pierce, I haven't left the Silver Street behind me.' Her voice held a positive certainty. 'And I've no wish to leave it behind me. I'm not ashamed of wheer I've come from and I'm not ashamed of my own people. I'm from the Silver Street and I'll never deny that fact, and them that doon't like it can bloody well lump it.'

The man shrugged helplessly. 'I fail to understand why all this should drive you to needlessly offend those who dwell in the circles that your marriage has raised you to, Mrs Josceleyne. It is not their fault that you were born and bred in Silver Street.'

'Maybe not, Doctor, but it's the fault of them and those like 'um that Silver Street and all the other streets like it in this town still exists like they does.'

Again the man shrugged. 'I must confess that there might be some degree of truth in what you say. But I fear that in this world there is nothing that either you or I can do to alter the way things are.' He smiled bleakly at her. 'All the Crusaders are long dead and buried, Mrs Josceleyne and the Holy Land is under the rule of the heathen.'

He lifted his top hat. 'I'll bid you good-day, and if I can be

9

of any further service to you at this time, then please do not hesitate to send for me.'

'Thank you, I will, Doctor,' she told him sincerely, and they parted.

Emma was still sufficiently bound by convention to move through the front rooms of the house and draw the heavy drapes across the windows to mark the presence of death within its walls. Then, the task completed she went down to the kitchen to find that Mrs Elwood's husband, who was employed by one of the local firms of undertakers, had arrived accompanied by the maidservant sent to fetch him.

'Does you want me to lay the old man out now, my duck?' he asked.

Emma nodded. 'If you will. And when you've finished you can come and have a drink with the rest on us.'

She looked at the bottles and glasses placed ready for use upon the wide white-scrubbed table and grinned mischievously at Mrs Elwood and the two maidservants. 'Right then girls, let's have a drop of "mother's ruin" shall we? Happy days are here again.'

The two young maidservants gazed at their mistress with admiring awe, and their eyes sparkled and they giggled in delighted unison as Emma handed them each a glass full of gin, then lifted her own glass and proposed. 'Here's wishing good luck and a safe journey to old Hector wheersoever he's bound for, heaven or hell.'

'It's got to be hell,' Mrs Elwood observed positively, then drained her own glass, and smacking her lips with satisfaction held it out for a refill.

She sipped at the fresh supply and then asked, 'When 'ull the funeral be, Emma?'

Emma shrugged her elegant shoulders and reflected for a moment or two, then informed casually, 'About a week from now probably. I'll telegraph Miss Miriam and Mister Franklin presently and give them the good news.'

There was an envious gleam in the older woman's eyes as she remarked, 'Well, at least you wun't be on tenterhooks to hear the will read, 'ull you, my duck. You already knows that everything's bin left to you, doon't you.'

There was savage satisfaction in Emma's expression as

she nodded. 'Oh yes. I knows what's in the will all right, Mrs Elwood. Everything that the old bastard owned comes to me.' A momentary bitterness hardened her features. 'And Christ only knows I paid a hard price for what he's left me. It's near on four years since I got wed to him aren't it.'

The older woman nodded agreement. 'Ahr, so it is my duck. Four years almost to the day, it must be.' She grinned salaciously. 'He had his bloody money's worth, didn't he?'

In her mind Emma relived the seemingly endless hours she had spent satisfying her dead husband's insatiable sexual appetites, and she shuddered involuntarily at the memory of his claw-like hands and wet lipless mouth ravaging her intimate flesh.

Mrs Elwood shrewdly divined her young mistress's thoughts. 'It's over and done wi' now, my duck, like I told you it soon 'ud be. And just look at you now. Twenty-two years old, and a rich widow. The world's your oyster now, aren't it. You can take your pick and pay whatever it costs with ease. You'm a lucky young 'ooman, so you am.'

Emma thrust her disturbing memories back into the recesses of her mind and smiled triumphantly. 'I know that, Mrs Elwood. I'm my own mistress now.' The hardness re-entered her eyes and when she spoke it was as if to herself. 'And I'll never again in my life call any man, master. That I swear.'

Chapter Two

The Clee Hills, Worcestershire.

The postman was sweating in his thick blue serge uniform as he trudged up the steep narrow lane towards the small isolated cottage tucked into a fold of the hillside.

In the front garden of the cottage Miriam Josceleyne sat on the low wooden bench, her back against the gnarled trunk of an ancient yew tree and with eyes closed enjoyed the warmth of the sun upon her face and the peaceful tranquillity of the summer day.

'Arternoon Miss Josceleyne.'

The man's rustic burr brought Miriam from her reverie, and she blinked against the sun's brightness as she focused her gaze upon the sweaty red face beneath the peaked shako.

'Good afternoon Mr Simpkin.'

'Got a telegraph message for you, Miss Josceleyne.' His expression was concerned, for he liked this quiet, frail little woman and he knew the contents of the telegram.

He came up the pathway and held out his receipt book together with a stub of pencil. 'If you could just sign here for it, Miss, I'd be grateful.'

She signed and handed the pencil back to him with a smile, then took the small brown envelope from his thick fingers. 'Thank you Mr Simpkin.'

He cleared his throat and shuffled his feet, then offered tentatively, 'I'd best wait to see if theer's any reply needs to be sent, Miss.'

'Very well Mr Simpkin.' She smoothed the flimsy sheet of paper and her faded green eyes scanned the words printed upon it.

She emitted a faint gasp of shock and raised one thin hand to her lips.

The postman coughed uneasily. 'It was sent yesterday evening, Miss Josceleyne, to Cleobury Mortimer. I ne'er got it until this morning, that's why theer's bin a bit o' delay in bringing it to you.'

The woman drew a long shuddering breath, and made a visible effort to master the shock of the message.

'Am you all right, Miss?' the man questioned.

She drew another long deep breath, and then replied evenly, 'Yes. Yes thank you, Mr Simpkin. I am perfectly all right.'

'Will theer be any reply, Miss?' he asked tentatively. 'Only I doon't want to werrit you at this time, but I'se still got me rounds to finish.'

She began to shake her head, then abruptly stilled that motion and told him hesitantly, 'Reply ... yes ... er ... yes.'

'I'se got an answer sheet here wi' me, Miss Josceleyne.'

'Thank you.'

Rapidly she printed: 'Received your sad news. Shall attend funeral.' She addressed it to: 'Mrs Emma Josceleyne, Cotswold House, Redditch.'

When the postman had been paid and had trudged away down the lane, leaving her alone once more, Miriam again devoured the telegram with her eyes, reading over and over the few words contained in it as if there was some hidden meaning in their content which she could perhaps discover. But there was nothing hidden there. Only a stark message.

'Mr Hector died this afternoon. Funeral to be held one week from today. Emma.'

Now that the initial shock had worn off Miriam was able to examine her own feelings, and found that there was no grief for her parent in her heart. Hector Josceleyne had been a harsh, unloving, tyrannical father who had long since destroyed any filial love that Miriam had felt towards him. There were faint regrets for what might have been, but she dismissed these as soon as they arose as being merely an exercise in futility. But as the minutes passed

13

and lengthened, an ever-increasing dread began to dominate Miriam Josceleyne; the dread of returning to Redditch after an absence of nearly two years; of returning to the scene of her shame; the scene of her degradation; the scene of bitter, heartbreaking memories. She physically trembled, and her eyes filled with tears as those memories now flooded back to rend her once again.

'No, no, no,' she whispered brokenly. 'I can't go back there. I can't. I can't. I can't.'

But even as she uttered those denials, she knew that she would go back because she was unable to fight any longer against the all powerful urgings of emotions that she had for so many many months tried fruitlessly to suppress.

Chapter Three

Miriam Josceleyne got down from her hired carriage and stood for several moments gazing at the front of Cotswold House, strangely nervous of entering the wrought iron gate and going up to the pillared portico of the front door.

'Shall I bring your box into the house for you, Miss?' the carriage driver asked.

She shook her head. 'No. Can you wait here for me please?'

The man grunted in grudging acquiesence. It had been a long day and he was anxious to be paid and begin the long journey home to Cleobury Mortimer.

Miriam drew a long ragged breath and nerved herself to face what she feared would be an ordeal. She pushed the gate open and crossed the stone-flagged space to the portico steps. She was not aware of the drawn curtains being twitched aside in the front drawing-room and the eyes that followed her brief progress. She tugged the brass bell-pull and heard once more the familiar discordant jangling of the cracked old bell. Her lips quirked mirthlessly as she thought how strange it was that she should now have to stand like a stranger before the door of her lifelong home and wait in uncertainty to find out if she could gain admittance.

'Miss Miriam, it's lovely to see you. Come in, doon't stand theer like a stranger. This is still your home you know.' Emma Josceleyne beamed in welcome and reached out her hand to draw the other woman into the shadowed hallway. She peered out at the waiting carriage, then ordered the two maidservants who had come to stand behind her. 'Milly, Becca, get Miss Miriam's baggage and

15

see how much the driver wants.'

'Oh no, I couldn't.' Miriam began to protest, but the younger woman completely disregarded her words and talking volubly drew her through the hallway and into the drawing-room.

'It's lovely to see you again, Miss Miriam. I'se thought about you manys and manys the time, and me and Mrs Elwood has talked about you often, and wondered how you was going on.' She broke off to shout loudly towards the rear of the house. 'Mrs Elwood? Mrs Elwoooddd? Come and see who's here!'

The fat cook came hurrying, wiping her floured hands on her voluminous apron, her flushed, sweaty face beaming with pleasure.

'Miss Miriam? How bist? Oh it's loverly to see you agen. Aren't it just! It's loverley, really it is. Does you want summat to ate? I'll bring you a cup o' tay directly.'

The genuine warmth displayed by the two women moved Miriam Josceleyne almost unbearably, and tears brimmed in her eyes. She let herself be pushed down upon one of the capacious armchairs, and within scant seconds found herself clutching a cup and saucer of steaming tea, and a plate piled high with cakes.

'Theer now, get this lot acrorst your chest my duck,' the motherly cook urged. 'It'll stay you until the supper's cooked and ready.'

'I've had your old room made ready for you, Miss Miriam,' Emma told her.

'But I've no wish to trouble you, Emma.' Miriam offered a weak protest. 'I can make arrangements to stay at one of the hotels.'

'You'll stay nowhere else but here, in your own home.' The young woman's black eyes sparkled fierily. 'Why the very idea of it? You staying in a hotel when your own place is here? I'll not listen to any more nonsense like that. Here you am, and here you stay, and that's final!'

'Missis Emma, the kerridge man's awaiting to be paid, and he's getting a bit riled about being kept hanging about,' Becca came to tell her.

'Getting riled is he? The cheeky bugger. I'll soon sort

16

him out.' Emma's quick temper sparked and she rushed from the room telling Miriam as she went, 'You just sit and have your tea, Miss Miriam. We'll talk presently.'

Left alone in the room, Miriam listened to the sound of Emma's voice shrilly berating the carriage driver and could not help but smile. Remembrance swept over her and she made no effort to keep it at bay. Remembrance of the day that Emma Farr, as she then was, had come to Cotswold House as a maidservant, little more than four years ago and had from that very first day displayed her remarkable spirit, sharp intelligence, and readiness to face up and to overcome whatever trials and tribulations life could hurl at her. 'You most certainly saved me Emma,' Miriam Josceleyne silently acknowledged. 'God only knows what would have become of me if I had not had you for my friend.'

Now for the first time since she had entered the house, Miriam's thoughts turned to her dead father, and a slight shiver passed through her as the old sense of fear and repulsion filled her once again. She frowned uneasily. 'Even dead you still have the power to keep me in fear of you, Father,' she whispered aloud, and her eyes went apprehensively to the ceiling above, which was the master bedroom of the house. Her father's room.

'You're lying up there now I expect.' The morbid thought that the dead man might be aware of her return caused her to shudder visibly, and although she berated herself inwardly for her own foolishness, she still could not stop herself from straining to listen for any movement in the room above.

'There, that's put that saucy bugger to rights!' Emma erupted back into the room, her beautiful face glowing with the excitement of triumphant combat. 'I sent him off with more than one bloody flea in his ear 'ole, I'll tell you.'

Her black eyes fell upon the untouched plate of cakes, and she said reproachfully, 'Why Miss Miriam, you've not even touched your cakes, and they're fresh made this very afternoon. Nor your tea neither! Come on now, get it down you or you'll offend Mrs Elwood, as well as me.'

Miriam tried to obey, but the thought of her father lying

above her separated by only floorboards and ceiling plaster dried her mouth and turned the succulent fruit cake into sawdust in her dry mouth. Again and again her eyes flickered upwards and Emma shrewdly divined what was in her one-time mistress's mind.

'You'se no call to worry about your Dad, Miss Miriam. He aren't in the house. I got Mrs Elwood's husband to shift the old sod down to Cresswell's Chapel o' Rest. With the weather being so hot he'd started to stink the bloody house out.'

Miriam did not know whether she wanted to laugh, or to cry, but as the younger woman's white teeth shone in an infectious grin, she could not help but smile back in relief.

'He was enough to put anybody off their food when he was living, Miss Miriam, ne'er mind bloody dead.' A reminiscent tone entered Emma's voice. 'Does you know I reckon that's one o' the best things about being rich. You can afford to put the dead 'uns in the Chapel o' Rest. Back in Silver Street we had to keep 'um in the house until we buried 'um. When my old Grandad died he stunk worse than any midden after a couple o' days. In the end we had to put him out into the back yard with a tarpaulin over him until we got the coffin.' She chuckled richly. 'And by the time we got the coffin the old bugger had swelled up that much that all us kids had to jump up and down on the lid so it could close and be nailed. Me Dad didn't half swear about it. The air turned blue. O' course me Dad never liked the old man anyway, him being me Mam's dad. Me Dad reckoned that the old man had swelled up just for badness and to cause him as much trouble as he could.'

Miriam could only marvel at the matter of fact way in which Emma related the macabre tale, and not for the first time realised that although the physical distance between Cotswold House and Silver Street could be measured in yards, the distance in life experience between the two places was an immeasurable gulf.

'We are two separate nations,' she thought. 'No matter that we live under the same flag, and share a common tongue. We are truly alien to each other.'

Aloud she asked, 'Have you heard from my brother?'

Emma nodded. 'Yes. Franklin telephoned his wife's brother to tell me that him and his family would be here for the funeral. But they'll be staying with his wife's brother.'

Miriam felt a distinct relief. Like her father, her elder brother, Franklin Josceleyne, had tyrannised her unmercifully and had always bullied her into subjugation to his will. She experienced a warmth of affection as she regarded the chestnut-haired young woman now seated opposite her. 'They both tyrannised me, Father and Franklin, until the advent of Emma. She knew how to handle them.' Sharp regret stung her. 'I wish I had been more like her when I was younger. How different my life might have been.'

But even as she dwelt on this thought, the knowledge that to be like Emma would have entailed her being born and raised in the town slums to suffer years of brutal hardship, deprivation and degradation, brought her back to reality. 'I could never have survived the life that Emma was forced to lead. I haven't got her courage, or her will-power.'

She realised that Emma was staring at her, and she flustered. 'Why do you look at me so intently, Emma?'

The younger woman smiled gently. 'I was just thinking that country life agrees wi' you, Miss Miriam. You'm looking better than I'se ever seen you look. Really bonny. You'll be turning all the men's heads, so you will.'

Miriam blushed, and despite her thirty-one years, briefly resembled the pretty young girl she had once been, before the long years of parental and brotherly tyranny had taken their toll, eroding her confidence, smothering all her joy of life, turning her into a fearful, nerve-racked old maid, without self-confidence, without hope. Now she laughed embarrassedly, pleased at the compliment, but not able to accept its veracity.

'You must not say such things, Emma,' she demurred. 'I am fast becoming an old maid, and am content to be so.'

'I doon't think James Whitehead 'ull be happy to hear you say that, Miss Miriam. He was always making sheeps' eyes at you, and I reckon he's still living in hopes that you'll

19

come back here to Redditch to live.'

Miriam's embarrassment deepened, but in an effort to overcome it she forced herself to ask, 'How is Mr Whitehead? Does he still practise his dentistry?'

In Miriam's mind there was another question clamouring for answer. Another name clamouring to be voiced. But she could not muster the courage to ask the question, or to voice the name.

'Oh yes, he's still pulling teeth and going to church five times a day and eight times Sunday.'

Emma's amused smile was tinged with cruelty as her knowing eyes studied the other woman. Although she possessed a deep and genuine fondness for Miriam Josceleyne and would have risked her own life to defend her, yet Emma could still be intensely irritated by the older woman's timidity and lack of confidence. Now this sense of irritation suddenly rose and intensified, and she could not stop herself from baiting cruelly. 'To be honest he's not my idea of a beau at all. I like a man to be a real man, with a streak of devilment in him. James Whitehead's too much of a mealy-mouthed little church mouse for my taste.'

Miriam Josceleyne made no attempt to reply. Instead she merely bent her head and kept her eyes fixed on the plate and cup and saucer she still held in her hands.

The submissive posture touched a softer chord in Emma's mind, and remorse flooded through her as she realised. 'I'm only acting like a bitch because I'm still jealous of Miriam and Johnny Purvis, and truth to tell I'm feeling guilty over the way I wronged them both.'

Aloud she said gently, 'Doon't pay heed to what I say Miss Miriam. I'm not really thinking straight these days, what with the funeral to arrange and everything. James Whitehead's a kind man, and a good living one, and I shouldn't have said what I did.'

Miriam was happy to accept the proffered olive branch. And now she forced a smile, and asked, 'Do you think I could go to my room and freshen myself, Emma? The journey was hot and very dusty.'

'Of course you must, Miss Miriam.' Emma rose with grateful relief that her cruel words had not precipitated an open rupture. 'You go on up and I'll send the girls after you with some hot water. You'll find towels already laid out and I'll tell Becca that she is to see to all your wants.'

'It's not necessary, Emma, I'm well able to attend to my own needs,' Miriam protested softly, but the younger woman would not be gainsaid.

'You'm back in your own home, Miss Miriam, and we all wants to make you welcome and to look after you. So please let us do whatever we can for you. It makes us all happy.'

Miriam smiled in surrender and acceptance.

Up in her old bedroom which was at the front of the house Miriam found that the maids had already unpacked her box, and laid out her toilet articles. After Becca had brought the hot water Miriam dismissed the girl with a smile and then washed the dust of travel from her hands, face and neck. She brushed her long dark-grey skirt and changed her simple high-necked, long-sleeved blouse for one similar. Then she carefully brushed and combed her long mousy hair and arranged it into a severely coiled bun at the nape of her slender neck. The air in the room was stuffy and stale and Miriam opened the casement window and sat before it gazing through the net curtains.

Cotswold House stood with its neighbours on the eastern side of the large open triangle of the Church Green, the hub from which the town of Redditch spread in all directions. Built on the northernmost spurs of a long range of hills bisecting the West Midlands plain and enveloped by the agricultural lands of the Worcestershire and Warwickshire border, it was an industrial town of hilly streets radiating from a flat central plateau. To the north and east the land fell sharply to the valley of the Arrow River; to the west the land undulated across thickly wooded hills; to the south it rose in a long ridgeway alternately widening and narrowing upon which, like necklace beads, were situated the satellite villages of Headless Cross, Crabbs Cross and Astwood Bank. It was collectively known as the Needle District, because although it lay away from the main streams of commerce and communications, it was the world's major producer of needles and fishing tackle. It also contained many other varied engineering factories and workshops within its boundaries. Miriam had spent the first 29 years of her life in this town, and although to the stranger's eye it might appear undistinguished and lacking in charm or architectural merit, Miriam loved it, and had never wished to leave its red-brick streets and noisy, grimy mills and factories and workshops.

Now she filled her lungs with the cool evening air, and her gaze moved over the recreation garden beneath her with its bandstand and small fountain, its shrubs and flowerbeds, then traversed across the dividing pathway, and the greensward graveyard dotted with tombs and shaded by hugely-branched elm trees, to the tall-spired Church of St Stephen, standing like a sentinel at the town's central crossroads. There was no traffic moving along the roadway around Church Green, and few pedestrains. At this hour people were resting and eating after the long day's labour, but Miriam knew that later, after they had eaten and rested, then the youth of the town would come flocking to Church Green to parade with linked arms, seeking romance and adventure and the air would be filled with the sounds of their banter and laughter. Later still, the numerous public houses, beershops and inns would disgorge their crowds of men and women and then the air might well echo to the shouts and screams of drunken dispute, and the bestial cries and oaths of savagely brawling men.

Inevitably Miriam Josceleyne's thoughts turned to her reason for leaving the town two years ago and she felt her cheeks burning as the flush of shame rose from her slender throat.

'I must have been mad,' she whispered bitterly. 'Stark, raving mad!'

Then the tears stung her faded eyes and harsh sobs tore from her throat and she whispered brokenly, 'Oh Johnny . . . Johnny,' and the ever-hovering anguish of heartbreak engulfed her yet again.

Chapter Four

The sparse attendance at Hector Josceleyne's funeral service in St Stephen's Church was an accurate indicator of how his marriage to Emma Farr had blighted the family's social standing in the Needle District. None of the great names of the district were represented. No Milwards, Allcocks, Woodfields, Holyoakes, Hemmings, Terrys, Chillingworths, Bartleets attended, and only a spattering of lesser luminaries.

In the family pew Franklin Josceleyne inwardly seethed with furious resentment at the absence of the town's elite, and glared with bitter hatred at the palled coffin containing his father's earthly remains.

'It's all your fault, you filthy living old bastard. It's your fault for marrying this damned slum whore,' he thought. His anger enveloped his sister. 'And it's your fault as well, Miriam, for behaving like a depraved slut, as you did, and making yourself a laughing-stock in this town.'

Beside him the young widow sat with a demurely bowed head, her features hidden by a thick black veil. Emma was well aware of her middle-aged stepson's feelings, and now she smiled with malicious pleasure.

Miriam Josceleyne sat on the widow's other side, dressed similarly in unrelieved black, and likewise heavily veiled. Unlike her elder brother she was uncaring about the loss of social status indicated by the absence of so many of those who at one time would have thronged the church. Indeed her thoughts were not present in the church at all, but instead were many miles away, centred on the grim prison where her one-time lover, John Purvis, was incarcerated. Tears brimmed in her eyes and in her being

23

she yearned for sight or sound of him.

The service ended and the mourners followed the coffin outside, to where the magnificently adorned hearse, drawn by a pair of glossy matching Flemish blacks, waited to receive Hector Josceleyne and carry him to his final resting place in the cemetery on the western side of the town. The horses whinnied restlessly, tossing their huge black head plumes as the coffin was placed inside the glass-walled hearse, and the wreaths and bouquets of floral offerings were piled on and around it.

A line of other funeral carriages stood waiting to take the mourners down to the cemetery. Emma experienced a sense of satisfaction as she regarded the impressive array of plumed horses, carriages, and the swarm of under-takers – men in sombre black frock-coats, black gloves and crepe-swathed top hats, those who were to march as mutes in slow cadence beside and in front of the hearse carrying long black wands.

'Well nobody can say that I aren't give the old sod a proper send-off,' she told herself, and behind the thick veil her black eyes eagerly scanned the large crowds of curious onlookers. 'I hope me Mam has come up to have a look. This 'ull make her really proud.'

For all her independence of thought and spirit, and newly acquired wealth, Emma was still a child of the poor and deeply indoctrinated with the mores of her class. A fine funeral was the dream and ambition of so many who spent their short brutish lives in the bitterest of poverty. Emma likewise could see no ironic paradox in the sacrifices so many of the poor made during their lives to ensure that that ambition for a decent, respectable funeral was achieved. She saw her shawled mother standing in a cluster of other poorly-clad women and waved to her, uncaring of the hisses of disapproval emanating from the mountainously fat wife and daughters of Franklin Josceleyne directly behind her.

Mrs Farr swelled with visible pride as she returned her daughter's greeting with a wave of her own work-worn hand.

'Hey Emma, it's me. It's me!' A small runny-nosed,

tow-headed street urchin screamed in delighted recognition of his elder sister, and Emma waved to him also and called: 'I'll come and see you later, Dickie, and bring you some sweeties.'

'Well really!' Mrs Franklin Josceleyne could contain her indignation no longer as she spat out, 'Cannot you conduct yourself with due decorum, young woman? This is your husband's funeral, not a slum fair day.'

Emma glanced scathingly at her attacker and retorted, 'Shurrup, you fat cow. I'll speak to who I wants, and when I wants.'

Before the other woman could recover from her shock, Cresswell the undertaker had come to usher Emma into the leading carriage directly behind the hearse. Miriam joined her there, but Franklin shook his head, and indicated that he would travel instead with his wife and daughters in the second carriage.

Emma chuckled and gibed, 'If I'd known you was to travel with that lot, Frankie, I would have ordered a carrier's cart for you all. You'll need it to squeeze your bloody missis and kids into as well as yourself.'

The short-statured little man, dwarfed by his towering wife and daughters, tugged angrily at his full beard and rose on to his toes as if endeavouring to grow taller.

Emma chuckled as she thought of the nickname the town wags had bestowed upon her step-son years before, 'The Short-Arsed Rooster'; then settled back in her seat and gloried in the sensation of riding like royalty in a fine carriage in front of admiring crowds.

After the burial the mourners dispersed, only a very few of the greedier or more daring spirits among them ready to risk the disapproval of public opinion by returning to Cotswold House to partake of refreshments. Franklin Josceleyne and his family were notable by their absence, and very soon those who had returned to the house made their excuses and slipped away.

Emma breathed a heartfelt sigh of relief when the last had left. 'Thank Christ that's over and done with.'

And instructed Mrs Elwood: 'Have what you and the

25

girls wants and then put whatever food's left into a basket. I'll take it down to Silver Street for the kids.'

She smiled at Miriam sitting facing her across the empty screen-fronted fireplace of the drawing-room. 'Am you glad it's over, Miss Miriam?'

The older woman nodded. 'Indeed I am. Although I must confess to a feeling of guilt.'

'Why?' Emma wanted to know.

'Because I couldn't bring myself to shed a single tear for my father.'

'Why should you weep for the old bugger. He never wept for anybody in his life, did he?' the young woman stated positively. 'And theer was nothing to weep for anyway. He'd lived his full span, and he'd had a good time of it as well.'

The robust honesty of the young woman cheered and strengthened Miriam Josceleyne's easily depressed spirit as always, and now she smiled gratefully. 'You're right, as you normally are, Emma. I've nothing to weep for, so why should I need to feel any guilt.'

'Why are you and Franklin at loggerheads?' she went on to ask curiously, for she had had no contact with her elder brother since she had left Redditch. 'Only when I left here I understood that he had fully accepted the fact of your marriage to my father, and that he was to continue to administer the estate?' Franklin Josceleyne had been the manager of the Redditch branch of the Metropolitan Bank of England and Wales, and had lived in the house adjoining its imposing dark red-brick building standing on the opposite side of Church Green to Cotswold House.

'He was going to administer it, and I was prepared to let him do just that. But soon after you'd gone he started to nag me about my spending, so I bloody soon put him to the right about,' Emma explained, then laughed in amusement. 'I thought he was going to bust a blood vessel when I told him that I was taking over the administration, and that in future he'd have nothing to do with the estate. And then, when he started blaggardin' me, I closed the account at the Metropolitan and withdrew everything and shoved it into the Capital and Counties Bank along the

26

road theer.' Again her white teeth gleamed and she laughed in delighted recollection. 'He went purple in the bloody face, so he did. I thought he'd drop dead of apoplexy. Especially when I told him in front of the teller that he ought to treat his new stepmother with more respect, and that he warn't the sort of son I'd hoped for when I got married.'

Miriam could not help but laugh herself at the vision of her brother's reactions.

'It warn't long after that that Franklin moved away to another branch of the Metropolitan over in Wolverhampton.' Emma sobered and a hint of bitterness glowed in her black eyes. 'The reason, he told folks, was that his missis wanted to be nearer her own Mam who was sick, but to be truthful, I doon't think that he could stand the shame old Hector had brought on the family name by marrying me.'

'Don't say such things.' Miriam's normal timidity metamorphosed into spirited protest. 'You've brought no shame on to this family. I am not ashamed to have you as relative. Quite the opposite in fact. I feel honoured by your friendship.'

For a brief moment Emma's mask of self-confident surety fell away, and the vulnerable young girl showed from behind it. 'It's good of you to say that, Miss Miriam. Really good.'

'Nonsense,' Miriam flustered, deeply moved and embarrassed by the display of naked feeling in the young woman's face. 'I am merely speaking the truth.'

There was an uncomfortable silence for some seconds and then Emma's customary air of confidence returned and she asked brightly, 'What will you do now, Miss Miriam? Will you come back to live in Redditch, now that your Dad's not here to torment you any longer?'

When the older woman hesitated in answering, Emma pressed on. 'Why doon't you come back and live with me here? You'd be more than welcome to. And we'd get on all right, shouldn't we. We always has done aren't we.'

For a brief while Miriam considered the proposition. There was much appeal in it for her. She was very fond of

Emma, and she knew that they could be happy enough sharing this big house. Her life in the rented cottage in the Clee Hills was very reclusive, and latterly she had been experiencing an increasing sense of boredom and emptiness of purpose in her days, as well as an ever-present, soul destroying loneliness to her solitary life.

Emma studied the play of emotions in the other woman's sensitive features and decided to speak bluntly. 'It's because of him that you'm not able to do what you really wants and come back here to Redditch to live, aren't it? It's because of John Purvis?'

The open stating of his name cut into Miriam Josceleyne with painful anguish, but paradoxically mingling with that sharp anguish came a burgeoning of relief. After a brief while she was able to nod and admit quietly, 'Yes, it's because of what happened between myself and John Purvis that I'm not able to return here.' Her green eyes beseeched for sympathy and understanding. 'I've suffered such shame and torment because of him, Emma, and every time I walked the streets of this town I felt that the whole world knew of my shame, and gloated on it.' She shook her head in distressed memory. 'He made a fool of me, Emma. A complete and utter fool. All the time he was professing his love for me, he was having connections with that Dolton woman.'

Memory was also tormenting Emma Josceleyne – the memory of her own treachery to her then mistress. The memory of how driven by pique and jealousy, she had concealed from the other woman that truth which would have given her comfort and hope in her time of greatest torment and need. Now, staring at Miriam Josceleyne's tortured eyes a terrible guilt swept over Emma, and she opened her mouth to confess what she had done on that day, but just as the words rose to her lips the door opened and Mrs Elwood bustled into the room.

'Am you two wanting anything to ate or drink afore I goes home? Because if you does then tell me now so I can get it ready for you.'

Miriam Josceleyne shook her head and rose to her feet. 'No thank you, Mrs Elwood. I want nothing. I'll go and lie down for a while, I've a terrible headache.'

The cook regarded the drawn pallid face and gushed sympathetically: 'Yes, you do that, Miss Miriam. You looks a bit peaky. But then, that's not to be wondered at, is it? A funeral always drags a body down. You'll be right as rain in the morning, when you'se had a good night's sleep. You just see if you wun't.'

Emma slumped back into her capacious chair with mingled chagrin and relief. 'I can always tell Miss Miriam tomorrow,' she assured herself. But in the recesses of her mind a faint voice whispered in contempt, 'But you won't tell her, will you. You won't tell her if you can avoid it. You'm too shamed by what you did to tell anyone, I reckon.'

Miriam Josceleyne sat at the window of her bedroom. The casement had been opened a few inches to admit the cool evening air and the dusk of the sky was deepening to night. Through the white net curtains she could see the shadowy figure of the lamplighter moving from one to another of the street lamps, and as he lifted his long pole to the great glass globes they suddenly filled with the hissing flames of ignited gas and threw out pale circles of light to drive back the darkness.

Her thoughts dwelt on the conversation she had had with Emma, and she marvelled at how she could at this moment think about her traumatic affair with John Purvis with calmness. It was as if the mere fact of speaking his name aloud and openly confessing her feelings about him to Emma had acted as an easing catharsis. 'Perhaps by openly acknowledging to Emma the way I feel about John Purvis, I've taken the first steps to ridding myself of those feelings. Perhaps by running away as I did from my life here, by acting the coward as I did, I've delayed the healing of my wounds.'

She toyed with this notion for some time examining its connotations and finally concluded, 'I should have stayed here and faced up to my shame. I should not have allowed the opinions of others to drive me from my home. After all, although I sinned in the flesh I harmed no one but myself.'

From the street below she heard the sounds of youthful voices and laughter, and she peered down at the circle of lamplight almost opposite her window where a group of young men and girls were flirting and bantering with each other. Miriam envied their light-hearted freedom, as the memories of her own constricted and rigorously disciplined youth flooded into her mind, bringing with them the sadness of unfulfilled desires. 'If I had been allowed their freedom, then perhaps I would have found love and happiness with a man. And I wouldn't be the pathetic, dried up old maid I've become.'

A gentle melancholy invaded her and she remained immersed in that emotion until tiredness overcame her and she went to her lonely bed.

Sleep was long in coming, and when it finally came it brought with it dreams engendered by her own deep-seated hungers. In the dreams she could not see the man's face, but could feel his hands upon her body, and his lips crushing her mouth and his maleness thrusting deep into her flesh, and she came awake with a cry of pleasure, and felt the moistness of her own juices upon the soft flesh of her inner thighs. A terrible sadness engulfed her as she realised that for her there could never again be the reality of the flesh, but only the phantasms of her mind.

For Emma Josceleyne sleep was also long in coming but her thoughts were pleasurable. 'I'm rich now, and I'm free. I can do whatever I wants, and theer's nobody in this world who can deny me. I'm going to buy me Mam a nice house, and see that the kids gets plenty of everything.' Her lips curved in smiling anticipation. 'If I meets a man that I fancies, then I'll have him. But I'll not be his servant, he'll be mine. Theer's nobody, man nor woman who I'm ever going to let domineer over me again.'

Sighing with utter satisfaction she drifted into dreamless sleep.

Chapter Five

At breakfast next day Emma again renewed her pleas for Miriam to stay at Cotswold House. 'What's the good o' you hiding yourself away in the Clee Hills? That aren't going to change anything, is it? And you've admitted yourself that it's a lonely life for you there among strangers.'

'But what will I do here?' Miriam protested weakly, because she was tempted to remain with Emma and Mrs Elwood.

'Why, you can do whatever you wants to, Miss Miriam. There's more to see and do here in Redditch than there is stuck away in the country.' Emma thought for a moment, then offered another argument, 'Listen, you'm a free woman now that old Hector's popped it, and you'se got money of your own that your Mam left you haven't you? There's no one who can make you live in any way but how you wants to live.' She paused for a few seconds, her black eyes shrewdly evaluating what effects her words were having, then went on. 'And it'll be cheaper for you to live here, won't it? You won't have to pay any rent, or household bills. Your Dad has left enough for us all to live in luxury for the rest of our days.'

Miriam shook her head in vigorous refusal. 'Oh no, Emma. I could not live here upon your income. That would not be fair, since, as you have pointed out, I have an ample income of my own.'

The young woman scented that her friend was weakening, and pressed home her attack. 'All right then, we can share the house expenses, if you prefer it that way.' She grinned mischievously. 'I'll not object to that, 'ull I? It'll give me all the more to spend on meself.' Artfully she switched her line of argument towards a lesser objective. 'I'll tell you what Miss Miriam. Let's agree to this, shall we – you stay here now for a few weeks and see how it suits you and if you finds that you'm unhappy here, then go back to the Clee Hills. But if you finds that it suits you here with me and Mrs Elwood then move in permanently. That's a fair enough agreement, aren't it?'

Miriam was shrewd enough to recognise that she had been outmanoeuvred and she smiled wryly, and nodded acceptance.

'Good!' the young woman gusted in satisfaction. 'Mrs Elwood 'ull be as pleased as punch when I tells her that you'm staying. The last thing she said to me last night was that I hadn't got to take no for an answer.'

'But I still need to return to Clee and fetch some of my things.'

Emma was not going to risk letting her friend go alone. 'That's no problem. It's Saturday now, so we'll hire a carriage for Monday and go together. I needs a change of air meself, and I've never seen the Clee Hills.'

Miriam smiled in total surrender.

'That's settled then,' Emma said, then recalled, 'I've just remembered that basket o' food I told Mrs Elwood to save. I'll take it down to Silver Street just as soon as I've finished me breakfast.'

An overwhelming curiosity to see Emma's origins at close quarters suddenly impelled Miriam to ask tentatively, 'Could I come with you, Emma? Do you know I've never in my life actually been into Silver Street? I've walked past the entrance in Red Lion Street of course, and peeped under the archway, but I've never actually set foot upon it.'

'It aren't the best of places for a lady like yourself to visit,' Emma answered doubtfully. 'It's very rough and dirty. I don't think your posh friends hereabouts 'ud take kindly to you visiting Silver Street.'

'I'd still like to come with you.' There was an unaccustomed note of stubbornness in the elder woman's voice. 'After all Emma, have not you just this minute told me that I'm a free woman now, and can do anything that I please.'

The young woman smiled ruefully as her own argument was turned against her. 'So I did say that, didn't I? All right then, Miss Miriam, you can come with me. But don't expect to find any rainbows at the end of that alley 'ull you. Because there's only muckheaps to be found there.'

The northern entrance into Silver Street was through an archway built on to the side of a public house, The Red Lion. Miriam Josceleyne felt a tremor of trepidation as she moved beneath the archway and into the long narrow alleyway with its continuous rows of mean hovels. The close confined space stank, and she was forced to lift her skirts high around her ankles and carefully pick her way to avoid treading on to human and animal excreta, pools of stinking liquid and a myriad of other discarded rotting wastes that had been tossed out of the dwellings. Frowsty heads were thrust from broken, rag-stuffed casements and battered doors as the inhabitants of Silver Street came to challenge these intruders into their domain. Miriam Josceleyne's trepidation mounted, even though Emma was instantly recognised by the self-appointed sentinels and greeted with warm friendliness. A horde of ragged, runny-nosed, scald-headed children came rushing to cluster around the two black-clad women, dirty hands raised and strident voices clamouring.

Emma laughed, and taking a large bag of sweets from her basket she dealt them out among the shrieking children, then chased them away. She led the way into one of the hovels and Miriam almost gagged at the foulness of the air pent inside its sooty, greasy walls.

Two women were in the tiny room sitting at a dirty table before a minute, rusted firegrate. As Emma entered, followed by Miriam, their haggard faces brightened.

'Thank Christ you'se come, Emmy!' one of the women uttered.

The young woman frowned. 'What's happened? Wheer's me Mam?'

'Her's upstairs, laying down,' the woman informed.

'Has me Dad been hammering her again?' Emma demanded angrily.

The woman nodded. 'Last night, when he come back from the pub.'

'The fuckin' bastard!' Emma's beautiful face was ugly with hatred as her shapely lips spewed forth a torrent of filthy abuse directed against her father.

Miriam flushed with embarrassment as the two haggard women stared at her with latent hostility in their eyes.

'You'm Miss Josceleyne, aren't you?' It was a statement rather than a question.

Miriam nodded confirmation.

'This 'ull be a bit different from what you'm used to, wun't it,' one of the women challenged aggressively.

'Fuck me, yes,' her companion sneered. 'The blokes her knows 'ud never give an 'ooman a kicking, 'ud they? They'm too lardy-da for that.'

And Miriam could only flush and bow her head, made flustered and uncertain by this undeserved aggression.

As they were speaking, Emma went up the stairs that were against the side wall of the front room, and her boots thumped across the ceiling above their heads, dislodging tiny particles of soot from the cracked plaster. There was a mumbling of voices from above, and then Emma called sharply: 'Miss Miriam? Miss Miriam, can you come up here for a minute?'

Thankful to get away from the women Miriam passed them with averted eyes and mounted the ramshackle staircase. The stairs led directly into the tiny front bedroom, and Miriam stared with pity and distaste at the dirty straw palliasses which filled the cramped floor space, and the foul-smelling rags and old clothes and sacks which served as bedding. The back room, even more minute, was filled with a plank bedstead, on which the woman was lying fully clothed, her old shawl acting as a coverlet.

Miriam caught her breath in horror as she saw Mrs Farr. Her head appeared grotesquely lopsided because one side of her face was hugely swollen with black-bruised flesh, and both eyes were mere slits. Abrasions and cuts still weeping watery blood covered her face and neck, and raw patches on her scalp marked where clumps of hair had been savagely torn out. As Miriam stared down with horror at the beaten woman, Mrs Farr moaned in agony, drawing her knees up, her raw-skinned hands kneading the great ball of her belly.

Miriam stared in question at Emma, and the younger woman spat out bitterly: 'Yes, the bastard kept on kicking her there, and she's nearly eight months gone.'

Suddenly Miriam's stomach rebelled against the stench and the sight of the tortured woman, and she retched and gagged as acrid bile filled her throat. With a strangled cry of apology she hurried down the stairs and out into the scarcely less rancid alley. She sagged against the wall, her stomach heaving, and then the bile erupted from her mouth; in an agony of shame she bent low, vomiting helplessly.

Sick and spent she felt hands grasp her arms, and concerned voices sounded in her ears. She was led back into the house and seated upon a broken-backed chair by her erstwhile aggressors, whose manner towards her had been transformed at the sight of her sufferings into a rough kindliness.

'Theer now, my duck. You sit still for a minute, and you'll be all right.'

'Here you bist, dearie, swallow this down you. It'll take the bad taste away.'

A cracked cup filled with tepid, musty-tasting water from the bucket in the corner of the room was held to her lips. She sipped at it gratefully, exchanging one foul taste for a lesser.

Emma came downstairs, her cheeks hot with angry colour, her black eyes fiery. 'I'm going to bring a carriage and shift me Mam to my house. She's not staying with that bastard Feyther o' mine for another day.'

Her listeners exchanged doubtful glances, and the taller woman told her, 'You'm talking sarft, Emmy. Your Mam 'ull never leave your Dad.'

'She bloody well will!' Emma declared passionately.

The other woman shook her tousled, frizzy hair. 'Even if her wanted to leave him, he 'udden't let her goo. You knows that well enough yourself, Emmy.'

'What the fuck is going on here?' The bowler-hatted

man in soot-thick clothing filled the low doorway with his bulk.

Emma faced her father defiantly. 'You doon't need to ask that. You knows well enough what's gooing on.'

The man tossed the bundle of canes, brushes and scrapers that he carried on to the floor in front of him, and lowered the heavy sack of soot from his shoulder. His red-rimmed eyes glared from his soot-grimed features at the other women in the room, and he jerked his head. 'Gerrout o' my house, you lot.'

Knowing his propensity for violence the two neighbours scurried out into the alley, where they stopped to stand with the rapidly gathering crowd of avid-staring onlookers enjoying this free entertainment.

Winston Farr stepped into the room and slammed the door shut behind him. He stared at the bowed figure of Miriam Josceleyne sitting on the broken chair, then growled at his daughter. 'What's you want here, our Emma? And what's you brought her here wi' you for?'

'I came to see me Mam and the kids,' Emma spat defiantly, her present anger overlaying the deeply engrained fear of her father's terrible rage. 'And I've seen what you'se done to her, you bastard!'

The man's fists balled in unspoken threat, but the presence of a gentlewoman such as Miriam Josceleyne made him wary. She would be listened to by the police and was in a position to bring all the power of the law against him should he offer her insult or harm. 'Her bloody well asked for everything her got,' he mumbled sullenly. 'I told her to shut her nagging mouth, but her 'udden't. So I did it for her.'

Emma wanted to spring at her father and tear the eyes from his head with her bare hands. But from bitter experience she knew that she stood no chance against his vastly superior physical strength, and that if she should venture to attack him, he would mete out to her the same treatment that he had meted out to her mother. Furious at her own impotence Emma spat at him: 'I'm going to bring the police on to you for this. And I'm going to shift me Mam from this stinking hole and bring her to live with me.

You'll not misuse her again, you rotten bleeder!'

He bared his decaying, tobacco-stained teeth in a contemptuous grin. 'You do that, you little slut! You bring the fuckin' police here if you wants to!' He laughed and sneered. 'The fuckin' police can't do nothing, and you knows it. A man's got a right to do what he wants wi' his own Missis. And as for you taking her out o' my house, well I'll tell you straight, I'll put the fuckin' cow in her grave afore I lets her leave me. And theer's nothing you or the bloody police can do to stop me. They carn't lift a finger until I'se done it, can they?' Again he laughed sneeringly, then once again jerked his head towards the door. 'Now fuck off out o' my house, you bloody slut, and take your mate wi' you.'

Slumped on the chair between the two antagonists, Miriam Josceleyne was literally shaking with fear. Feeling faint and nauseated, she suddenly pushed herself upright and begged brokenly, 'Please Emma, please let us go from here. I cannot stand it any longer. Please let us go.'

Emma stared wildly at the pallid-faced, trembling woman and was torn in two directions, one side of her clamouring to remain and continue this confrontation with her father, the other gentler side beseeching her to take Miriam Josceleyne away from this scene of threatening violence.

'Please, Emma! Please!' Miriam Josceleyne begged, her eyes frightened and pleading.

Reluctantly, Emma broke eye contact with her father, and nodded. 'All right, Miss Miriam. We'll go.'

She took the other woman's arm and led her to the door. Opening it she ushered Miriam Josceleyne out into the alleyway and followed her, turning her head as she did so to challenge Winston Farr's triumphant grin. 'You aren't heard the last o' this you bastard! I'll be back!'

'Not if you knows what's good for you, you wun't, you bloody little slut,' he jeered, and lurched forwards to kick the door shut in her face with a resounding slam.

The crowd escorted the two women back to the arched entrance of Silver Street, voicing their support and encouragement to Emma.

'You'm a good wench, Emmy.'

'Ahrr, you told him straight didn't you, my duck.'

37

'He's a bad bugger, so he is. You'd do best to keep well away from him, my wench.'

'Your Mam 'ull be all right, now that her's seen you, Emmy.'

'Her's lucky to have a daughter like you, so her is.'

Emma and Miriam reached the arch and went under it into Red Lion Street. Emma nodded her thanks to the two women. 'Will you get word to me if he starts battering her again today?' she asked, and they agreed vociferously.

'We 'ull, my duck.'

'We'll send word to you straight off.'

'Thank you.'

With a heavy heart Emma led the badly shaken Miriam Josceleyne back towards the peaceful safe haven of Cotswold House, and as she did so vowed silently. 'I'll have you for what you'se done to me Mam, you bastard. You might be me Father, but I still hates you. I'll get you for what you'se done to me Mam, I swear it. I'll get you back, just wait and see.'

For her part, Miriam Josceleyne felt only relief that she had left the slum behind her. But as she neared the haven of Cotswold House a sense of anger began to burgeon within her. Anger that in this modern age men could so ill-treat and abuse their wives with apparent impunity. 'Those poor women in Silver Street are powerless, and no one in authority cares. Not the police, the church or the politicians. It's not fair. It's not just. Even though they are poor, they have the right to decent treatment from their menfolk.' She thought of her own life and frowned. 'It's not only the women of the poor who are ill-treated by their menfolk though, is it? Even those like myself who were lucky enough to be born into comparative wealth and social standing can still be badgered and beaten without redress. It's time women had more power over their own lives.'

The old familiar sense of helplessness invaded her. 'But how can they achieve that? There is no way open to them. Men rule this country. They make the laws, and they enforce those laws. Women can do nothing.'

Chapter Six

Evesham Street ran north from Church Green crossroads and was one of the main shopping thoroughfares of the town. Although it was Saturday morning the shops were not unduly busy; the main business would begin in the late afternoon when the workers were paid and released from their week's toil to celebrate their scant hours of freedom until the advent of Monday.

Almost at the northern end of the long flat street, where it joined with the lower slopes of the continuing Front Hill, The Redditch Meat Company's outside display of hook-hung sheep and pig carcasses sweated in the heat.

As she neared the shop, the dark eyes of Cleopatra Dolton dwelt sourly on those hanging carcasses; she halted directly in front of the open display window to briefly study the swarms of flies that were buzzing around the laid out trays of chops, and steaks, and sausages, and variously cut joints. Frowning, she entered the premises, with one hand deftly gathering the folds of her skirts to twitch the hems clear of the thick layer of sawdust strewn upon the floor.

There was no one in the shop but through the open door which led to the rear rooms of the building, she could hear a shrill whistling.

'Are you there, Clarke?' she called sharply, and the whistling stilled abruptly. An elderly man dressed in the striped blue apron and ribboned straw boater of a butcher came through the open door.

'Ozzie's not here, Mrs Dolton. He's down at the yard.'

'What's he doing down there?' she demanded.

The old man's lined grey face was surly. 'Sticking them

pigs he bought yesterday at Bromsgrove Mart.'

The woman nodded. Then scolded: 'Why haven't you wrapped those carcasses outside there with muslin cloth? And why are the trays uncovered? The meat will be flyblown before the day's done.'

He scowled resentfully at his employer. 'I'se only got one pair of hands, Missis. And I'll have to haul all of them carcasses down agen to wrap 'um. And they'm bloody heavy, I can tell you. I doon't know as if I'll be able to manage to hoist 'um up agen by meself.'

'Don't you take that tone with me, Walter Spiers,' she snapped warningly. 'Or you'll be looking for another place. If you're not able to lift the carcasses, then perhaps I'd better replace you with somebody who is strong enough to lift them.'

For brief seconds their eyes locked, and then the man broke off the contact and grumbling beneath his breath, rummaged in a wooden locker and fetched out a large roll of muslin net.

Satisfied that she had quelled his rebellion Cleopatra Dolton swung on her heels and walked out of the shop.

Walter Spiers raised two fingers in an obscene gesture at her retreating back. 'Fucking miserable cow!' he spat. Then used his long-bladed knife to cut pieces of muslin net to cover the trays, hacking savagely at the material as if he wished it were the throat of his employer.

Cleopatra Dolton halted momentarily in the street outside and briefly debated with herself.

In the doorway of the neighbouring grocers the pimply-faced young shopman stared hungrily at her slender waist, rounded hips, and the proud full breasts thrusting out against the thin black silk of her bodice. Despite being nearly forty years of age, Cleopatra Dolton was a woman to tempt any man with her black hair, dark eyes, olive skin and shapely body. The black of her widow's weeds only emphasised her exotic appearance, and the young shopman's erotic fancies simultaneously delighted and tormented him as he watched her walk slowly away, her sombre coloured parasol held above her wide-brimmed hat, and her hips undulating sensually as she moved.

The pig shrieked in outrage as rough hands grabbed and dragged it tugging and struggling from its thick-barred wooden cell, and the men laughed and cursed in turns as its heavy bulk cannoned painfully against them.

'Get the bugger on to the bench, 'ull you, and stop fartin' about,' Ozzie Clarke shouted irritably. 'Tommy, bring the bucket here.'

The small ragged urchin holding the big wooden pail hung back, fearful of coming close to the shrieking, bucking beast, and his gaze constantly flickered between the pig and the big man standing stripped to the waist, his muscular torso glistening with sweat in the sunlight.

'Hup now! Hup now!' Shouting in unison the men bodily lifted the animal and smashed it down upon the squat bench. Muscles strained and breath grunted in effort as they fought to turn the pig on to its back and hold it steady.

Ozzie Clarke scowled at the frightened urchin. 'Get that bucket under its yed, you little bleeder, afore I fists you one.' In his right hand he held a knife with a long pointed blade honed to razor sharpness.

'Get that bucket here, blast you!' he shouted in sudden angry outburst, and the urchin's fear of the shrieking animal was over-borne by his fear of the angry man, and he shuffled tearfully forwards and set the bucket under the animal's head where it overhung the end of the bench.

'Now make sure you catches all the blood,' Ozzie Clarke exhorted. 'It won't bloody hurt you, you windy little bastard.'

With his left hand he grasped the snout of the screaming animal and then selecting his spot slid the knifeblade into the beast's neck with almost surgical precision. The pig shrieked and convulsed and the men holding it shouted out in alarm as the convulsions threatened to tear the great body free from their restraining hands. The bright hot blood sprayed from the wound, and then began to gout out in rapid pulses, splashing down into the bucket, steaming and frothing.

41

The urchin screwed up his grimy features and wailed pitifully as spatterings of blood hit his face and throat and chest; but still he grimly clutched the bucket as Ozzie Clarke twisted the knife blade to increase the flowing of blood.

The animal still twitched and jerked in the throes of dying as it was lashed up by its hindquarters to a heavy beam and hung head downwards with the bucket still underneath its snout to catch the last drainings of blood. The men brought flaming torches of twisted straw and began to singe the tough bristles from the thick skin and the stench of burnt hair and scorched flesh filled the air. A little distance from the bench a small crowd of ragged children watched with avid eyes, some whooping with gleeful excitement, others silent and afraid as they witnessed agony and violent death.

Once the singeing of the bristles had been completed, Ozzie Clarke tugged off the detachable gristle covers of the pig's toes and flung them to the watching children, who fought each other to snatch up the gory trophies, which the winners greedily sucked and gnawed with every appearance of relish.

The second pig was dragged out mad with terror as it scented the blood of its fellow. But all its struggles were rendered powerless and its shrieks were quickly silenced by the deadly hand and knife.

When it too had been lashed up to the thick beam, Ozzie Clarke grinned in triumphant satisfaction, as did his helpers. It was as if the bloody killings had satisfied deeply buried, but still potent, atavistic hungers within their beings.

As Ozzie Clarke used his knife to scrape patches of singed hide free from the remnants of bristles, one of the helpers tapped him on the shoulder, and jerked his head towards the entrance to the yard.

Ozzie Clarke saw the black-clad figure standing just inside the entrance and reacted with his customary mixture of lustful wanting and sharp resentment. 'Jesus. Christ, what bee has she got in her bonnet now?' He knew that for his employer to come down to the yard it meant that there was something angering her.

42

He issued brief instructions to the men with him, and playfully cuffed the head of the bucket holding urchin. 'Theer now, Tommy,' he grinned. 'You wun't be feared of catching the blood agen, 'ull you. You showed that you got pluck today.'

The urchin visibly swelled with gratified pride, and chortled in gap-toothed delight when the man handed him a silver sixpence.

Still grinning at the small boy's reaction, Ozzie Clarke turned and walked slowly towards the waiting woman.

Her dark eyes dwelt appreciatively on his pale, splendidly muscled body, and the red splashes of blood mingling with the sweat trickling down over his chest and arms. She felt a frisson of sexual excitement. 'He looks like a victorious gladiator coming from the arena.'

He reached her and grinned, and for a disquieting moment she wondered if he could detect the sexual stirrings he had aroused within her.

'Morning, Missis Dolton. What can I do for you this fine day?' he greeted, the grin still wreathing his handsome sun-bronzed features.

With his thick, brown curly hair, fine physique and personable manner, Ozzie Clarke was a man who enjoyed considerable success with women, and it was a source of piqued resentment for him that his charms did not seem to impress his employer. On several occasions her manner towards him had led him to think that she too was ripe for conquest. But each time he had responded to her inviting manner with a verbal advance she had turned upon him with a cold rebuff, causing him to feel both humiliated and angered.

Now, as he looked at the beautiful face before him he struggled to suppress the desire he felt for her. 'You'll not make a mug out of me again, Cleopatra Dolton,' he told himself firmly.

The woman was annoyed with herself in case she might unconsciously have betrayed the fact that this man could excite her sexually; and that self-directed annoyance caused her to stare at him frostily, and speak with curt hostility. 'I've just come from the shop, Clarke. The meat was uncovered, and in this heat it's attracting swarms of flies. Don't let it happen again.'

Ozzie Clarke reddened with embarrassment, uncomfortably aware that the other men in the yard could not help but overhear her penetrating voice.

'I was going to cover it after I'd finished with the pigs, Mrs Dolton,' he began to explain. 'We couldn't do it earlier because we were waiting for the muslin to be delivered. Alfie Walter had run out of stock so I had to order it from elsewhere. That's why there was a delay in delivery.'

She scathingly waved aside his explanation. 'Spare me your excuses, Clarke. I don't pay my managers to make excuses. I pay them to do their jobs properly, and if you can't do the job as I want you to do it, then perhaps I'd better find someone else who can.' She paused, and her dark eyes were challenging, as if daring him to argue further with her.

The man swallowed hard, and with an immense effort kept his own quick temper in check. Jobs were hard to come by these days, and despite her uncertain temper Cleopatra Dolton paid good wages.

'It wun't happen again, Missis Dolton,' he muttered sullenly.

'Make sure that it doesn't,' she snapped, then turned and walked away.

Ozzie Clarke gazed at her shapely buttocks beneath the tight-hipped black silk gown, and his tongue slid over his lips as his vivid imagination took wings. 'Just one night, Cleo Dolton. Just one night wi' me and you'd be singing a different tune. I'd fuck all that bad temper out of you.'

The men winked and sniggered to each other as he rejoined them, and one baited: 'I reckon you'm giving her one, Ozzie. That's why her come down here, just to make sure you warn't having it off wi' some other bit o' skirt.'

'Ahrrr, that's got to be right, Amos,' another man agreed. 'You'se only got to hear the lovesome ways her talks to him to know that he's got her just wheer he wants her.'

Ozzie Clarke's customary good humour reasserted itself, and he grinned at their bantering.

'I'll tell you summat,' the first man stated. 'I only wish I was giving Cleopatra Dolton what for.'

'Ahrr, so does Ozzie,' the second man quipped, and the whole gathering roared with laughter and Ozzie Clarke laughed as heartily as any.

Cleopatra Dolton came out of the long covered entry back on to Evesham Street and turned southwards towards the central crossroads. She was conscious of the fact that men's and women's eyes followed her sensuous progress, and that those eyes expressed differing reactions to her – some admiration, some sexual hunger, others hostility and scorn. For her part she looked neither to right nor left, answering the occasional greeting of an acquaintance with a curt nod. She kept her head high and her body erect, and she radiated an aura of what many took to be arrogance, but which was in reality a defensive shield against a world that had cruelly abused her.

She reached the central crossroads and glanced along the road running eastwards. It was known as 'Market Place', and today being Saturday the travelling stalls and pedlars that gave it its name were already crying their wares. Like the shops, their main business would not commence until the release of the workers but still there were numbers of men, women and children strolling and shopping.

On impulse Cleopatra Dolton walked down Market Place looking at the pots and pans, the cheap crockery, the foodstuffs, assorted fruits and vegetables, the second-hand clothes, the patent medicines and all the other myriad items placed out for sale.

Behind the row of stalls in the green-sward graveyard beneath the great grey bulk of St Stephen's church, three young women, dressed in plain skirts and blouses, with straw boaters on their heads stared through the gaps in the market stalls at the passing shoppers. They argued with each other in low voices.

'I say we should do it now.'

'But there aren't many people here.'

'That doesn't matter.'

'But surely it would be best if we waited until the crowds are larger. That way we shall attract more attention.'

'We can do it again later, can't we. We're only wasting time by waiting until there are more people.'

'Yes, Laura's right, Beattie. We're just wasting time if we wait.'

After a moment of hesitation the objector nodded. 'Very well. Let's do it.'

On the ground at their feet was a large carpetbag and a wooden soapbox. Beattie, a short, plump girl, knelt and took several small rolls of white cloth from the bag. She shook out the rolls of cloth to display the large black letters stencilled upon them.

'Right then.' Her face was pale and her voice was strained with nervousness but she spoke determinedly: 'Let's put these on.' Beattie swallowed hard, and with trembling fingers tied the lettered cloth across her large breasts.

'How does it look?' she wanted to know, and the other girls smiled tensely.

'Fine. It looks very fine.' This was Laura, tall and slender, with grey eyes and a wide brow, and an air of elegance in the way she spoke and carried herself.

The third girl, Emily, was more like the plump Beattie in appearance – short in stature with dark hair and bright bird-like eyes which now held a fearful excitement. She drew in a long shuddering breath as if nerving herself for what lay ahead.

'Come on then.'

All three now wore the lettered white cloths across their breasts. Beattie carried the carpetbag and Laura the soapbox, while Emily held another unfurled white banner before her, its big black-stencilled letters proclaiming the same slogan as their breastplates of white cloth.

'VOTES FOR WOMEN! VOTES FOR WOMEN! VOTES FOR WOMEN!'

Their voices rang out in unison, hurling the slogan along Market Place. Surprised faces turned to stare.

In the middle of the roadway, where Market Place joined the central crossroads, the three girls halted. Laura laid down the soap box and stepped upon it while her two friends ranged themselves on each side of her, fluttering their home made banners in front of their bodies, as if to flaunt them in challenge.

'Ladies and gentlemen . . .' Laura's high-pitched voice cracked with nerves and she coughed and steeled herself to begin again. 'Ladies and gentlemen, I want to bring to your attention the wicked injustice that is being perpetrated against the women of this country . . .'

Eager to view this unexpected free entertainment, a crowd quickly gathered in front of the trio of young women. Laura became more confident as she spoke and her shaky voice strengthened.

'Half of the adult population of this country have no voice in its governance. Women cannot vote in any election. No matter how worthy a woman might be, she has no voice in electing the Members of Parliament who rule over her . . .'

Cleopatra Dolton was returning towards the central crossroads when she became aware that ahead of her a crowd had gathered. She unconsciously hastened her steps towards the crowd and joined its rear fringes. She regarded the tall, attractive, blonde-haired young woman standing upon the soapbox speaking so passionately, and her own interest quickened as she heard.

'. . . Is it any wonder that so many women are mistreated and exploited when they are so totally bereft of any power or influence in the political life of our country? And so long as women remain without the right to vote, then so long will that mistreatment and exploitation continue unabated . . .'

The young woman's voice rang out clearly and the message it carried to Cleopatra Dolton's ears struck an answering chord.

'. . . Women are forced to be the slaves of their employers, to labour for a pittance that is not sufficient to keep body and soul together, because those employers know well that their women employees have no political power. They have no vote, and because they have no vote they can do nothing to change the laws of this land. They have no power to demand new and more just laws, which would compel their exploiters to pay them a fair wage.'

47

Here and there among the crowd, heads nodded in agreement and support, but for the most part the faces that Cleopatra Dolton could see were either amused, hostile, or indifferent.

The speaker directed her next words towards the male element of her audience. 'It is you men who must help your womenfolk to gain the voice they need . . .'

'My old 'ooman doon't need any gain in her voice. Her's got more nor enough already,' a man shouted, and the crowd erupted with laughter.

The speaker's pale skin flushed and she looked flustered as another jeering shout sounded from the crowd.

'Wheer's your man? Why aren't he here helping you to gain more voice?'

Laura hesitated, then replied: 'I have no man. I can speak for myself.'

'That's what you needs, aren't it, Missy. A man! Perhaps if you had one he'd be able to knock a bit o' sense into your yed!'

Now Laura made a cardinal error, and allowed herself to be provoked into an individual confrontation.

'It's you who needs sense knocking into your head!' she retorted angrily, and the man's face hardened.

'You mouthy bitch!' he bellowed. 'I'll teach you to insult me.' He bent swiftly and snatched up a piece of refuse from the ground, then hurled it into the face of the tall young woman.

It struck her high on her broad brow and she cried out and lifted both hands to her head. Instantly the rougher elements among the crowd seized on their opportunity for creating uproar. Bellowing with delight, they also snatched up and hurled whatever came to their hands at the three young women before them.

In scant seconds their targets were liberally besmeared with dirt and rotting refuse. As they cowered away from the barrage, their obvious fear brought the cruelty of their tormentors to the surface, and they surged around the young women, howling execrations and jeering with brutal laughter. A youth darted forward and tore the banner from Emily's hands, another youth followed suit and attempted to snatch Beattie's banner, but she resisted fiercely and he cursed her vilely and struck her savagely with his fist, sending her toppling over on to the ground.

As Cleopatra Dolton saw the blow, her own fury erupted. For nearly all her life she had been the victim of men's brutality, and the sight of the attacker's slack-lipped brutish grin as the girl went sprawling brought a red haze across Cleopatra's sight, and she exploded forward through the crowd.

But before she could reach the youth, the crowd swirled and eddied violently and bodies thudded into her, sending her staggering sideways. Policemen suddenly materialised and surrounded the three young women to grasp them roughly and bundle them away. The excited crowd followed on, catcalling, shouting, jeering, and Cleopatra Dolton went with them.

The policemen frogmarched their prisoners along the eastern side of Church Green then swung westwards down Church Road, a long cul-de-sac on which stood the Public Hall, the Post Office, the Literary Institute and the Police Station. The policemen and prisoners disappeared inside the Station, and a sergeant and constable came out to disperse the crowd.

'Come on now, move along. There's nothing more to be seen. Move along. Move along. Gerrof wi' you Benny Lewis, and you Billy Williams, or you'll be seeing the inside o' the bloody cells. Move along now. Move along!'

Reluctantly the crowd slowly moved away back towards Church Green, their voices raised in loud and excited discussion of what had occurred.

'Bleedin' suffragettes! They wants a good fuckin', the lot on 'um!' a red faced man with a drooping walrus moustache declared emphatically, and his statement was greeted with almost universal approbation.

'I knows what I'd do wi' any 'ooman o' mine that behaved like that. I'd take me belt to her.'

'And I 'ud, and a double ration o' me boot up her arse, as well!'

Cleopatra Dolton's earlier fury had abated now, and she

listened to the blustering statements with a cold contempt. She moved on with the crowd, her mind filled with the courageous way the young woman had spoken, and what she had said. Then she came to an abrupt halt, and turning on her heels, went back towards the Police Station. When she reached it she ignored the constable posted on watch outside its walls, and crossed to the opposite side of the road. With her parasol held to shield her head from the sun she stood patiently waiting.

While Inspector Charles Howard listened to the report of the senior constable present, his eyes regarded the three dirty, dishevelled young women before him with an increasing distaste. When the man had finished, the inspector nodded brusquely and spoke directly to the tallest of the girls. 'What's your name?'

Her grey eyes were angry, but she replied in a level voice: 'Laura Hughes,' then continued, 'and I wish to protest in the strongest possible terms about the treatment I and my friends have been subjected to.'

'Hold your tongue, girl!' the inspector snapped curtly. 'I only require an answer to my question, nothing more.'

The anger in the grey eyes spilled over into the young woman's voice. 'I will not hold my tongue! I have the right to speak!'

'You'll find yourself speaking to the walls of a cell if you don't keep quiet!' the big policeman threatened.

'Shhhhh, Laura!' Emily whispered fearfully, and Beattie added her own frightened pleas.

'Yes Laura, do be silent!'

The tall girl subsided with ill-grace, and Howard turned his attention to her companions. 'Your name?'

'Emily May Shuttleworth, sir.'

'And yours?'

'Beattie Cartwright, sir.'

'You're not a Redditch woman are you?' His question was directed at Beattie, one of whose bright bird-like eyes was swelling and discolouring from the blow she had received.

'No sir. I live at Alvechurch. Emily is presently staying with me.' She named a village some four miles distant on the main route to Birmingham.

'Where in Alvechurch?'

'At my Father's house in the Withybed Lane, sir.' Beattie's eyes filled with tears which began to spill down over her plump cheeks. Howard nodded, and beneath his full moustache his lips twitched in wry amusement at the woebegone spectacle the young woman presented.

The sight of her friend's distress caused Laura to erupt once more. 'Why have you arrested us, Inspector? When it is we who have been assaulted. You can see for yourself the injury done to my friend.'

The man's breath hissed sharply in irritation. 'You have not yet been arrested, young woman. You have merely been taken into protective custody. However, should you continue to make unwanted, and unasked for interruptions, I most certainly shall have you arrested.'

'On what charge?' Laura demanded, unintimidated by his threat.

'On several charges of disturbing the public peace, and resisting arrest, and obstructing police officers in the performance of their duties. Those will be the initial charges, and I can doubtless think of others to lay against you in due course. Have I made myself perfectly clear?'

Actual terror showed on the faces of the other two girls, and again they begged their fiery friend to be quiet.

Torn between disgust at their fear, and sympathy for their distress, Laura relapsed into disgruntled silence.

A few more questions from the inspector elicited all the information he needed to come to a decision regarding two of the young women. They were both from respectable, middle-class families. Beattie Cartwright's father was a wealthy businessman whom Howard knew personally. Emily Shuttleworth was an old schoolfriend of Beattie's, and her parents were landowners in Herefordshire. She was staying with Beattie for a holiday.

Laura Hughes gave Howard pause for more thought, however. A few years older than her companions, she was a school teacher who had recently moved to Redditch to take up a post at a private girls' school, Grafton House, which was owned by two spinstered sisters, the Misses

Amelia and Annabel Grose.

'Well now, what's to be done with you?' He frowned at the three girls. 'This is a serious matter.'

Beattie Cartwright's tears fell freely, and she whimpered fearfully. 'You won't tell my Father about this will you, sir. Please don't tell him.'

Laura Hughes snorted impatiently and spoke out forcefully: 'Inspector, I am solely to blame for these two being here. I persuaded them both to accompany me, and I wish to accept full responsibility for anything that has happened. If there are to be charges then let them be brought only against myself. These two were acting under my influence, and my direction.'

A grudging respect entered the policeman's mind. At least this young woman was showing courage, no matter how arrogantly she behaved.

He considered further, and then offered: 'I am prepared to release all of you without charge in return for certain undertakings on your behalf.'

They listened in silence, hope growing in the two younger women's faces.

'If you will give me your word that there will be no repetition of this behaviour, then I will merely bind you over and release you to go home.' He stared interrogatively at each of them in turn.

Beattie Cartwright and Emily Shuttleworth eagerly assented to his proposal, but Laura Hughes only frowned, and stubbornly shook her head. Her friends stared at her in shocked dismay, and volubly begged her to agree. But she stayed silent, and refused even to look at them.

The policeman appeared to lose patience with her, and ordered a constable.

'Lock this one up.'

Laura Hughes allowed herself to be led away without protest, and her friends uttered faint cries of distress.

Howard spoke to them with a rough kindliness: 'There now, there is no need to distress yourselves. She will come to no harm, I assure you. But I would advise you to discontinue your acquaintanceship with that young woman. She is entirely unsuitable as a friend for gentlewomen like yourselves. I know that your Fathers would concur wholeheartedly with what I say. Now go back home, and don't behave so stupidly ever again. You'll hear no more of this matter so long as you do as I have advised.' He nodded to a constable who ushered the two girls out of the room and through the corridor to the street outside.

A little distance opposite the Police Station, Cleopatra Dolton saw the young women exit from the building and crossed the roadway to intercept them as they hurried with bowed heads towards Church Green. 'Excuse me, where is your friend? Why is she not with you?' she asked.

The two dirt-smeared, tearstained faces stared at her in alarm, then the plumper girl said: 'She's still inside. They've locked her into a cell. Now please let us pass. We've no wish to say anything else to you.'

Cleopatra drew aside and they hurried on past her. Her curiosity was fully aroused now. Why should the tall girl have been put into a cell and these others released? For a moment she toyed with the idea of going into the Police Station herself to find out what was happening to the young woman. Then dismissed that idea for the present. 'I'll wait a while longer to see if she comes out,' she decided, and settled herself once more to her weary vigil.

Inspector Howard left Laura Hughes locked up for an hour before having her brought to his office once again.

'Now then, young woman, are you prepared to give me your undertaking to abandon any further attempts at public speaking?'

She met his stern gaze without any sign of timidity. 'No, I cannot do that.'

He sighed wearily. 'Why?'

'Because I have taken a solemn oath to uphold the cause I serve,' she stated spiritedly.

'What oath? And for what cause?'

'The oath to fight for justice for women. I am a member of the Women's Social and Political Union.'

'You are a suffragette?' There was contempt in the man's voice.

'Yes, I believe that is the term we are now known by.'

53

The policeman could not restrain a snort of derision. He was not a believer in universal suffrage. In fact he considered that there were many men who should not be allowed the right to vote, never mind extending that right to a pack of empty headed, hysterical women. However, in the execution of his duties he was essentially a fair minded man, and he had no desire to persecute this stubborn, irritating young woman. Summoning his patience he said quietly, 'Miss Hughes, by your actions this morning you created a disturbance in the centre of this town. Strictly speaking you should be charged with the offence of disturbing the peace. However, I am inclined to take a lenient view of the matter, since you and your friends have to some extent already suffered as a result of your actions. All I require of you now is your undertaking to refrain from any more of this nonsense.'

Laura Hughes's dirty face scowled and she pointed her forefinger at her bruised brow. 'Is the man who did this to me also going to be prosecuted, Inspector? And the brute who struck Beattie Cartwright to the ground?'

He regarded her ambiguously. 'Can you identify the culprits? Can you give me their names?'

'Of course I cannot give their names,' she rejoined angrily. 'They are strangers to me. But your officers could doubtless discover their identities if you were to order them to make enquiries.'

'My officers are already making enquiries, Miss Hughes.' He was stung by the imputation that he was laggard in his professional duty. 'And when the culprits are identified, then they will be duly charged.'

Her expression of scornful disbelief provoked him to anger, and he reacted accordingly.

'Very well, Miss Hughes, either you now give me the undertaking that I require from you, or you will be arrested and charged with causing a disturbance of the peace. I should make it clear to you that in this case other charges may well follow.'

'I'll not give you any such undertaking,' she reiterated stubbornly.

The man's lips compressed into a harsh line, and he

bellowed: 'Sergeant Brunton, come here will you.'

When the sergeant appeared from the other room, the inspector formally arrested and charged Laura Hughes and instructed the sergeant to return her to her cell.

'Can she be granted bail, sir?' the sergeant queried.

His superior nodded. 'Yes. But not on her own recognizance.'

The elderly sergeant frowned slightly, but made no reply and led the young woman out of the office.

In the cell block he asked Laura, 'Does you have anyone that'll stand as surety for your bail? I can get word to them if necessary.'

The young woman shook her head doubtfully. 'Not here in Redditch. I can't very well ask my employers to stand as surety for me. I'm sure that once they learn about me being arrested then my employment will be instantly terminated anyway.'

The sergeant's manner was sympathetic. 'You shouldn't have angered Inspector Howard like you did young 'ooman. He aren't a bad hearted chap normally. He would have bailed you on your own recognizance if you hadn't upset him. I doon't like seeing a decent, respectable young 'ooman like yourself locked up in here like this. I'se got a daughter o' me own who'se about your age, and it 'ud grieve me sore to see her in this predicament.'

Laura shrugged her slender shoulders, affecting an uncaring bravado, which she was far from feeling. 'It doesn't matter to me being in here, Sergeant.'

But inwardly the gravity of her situation was now striking home to her, and her heart sank as the cell door was slammed and locked behind her. A wave of weariness overcame her and she slumped down on to the wooden pallet that served as a bed.

'I've lost my job, that's for sure, and my lodgings,' she thought apprehensively. 'And I might even end up in prison, because I've no money to pay any fines.' Momentarily her courage deserted her. A lump rose in her throat and she could not stop herself from bursting into tears.

Half an hour later, Sergeant Brunton left the station to check his constables on their beats.

Cleopatra Dolton saw him, and knowing him quite well she had no hesitation in approaching him.

Although visibly surprised by her interest in the young woman, Sergeant Brunton readily explained what had happened to her.

'Can I stand for her bail and surety?' Cleopatra asked.

'Why should you want to do that, Mrs Dolton? Her's a stranger to you, aren't she?' the sergeant wanted to know.

A mirthless smile briefly touched the beautiful woman's lips. 'Perhaps it's because I know what it's like to be a woman in a man's world, Sergeant Brunton.'

He returned with her to the Police Station. As soon as the formalities of bail and surety had been completed she asked him, 'Can I ask a personal favour of you, Sergeant Brunton?'

He grinned bluffly. 'Well, you can ask, Mrs Dolton but I can't guarantee that I can grant it.'

She smiled in return. 'It's nothing much, Sergeant. I just want you to give me time to get clear of Church Road before you release the girl.'

'But doon't you want to speak to her?' he queried in mystification. 'At least let her thank you for what you'm doing for her.'

She shook her head. 'No, I want no thanks, Sergeant. However, you might tell her that if she has no objection, I would be very interested in talking to her about what she is doing. You can give her my address if you will, and tell her that I'm at home every evening, so she can call at her own convenience. But please make it clear to her that she is under no obligation to do so.'

She smiled her thanks to the man and then walked out of the building, leaving only the faint scent of her perfume as a memento of her presence.

Chapter Seven

By late Saturday afternoon Emma Josceleyne was still suffering from the despondency which had afflicted her after that morning's visit to her mother.

'I'll just have to accept the fact that me Mam 'ull never leave that bastard of a Dad of mine, Mrs Elwood?' she told her confidante as they sat facing each other across the kitchen table, a shared bottle of gin between them.

The older woman clucked her tongue sympathetically.

'You know what annoys me most though,' Emma went on, 'it's the fact that whatever money I gives her to use for herself and the kids, that bastard gets most of it off her and pisses it up against the wall. I thought that when they had more money to spend on food and that, then he'd treat her better, because he 'udden't have to work so hard himself to feed 'um all. But he's worse to her now than he was afore.'

'Well, it's his pride, aren't it, my duck,' the cook averred with an air of wisdom.

'What do you mean, his pride?' Emma challenged hotly. 'How can any man be proud of knocking his Missis about?'

'Nooo, you misunderstands my meaning,' Mrs Elwood protested. 'What I means is that the bugger's pride is hurt because he has to rely on you to support his Missis and kids.'

'He 'uddent have to rely on me if he'd stop throwing his money away on the booze, and sweep a few more bloody chimneys instead o' spendin' all his time in the pub.'

'That's the way of a man, my duck,' the cook sighed resignedly. 'It always has been and always will be.'

Emma also sighed and then made a conscious effort to

dispel her gloomy mood. 'Ah well.' She forced a smile and took a large gulp of gin. 'There's nothing I can do for me Mam, except to make sure she's got some money in her pocket. It's her own choice to stay with the old bastard!' She shook her head in puzzlement. 'But why she does stay is a bloody mystery to me.'

'There's a good show at the Public Hall tonight, my duck,' Mrs Elwood informed. 'Chinese acrobats. Has you ever seen 'um?'

Emma shook her head.

'They'm supposed to be wonderful to see,' Mrs Elwood told her. 'At least that's what Willy Treadgold told my old man.' William Treadgold was the lessee and manager of the Public Hall.

'Willy Treadgold 'ud say that a bloody snail crossing the stage was wonderful entertainment if he thought he could sell tickets for it,' Emma chuckled disparagingly.

Nevertheless her interest was aroused, and she went on, 'Mind you, I wouldn't mind having a bit of a night out.'

Her companion's fat face frowned uncertainly. 'That 'udden't be proper, my duck, for you to goo out gallivanting. Not when you'se only yesterday buried your husband. What 'ud folks say?'

'I couldn't give a bugger what anybody might say.' The young woman's beautiful face was scornful, and the older woman's objections only served to make up her mind. 'I'm going to go to see those acrobats tonight,' she declared firmly. 'Does you want to come wi' me, Mrs Elwood? I'll treat you.'

The woman puffed out her fat cheeks and chuckled admiringly. 'You'm a case you am, Emma! You'm a real bloody caution!'

'Well, does you want to come?'

The cook shook her frizzled head regretfully. 'I'd love to come wi' you, my duck. But I carn't. Me and Elwood has got to goo and visit with his brother. It's been fixed up for ages.'

'That's a pity.' Emma was genuinely disappointed. 'Never mind, I'll take Miss Miriam.'

Mrs Elwood's eyes widened incredulously. 'Miss

Miriam? Goo to see a Music Hall turn? Her 'ud never do that! Especially not when her's just buried her Dad!'

Once again the other woman's objections only served to make Emma more determined to have her own way. 'Oh yes, she will come with me,' she declared positively. 'She'll come all right, even if I have to drag her there.'

'My lords, ladies and gentlemen, tonight for the grand finale, and for your entertainment, wonderment and delight, I have engaged the foremost act of its kind in the entire world! Regardless of the enormous expense, I was determined to provide my patrons here in Redditch, namely yourselves, ladies and gentlemen ... I was determined to lay before your discerning tastes the finest entertainment that the world can provide.' The short and stocky figure of William Treadgold bellowed from the front of the stage, resplendent in full evening dress, his starched white shirt front glistening in the footlights.

'The act that you are about to see has performed before all the crowned heads of Europe and Asia. Chung Han Lee is a Yellow Button Mandarin and his troupe are all of noble blood. As a small boy he was adopted by the Dowager Empress of China and when that lady realised how talented he was as an acrobat . . .' Treadgold bellowed on and on and the crowd quickly became impatient with his verbosity.

'Shut your bloody trap 'ull you, Willy Treadgold! And let's see them bloody Chinks!' a voice bawled from the darkened stalls of the cavernous auditorium, and was immediately followed by others.

'Let's have them bloody Chinks on!'

'Gerroff Treadgold!'

'Bring on the Chinks! Bring on the Chinks!'

The cry was taken up from all sides and boots thundered in unison on the wooden floor, creating a thunderous uproar and raising clouds of dust. 'BRING ON THE CHINKS! BRING ON THE CHINKS! BRING ON THE CHINKS!'

The Manager accepted defeat and signalled to the orchestra conductor in the pit below the stage front. The man raised his baton and the musicians struck up a tune with much clashing of cymbals to suggest the mystic Orient. The great stage curtains swept back to reveal an empty stage with a painted backdrop of pagodas and colourful dragons. Then, with a suddenness that struck the noisy crowd into stunned silence, pigtailed men clad in shimmering, loose-fitting costumes erupted on stage in a glittering whirling kaleidoscope of vaulting, somersaulting cartwheeling bodies.

In one of the dark sideboxes above the stalls Miriam Josceleyne drew breath sharply in delighted wonderment, and her nervous embarrassment at being in the hall was overlaid and forgotten in her enjoyment of the spectacle onstage. Beside her in the box, Emma threw her dark veil back from her face so that she could see more clearly, and crowed and applauded like a child as the troupe performed their miracles of muscular dexterity and strength. As time went on Miriam Josceleyne also threw back her own black veiling and allowed herself a clearer view.

Emma had become completely absorbed and was leaning over the boxfront and the bright lighting of the stage reflected upon her features. In the stalls beneath her a man glanced up and saw the rapt, beautiful face. He nudged his companion then whispered in his ear. The other man stared up at Emma, whistled in admiration, then answered his companion's urgent questions with shrugs of ignorance. The second man again turned his full attention back to the stage, but the first man had lost interest in the acrobats, and instead sat staring fixedly at the sidebox and its beautiful occupant.

Even before the final act had ended the man rose from his seat and left the hall. He crossed the street and stood on the steps of the Post Office entrance, from where he could see the length of the Hall's road front.

A police constable came from Church Green and passed by. His eyes studied the man standing on the steps with professional interest, noting the expensive laundered linen, well-cut suit, fashionable Homburg hat, gloves, gold-nobbed cane and highly polished boots.

'Good night, Officer.' The accent was that of a gentleman, and the policeman decided that there was nothing suspicious in his presence there.

'Good night, sir.' He saluted and passed on.

From within the Public Hall, the strains of the national anthem denoted that the night's performance had ended and shortly afterwards the happy, noisy crowd spilled from the main doors and subsidiary exits.

The watching man's late companion came hurrying across the roadway.

'Why did you leave early, Mr Vivaldi? Aren't you feeling well?'

Harry Vivaldi's swarthy features smiled, but his lustrous dark eyes were resentful of this distraction from his vigil.

'I'm fine, thank you. I'll come and see you tomorrow.' There was dismissal in his tone, and the other man recognised that he was unwanted there.

'All right then, Mr Vivaldi. I'll see you tomorrow then.'

Vivaldi ignored him, his eyes were searching the crowds, and the man frowned resentfully as he walked away.

'He's an ignorant bleeder, he is,' he told himself disgruntedly.

Vivaldi grinned in satisfaction as he saw the two black-clad women come out from the main entrance, their arms linked, and heads bowed as they hurried past him. He left his vantage point and followed the pair.

Their journey was a short one along the road to the Church Green. They went through the intersecting pathway and into the large porticoed house in the buildings facing the Recreation Garden.

Vivaldi strolled past the house a couple of times, examining its opulent exterior, taking in the name lettered in elegant script above its porch. 'Cotswold House,' he murmured. 'Cotswold House. And very nice too. I'm going to make it my urgent business to find out all I can about you.'

Smiling speculatively, he strolled off into the darkness, threading his way through the crowds of drinkers being reluctantly forced out of the closing public houses. He passed along Red Lion Street and the arched entrance to

61

Silver Street and took the next turning to the right into a street of tall back-to-back houses and factories known as George Street.

A little distance along the street he entered a covered entry and fumbled his way along its pitch blackness to emerge into a cramped and rancid-smelling court. He frowned in disgust as his nostrils filled with the foul stench from a broken-doored privy which stood only a couple of paces from the fronts of the houses. There were four adjoining tenements in the narrow court, built back-to-back with the houses on George Street. Harry Vivaldi entered the second house in the row.

'Where the bloody hell have you been? Chasing after some slut or other, I'll be bound!' The speaker was sitting by the side of a small table, which together with two straight-backed wooden chairs and a battered dresser comprised the furnishings of the cramped room. She was a woman in her forties, once pretty, now fast becoming fat and blowzy, her hair hanging in greasy tendrils around a blotched, pimpled face.

He pursed his lips in distaste as he regarded the shabby room which was poorly lit by a hissing gas jet, the fumes from which filled the stale air. His eyes were bleak as he answered his mistress. 'No, I've not been chasing after skirts, Bella. I've been having a business meeting.' He forced himself to smile at the woman and summoning all his willpower he bent and kissed her mouth, trying to ignore her sour breath and the sweaty odours of her unwashed body.

Then he pulled back a curtain hanging across an alcove in the wall which had been made into a makeshift wardrobe, and proceeded to take off his hat, outer clothing, shirt and boots and carefully hang, fold and place all the items within the alcove. Dressed only in his vest and long johns he seated himself at the table across from the woman and asked, 'Have you got anything to drink in the house?'

She scowled sullenly, but after a moment or two bent low, and gasping with the strain of compressing her corpulent body, she pulled out a jug from beneath her chair and handed it to him. 'Don't swill it all down in one go,' she warned wheezily. 'Because there's no more. Billy Kibler's stopped our slate until we pay what we owe him.'

He smiled brilliantly at her, displaying white even teeth and told her, 'What would I do without you, my sweetheart.' Then he lifted the jug and drank deeply of the beer it held.

The woman watched him drinking. In her unguarded expression there was reflected all the poignant yearning of the love she bore him. He was in his mid-twenties, lean-bodied and darkly handsome. His colouring and features were those of his Mediterranean ancestors, although he himself was the son of third generation immigrants who had long since lost all ties and loyalties to their ancestral homeland of Italy and regarded themselves as British.

Now that her man was safely home Bella Thomas's ever-knawing fear of losing him to another woman was temporarily eased, knowing that for tonight at least he would be sharing her bed.

'What business, Harry?' she questioned eagerly.

For a moment he looked blankly at her then smoothly recovered himself and answered airily, 'Talking Machines. I've been discussing a partnership in Talking Machines with a man I know.'

It was her turn to stare blankly. 'What are they?'

He ejaculated impatiently: 'You know well what they are, you silly cow. Gramophones and Zonophones.'

Her expression became animated, and traces of her youthful good looks were clearly discernible as she exclaimed excitedly: 'Ohh yes! Of course! How stupid I am!' then questioned eagerly: 'who is it who's offered you a partnership?'

'A chap name of Ernie Field. He's got a shop on Prospect Hill. I've got to meet him tomorrow and discuss the final details.' He frowned slightly. 'There's one thing that might stop me from getting the partnership though.'

The woman sobered instantly, and asked grimly, 'How much, Harry?'

He scowled petulantly. 'Why must you always bring

63

money into it?'

She displayed a flash of temper. 'Because it's always me that has to find the money from somewhere, isn't it!'

He made a show of staring contemptuously at his surroundings and sneered, 'Judging by this you're not doing a very good job of finding it these days, are you, my sweetheart.'

'You rotten bastard!' she shrieked furiously. 'You've taken everything I had, and spent it on your sluts and whores. You're nothing but a bloody ponce! You've been the ruin of me! I was a respectable married woman when I took up with you, and you've destroyed me!'

His dark eyes were cruel as he jeered, 'Destroyed you? A respectable married woman? You were a broken-down variety turn who'd managed to hook a bloody shopkeeper, so don't give me that respectable married woman nonsense.'

'I was never a whore, living in sin like I am now!' she argued doggedly, but her initial fury was fast becoming overlaid by fear that she might drive him away for good. Of late he had been showing increasing signs of restlessness and discontent, and she was so besotted with him that she felt that she would die if she ever lost him.

'Never a whore?' he scoffed viciously. 'That's all you ever were. Don't try telling me that you were a success on the Halls. You were a third-rate clodhopper who only ever got on the bottom of the bill. And you only got those bookings because you slept with any bloody manager who'd engage you. And when you got too long in the tooth for anybody to want to shag you, and you couldn't get any more bookings, why then you hooked that poor simple-minded sod who wed you.'

Her fury ebbed and disappeared and her expression was tragic. Yet there was a pathetic dignity emanating from her as with tears brimming in her eyes she told him hoarsely, 'Don't you go blaggarding Albert Thomas. It's his money that's bought you the clothes on your back, and put a roof over your head, and kept your belly filled for these last three years.'

These simple truths threatened to puncture Harry

64

Vivaldi's overweening self-esteem, and goaded him to shout: 'Whatever money you've given me is only a loan until I get on my feet! I'm going to pay you back every bloody penny, don't you worry about that. Every soddin' penny of it!'

Through the thin brick wall that separated them from the house next door, there sounded a furious muffled bawling and the wall almost shook under the volleyed impacts of heavy thumping blows.

'Look what you've done now!' Bella Thomas hissed accusingly. 'You've woke the whole bloody street up! Can't you be quiet?'

Harry Vivaldi's initial impulse was to slam his chair against the wall and bellow back at the irate neighbour. But then he recollected that the man was a mightily-muscled coal heaver, with a reputation as a fearsome brawler, and he thought better of that impulse.

For some time the couple remained motionless staring at each other, each waiting for the other to weaken. As always it was Bella Thomas who did so. Reaching out her hands towards him she beseeched, 'Don't let's fall out, Harry. You know that I love you. Don't be cruel to me.'

For all his vicious verbal attacks on her, the young man's nature was more petulant than cruel, and so long as he got his own way he was normally pleasant and indulgent towards women. Also, he knew that he still needed this meal-ticket. He forced his anger down and stared at her in sad reproach. 'Why do you always becall me so, Bella?' he asked huskily. 'I've done nothing to deserve this tonight. It's not my fault that I'm strapped for cash just now, is it? I try my best to find a good job. I hate being dependent on you, like I am at present. I feel ashamed that I can't give you all the things that I want to give you, sweetheart. A nice house and jewellery and fine clothes. I want to make you proud of me, Bella, really I do. I hate it when we quarrel like this and say such cruel things to each other. Because I don't mean what I say, it's only my temper that makes me say such terrible things. I don't mean them.'

Relief and thankfulness made Bella Thomas utter a sobbing cry, and she stumbled into his outstretched arms, hugging him fiercely and smothering his face with kisses. 'Don't you worry about the money for your partnership, my darling,' she told him over and over again. 'I'll go to Brum' tomorrow and see my husband. He'll give me the money.'

Harry Vivaldi closed his eyes and silently offered up a prayer of gratitude. The shopkeeper, Albert Thomas, was as besotted with his erring wife, as she was with Harry Vivaldi, and could never refuse her when she asked him for money – living as he did in the pitiful hope that one day she would return to him.

Now Bella Thomas's kisses became greedier and her breathing quickened to hoarse panting.

'Take me to bed, sweetheart,' she begged hungrily. 'Take me to bed.'

Wordlessly he led her up the narrow staircase and stripped the many layers of clothing from her fat body. The knowledge of his domination over her acted as an aphrodisiac upon his senses, overriding his distaste for her acrid-smelling flesh and sour breath, and he took her with a savage urgency, excited sexually by his physical and mental mastery of her.

Afterwards as he lay beside her, listening to the wheezy snortings of her breathing, he mentally compared her to the image of the beautiful young woman he had followed from the Public Hall, and he promised himself, 'I'm going to get to know that one if it's the last thing I do. I'm going to get to know her.' He grinned to himself. 'And then it will be goodbye to this fat cow.'

Still grinning he turned over on to his side and settled himself to sleep.

Chapter Eight

Laura Hughes awoke in her attic bedroom to the sounds of the bells of St Stephen's Church calling the faithful to prayer. Her brain still enmeshed in the confused dreams of sleep, she blinked drowsily and stretched her slender body, then memory flooded back and she came upright in her narrow bed.

Mentally she debated her best course of action, and decided that there was no point in avoiding the unpleasant realities of her situation. 'I'll go and tell the Groses about what has happened,' she smiled mirthlessly, 'and then I'll resign before they can dismiss me.'

She visualised the stern features of her employers, and could not repress a slight tremor of apprehension. Strong men had quailed before their icy gaze and brave though Laura was she did not relish the coming confrontation.

She got out of the bed and drew her nightdress over her head then examined what she could see of her naked body in the mirror of the washstand. She clucked her tongue critically. 'You look like a scrawny plucked chicken, Laura Hughes,' she told herself disparagingly. Many people would have thought that she was being over-critical of herself, but in an age when fashionable beauties flaunted large breasts and wide hips, Laura considered her own small high breasts and narrow hips to be too boyish to be attractive.

She poured cold water from the large jug into the wide, deep bowl on the marble washstand and using a flannel and harsh yellow soap, she scrubbed herself from head to toe. Then cleaned her teeth and brushed her hair. Still naked she ruefully examined her soiled clothing. 'I don't think some of these stains will wash out,' she thought sadly. 'This blouse is ruined, and probably the skirt as well.'

This represented a serious depletion of her scant wardrobe and she had no money to buy replacements for the ruined articles.

She dressed herself in her prim, dark blue Sunday gown, and then steeling herself to face the uncomfortable interview, left her attic and went downstairs.

Grafton House stood in Worcester Road which ran down westwards from Evesham Street, close to the central crossroads. It was a large, rambling building; the ground floor served mainly as schoolrooms, the first floor as living quarters for the Misses Grose, the second floor as storerooms and bedrooms for guests and boarding pupils, although none of the latter were in residence at present. The attics were staff quarters. The present staff consisted of Laura and a living-in general maid.

Laura encountered Primrose the maid on the second floor landing. Laura had been ironically amused by the contrast of the flowery name with the tall, raw-boned, dour-faced middle-aged woman who bore it. Primrose stared at the large bruise on Laura's forehead, and sniffed. 'I was just coming up to get you, Miss,' she said. There was a gleam of malicious satisfaction in her small eyes. 'Miss Amelia and Miss Annabel wants to see you straight away.'

Laura nodded curtly. There had been a mutual dislike between herself and the maid from their very first meeting.

Primrose could not resist adding triumphantly, 'I expect they wants to see you because of what happened in the Mart yesterday. They must have been told about it when they went to early service this morning. It's the talk o' the town, so it is.'

Laura seethed inwardly at the other woman's obvious spiteful satisfaction but forced herself to smile sweetly at her, and reply gaily. 'I'm glad to hear that, Primrose. It was great fun. I enjoyed every moment of it.'

The woman glared at this light-hearted reaction, and sneered: 'Well, I hopes it's just as good fun for you when you'm walking the streets carrying your box.'

'It will be, Primrose. It will be,' Laura answered smilingly, then walked past the woman and tapped on the door of her employers' private quarters.

The almost identical sisters were sitting stiffly upright, side by side on two armless chairs. Dressed alike in sombre black, with jet jewellery, their iron-grey hair severely bunned on top of their heads, their hands clasped on their laps. Their pale grim faces turned towards Laura as she entered the room and their hard eyes stared bleakly at her.

'Miss Hughes, be good enough to explain what happened yesterday,' Miss Amelia commanded.

Laura swallowed hard to dispel the lump that had arisen in her throat. Despite her own resolve not to be intimidated, she was still made nervous by this formidable pair.

'Well, Miss Hughes? We await your explanation.' Miss Annabel frowned.

Laura felt herself flushing, and this realisation brought with it a rush of self-directed anger. 'Why should I let these two harpies frighten me,' she challenged herself, and then blurted out: 'I and my friends were assaulted by some hooligans, and the police took us into protective custody.'

Now that the confrontation had finally begun, Laura's confidence returned in a rush and she was able to meet their hard eyes with a defiant stare.

'Why were you assaulted by these hooligans?' Miss Amelia demanded.

'Because I spoke out about the injustices that women are subjected to in this country,' Laura stated firmly.

'If you and your friends were the victims of assault, why is it that the police are charging you with creating a disturbance, Miss Hughes?' Miss Annabel wanted to know.

'Because I refused to submit to the conditions for my release which the police wished to impose upon me.'

Both sisters raised their eyebrows in silent interrogation, and Laura went on to explain in detail all that had occurred both before and after being taken into custody.

'And when are you to appear before the Magistrates?' Miss Amelia asked.

'Wednesday morning next, at half-past eleven.'

The sisters exchanged a long look as if communing by telepathy. Then their faces turned again to Laura.

It was Miss Annabel who acted as spokeswoman. 'We appointed you to your present position as an act of Christian charity, Miss Hughes. Knowing that you possessed no living relatives we were prepared to offer you shelter and employment. Because your late father, the Reverend Hughes, had been known to us we trusted that his daughter had inherited his own blameless character and strict moral rectitude. He was a truly Christian gentleman, Miss Hughes.'

Miss Amelia nodded her head in silent agreement with her sister's words, as Miss Annabel continued. 'It is clearly apparent that our trust has been misplaced, and abused. You will therefore leave this house. Naturally we cannot supply you with references which might enable you to obtain a similar position elsewhere. We would be failing in our duty to any prospective employer if we were to give you a character. We bid you good-day, Miss Hughes. Kindly vacate your room immediately.'

Quick resentment flared in Laura's mind. 'I accept that you have the right to dismiss me from your employment. But you do not have the right to dismiss me without paying me the wages you owe me. You have made no mention of when I am to receive them.'

'You have forfeited any entitlement to remuneration by your improper conduct, Miss Hughes,' Miss Amelia said sharply.

'I've been here for more than two months,' Laura protested. 'And you yourselves have both stated that you were satisfied with my work. I am entitled to that money.'

The sisters again exchanged a long stare of silent communication. Then Miss Amelia said coldly, 'I repeat, you have forfeited any entitlement to wages by your own wicked conduct. If you continue to dispute this, then we shall have no other recourse open to us but to immediately telephone to the Police Station and have you arrested. Now kindly go from this house.'

Laura's expression mirrored her incredulity. She could hardly believe that she was hearing the words correctly.

'Arrested?' she exclaimed. 'You are threatening to have me arrested because I am asking for what is rightfully mine? I can't be arrested for that.'

The sisters regarded her coldly, and Miss Annabel answered, 'You are behaving in a threatening manner towards us, Miss Hughes. From my reading of the law I am confident that that constitutes good and sufficient reason for having you arrested. And there is another witness to your threatening behaviour.'

'Another witness?' Laura repeated, and the two sisters simultaneously nodded towards the door behind her.

She half-turned and saw that Primrose had come silently into the room and was standing with her back to the door. A sense of helplessness suddenly invaded Laura as she realised her own impotence. Anger burned, but knowing its futility, she nodded in bitter acceptance, and without another word she left the room and returned to the attic to begin packing her meagre belongings into her travelling box. As she folded her few items of clothing and laid them in the wooden box, she thought worriedly about what she was going to do now. She had only pennies in her purse, and nowhere to go. She thought briefly of going to Beattie Cartwright's house, but rejected that notion almost instantly. 'Her father would not let me across the doorstep. And I don't want to involve poor Beattie in any more trouble.'

She lifted the scrap of paper that Sergeant Brunton had given her the previous evening and read again the name and address of her benefactor. 'Mrs Cleopatra Dolton. The Elms. Red Lane.' She murmured the words, trying to visualise the woman who had been prepared to stand as bail and surety for a complete stranger.

Laura had intended going to that house later in the day to thank Mrs Dolton for her kindness. But now, after what had occurred, she was reluctant to do so until she herself had found another place to live, and some means of support.

'I would be too tempted to ask her for help,' she realised, and her fierce pride rebelled at the prospect. She was honest enough to admit that in her desperate situation, the temptation to ask for further help would probably prove to be overwhelming. 'I can't risk it,' she decided. 'I can't risk going there now.'

She heard the clumping of heavy footsteps on the staircase and then the door was pushed open and Primrose entered the room.

'Am you ready to leave?'

Laura ignored the woman and finished packing her box. She closed its lid and tightened the long leather straps around it. Then shrugging into her long mackintosh and putting her straw boater on her high-piled hair, she hefted her unwieldy luggage and went from the room and out of the house.

'Good riddance to bad rubbish,' Primrose mouthed behind her, and the door slammed.

The slamming of the door sent a shiver of loneliness through Laura's mind. She was now homeless, friendless and virtually penniless, in a town in which she was a comparative stranger.

The sun was high and very hot, and Laura started to trudge slowly up the slope towards Evesham Street. As she walked she tried to plan her next move, but it was as if her brain was refusing to function rationally and only random, jumbled thoughts and memories came to her. At the top of the slope she turned left past the Vine public house, stepping to the outside of the pavement to skirt the men lounging against its walls, waiting for its doors to open. With her head bent and immersed in her own unhappy reverie, she did not notice the shabbily dressed woman who came towards her from the crossroads and who stared with sudden recognition, then, when Laura had walked some distance further on, who turned and began to follow her.

The tall trees surrounding St Stephen's church offered a shaded haven from the blazing sun and Laura crossed the road and moved beneath the shelter of the huge branches. When she reached the Recreation Garden, she saw the benches placed around the walkways and experiencing a sudden weariness, she entered the garden and seated herself on a shady bench. She fumbled in the cluttered pockets of her long mackintosh and unexpectedly found a few extra coins. She regarded them with considerable thankfulness. 'Well, I've got three shillings and fourpence altogether now. At least I won't starve for a couple of days.'

The shabbily dressed woman who had followed her walked slowly along the roadway outside the garden fence and surreptitiously watched her quarry. At the apex of the triangular garden the woman slowed and halted, and then turned to retrace her footsteps, all the time keeping her eyes fixed on the young woman sitting with bowed shoulders on the bench. When she came to the pathway bisecting the garden from the churchyard, the shabby woman came to a decision and walked briskly into the garden and up to Laura Hughes.

'Begging your pardon, Miss,' she spoke hesitantly, as if fearful of rebuff.

Laura blinked up at this stranger, whom she judged was about her own age, but whose thin face was prematurely worn and bore the greyish imprint of ill-health.

'Yes, what is it?' She spoke more brusquely than she intended and the shabby woman appeared to flinch nervously.

'I'm sorry, I didn't mean to sound so ill-tempered,' Laura apologised instantly, and the other woman smiled timidly, disclosing sadly decayed teeth.

'That's all right, Miss. Theer's no harm done.'

Again she lapsed into silence, as if uncertain of how to proceed, and Laura made herself smile and ask encouragingly, 'Did you wish to speak with me?'

The thin face suddenly radiated eagerness, and the woman nodded jerkily. 'Yes, I wants to ask you if you'm the young lady who was speechifying in Market Place yesterday?'

'Yes, I'm she,' Laura confirmed, then added ironically, 'at least I'm the one who was trying to make a speech.'

'I thought it was wonderful,' the woman breathed admiringly. 'What you was saying was wonderful, Miss. I wanted to hear more, and when them roughs went for you, I was so angry I felt like killing 'um.'

The patent sincerity in the woman's voice and face ignited a sudden flame of gratitude in Laura's heart, and acted like a tonic upon her jaded senses. She smiled warmly and patted the seat beside her.

'Won't you sit down, Miss? Miss?'

'It's Rosie, Miss. Me name is Rosie Spiers.'

'I shall call you Rosie,' Laura told her, 'and you must call me Laura.'

For a while they sat by side, exchanging brief sideways glances, smiling to mask their unease when their eyes met.

Finally Laura grew impatient with herself for her own unease, and said briskly, 'This is silly, sitting here without talking. Tell me about yourself, Rosie. I'd really like to hear more about you.'

When the other woman proved shyly reluctant, Laura urged gently, 'Please tell me, Rosie. It's not every day that I meet someone who enjoys my attempts at making speeches.'

As if the word had broken a mental dam in Rosie Spiers's mind, she began to speak; hesitantly at first, then with increasing confidence and fluency as Laura encouraged her.

She was a seamstress, living with her twin brother in a slum court off the Unicorn Hill. She was Laura's own age, twenty-five. Her parents had been middle-aged and had already raised a large family when the twins had been born to them. Both parents were still living but they had been forced by old age and infirmity to go into the Union Workhouse, in Bromsgrove, some six miles to the west of Redditch. Rosie could read and write, although with some difficulty.

'I only had board school learning you see, Miss. And because I had to help keep the house gooing, I missed a lot of lessons.'

'And your brother, what work does he do?' Laura was fascinated by her new friend's story, mentally contrasting the difference in their lives, and acknowledging how sheltered and easy her own life had been in comparison with that of Rosie Spiers's. 'At least until now,' she thought to herself wryly.

Rosie hesitated before answering Laura's question concerning her brother. Then she drew a long breath and spoke as if making a guilty confession: 'Me brother doon't do any work, Miss. He aren't capable.'

'Call me Laura,' Laura corrected sternly, and then queried, 'is he ill, your brother?'

Rosie seemed near to tears as she shook her head. 'Not poorly in health, no.' She coughed and wiped her thin hand across her reddening eyes. Then blurted out: 'He's a natural. He aren't right in his yed.' She hurried on defensively, 'He aren't a danger to anybody, excepting himself, poor soul. But he's simple yedded. By rights he should goo to the loony bin, I suppose. The doctors at the hospital said that he should be put away. But I couldn't bear to think of him being locked up like that. 'Specially now, after me Mam and Dad's had to goo into the work'ouse. He's all I got left in the world, you see. I aren't got anybody else.' She sniffed loudly, and rubbed hard at her eyes with both hands. 'I'm sorry to be like this,' she muttered brokenly. 'I'll be all right in a minute.'

Laura said nothing, and left the other woman to recover herself.

When Rosie Spiers had stemmed her tears, Laura asked gently, 'Where is your brother now, Rosie?'

'He's at home. Me neighbour's a good soul. She looks after him for me when I has to goo and do me shopping, or see about me work.'

Laura's vivid imagination was already picturing in graphic detail the life that this shabby woman must lead, and her heart welled with mingled pity and admiration. 'Compared to her, I am the most fortunate creature breathing,' she admitted to herself. 'My present troubles are piffling when I think what she has to endure.'

Again they sat in silence, but now it was free of any unease and both women experienced a sensation of contentment in each other's company.

This time it was Rosie Spiers who broke the silence. Indicating the wooden box she asked: 'Are you going away anywheer, Laura?'

Laura smiled ruefully. 'I don't know what I'm going to do, Rosie.' She went on to explain what had happened that day.

'. . . so even if I had the money to leave Redditch, I couldn't do so before Wednesday. Because I have to appear before the magistrates on that day.'

Rosie pondered what she had heard and then offered diffidently, 'I hope you wun't take this amiss, Laura, but I could always fix you up with a bed in my house.' She blushed with embarrassment. 'O' course, me brother 'ud be theer. But he can share my bed. You'd have a room to yourself. It aren't what you'm used to, I know. After all, you'm a lady, aren't you, and used to better things. I'm afraid that you'll think I'm insulting you by offering.'

'I most certainly do not,' Laura protested indignantly, and instantly made up her mind to accept. 'I'm most grateful to you, Rosie. and I gladly accept your kind offer. But on one condition. You must allow me to pay for my lodgings.'

It was Rosie Spiers's turn to protest. 'Oh no, I couldn't take anything from you. The lodging I'm offering is too rough to take anything for it.'

'I shall pay!' Laura stated positively, and waved aside any further protest from her companion. 'Right then, shall we be off?'

Rosie smiled shyly, and nodded agreement.

The court where Rosie lived was in Hill Street, an alleyway leading off Unicorn Hill which fell away to the west from the central crossroads.

As the young women passed by the Unicorn Inn, a little distance from the crossroads, they were forced to run a gauntlet of curious stares from the loungers outside the public house.

'Does you want me to carry your box for you, sugarplum?' a youth shouted cheekily.

'Doon't you let him, sweetheart, he'll want too much for doing it,' one of the youth's friends warned jokingly.

'Ahrr, and it wunt be money he'll be wanting neither,' a third man bawled, rubing his crotch suggestively. His sally was greeted with roars of lewd laughter from the other loungers.

There was another public house, the Lamb and Flag, on the corner of Hill Street, and its frontage also was lined with lounging men. Laura frowned with misgivings when she saw the unshaven, brutish-looking faces louring hostilely at Rosie and herself as they neared the corner.

Her misgivings became laced with actual fear when a burly man, with a tough, unshaven face, a muffler knotted around his collarless throat and a broken-crowned bowler hat pulled down low over his bleared eyes, stepped directly into their path and forced them to a halt. Laura was about to challenge him angrily, but ignoring her, he growled harshly at Rosie. 'Has you seen our kid, Rosie?'

'No.' Rosie looked suddenly anxious. 'Why?'

'I sent him to find you, my duck. Your Tommy took a bad fit just arter you'd gone out, and we had to tie him down.'

'Oh my God!' Rosie's thin hands went to her mouth in dismay, and the man clumsily patted her thin shoulder, and roughly comforted.

'Now doon't get moithered, girl. He took no harm, only bit his tongue a bit, that's all, afore I could get some rag atween his teeth.'

'He didn't hurt Maria, did he?' Rosie questioned worriedly.

The man laughed in genuine amusement. 'Hurt my Missus? Fuck me, girl, it 'ud take the Brigade o' Guards to hurt that old cow.'

'Thanks, Eddie, for looking after him. I'm ever so grateful.'

'That's all right, duck.' The man waved her thanks aside. 'But you'd best gerron home right away. He'll be all right when he sees you.'

Rosie hurried up the narrow, deeply-rutted street, and Laura followed. A faint sense of shame gnawed at her.

'Let that be a lesson,' she told herself, 'not to keep on judging people by their appearance. That man might look like a brute, but he's proven himself to be a good person.'

The court was a cramped, dank oblong of huddled tenements, with rag-stuffed broken windows, and splintered doors. No sun lightened its gloom because its rays were blocked by the high walls of a grain store. The entire centre space was filled by a reeking uncovered rubbish heap, bounded by low walls fashioned from baulks of rotting timber, through the gaping cracks of which oozed stinking liquid wastes to puddle and saturate the ground. Several tiny ragged children were jumping with bare feet into the puddles and shrieking with glee as the filthy mud spattered all around them.

Rosie disappeared through a low doorway and Laura paused for a moment or two to take in her surroundings. The stench seemed to clog in her throat and made her nauseous. But she clenched her teeth and swallowed hard, telling herself: 'You'll get used to it. Just remember beggars can't be choosers.'

From inside Rosie's house she could hear the sounds of female voices raised in harsh discordance, and with a feeling of trepidation she ducked her head under the low doorway and entered.

To her surprise the small room was empty of people, the voices were coming from the rear of the cottage. Laura looked around her, surprised and pleased to see that although only meagrely furnished with a couple of three-legged stools and a minute table, the place was clean, the walls whitewashed and the unpainted woodwork scrubbed. Above the mantelshelf, pinned to the wall, were some needlework samplers, colourfully embroidered with flowers and mottoes, and on the shelf stood a couple of old chipped vases filled with sweet-smelling wild flowers. On the other walls were hung bunches of fragrant herbs. Her respect for Rosie Spiers intensified.

She moved to the connecting doorway and peeped into the rear room. It was a narrow scullery, fitted with a long stone sink, and some shelves on which rested Rosie's pathetic collection of battered and dented tin pots and pans, and cracked and chipped crockery.

Laura would learn later that the tenements had no direct water supply, and every drop of water used for washing, cooking and cleaning had to be carried from a solitary hand-pump halfway down the street. There were no privvies or waste pipes in the courts either, and the people who lived there were forced to use buckets for their personal offices, which were then emptied wherever the individual decided was most convenient. For the most part this was on the big rubbish heap in the centre of the court. Any cooking was done at the small fireplace in the living room, on the minute cast-iron range which incorporated a tiny oven and hot-plate. Beyond the rear of the scullery was a tiny shared back yard with rope lines slung across its width and length to hang and dry wet clothing and bedding.

In the scullery Rosie was facing two women. Maria Cull, the wife of the man who had accosted them, and physically a female version of her husband, was haranguing Rosie.

'He'll have to be put away, my wench. He'll drag you down in the end. He's getting too much for you to handle. It took me and Ethel here, and my old mon to hold the bugger and get him lashed down. And we had an hell of a job to do it, as well, I'll tell you.' She sought confirmation from her companion.

'Aren't that so, Ethel?'

Ethel's grimy, greasy head nodded vigorously. 'Maria's right, my duck,' she said vehemently. 'Your Tommy's getting worse, God help the poor benighted bugger. It aren't his fault, we all knows that, but he's getting to be a bloody menace, my duck. He'll end by killing you in one of his bloody turns. You should ought to have him put into Barnsley Hall wi' the rest o' the bloody loonies. That's the proper place for him.'

Inarticulate cries suddenly sounded from the room above their heads, and a heavy thumping shook the thin floorboards.

'Fuck me, the bugger's got loose again!' Maria Cull cursed angrily. 'Come on Ethel, and you, Rosie. It'll take all on us.'

For the first time she noticed Laura, and questioned: 'Who's this then?'

'It's my friend, Laura,' Rosie explained.

'You'd best come up as well,' Maria Cull ordered. 'The more on us the better. He's really strong when he's like this.'

79

She led the way up the ladder-like staircase, and Rosie turned to Laura. 'I'm sorry!' Her face was filled with shame and distress. 'You doon't have to come. You must leave.'

Although Laura was more than a little afraid of what might lay ahead of her, there was at the same time a wild excitement beginning to course through her being. 'This is really living!' she told herself with a burgeoning exhultation. She felt an insane desire to laugh aloud, and unable to credit what was happening to her emotions, she could only shake her head wildly, and tell Rosie: 'I'm coming with you, Rosie. I'll not be denied.'

Then she followed Ethel up the stairs. She briefly glimpsed the front room, with its narrow bed and wooden box for a dresser, then plunged through to join the other women wrestling across the bed with the thrashing body of Tommy Spiers.

The young man was still bound with ropes, but had managed to get one arm free, and was flailing wildly about him, and kicking furiously with his bound legs.

'Lay across his legs!' Maria Cull shouted to Laura, her own hands desperately trying to hold the lunatic's mouth closed so that he could not bite, while Ethel fought to pinion his free arm.

Laura did not stop to think, but hurled herself forwards bodily. His knees thudded painfully into her stomach, and she gasped for breath, but pressed her full weight downwards, grasping the edge of the bedstead with her hands and exerting all the strength she could bring to bear.

'Grab that piece o' wood, Rosie, and be ready to shove it in his mouth when I tells you to,' Maria bawled. 'And make sure you gets it well in, or he'll bite your bloody hand off!'

Laura lost all count of time as the violent struggle went on, and then it was suddenly over, and the man was once again lashed securely to the bedstead, powerless to inflict injury either to himself or to others.

Bruised and almost spent, Laura levered herself upright, and stood looking down at the bound figure. A sense of amazement filled her as she regarded his thin, undersized body, with its stick-like arms, and puny chest. 'Where did all that strength come from?' she wondered aloud.

Maria Cull shook her head. 'I dunno, girl, but I wish I could have some on it for the next time when my old mon comes home drunk and nasty.' she chuckled grimly. 'Like he 'ull tonight most probably.'

She spoke in a kindlier tone to Rosie: 'I'll have to be getting off now, my duck. I'se got to get my old mon's dinner ready for when he comes back from the pub, there'll be bloody ructions else.'

'An me as well, I'll have to goo now,' Ethel added.

Both women bade Laura a farewell, examining her with curious eyes as they left.

Rosie Spiers stared shamefaced at Laura and once more began to apologise for what had happened, but Laura gestured her to silence.

'I doon't suppose you'll be wanting to lodge here now, 'ull you,' Rosie said glumly.

Laura looked at the bound man, his eyes bulging wildly in his thin pock-marked face as he snorted for breath. Then her gaze travelled around the poverty-stricken room, noting the neatly patched bed covers, the bare clean-scrubbed floors and walls, the washed underside of the uncovered roof tiles. She caught the scents of the hanging herbs and wild flowers that were festooned all around the tiny house, and she smiled, and said gently, yet very very firmly: 'Wild horses could not drag me away from here, Rosie. I intend to stay for just as long as you will have me.'

During the rest of Sunday morning and afternoon Laura helped Rosie with the household tasks and the care of Tommy Spiers. The question of how they should arrange sleeping quarters arose. There were two beds in the house, a double and a single. Rosie said that she and her brother would share the double bed in the front room, leaving Laura the rear bedroom to herself with the single bed.

Although Rosie had previously said that she would be sharing a bed with her brother when she had offered her new friend lodgings, Laura had not really given the proposal any thought. Now, faced with concrete reality, she found the idea repugnant to her sense of morality. Of course she had always known that the poor slept promiscuously mixed together, but she had never before personally experienced this fact at first hand. Childhood memories of her father inveighing against the sin of incest rose up in her mind to torment her. It was an accepted belief among the middle classes that the poor practised incest on a wide scale, and indeed that belief was well-grounded in actual fact. Contained in the police and the Registrar General's records were many cases of young women and girls being made pregnant by their own fathers, brothers and other male relatives.

Laura's uneasy thoughts were reflected in her eyes, and Rosie Spiers was sensitive enough to divine what was troubling the other woman.

'Tommy's a babby in everything except his years, Laura,' she said softly. 'And to me he's like my own babby. There's nothing wrongful or wicked in me and him sharing a bed. It aren't man and woman sharing, it's mother and babby.'

Laura blushed to the very roots of her hair with mortified shame, and she started to babble out denial, apology and excuse.

Rosie now displayed a depth of understanding and a dignity that even in the midst of her own shame and confusion invoked in Laura a touch of awe. 'Theer's no need for you to say anything, Laura.' The thin, grey face contained no hint of reproach. 'This is all new to you, the way that we lives here in Hill Street. But you'll find that the people here am very much the same as the rest o' the world. There's good, bad and inbetweens.' A hint of a smile quirked her lips. 'Mind you, we looks a bit rougher than the folks who lives in Worcester Road, I'll give you that.' Rosie paused, deliberately turning to rearrange the flowers in the chipped vases, giving Laura time to compose herself. Then she turned back and smiled.

'Let's have a cup o' tay, shall us?'

By the time the tea had been brewed and they were perched on the three-legged stools sipping their cups of the dark sweet liquid, Laura was at ease once more.

Inwardly she was resolved that she would never again prejudge any situation until she knew the full facts of it.

Her thoughts turned to her mysterious benefactor of the previous day, and she asked Rosie casually, 'Do you know a woman named Cleopatra Dolton, Rosie? Mrs Cleopatra Dolton?'

'Oh yes. The Queen of Egypt, we calls her.' Rosie grinned, and then queried in her turn, 'Why, do you know her yourself?'

Laura shook her head. 'No, I don't know her, but it was she who stood as bail and surety for me.'

Now Rosie's expression denoted shocked surprise, causing Laura to question sharply, 'Why do you look so shocked, Rosie?'

After a few seconds Rosie answered thoughtfully, 'I was surprised that she would have done such. Because she's got the name of being a hard-hearted woman.' She peered curiously at her companion. 'Does you know the story of her?'

'No.' Laura shook her head.

'Well, her's a widow-woman. And her's got a fair bit o' money. Them butchers' shops, the ones called 'The Redditch Meat Company', they'm all hers. She's got three boys that she's sent away to be schooled at one of them gentry schools.'

Laura listened, but could not yet see any reason for her friend's shocked reaction to the woman's name. Then Rosie informed her. 'Cleopatra Dolton had a fancy man, name of Johnny Purvis, and about three years past, Arthur Dolton, her husband, caught her and Purvis in bed together and there was a fight. Arthur Dolton got killed. Johnny Purvis was convicted o' manslaughter and sent to jail.' Rosie's eyes were speculative. 'But there's a lot of folks hereabouts who thinks it shouldn't have been him who was sent to jail.'

Laura's eyes were wide with enthralment. 'Why do they think that?'

Rosie's thin shoulders shrugged high. 'Well, they thinks that it was all her fault that it happened. That she led Johnny Purvis on and tormented her husband until it was bound to happen, that one of 'um would kill the other.'

'And what do you think, Rosie?'

The worn, grey face filled with sympathy. 'I think that no matter what happened, she was bound to be blamed for it. Women always am blamed, aren't they, because they've got no voice in this world. There's nobody to stick up for them, is there?'

Fierce determination flared in Laura's eyes. 'We are going to change all that, Rosie. Just you wait and see. We'll make the world listen to our voices, whether it wants to or not. We'll make it listen.'

Chapter Nine

Harry Vivaldi sauntered along Market Place casting appreciative glances at his elegant reflection in the shop windows. Although the Monday morning skies were grey and overcast, his own mood was light and sunny. Bella Thomas had gone to Birmingham on the early train, and the young man was confident that she would once again be successful in extracting money from her husband. In the meantime he was enjoying the fact that she was miles away, and so could not be surreptitiously following him, as she so frequently did.

For nearly an hour now he had been promenading through all the principal thoroughfares of the town centre. But at this hour there were few diversions to be found in the streets, with a dearth of pretty women to ogle, and Harry Vivaldi was becoming a little bored. He walked around the large triangle of the Church Green, and up and down the Recreation Garden, centering his attention on the Cotswold House, hoping for some sight of its occupants, but it remained disappointingly devoid of any signs of life behind its drawn curtains.

He stood at the apex of the Green and stared down Prospect Hill and over the Arrow valley and the sweep of countryside beyond. He remembered the story he had told his mistress on Saturday night, concerning his potential partnership, and grimaced wryly. It was not a partnership that Ernie Field had offered, but the possibility of a job as a salesman and demonstrator of 'Talking Machines'.

'It's lucky the old cow forgot that I was supposed to settle the details yesterday.' Vivaldi congratulated himself on his good fortune. 'She would have nagged me blind if she hadn't done.'

He now thought about the possible job. As well as working in the shop on Prospect Hill he would also play the machines at private houses. Talking Machines were still a popular novelty, and many people entertaining their friends at home in the evenings, or holding a party or small dance, engaged the proprietor of a Talking Machine to attend with a collection of records. It was far cheaper than paying a band of musicians to play for the gathering.

Vivaldi pursed his lips thoughtfully. 'It would get me into a lot of houses around here, wouldn't it. And I'd get to meet a lot of women at the parties.'

He turned to look over his shoulder at Cotswold House. 'Maybe even in there as well. She looked a lively girl who'd enjoy parties.' He grinned to himself and went on down the hill to Ernie Field's shop.

Field was a stoop-shouldered man with thinning ginger hair. Harry Vivaldi had made his acquaintance in one of the local public houses some weeks previously when he and Bella Thomas had first moved to live in Redditch. The two men had drunk together on several occasions since then. The shopkeeper had been impressed with Harry Vivaldi's elegant appearance and personable manners, and at their last meeting during the past week had mentioned the possibility of a job.

Now he greeted the young man's entrance with a smile. 'Hello there, Harry. I aren't seen you for a bit. I thought you might be in The Sportsman last Saturday night, but you weren't there.'

Harry shook his head. 'No, I met a chap who had a couple of tickets for the Public Hall, so I went with him to see those Chinese Acrobats.'

They talked about trivia for a few minutes, and then Vivaldi said casually, 'I've been giving some thought to that job you offered me.'

'Oh yes.' A guarded look came into Field's watery blue eyes. Anything that smacked of money having to be paid out made him wary. 'Well, it warn't exactly a firm offer I made, Harry. It was more of a possibility.'

Harry Vivaldi smiled inwardly, and thought to himself, 'You fucking peasant! Now it's come to the crunch you're worried about paying out wages, aren't you.' Aloud he said easily, 'Oh, I know that, Ernie. But let's say I'm interested in the possibility. What sort of money could I earn, if the possibility became a fact?'

Ernie Field drew a long breath, then said vaguely, 'Well, that 'ud be up to you really, Harry. The more sales you made, then the more you'd earn, obviously.'

'I'd get commission then, would I?' The young man sought confirmation.

'Oh yes. You'd get a good commission,' Field nodded. 'You'd get commission on every machine that you sold, and on the records, and even the needles. Then there'd be the gratuities as well, on top of all that.'

'Gratuities?'

'Yes, when you did an evening party, if they took a collection for you, or gave you a tip, then you'd keep half of whatever they give you.'

'Only half?' Harry affected surprise, but inwardly was grinning broadly, amused by the other man's miserliness.

'I have to think about the wear and tear on my machines and records, and the cost of the needles, haven't I,' Field said hastily. 'Half the gratuities doon't even begin to cover that.'

Harry Vivaldi could not help but bait his companion. Assuming a doubtful expression, he remarked, 'Well, if half wouldn't even begin to cover the wear and tear, then the gratuities must be bloody small ones, Ernie.'

For a moment the other man was taken aback, but then he looked at Vivaldi and a sly gleam came into his eyes. 'There's some blokes gets more than others might, if you get my meaning, Harry. Now a good-looking young chap like you 'ud do very well. There's a lot of older women who'd have a soft spot for you, I should think. And they'd be happy to give you a bob or two extra if you provided a good evening's entertainment. If they liked the programme, they'd even have you back to do an extra performance. It's happened before to my certain knowledge, Harry.'

Field's words sparked off a whole new train of ideas in Harry Vivaldi's mind, and his imagination suddenly soared. 'The old bastard might have something there,' he thought excitedly, knowing from experience how many older women were partial to his good looks and easy charm. 'Who knows what could happen? I could meet some rich old dear and do very well for myself.' Outwardly he betrayed no sign of his inner excitement.

'What basic salary were you thinking of paying me, Ernie?'

'Oh I couldn't afford to pay you any salary, Harry. The business wun't be able to afford that,' Field blustered defensively. 'Times are very hard at present. It's all I can do to keep this shop going.'

'So I'd have to rely on commission and tips then, would I?' Harry pressed.

Field nodded.

Harry Vivaldi had already made up his mind to accept the job. He knew that he could continue to live off Bella Thomas, so he was not too concerned about the lack of basic salary. What was more important to him was the exciting prospect of gaining such an easy entrée into the local households and families.

Now he feigned doubt and reluctance. 'Well, I don't really know what to say, Ernie. I'd like the job, and I think that I could do very well at it; and make a lot of money for you in sales. But it's still very uncertain, isn't it? As you point out, times are very hard, and I might well find that it won't be possible to make a decent living.'

The shopkeeper felt a twinge of anxiety. He believed that this young man would do very well for him. A handsome face would attract business from a certain type of woman. Bored, middle-aged housewives seeking the frisson of excitement in having dealings with a handsome young man were to be found in plenty in this district.

Vivaldi sensed the other man's anxiety, and decided to press his luck. Shaking his head with well-feigned regret he said, 'I'm sorry, Ernie. I really am. But I think that I'll have to go elsewhere. I've had another offer, and although I'd much prefer to work for you, the other job pays a basic salary as well as commission.'

'Who's offered you a job? And how much is he going to pay?' Ernie Field demanded.

Harry shrugged. 'I'm not really supposed to tell anyone about it, Ernie.' He smiled as one shrewd man of the world to another. 'I expect I've been sworn to secrecy so that nobody else will top the money the chap's prepared to pay.' He turned away as if to leave. 'I'll not take up any more of your time, Ernie. Thanks for your offer anyway.'

He reached the door, and when Field made no move, felt a sickening sense of error. He inwardly cursed himself. 'You stupid bastard! You've fucked it right up!'

'I'll give you seven and a tanner basic, and five pence in the pound commission, on machines and records.'

Relief coursed through Harry Vivaldi, and he halted. Still looking out into the street he asked, 'What about needles?'

'Three pence in the pound,' Field told him.

Harry Vivaldi turned round and proffered his hand. 'It's a bargain, Ernie. When do I start?'

Field looked at the clock. 'You can start right away, Harry. But I'll have to dock you a shilling because half the day's gone.'

The young man frowned slightly at this portent of his new employer's code of practice, but then smiled.

'Fair enough, Ernie!' Inwardly he promised to regain that shilling at the earliest opportunity, and as many others as he could possibly cheat the business out of.

The hours passed very quickly for Harry as he enthusiastically set himself to learning all that he could about his new trade. He possessed an agile and retentive brain, and rapidly familiarised himself with the wide array of Talking Machines held in stock: Vodaphones, Gramophones, Graphaphones, Zonophones, Phonographs, manufactured by companies like Edison, Bettini, Bell, McDonald, Cros. Some costing only seventeen shillings, others as much as fifty pounds, a full year's earnings for many working men. Some machines, such as the Gramophones, were purely for playing cylindrical records, others like Phonographs and Graphaphones were both recording and playing machines.

To Harry Vivaldi's surprise, Ernie Field proved to be a willing teacher, ready to share his own extensive knowledge of the trade with his new assistant, paradoxically as generous with information as he was mean with money. With an obvious pride he displayed his large stock of recordings.

'I've got the lot here, Harry. There's not a shop in the Midlands that can match my stock list. And I doubt if there's many that can in the whole country, including London.'

Despite his innate cynicism the young man could not help being impressed as he read the labels on the record covers: Sarah Bernhardt, Campanari, Ancona, Caruso, Plancon, Mark Twain, Evie Green, Marie Lloyd, and many other singers and narrators to suit all varieties of tastes. There were rows of orchestral and solo instrument recordings. Brass band and dance music. Comic singers and 'Nigger Minstrels'. Comic monologues and tragic epic poems. Operas and operettas. Ballads and love songs. There was even a large selection of foreign language lessons.

'What d'you think of it, Harry?' Ernie Field sought for praise, and the young man was sincerely willing to tell the shopkeeper what he wanted to hear.

'Very impressive, Ernie. Very impressive indeed!'

Despite the impressive stock, however, customers were few and far between that day, and those that came to the shop purchased only a few diamond point playing needles, or made enquiries about prices of machines and records. At nine o'clock that night Ernie Field glumly said, 'We might as well lock up, Harry. It's costing more in gaslight than it's worth to stay open.'

To his own surprise Harry Vivaldi found that for the first time in his life he was reluctant to leave a workplace. He would have liked to stay on by himself and experiment with recording his own voice, and play selections from the record stocks.

As he walked slowly up Prospect Hill he felt envy and contempt for his employer. 'The bastard doesn't know how lucky he is to own a business like that. It's the entertainment of the future, it really is. If he was to spend money on advertising and promoting it properly, he could make a bloody fortune.'

Back in George Street he found Bella Thomas waiting for him. Before she could speak he told her sharply, 'I've been at work, Bella, not gallivanting. So don't start blaggarding me. I'm in no mood for it.'

She regarded him nervously and hastened to mollify him. 'I wasn't going to say anything, darling. I don't mind you going out to enjoy yourself. You know I don't.'

He stared at her suspiciously. This mealy-mouthed subservience was normally present only when they had had a prior dispute. Then understanding dawned, and he accused, 'He wouldn't give you any, would he? You've come back with nothing?'

She shook her frizzed head. 'No, he did give me some. Only it aren't very much. He says business is very bad for him at present.'

The young man's initial impulse was to throw a tantrum, but then he suddenly realised that he could turn this situation to his own advantage. He bit back the angry abuse that hovered on his lips, and instead asked quietly, 'How much did he give you, Bella?'

'Five quid.' She gulped, and physically flinched as he snorted loudly.

'Five quid! What good is five measly quid!'

He began to pace up and down the limited floorspace, three steps and turn, three steps and turn, three steps and turn, and the woman's frightened gaze never left him, and her painted Cupid's bow of a mouth trembled as her mascaraed eyes brimmed with threatening tears.

When he sensed that he had tormented her sufficiently, he halted and slumped down on the chair facing her across the table.

'Well, this has placed me into a very difficult position, Bella,' he sighed regretfully, and seeing her tears begin to fall was forced to bite his lips to prevent himself bursting into contemptuous laughter. 'What a stupid, gullible cow she really is,' he thought, then aloud spoke tenderly to her.

'I'm not blaming you for this, sweetheart. I know it's not

91

your fault that your old man is such a stingy bastard.' He shook his head regretfully. 'But this means that I've lost the partnership. I've lost the chance of making a success of myself.'

'I'm sorry, Harry. I'm really really sorry!' She snatched his hand between her own and smothered it with slobbering kisses. 'I did my best, Harry. I swear to you I did my best to get the money from him.'

Hiding a grin he told her: 'I'm sure you did your best, sweetheart. And don't you worry about me. I'll see Ernie Field first thing tomorrow and explain the situation to him. Explain how badly I've been let down.' He gave her a brave, tremorous smile. 'Perhaps he'll still give me a job. He likes me well enough. I suppose I can get used to being just a counter jumper.'

Bella Thomas stared at his handsome face with besotted adoration. 'I don't deserve a man like you, darling. You're the best, kindest man I've ever met,' she choked out.

'There now,' he patted her jowly, powdered cheek comfortingly, 'so long as we've got each other, then nothing else really matters, does it, honey?' He steeled himself to lean over the table and kiss her wet lips, then suggested diffidently, 'Of course, it would be a considerable help if you could get some sort of work, just until I can get on my feet again, sweetheart.' He smiled wanly. 'I don't suppose being Ernie Field's counter jumper will pay very much.'

'I will, darling. I'll go looking for a job first thing in the morning. I'll find something, you'll see,' she promised fervently. 'I know they're looking for women down at the B.S.A. works. I'll go there first thing tomorrow.'

Her slavishness suddenly brought a stirring of desire and a quickening in Harry Vivaldi's groin, and he leaned forwards to kiss her mouth again, but now its hot wetness excited instead of repulsed and he pulled her roughly after him towards the stairs.

Chapter Ten

Now that she had obtained lodgings, Laura's next priority was to find work, but the knowledge that she had not yet thanked her benefactor kept nagging at her mind, so early on Monday morning she decided to go and see Cleopatra Dolton, before beginning her search for employment.

She walked down Unicorn Hill and over the railway station bridge at its bottom, crossed the flat valley and halted on the lower slopes of leafy Red Lane with its large houses fronted by well-tended lawns shaded by trees.

Laura was eager to see the subject of Rosie Spiers's lurid story, and wondered how the occupants of these opulent houses regarded a presence of such notoriety dwelling in their midst.

The young maidservant who opened the door stared at Laura suspiciously, and upon hearing that she wished to see the mistress of the house, demanded to know her name.

Then snapped, 'You'll have to wait theer.'

And closed the door in Laura's face.

It was not the maidservant who reopened the door however, but Cleopatra Dolton herself.

Laura regarded the beautiful face and sensual, shapely body, the limpid eyes and olive skin so dramatically enhanced by a sombre-coloured gown, and could understand why some men might kill to possess this woman.

'Come in, Miss Hughes.' The husky voice was in keeping with the sensual appearance. 'I must apologise for my maid leaving you standing out here. But not all callers are welcome.'

Cleopatra Dolton led her visitor into the drawing-room, and rang for the maid.

'Bring us some tea please, Dolly?' she asked, then added, 'unless you would prefer coffee or perhaps something else, Miss Hughes.'

'No thank you. Tea will suit very well, Mrs Dolton.'

Laura could not help but stare at this exotic creature who had been the central figure of such drama.

They remained silent until the maid had brought in the tray of tea things and had left the room once more. Cleopatra Dolton served Laura with tea and then for the first time smiled wryly and said, 'I see by your expression that you have heard something of my history, Miss Hughes.'

Laura flushed hotly with embarrassment at her own bad manners in staring so avidly at her hostess, but Cleopatra Dolton hastened to reassure her. 'Please, don't let my candour embarrass you, my dear. I'm used to people staring at me as if I am some character from a penny dreadful.'

She chuckled with genuine amusement, and after a few seconds Laura was able to return her smile and say, 'I'm sorry I was behaving so rudely, Mrs Dolton.'

The older woman nodded acceptance of the apology, and Laura went on, 'I wanted to thank you for your kindness towards me, and to assure you that I shan't prove undeserving of it.'

'I'm sure you won't.' Cleopatra Dolton's manner became brisk and businesslike. 'Now Miss Hughes. I want you to tell me all about this movement you are a part of. The Women's Social and Political Union is it not?'

Laura looked searchingly at the older woman as if seeking to understand her motives in making the request, and Cleopatra Dolton told her, 'I was among your listeners in Market Place on Saturday last, Miss Hughes. Even though you were only able to speak briefly I was greatly interested in what I heard. From my own personal experience I know how powerless we women are, and I deeply resent that powerlessness.'

Satisfied, Laura began to speak. Calmly at first, and then

94

with an ever increasing fervour and enthusiasm. 'Two years ago my father and I were living in Manchester, and I attended a meeting there held by the North of England Society for Woman Suffrage. Miss Esther Roper was the principal speaker, and what she said that evening was a revelation to me. She talked of how women were treated in this country. How they were exploited and brutalised and held in virtual bondage. She described the awful lives of the women in the slums of Salford and Liverpool and Manchester, and all the other slums throughout the land, and she said that until we women obtain a voice in the government of this country, then we shall never be free. We will never be able to live our lives in the way that we would choose to live them. She said that we must fight for the right to vote. Because only then would we be able to influence those who ruled us, and force them to alter the laws that keep us bound in our slavery.'

The young woman's eyes were shining and her colour had heightened as she relived that time of her conversion to this cause that she now devoted her life to.

'After that first evening I attended many meetings, all over Cheshire and Lancashire. I came to know Emmeline Pankhurst, and her daughters, Christabel and Sylvia, and I met Mrs Fawcett and Miss GoreBooth. I even met Mr Keir Hardie of the Independent Labour Party.'

She frowned. 'Initially we had the hope that the Labour Party would fight shoulder to shoulder with us to obtain full suffrage for all men and women in this country. But they were quickly proved that they were like all the other political parties. They refused to accept women as members of the Independent Labour Party, and insulted our intelligence by the excuses they gave us in explanation of that refusal. That's when Mrs Pankhurst decided to form a new organisation. Which is the one I now belong to – The Women's Social and Political Union.' Her voice faltered and she fell silent.

'Why have you stopped?' Cleopatra Dolton asked. 'Do go on.'

The young woman appeared to be curiously deflated, and her tone had lost all its fervency when she answered,

'There's nothing more to be told, Mrs Dolton. We suffragettes spend our time making speeches and lobbying politicians, and we get nowhere. People either ignore us, or jeer and mock us, and sometimes attack us physically. And the very women who stand to gain most by obtaining the right to vote, are the ones who seem to care the least.'

'What do you think you should be doing, instead of lobbying politicians and making speeches?' Cleopatra Dolton asked perceptively.

A fanatical gleam came into the young woman's eyes, and the fervour throbbed once more in her voice. 'Our organisation should become a militant force. Instead of pleading and begging we should be demanding and threatening those who stand in the way of our objectives. We should be forcing the politicians to give us the vote, by using whatever methods are necessary to achieve our aims.'

'Even violent means?' the older woman asked curiously.

'Any means, so long as no harm is done to innocent people,' Laura stated vehemently.

Silence ensued as each sat immersed in their own thoughts. It was the older woman who was first to speak.

'How is your movement financed and directed?'

'We finance it ourselves. Each member gives whatever she can afford. Then we have a committee, Mrs Pankhurst is the chairwoman. She is accepted by most of us as the leader of the movement.' Laura grinned ruefully. 'But there are many strong-minded ladies in our ranks who do not take direction kindly. To speak truthfully, we are not really disciplined. Many of us tend to go our own ways in the actions we take.'

'Yourself included?' Cleopatra Dolton smiled.

Again Laura grinned ruefully and confessed, 'Yes, myself included. I've been trying to organise a branch of the movement locally, but I haven't been officially appointed as a Branch Organiser by the committee.' She laughed in self-disparagement. 'That's just as well considering my lack of success so far. I've only managed to recruit two members, and I fear that they have both now abandoned the movement.'

Again silence fell, then Laura said, 'I must go now, Mrs Dolton. I have to look for work.'

Cleopatra Dolton nodded understandingly. 'You have lost your employment with the Misses Grose I take it.'

'Yes.'

'And where are you now living?'

'In Hill Street, with a girl named Rosie Spiers. She's befriended me.'

The older woman smiled bleakly. 'I know Hill Street, and I know the Spiers family. A relative of theirs works for me.' She rose gracefully to her feet and regarded her companion closely. 'Do you need money?'

Laura shook her head emphatically. 'No, thank you. I shall manage.'

Recognising the younger woman's fierce pride, Cleopatra Dolton did not press the matter.

She walked with her visitor to the front door and opened it for the other to pass through.

When Laura began to wish her goodbye, she told her, 'I am in agreement with the aims of your movement, and if you need any financial aid to form a branch of it here in Redditch, then I would be prepared to contribute something to the fund.'

'That is very kind of you.' Laura's surprise at the offer showed in her expression. 'You would become a member?'

Cleopatra Dolton shook her head and the bleak smile touched her lips once more. 'No, my dear. I could not openly join you. My being a member would damage your cause here in this town. No respectable woman would wish to be associated with any organisation of which I was a member. It would be better for all concerned if my interest and financial contributions remained a secret between you and I.'

Fresh hope flooded through Laura Hughes at this manifestation of support. 'Thank you very much, Mrs Dolton. You've given me just the encouragement I needed at this time. I will certainly call upon you for a contribution at sometime in the near future.'

'Make sure that you do,' Cleopatra Dolton instructed firmly, and closed the door.

Laura felt like singing with joy as she walked away from the house. 'That's definitely an omen of success,' she told herself gleefully. 'I'll find work, get the magistrates' court over with, and then begin looking for recruits.'

As she walked back up Unicorn Hill towards the town centre, Laura's sense of joyful hope began to ebb away as she faced the harsh reality of finding work. Without references she had no chance of obtaining any sort of teaching or tutorial post, and the realisation struck home to her that she lacked any manual skills which might gain her employment.

She knew that in the Redditch district many hundreds of women were employed in the fishing tackle and needle industries, but much of the work that these women did was of a highly skilled nature requiring training and long practice. Even the simpler types of work needed a manual dexterity which she herself did not possess.

'I'm not even dextrous with a needle and thread, never mind needle boxing or hooks to gut work,' she accepted glumly.

The notion of becoming a shop assistant she instantly discarded. 'What shopkeeper would keep me in their employment after I've appeared in a Police Court.'

'Perhaps I could become a typewritist?' She smiled with bleak self-mockery at the thought. 'I don't know how to use a typing machine of course, but surely that wouldn't matter.'

Immersed in her own troubled thoughts, Laura did not notice the elderly police sergeant standing outside the Unicorn Inn. Ivor Brunton recognised the slender young woman trudging wearily with her head bowed and clucked his tongue sympathetically as he noted her depressed expression. He knew that she had lost her employment and accommodation, and considered that she had been harshly used by those formidable ladies. When she neared him he stepped out to speak with her.

'Good morning, Miss Hughes.'

Startled from her reverie Laura stared blankly at the man for some seconds, then nodded politely.

'Good morning, Sergeant.'

'And where are you off to, Miss?' he asked jovially.

Her expression became guarded and she replied warily, 'I'm just taking a stroll, Sergeant.'

There was something in her posture and general appearance that reminded him strongly of his own beloved daughter, and impelled by this he was driven to find out if she was all right.

'I hear that you've left your lodgings with the Misses Grose?' It was statement rather than query, and again Laura replied warily.

'Yes, that is so, Sergeant.' Then fleeting anxiety flashed in her eyes and she asked, 'Was I supposed to notify you that I had done so, Sergeant? Only I left there yesterday, and I had to find somewhere else to stay.'

He smiled reassuringly. 'Well, strictly speaking I suppose you should have told us that you'd changed your address, Miss, you being on bail as you are. But never mind, you can tell me your new address now, and I'll make a note on it.'

Nodding, she told him her address, and again he grinned kindly at her. 'That's all right then, Miss.' He paused, as if uncertain and stared speculatively at her for some moments until she began to feel nervous under his scrutiny.

'Is something the matter, Sergeant?' she asked.

He puffed out a noisy breath from between pursed lips, and grimacing, told her: 'Now strictly speaking, Miss, this is none o' my business, but I've a daughter of about your age, and I 'udden't like to see her in the predicament you'm in. So don't take my words amiss, I'm only thinking of your welfare.'

'What is it, Sergeant? What have I done now that might cause me further trouble?'

'Now you mustn't moither yourself.' He hastened to soothe her. 'It's only that I was wondering if you've sufficient money to pay any fine the bench might impose on Wednesday. Normally for the type of offence you'm being charged with they fines a sovereign. But it's Mr William Yeomans presiding on Wednesday and he can be a bit of a tartar. He's a very strict gentleman is Mr Yeomans, and he's hard on them who causes upsets in the

99

streets. So he might well impose a heavier fine on you, and if you can't pay, then it's prison.'

In the past, Laura had always pictured herself suffering imprisonment, even injury and death for her cause. In those pictures she had been a noble, heroic figure, daring her enemies to do their worst, and going to her fate with a defiant laugh. But now, abruptly, came the realisation that this was no longer a matter of imaginary pictures. Instead it was a concrete fact. She thought of her dead father, and the shame he would have experienced at having his only daughter sentenced like a common felon, and a sudden sense of shame at how she was betraying all his moral strictures assailed her. Her heart sank, and fearful dread seized her as she realised that by this time on Wednesday next, she could be on her way to prison. A sensation of actual fear shuddered through her and she asked faintly, 'How long will he imprison me for if I can't pay the fine?'

He shrugged. 'Hard to say, Miss. Perhaps a month, perhaps longer?'

Laura fought desperately to master her fear and to present a brave face to him. She tried to shrug carelessly but the tremor in her voice betrayed her trepidation.

'Well, so be it, Sergeant. I've no money to pay any fine with. And no means of earning any at present either.'

Ivor Brunton's eyes were kindly as he recognised what she was feeling, despite her brave attempt to conceal it. 'If you could find work before Wednesday, or even get the promise of it, then you could offer to pay the fine off in instalments, Miss. I'm sure the bench would accept that. It 'ud certainly be better than being stuck in jail, my dear. You'll meet only shame and degradation in there. I 'udden't like to see a well brought up young gentlewoman like yourself stuck in there wi' a load of scum like you'll be with.'

She shook her head helplessly. 'I want to find work, Sergeant. Indeed I must find work to support myself. But I don't know where to go in search of it. I've no references now, and no manual skills to offer, and with a Police Court hanging over my head, who will trust me enough to give me any sort of employment?'

Again he stared at her speculatively for some seconds, and then asked, 'Am you fussy about what sort of work you'm prepared to do, Miss?'

She shook her head vigorously. 'Not at all, Sergeant. I'll do anything, so long as it's decent and respectable work.'

He pursed his lips and appeared to ponder on what she had said, then suddenly clucked his tongue loudly, and told her: 'Right then, my dear. I just might be able to help you. You goo and sit in the Recreation Garden and enjoy this sunshine until I comes to you there. Goo on now, I'll not be long in coming.'

She allowed herself to be ushered onwards towards the centre crossroads, and feeling strangely dazed, did as she had been bidden.

Within an hour the sergeant came in search of her.

'Now my dear, I've had a word wi' a chap I knows, and he's prepared to give you a trial,' he informed with a smile.

'Trial? Doing what, Sergeant Brunton?'

'Working as a waitress and general assistant in his restaurant. I know that strictly speaking it's not suitable work for a gentlelady, but like you said, you'm prepared to try anything that's decent and respectable.'

Laura hesitated, then asked: 'Does this gentleman know that I'm to appear in the Police Court?'

He nodded. 'I've explained all that to him, Miss Hughes.'

Laura's thin face glowed with her gratitude. 'Thank you very much, Sergeant Brunton, I'm very happy to accept. And I'm deeply grateful to you for all your kindness to me.'

The policeman waved away her thanks, and urged, 'You must goo straight and see him now. His name's Reginald White. The restaurant's on the top of Unicorn Hill there.'

'I know it,' Laura told him, and with a final word of thanks she hurried away.

101

Chapter Eleven

The trip to the Clee Hills to fetch Miriam Josceleyne's belongings had left Emma feeling restless, and now as she faced the older woman across the breakfast table the thought of spending this Wednesday cooped up in the house tormented her unbearably. Her dark eyes held a lurking resentment in their lucent depths as she regarded her companion contentedly sipping a cup of tea.

'I love you, Miriam,' she thought, 'but there's times when you make me want to shake a bit of life into you.' Aloud she asked, 'What are we going to do today, Miriam?'

Miriam Josceleyne smiled and her green eyes were warm as she answered, 'What would you like us to do, Emma?'

The young woman pouted and tossed her head pettishly. 'Anything rather than sit about the bloody house all day long. I'm like a prisoner here.'

'I hardly think that you can be termed a prisoner, Emma,' Miriam protested gently. 'Why, we only returned from Clee yesterday.'

'Yes, but that was yesterday, warn't it. It's today now, and I want to do something exciting with it.'

Mrs Elwood had entered the room while the young woman was speaking, and now she grimaced. 'You'd oughter remember that you'm a widow, my wench, who only buried your husband last Saturday. You'd oughter show a bit o' decorum and proper respect.' She shook her head. 'I dunno what folk 'ud think if they was to hear you now, I really don't.' She mimicked the younger woman's words: 'I wants to do summat exciting.' Then she scowled and berated: 'You want to try acting like a proper lady, my

102

wench, and not like some Silver Street baggage. You'se got a position in life now, and you must live up to that position and act accordingly.'

Emma's customary good humour reasserted itself and she showed her white even teeth in a broad grin. 'Well, I does, Mrs Elwood. Doon't forget I bin acting like a proper lady for the last four years.' She threw out her arms and arched her body, causing her high pert breasts to strain against the bodice of her dress. 'But I'm bored with acting like a proper lady, and I wants a bit o' fun now.' She appealed directly to Miriam: 'Let's go out somewhere, Miriam. Let's do something different today. Something we've never done before.'

'Phoo, I reckon there aren't a lot o' things that you aren't done afore, my wench,' Mrs Elwood averred forcefully. 'Now, if you'se finished your breakfast I'll clear this lot away.' She began to collect and stack the dirtied crockery on her large tray.

Miriam Josceleyne sat back in her chair and watched the brisk capable hands at work, and sighed with contentment. 'I've come home. I've come back to where I really belong,' she told herself.

'That young 'ooman is up before the beaks today,' Mrs Elwood told them.

'What young woman?' Emma wanted to know.

'Why, the one who caused all the ructions in Market Place last Saturday. The suffragette.'

'What ructions?' Emma challenged.

'O' course, you haven't heard about it have you,' Mrs Elwood scolded herself. 'More fool me for not thinking afore I spoke. It happened while you was all down at the cemetery. From what I've heard this young 'ooman and some others marched up as bold as brass and starting speechifying about votes for women. O' course, some o' the chaps that was theer took exception to that, and set about 'um. Then the police come and took all the women to the lock up. My old man is a friend of Ivor Brunton's. And when he come back from the pub last night he told me that Ivor Brunton had told him that the one young 'ooman was to come up afore the beaks this morning and answer the charges against her.'

Miriam Josceleyne's interest was sparked. She had read of the emergence of women's suffrage movement in the north and midlands, but had had no direct encounters with any of its members herself.

'What else do you know about this young woman, Mrs Elwood?' She questioned, and listened intently to the information the cook had garnered at second hand from her husband and concerning Laura Hughes.

Emma was contemptuous. 'Phew, I think these suffragettes are nothing but a load of frustrated spinsters. Having a vote won't change things for women in this country. You've got to beat the bloody men at their own game. They all want the same thing, and you've got to make them pay the price to get it. All this nonsense of having a vote wun't do a blind thing to make women's lives any better. What does these suffragettes know about what life's like for women like me Mam. What good 'ull having a vote do for me Mam and the rest on 'um in her boat. No, they'm just a load of bloody idiots, if you asks me.'

Colour rose in Miriam's pale cheeks, and she answered with uncustomary tartness: 'I think you misjudge the suffrage movement, Emma. They are trying to achieve some dignity and status for women.'

Irritated by this challenge, Emma retorted sharply, 'Well, I 'udden't call being plastered with rubbish and knocked about by a load o' roughs, and then being carted off by the police as acting dignified, Miriam. Or achieving any status for that matter. They'm just making bloody fools of themselves if you ask me.'

Miriam recognised the futility of further argument at this time, and shook her head. 'I fear that we shall have to agree to differ on this point, Emma.' Turning to Mrs Elwood she asked, 'At what time does the court begin?'

'About eleven o'clock, Miss Miriam.'

'Thank you.' Miriam nodded, and told Emma, 'I'll see you later then, my dear.'

The girl's dark eyes were curious. 'Are you thinking of going to the Police Court then?'

Miriam nodded.

Emma's eyes glinted and she clapped her hands delightedly. 'Then I'll come with you, Miriam. It's something different to be doing today, aren't it.'

Before the elder woman could even begin to formulate an answer, the girl was going out of the room talking excitedly: 'I think I'll wear my new gown, and my new hat, and I'll take a parasol but without any mourning streamers on it.'

Mrs Elwood smiled at Miriam. 'Her's a caution, aren't her Miss Miriam?'

Miriam's answering smile was fond. 'Indeed she is, Mrs Elwood. Indeed she is.'

Sergeant Ivor Brunton stood in the yard of the Police Station in Church Road and checked the list of names he held in his hands against the motley collection of humanity assembled before him. He clucked his tongue in apparent regret as he noted familiar faces, and exchanged remarks with some of the regular clientele.

'You wants to take more water wi' the gin in future, Maggie.'

'My Christ, Tommy, that's a fine shiner you've got there.'

'Up to your old tricks again I see, Benton. How long have you been out this time?'

The shabby-coated man he last addressed shuffled his feet and bared decayed teeth in a snarl of resentment.

'Three weeks, as you well knows, Brunton.'

'It's Sergeant Brunton to you, my buck,' the policeman reproved sternly, then grinned and jeered, 'lasted three weeks this time, did you. My Christ, you'm becoming a reformed character.'

The man snarled and muttered beneath his breath.

The policeman quickly checked out the remainder of his list and then told the small assembly: 'Right then, some of you already knows the drill. But for them who doon't, this is what happens. When your case is called you'll be fetched inside to the court and put into the dock. The Clerk of the Court, Mr Eustace Browning, will read out the charge against you and ask you how you plead, guilty or not guilty. You'll call him sir, and if any of the magistrates should speak to you, then you'll address them as your worship. When your case has been dealt with you'll either be put in the cells, or I'll bring you back out here and tell you anything you might need to know about paying your fines etcetera.'

He paused and swept his gaze across the faces before him, then asked: 'Is that clear to everybody?'

A murmur of assent from several was his answer, coupled with grimaces of hatred and muttered curses from a few, which the policeman chose to ignore.

'Chambers, come out here,' he shouted, and a constable appeared from the door which led into the small courtroom.

'Yes, Sergeant?'

'You stay here and keep an eye on our guests,' the sergeant ordered, and grinned mockingly at the recidivist. 'Benton here might take a notion to do a runner else, mightn't you, Benton?'

The man scowled viciously, but made no reply.

Laura had been standing slightly apart and to the rear of the group, and now as the constable took up his stance before the courtroom door she moved further away from the rest and began to pace nervously up and down the yard.

The sergeant moved to her and brought her to a halt. His eyes were kindly as he asked in a low voice, 'How are you feeling, Miss Hughes?'

She smiled tremulously. 'Very nervous, Sergeant Brunton.'

He nodded understandingly. 'Well, just between you and me, my dear, I think that you'll only be fined a pound, and given a talking to by the bench. But you listen to me now. Doon't you go getting on your high horse and giving the bench any cheek. Because that 'ull only make things a sight worse for you.'

'Very well, Sergeant,' Laura agreed submissively, and then added, 'no matter what happens, Sergeant, I'd like to say thank you for all your kindness to me.'

He smiled gently. 'That's all right, my dear. Like I said,

I've a daughter o' me own. Now you remember what I've told you, and don't go answering the magistrates back, no matter what they might say to you.' He lowered his voice to whisper conspiratorially, 'You wun't be able to get any votes for women if you'm locked up, will you, my dear?'

He turned to leave her, adding as he did so, 'I've put you on top of the list of cases, so you'll be called in very shortly. Just bear in mind what I've told you now, and it'll be over and done with in two shakes of a mare's tail.'

WH Yeomans Esq., flanked by his two fellow magistrates, glowered down from his elevated chair at the slender, neatly-dressed young woman in the prisoners' dock.

'Laura Hughes, you have pleaded guilty to the charge of causing an obstruction on the King's highway. From the evidence I have heard, I'm of the opinion that there should have been further charges brought against you.' His angry stare switched momentarily to the burly, military-moustachioed Inspector Howard, who met the magistrate's bloodshot glare with a bland expression of innocence. 'However,' he went on, 'if the police in their wisdom have not seen fit to bring those further charges, then there is nothing to be done about it.' Again Yeoman's bloodshot eyes glowered upon Laura, and she could not repress a shiver of nervousness in the face of his unconcealed malevolence.

'The court has been informed that you are of a good family, the daughter of a clergyman. Does your Father know to what depths of depravity and wickedness his daughter has so wilfully descended to, I wonder.'

Stung to anger by the man's arrogance and bullying, Laura spoke out heatedly. 'My Father died two years ago. I'll thank you not to bring his name into this. What I do has nothing to do with my Father. My views are my own, and do not reflect the views my Father held whilst he was alive.'

For a brief moment Yeomans was taken aback by her defiant retort, and a rustle of sympathy and support for the girl ran through the well-filled spectators' benches. The magistrate shook his head and took a few moments to

107

compose himself. Then scowling, he continued, 'If you interrupt me again, young woman, I shall myself have you charged with contempt of this court, and you will be punished accordingly.'

Laura's anger still seethed and she was about to reply spiritedly when her eyes caught the warning stare of Sergeant Brunton, and the almost imperceptible shaking of his head. With an immense effort of will she controlled her own fury, and remained silent. But could not bring herself to break off her defiant visual confrontation with Yeomans's threatening glare.

To Yeomans's left his fellow magistrate, Ernest Cadbury, knowing his colleague's propensities towards ungovernable rage, and consequently intemperate actions, leaned across and whispered urgently in Yeomans's large ear.

Yeomans grunted surlily in reply, but then the other magistrate followed suit, and overborne by numbers, Yeomans subsided with bad grace.

'I fine the defendant the sum of one pound,' he announced. 'Or 14 days' imprisonment in lieu. You may step down.' He growled at Laura.

She remained standing in the dock, and the magistrates stared at her in concerted surprise.

Eustace Browning, Clerk to the Court, got to his feet and challenged Laura, 'What is it, young woman? Have you not understood what His Worship has said?'

Laura swallowed hard, her earlier anger ebbing fast to be replaced by nervous anxiety. 'If you please, sir,' she uttered in a voice made husky by a suddenly parched throat and mouth, 'may I have time to pay?'

From the well of the courtroom a man laughed jeeringly, and Laura crimsoned in embarrassment.

Yeomans's thick lips quirked in a triumphant sneer. He exchanged quick glances with his fellow magistrates, then leaning bodily towards the young woman in the dock he told her mockingly, 'Of course you may have time to pay. This bench always endeavours to accommodate defendants who mock and defy its rulings. The Court allows you one hour to make payment, failing which a warrant will be issued for your arrest for wilful non-payment of your fine. And that offence will undoubtedly result in imprisonment. Now stand down.'

Laura opened her mouth to protest, but from the corner of her eye saw the frantic jerking of Sergeant Brunton's head, and closed her lips and turned and hurried from the dock.

From her seat on one of the hard backless benches to the rear of the courtroom, Miriam Josceleyne had watched and listened to the bullying treatment of the young woman with ever-mounting anger.

'It's intolerable,' she whispered to Emma sitting beside her. 'That man is nothing but a vile bully.'

Emma grinned and shrugged uncaringly. 'It's sticks and stones that break your bones, Miriam,' she whispered back. 'A bit of mouthing never killed anybody yet.'

'But he was most insulting to the poor girl!' Miriam exclaimed indignantly.

Emma only chuckled. 'Jesus Christ! I've bin blaggarded a sight worse than that on any day o' the week. She should have told the old bastard straight, and give him his bloody character! That's what I'd have done, make no mistake. I'd soon have put him to the right about.'

Miriam Josceleyne sighed as once again she realised the vast gulf of experience which yawned between herself and her young friend.

'Perhaps I am overreacting,' she told herself ruefully. Then after a moment or two she whispered, 'Will she really go to prison if she fails to pay the fine?'

Emma nodded judiciously. 'I should think so, Miriam. My Dad has always been sent down when he never paid his fines. And he sweeps Yeomans's chimneys for him as well, but that's never stopped the old bastard from putting me Dad inside for a seven or fourteen.' She paused for a moment, then added with a gamine-like grin, 'Mind you, the old bastard did me Mam a favour whenever he put me Dad inside. At least it give her a holiday from the bad bugger.'

An idea was germinating in Miriam Josceleyne's brain, and suddenly she whispered urgently, 'Can someone else pay the fine for her?'

Emma nodded. 'Yes. If there's anybody sarft enough to do it. So long as they gets their money, they doon't give a bugger who pays it.'

The idea came to full flower, and Miriam told her friend, 'I'm going to pay it. I'll not let them send her to prison.'

Emma stared in shocked surprise. 'But you doon't even know the wench?'

Miriam shook her head dismissively. 'That doesn't matter. I'd like to talk to her, and to hear what she has to say about women's suffrage.'

The younger woman rolled her sparkling black eyes upwards in mock dismay. 'Oh nooo!' she groaned theatrically. 'You've been infected as well!'

'Shhhh!' the young constable standing just inside the street door warned severely, only to blush when Emma cheekily stuck her tongue out, then winked lewdly at him.

Miriam tried to look sternly dignified, but could not suppress a giggle at the shocked expression on the young policeman's brightly glowing face. Then, on impulse she said, 'Come Emma, let's go and pay the young woman's fine, and see if we can find her. I want to meet her.'

Not loath to seek fresh interest Emma readily concurred, and the two women rose and went quietly out into the street.

Laura's thin face was clouded with worry, but although Sergeant Brunton was sympathetic to her plight, at this particular moment his courtroom duties only allowed him the time to snatch a few words with her.

'If I was you, Miss, I'd ask Reg White if he can advance you a pound out of your wages.'

Laura nodded disconsolately. 'I will Sergeant.'

Then the policeman returned inside the court building and Laura grimaced wryly. 'A pound advance, when my wages are only five and sixpence a week. I can't see Mr White paying me a month in advance, and then I still have to pay my way.'

She sighed wearily and pondered on what she should now do. It seemed pointless to return to her work when in one hour's time there would be a warrant issued for her arrest. She was still standing undecided when the two women dressed in mourning came out of the courtroom door and approached her directly.

'Miss Hughes, I do hope you'll forgive my forwardness in addressing you without introduction.' It was the elder woman who spoke in a soft timid voice, appearing nervous of rebuff. 'My name is Josceleyne. Miss Miriam Josceleyne, and this lady . . .' she indicated the startlingly beautiful young woman beside her, 'this lady is Mrs Emma Josceleyne.' She lapsed into silence, her hands nervously twisting the handle of the furled parasol she held before her.

Laura forced a polite smile. 'I'm happy to make your acquaintances. But if you'll forgive me I have much to think about at this moment. There are pressing matters I must attend to.'

'If it's the fine you'm moithering about, my duck, then there's no need for you to worry your head about it.' Emma grinned, and momentarily resembled an engaging street urchin as she winked broadly. 'We'em not about to let that old bastard in there put you in jail for the sake of a quid. Here,' she took a gold sovereign from her dainty purse and pressed it into Laura's hand, 'goo into the office theer, and pay it straightaway.'

Laura's thin face was nonplussed. 'But, I cannot take . . .' She began to protest but the beautiful young woman carelessly brushed aside her words and taking Laura by the arm led her towards the court office doorway. She gave Laura no opportunity to make any further demurrals and once the fine had been paid she again took Laura's arm and led her out into the street.

'You'll come and have a cup of tea with us, Miss Hughes,' Emma invited. 'Miriam here has a deal o' questions to ask you about the suffragettes, haven't you, Miriam?'

Miriam's expression was still timid and her manner diffident as if awaiting reproof, but she smiled nervously and nodded. 'Well, I am most interested in the suffrage movement, Miss Hughes,' she murmured breathlessly. 'And I would greatly enjoy hearing whatever you might be able to tell me concerning it.'

By now Laura had regained her composure, and she

111

smiled at the two women. 'Firstly let me thank you for loaning me the money to pay my fine with. I shall of course return it to you as soon as I possibly can.' She spoke directly to Miriam. 'I'd be most happy to tell you about the Women's Social and Political Union, Miss Josceleyne, but would it be possible for me to do this at some later date? I must return to my work now, and have little or no time to spare.'

Miriam nodded jerkily. 'Yes, of course, Miss Hughes.' She glanced towards Emma in unspoken question.

Emma smiled and said, 'We live at Cotswold House, just across the Green theer. Come there on any evening you've a mind to.'

Laura smiled warmly. 'Yes, I'd like that. I can come tomorrow evening, if you wish.'

'Yes, that'll do fine,' Emma told her. 'Come about eight o'clock. We'll be looking forward to seeing you, won't we, Miriam?'

The elder woman flushed, but smiled and nodded, and with final words of thanks, Laura hurried away.

Emma smiled with fond exasperation at her friend. 'Jesus Christ above, Miriam! What use 'ull you be in getting votes for women if you can't even talk to another woman without blushing and trembling. You've got to be more confident and easy with people, my duck.'

Miriam accepted the remonstrance with good grace, and smiled. 'I'll try, Emma. Really I will. I'll try.'

Emma linked her arm through Miriam's and hugged it close to her side. 'Come on, my duck, let's have a wander round the town and see what's happening.'

Chapter Twelve

The bright morning sunshine did nothing to lighten Harry Vivaldi's dark mood as he walked along Red Lion Street on his way to work. His head throbbed from the after effects of the previous night's heavy drinking and he scowled as he considered the emptiness of his pockets.

'I shouldn't have let myself be drawn into playing cards with those bastards. I'm bloody sure they switched those two aces in the last hand.' His scowl metamorphosed into an apprehensive grimace as he saw the burly, flat-capped man coming towards him from the direction of the Church Green, and his eyes flickered from side to side in search for some avenue of escape. Some yards in front of him, the arched entrance to Silver Street offered a haven and he quickened his pace, but a raucous bellow brought him to a reluctant halt, and he forced a smile of greeting as the burly man hurried up to him.

'I was just coming to see you, Mr Vivaldi.' The man's tough features were grim and challenging. 'You knows what I wants, doon't you?'

Vivaldi assumed an expression of puzzlement. 'No, Mr Louch.'

'You owes two weeks' rent,' Louch stated bluntly. 'And Mister Neasom says that the terms you agreed on when you took the house was payment in advance by the week, Mr Vivaldi.'

Vivaldi shook his head in bewilderment. 'I know that was the agreement I signed with Mister Neasom, and I've complied with it to the letter.'

The tough features wore a knowing sneer. 'I'se bin round to the house three times in the past week, Vivaldi,

113

and aren't bin able to raise an answer.' Louch pulled a dog-eared notebook from the pocket of his capacious jacket and brandished it beneath Vivaldi's aquiline nose. 'It's all in here, Vivaldi – rents owed, rents paid, rents unpaid. And you'm down as unpaid for two weeks now.' His manner became distinctly threatening. 'Now as you knows, I'm Mr Neasom's rent collector, and his debt collector as well. And I only gets paid on commission on what I collects. If I don't collect, I don't get paid. And if I don't get paid, why then, I gets very riled up. And when I gets riled up then I'm liable to do more than a bit o' damage to them that's riled me up, Mister. Theer's many a one hereabouts who can vouch to the truth o' that.'

Harry Vivaldi's olive complexion became a paler shade of green, and he swallowed hard. 'Now Mr Louch, if you'll only hear me out, I think I begin to understand what has happened here,' he gabbled breathlessly.

The burly man stared hard, and challenged: 'What? What's happened here?'

'It's not my fault, Mr Louch.' Vivaldi's mind was racing, and he struggled to enlist the other man's sympathy. 'It's that woman who I've got staying with me. I've given her the rent money every week since I took the house, and she's assured me that she's paid it regularly. This is the first I've heard about this matter.' He simulated a flash of anger. 'I'll bloody well flay her. She must have spent the money on other things.' He essayed a wry shrug as from one man of the world to another, and lowered his voice as if imparting a confidence. 'Just between you and me, Mr Louch, the drink is her problem. She's an old friend of my family's, and out of kindness I took her in and gave her shelter when she came weeping and wailing to me. There's nothing between us, you understand. She's only a sort of non-paying guest.'

Louch's expression was one of sneering disbelief, but he made no reply, and emboldened, Harry Vivaldi went on, 'Look here, Mr Louch. How much rent is owing exactly?'

The burly man glanced briefly into the dog-eared notebook. 'Counting today, eight shillings and threepence.'

Vivaldi slapped his jacket's pockets and scowled. 'Damn it, I haven't got my pocketbook with me,' he sighed impatiently. 'And I'm late for work as well, so I can't really go back to the house for it now.' He appeared to ponder for a moment, then suggested, 'Look, Mr Louch, I shall be finishing work at about eight o'clock this evening, how will it be if I bring the money round to your house then?'

The rent collector considered the suggestion with a bleak frown, then nodded reluctantly. 'I lives at 43 Walford Street. I'll be there at eight o'clock. Just make sure you am as well.'

Vivaldi nodded vehemently. 'You may rest assured that I will be, Mr Louch. And that the money will be paid in full the very moment I come there.'

The rent collector nodded grimly. 'It had better be, Mister. Or else I'll be really riled up.' He jerked his head in dismissal.

His heart thudding with relief Harry Vivaldi went past the other man, and with hurried footsteps put as much distance as he could between them.

As he rapidly paced towards Field's shop the young man sought desperately for some way out of his predicament, cursing what he perceived as his undeserved bad luck. 'It's all that fat cow's fault,' he told himself bitterly. 'If she'd managed to get a few quid more out of her bloody stingy husband I wouldn't be in this situation. She's just a bloody burden to me, that's all she is. A bloody burden!'

The fact that he had wasted all the money that Bella Thomas had obtained from her husband in drinking and gambling did nothing to assuage Vivaldi's rabid resentment. While the further fact that it was he who took whatever money Bella Thomas was able to earn from her, leaving her with nothing at all to spend, did not occur to him at this moment in time.

'You're late, Vivaldi!' Ernie Field grumbled as the young man entered the shop. 'You should have been here at quarter to eight, and it's ten past now. That's another sixpence I'm docking from your wages, my lad. If you goes on like this you'll have nothing to draw at the end of the week, 'ull you.'

For a fleeting instant Harry Vivaldi was sorely tempted to tell Field what he could do with his job. But the thought of the trouble he was already in restrained him from giving voice to that impulse.

'You never swept the shop out last night either, my lad. You'd best get it done now afore we gets a customer,' his employer snapped peevishly.

The young man sighed self-pityingly, and did as he was bidden, inwardly cursing as the dust from the broom coated across the high polish of his elegant boots and collected on the bottoms of his narrow trousers.

He finished the sweeping and returned the broom to its cupboard then went to the counter and, taking a piece of rag from the shelf beneath it, wiped his boots clean and flicked the dust from his trousers. Glumly he resigned himself to the long long day which stretched ahead of him, and then his heart leapt as he heard his employer telling him, 'Now, I's got to goo up to Brummagem by the nine o'clock train. There's a bit of urgent business come up. Does you reckon you'll be able to manage the shop by yourself until I gets back?'

Harry smiled broadly. 'Oh yes, Mr Field. I'll manage very well.'

The older man glowered suspiciously. 'My lady wife 'ull be looking in during the day to keep an eye on you. So I doon't want to hear from her that you bin slacking. You can polish up the stock, and clean out the back room if trade is slow. And I won't be that long away. The business in Brummagem 'ull not take long to settle. So I could be coming back at any time. Just you bear that in mind, my lad.'

The young man nodded submissively. 'I'll do that, Mr Field. You've no call to worry on that score. I'll not slack.'

'Just make sure that you doon't,' the other man warned, and taking up his bowler hat and umbrella went miserably away.

It was as if a black cloud had been lifted from Harry Vivaldi's spirits, and he came from behind the counter and cautiously peeped out of the door to ensure that his employer was definitely walking up the hill. For a few

116

moments he watched Field's rounded shoulders receding into the distance, then he grinned broadly and made a lewd gesture of farewell with his fingers. Whistling gaily he walked back into the centre of the shop and stood staring speculatively around him.

In his top pocket he had a half-smoked cheroot and now he took it out and lit it using a lucifer match which he struck raffishly on his boot heel. He drew strongly on the thin brown tube and exhaled a cloud of smoke, sighing with satisfaction. The prospect of Ernie Field's wife appearing he dismissed with a contemptuous shake of his head. The woman was a self-proclaimed invalid, who hated her tyrannical husband and refused on the grounds of her sickly health to take any part in helping him with his business.

'No, old Ivy won't be coming in here today, that's as sure as God made little apples, that is.' Harry Vivaldi grinned to himself.

Then the brief euphoria engendered by his employer's unexpected absence abruptly deflated as the memory of Caleb Louch's threatening features obtruded upon his mental vision.

'Where the hell am I going to get eight and threepence from by tonight?' he thought hopelessly. 'I've as much chance of getting that as of flying to the moon.' The thought of what Caleb Louch's fists and boots might do to him caused Harry Vivaldi to wish fervently that he was indeed capable of flying to the moon. 'At least the bugger couldn't get hold of me there.'

Another disquieting thought struck him with dread: 'He'll kick me and Bella out into the street as well, after he's given me a hiding, and then where will we go?' He began to rack his brains for some solution to his problem, and ever wilder ideas came and were discarded as hopeless in frantic succession.

'Perhaps I could pawn my suit, or Bella's clothes? Maybe I could sell the furniture? I wonder if I could borrow from a moneylender?'

Then a woman entered the shop, and his heart leapt as he recognised the beautiful young woman who lived in

Cotswold House. Hastily discarding his cheroot by popping it down the horn of the nearest gramophone he advanced towards her and smiled in welcome.

'Good morning, Madam, can I help you?'

Emma Josceleyne's black eyes studied the good-looking young man with interest. 'Well aren't you the pretty boy,' she thought appreciatively. Then her eyes sparkled with amusement as she noticed the smoke curling upwards from the gramophone horn, and she told him, 'I think you'd better put that fire out before you attend to me.'

Shocked, he turned and grabbing the gramophone rushed past Emma and out into the roadway where he shook the burning cheroot out on to the ground and stamped it to shreds.

He felt like cursing aloud in chagrin at appearing so clown-like when he returned inside to find the beautiful young woman smiling with amusement at him. Then the humour of the situation struck him also, and he relaxed and laughed aloud at himself. 'That'll teach me not to sneak a smoke,' he said wryly, and Emma joined in his self-deprecating laughter.

'Now Madam, how can I help you?' Vivaldi smiled, and was shrewd enough to recognise from the gleam in her eyes that this young woman found him physically attractive.

'I'm interested in buying one of these Talking Machines,' she told him.

Harry Vivaldi's thoughts raced as he suddenly glimpsed a chance of saving himself from Caleb Louch's fury, and also at the same time of inveigling himself into a closer acquaintance with Emma Josceleyne.

He smiled charmingly. 'Well Madam, we do have the most comprehensive selection of Talking Machines in the Midlands, possibly in the country.' He hesitated a moment, then went on to enquire tentatively, 'The price range is very wide; we have some machines at less than a pound, and the very latest and most advanced machines selling at 50 pounds. Might I ask the price area you are interested in?'

'I want the very best machine you have,' Emma

answered without hesitation.

'There are several types that I could equally recommend. Would you care for a demonstration?' Vivaldi offered.

She frowned slightly. 'I've no time to spend at present.'

The young man instantly seized upon this opportunity. 'I could bring a selection of our finest machines to your home, Madam, and demonstrate them to you at your pleasure.'

Emma nodded. 'Yes, that would suit me. Come this afternoon at about three o'clock.' From her purse she took an expensively embossed card and proffered it to him.

He scanned its ornate lettering. 'I'll be honoured to do so, Mrs Josceleyne.' He bowed slightly.

As she walked towards the door he followed quickly behind her and queried, 'Do you have any preference in the recordings you would wish to hear, Mrs Josceleyne?'

She shrugged her shapely shoulders. 'Not really. Anything that's lively.'

Again he bowed as he ushered her from the premises. 'Very well, Mrs Josceleyne, I'll bring a selection with me. Until this afternoon then.'

Her dark eyes dwelt on his face for several moments, and speculation lurked in their shimmering depths. Then she nodded a farewell, and walked away.

He remained in the shop doorway watching her retreating figure, admiring the trim un-corsetted waist and shapely hips.

'By God, I could fall in love with you, Mrs Josceleyne,' he murmured aloud, then frowned uneasily and admonished himself. 'Now don't you go getting all spoony, Harry boy, she's only just another bit of skirt that's all. You've got to keep your wits about you my son, and keep your priorities in the right order. And number one priority at this moment, is to get that bastard Louch off your back.'

Chapter Thirteen

The visit of Laura Hughes to Cotswold House had had a profound effect upon Miriam Josceleyne and although a week had now passed she could still recall every impassioned word that the young woman had uttered. To Miriam Josceleyne, made timid and stripped of self-confidence by men, the young woman's demand for equality with the male sex, and her arguments to support that demand had been both revelation and an inspiration. During the succeeding days Miriam Josceleyne had thought long and deeply and a spirit of resolution had germinated and come to flower within her. A resolution that she would join with Laura and make common cause with her and the other suffragettes, that she would join the Women's Social and Political Union and become an activist in the movement's struggle. Up until now she had not voiced anything of her thoughts to anyone else; she had wanted to be completely resolved in her own mind about what she intended to do before telling Emma or Mrs Elwood.

Now, sitting in the drawing-room of Cotswold House she was waiting for Emma to return from her shopping expedition. Trying to exercise patience, but finding it hard because she was now ready to tell Emma about her decision.

The outer door opened and slammed shut and the young woman came bustling into the room with a flurry of silken petticoats and a flush of excitement.

'We shall be having a visitor this afternoon, Miriam,' she announced with dancing eyes. 'I've decided to buy a Talking Machine, and a very handsome gentleman is coming to demonstrate it for us.' She paused and stared hard at the seated woman, whose expression had suddenly become doubtful.

'What's the matter? Has something upset you?'

Miriam shook her head and smiled apologetically. 'No my dear. It's only that I shall not be here this afternoon.'

'Why not? Where will you be?' Emma demanded.

'I'm going to Foxlydiate,' Miriam informed. 'To Foxlydiate House actually, to meet Lady Isobel Margesson.' She held out a sheet of headed notepaper. 'See, she has invited me to call on her today.' The hamlet of Foxlydiate was some miles west from the centre of Redditch towards Bromsgrove Town.

Emma grinned and teased good naturedly: 'My oath! Aren't we moving up in the world? A titled lady no less. So my company isn't good enough for you any more, is it?'

Miriam smiled at the teasing. 'You know better than to suggest that, my dear.'

'How did you come to get invited to her house then?' Emma's curiosity was sparked. 'You never told me that you knew her.'

'I don't. But I wrote to her earlier this week. She's the President of the Redditch branch of the Women's Suffrage Society. That's why I want to meet her now.'

The younger woman's black eyes were shrewd. 'That Laura Hughes made a big impression on you, didn't she, Miriam? I could tell that, even though you said nothing.'

Miriam nodded. 'Yes, she did. So much so in fact that I've decided to join her movement.'

Emma laughed incredulously. 'You, become a suffragette? Marching around with banners and screaming for the vote?' She shook her head forcefully. 'That's not for you, Miriam. You're too ladylike for all that bloody nonsense.'

Miriam savoured the unaccustomed surging of confidence she found within herself, as she answered firmly: 'I do not regard it as nonsense, Emma. And I trust that I'll be able to do my share of parading with banners, if that is necessary.'

The young woman chuckled and shrugged her

shoulders. 'Well, sooner you than me. I've got other fish to fry right now.'

The swarthy handsome features of Harry Vivaldi imposed themselves upon her mental vision, and she felt a frisson of sexual desire as her vivid imagination pictured his lithe body pressed against her own nakedness. After four years of submitting to the weak and shrivelled flesh of Hector Josceleyne, Emma hungered to enfold smooth muscular strength in her arms, and to feel the vigorous ardour of a young man between her thighs. Her full lips parted moistly and her breath quickened as the vivid mental pictures took on almost physical reality, and then she became aware that Miriam was regarding her curiously. She thrust the disturbing pictures from her mind and covered her momentary discomfiture by taking off her broad-brimmed, black-feathered hat, and discarding her black shoulder cape. 'What time are you going to Foxlydiate?' she enquired.

'I'm waiting for Mr Elwood to bring the trap, I've hired him to take me there.'

Inwardly Emma was pleased to hear that her friend would be absent that afternoon. It meant that she could flirt with the handsome Harry Vivaldi without the constraint of Miriam's presence. She sighed with barely concealed impatience for him to come, then decided to use the intervening time in making herself look truly beautiful. She feigned a slight yawn and smiled at her companion. 'Do you know, I feel quite tired. I think I'll go and lie down in my room for while.'

Left alone once more, Miriam was forced to admit to a feeling of relief that Emma had not invited herself to accompany her to meet Lady Isobel Margesson. Although Miriam loved the young woman dearly, she knew that Emma would not be able to take the matter of women's suffrage seriously, and this afternoon Miriam was hoping for a serious conversation with her hostess about the Women's Suffrage Society.

Chapter Fourteen

Back in Ernie Field's shop Harry Vivaldi was exultant at his good fortune. 'This is my big chance,' he kept on telling himself. 'This is the chance I was praying for.'

He stared at his reflection in the shop mirror and frowned. 'My hair could do with a trim, and this collar's looking a bit grubby. I'll need a good wash and brush up before I go to Cotswold House. A bit of Russian pomade for my hair, and a splash of cologne water.' As an experienced seducer he knew the value of fastidious personal hygiene and pleasantly scented flesh.

'What if old Ernie comes back before three o'clock?' The thought caused him considerable disquiet, and he tried fruitlessly to remember the times of the train arrivals from Birmingham. A further possible difficulty then presented itself. How was he to carry the talking machines and records up to Cotswold House? Normally if there were several deliveries of goods to be made around the district Ernie Field used the handcart which was kept in the yard at the back of the shop. Resentment flooded through the young man, causing his full lips to narrow into thin bitter lines. 'What'll it look like if I go to Cotswold House pushing the handcart like a day labourer? I can just imagine how Emma Josceleyne would regard me if she saw me pushing the sodding thing. I need to pay somebody to push it for me.'

Harry Vivaldi's fingers patted his empty pockets, and his eyes went to the cash drawer set into the tall narrow counter at the rear of the showroom.

He opened the drawer and checked its contents. There were copper and silver coins amounting to the sum of two pounds in the compartmented tray.

'I can use that,' he told himself, but as he reached down to lift some of the coins, his hand slowed and halted, and withdrew with empty fingers. 'The old bastard will give me the sack if I take anything from here,' he realised. He knew that his employer had discharged a previous assistant for taking only pennies from the cash drawer without previous permission, even though the pennies were used on shop business.

He slammed the drawer shut in a fit of petulance, and stood with his fists clenched, staring angrily out at the sunlit world beyond the shop's bowed windows. 'And how am I going to be able to get my hair trimmed, and get a new collar, and buy some cologne water?' He shook his head furiously, and then a tiny voice in his mind whispered: 'And how are you going to get the eight and threepence for Caleb Louch?'

'Fuck Caleb Louch!' he ejaculated fiercely, but then the memory of the man's formidable reputation assailed him, and a tremor of fear overlayed his resentful defiance.

'Fuck him!' he repeated, but now it was more of a whimper than a warcry.

He sighed heavily and started to pace up and down between the tall stands laden with Talking Machines, records and boxes of needles. The more Harry Vivaldi considered his present predicament, the more hopeless it appeared to him. And it was that very hopelessness that steeled him now to desperate measures.

'There's nothing else for it. I'll have to use the money from the cash drawer. I'll just have to take a chance on it, that's all. If the old bastard comes back, then that's just too bad. I've got no choice in the matter anyway, have I? It's either take a chance, or face bloody Caleb Louch without his rent, and I'd sooner take a chance than do that. If I can sell Emma Josceleyne a machine, I can add a quid to the price. I can make out two separate receipts, one with the right price for Ernie Field, the other for her price. I'll just have to copy her signature. That shouldn't be too hard for me, I've had enough practice at copying signatures after all.'

The more he thought about this plan, the more promising it began to appear. 'I've just got to hope that old Ernie gets delayed in Brummagem. If he don't come back early, then it'll all be all right, and I'll be clear and dry.'

His mercurial spirits began to rise sharply, and on impulse he decided: 'There's nothing to be gained from hanging around waiting any longer. First thing is to get my hair trimmed, buy a new collar and some cologne, and then go home and have a good wash and brush up. I'll find somebody to push the handcart when I'm on my way back here.'

Going to the drawer he took all the coins from it and slipped them into his trouser pockets. Then put on his elegant Homburg hat, lifted his Malacca cane, locked the shop door behind him, and went jauntily up the hill towards the town centre and into a barber's shop.

When later he entered the stale smelling room in George Street, he found Bella Thomas sitting at the table. Her painted Cupid's bow mouth twisted angrily when she saw him. 'What are you doing home at this hour? Have you got the sack?'

He scowled at her querulous expression. 'Don't you bloody well start,' he warned, then ordered her, 'Fetch me some clean water to have a wash in. I've got an important business appointment to go to.'

'That's a likely story!' she jeered, and her aggressive tone caused him to pause and stare curiously at her. He noted the fury burning in her bloodshot eyes.

'What's the matter with you?' he demanded. 'Why do you glare at me so?'

'That Caleb Louch as bin here,' she spat out. 'You haven't bin paying the rent, have you, you bastard!'

His swarthy face flushed dully, and he made no immediate reply. He eyed her warily, knowing from past experience that in her present mood she could well turn violent and attack him physically. With his visit to Cotswold House before him he could not risk having his one good suit either soiled or torn in a fight with her.

'I'm going to pay him in full tonight,' he growled sullenly.

'What with? Fucking buttons?' she screeched and came to her feet, her fat jowls quivering with the force of her fury. 'There's not a penny piece in the house to buy a bit of grub even, and now I find out that we'em to be kicked into the bloody street, because you aren't paid the bloody rent for weeks on end. You've spent all the money I give you on whoring and drinking you filthy rotten bastard!'

The young man recognised that this was the critical moment before the explosion of rage which would bring her flying at him, fingers hooked to tear at his eyes, mouth spewing shrieked obscenities.

'It's no good, I can't risk the cow messing up my clothes,' he accepted glumly, and pulling coins from his pocket he slapped them down on the table between them. 'There's the bloody rent money,' he shouted. 'And money for the bloody housekeeping.'

The sight of the coins took her aback. This was the last thing she could have expected. Vivaldi took advantage of the moment and spoke rapidly. 'That's the reason I've come back here at this hour, Bella. To bring you this money. I saw Caleb Louch this morning, and I told him that he wasn't to come bothering you about the rent. I told him that I'd be paying him everything we owed tonight, just as soon as I'd finished work.'

He paused to evaluate the effect of his words, and satisfied that he had averted physical attack, allowed an aggrieved note to enter his voice. 'The reason that I didn't pay the rent before now, was that I lent a chap some money, and he didn't pay me back as he promised to. I've had to chase after him this morning in my dinner break to get it off him. Then, when I got back to work I remembered that you hadn't got any money for food for yourself, and so I came back now to bring you some, so that you wouldn't have to wait until I'd finished tonight before having something to eat.'

He shook his head and added bitterly, 'For all the thanks I get, I needn't have bothered, need I. Even when I do me best you always think that I'm doing wrong by you.'

Bella Thomas's anger died within her, and she experienced a genuine remorse. 'Oh Harry, darlin', I'm sorry. Really I am. I'm sorry.'

He shook his head, an expression of grievous hurt on his face.

The fat woman came to him with outstretched arms, her eyes filling with tears of contrition. 'I'm sorry, darlin'. Don't be angry with me, I couldn't help it. I'm sorry. Truly I'm sorry.'

He allowed her to hug him close, then mindful of her face rouge smearing upon his jacket, he pushed her away. 'It's all right, Bella. Let's just forget it, shall we,' he told her. Then became brisk: 'Come on now, gal, fetch me that water. I've got to be quick and get ready for that business appointment.'

She hurried to do his bidding, and his lips twisted contemptuously as he watched her scurrying out into the yard to fetch water from the pump and told her silently, 'I still need you for the present, you fat sow. But once I've got myself in with Emma Josceleyne, then I'll kick your arse back to your bloody husband so fast, that you won't have time to blink even.'

While he washed and prepared himself, patting liberal splashes of cologne on to his cheeks and throat, and carefully tying his tie and brushing his pomaded hair, she hovered adoringly around him, talking constantly.

He hardly bothered to heed her words until she told him: 'Oh, and I reckon I've found a job for certain. I'm to goo round this afternoon for the final word.'

'What job is that, sweetheart?' He forced himself to smile kindly.

'At the Steam Laundry, down St Georges Road there. They reckon that it's bloody hard work, and the money aren't very much, but at least it'll be something, won't it, darlin'? It'll help you a bit, won't it?'

Her beseeching for his approval momentarily touched some softer chord within Harry Vivaldi's soul, and there was some genuine warmth in his voice as he told her, 'Of course it will help me, sweetheart. Of course it will.'

He had to evade her clutching arms. 'Now don't go messing me up,' he remonstrated sharply. 'I've only just got this tie as I want it.'

To soften the rebuff, he struck a pose and asked her,

'Well then, how do I look?'

All the fierce hunger of her love for him shone in her eyes, as she assured him fervently. 'You look like a prince, darlin'. Just like a prince!'

When he left the house she followed him through the covered entry and stood to watch him walk down the street. Harry Vivaldi, filled with the happy anticipation of his coming meeting with Emma Josceleyne, felt sufficiently kindly towards his mistress to turn and wave to her fat dowdy figure before disappearing around the corner into Red Lion Street.

Chapter Fifteen

Mrs Elwood sniffed loudly as she entered the drawing-room, and her eyes slitted in puffy balls of fat stared suspiciously at the young woman. Emma was leaning back on the huge *chaise-longue*, dressed in a pastel-shaded lilac gown, which set off her flawless complexion and glossy high-piled chestnut hair to perfection.

The older woman sniffed again, and Emma's white teeth gleamed in a teasing smile. 'Have you got a cold, Mrs Elwood?' she enquired sweetly.

'Humph!' the cook snorted disgruntedly. 'Even if I had, which I aren't, I'd still be able to smell that muck you'm plastered with. It stinks the whole house out, so it does.'

'This muck, as you calls it, is a very expensive French perfume, and it's all the rage in London. All the high society women are using it. Even the Countess of Warwick so I'm told.' Emma's black eyes twinkled with mischief. 'And if it's good enough for the King's fancy woman to use, then I'm sure it's quite good enough for me.'

Mrs Elwood's lips pursed as she stared balefully at the expensive gown, the silken folds of which moulded to the younger woman's shapely body and rounded thighs.

'And that bloody dress you'm wearing shows more than it hides, my wench,' she accused. 'It's not decent.'

Emma glanced complacently down at herself, and then widened her eyes as if in shock and fingered her high collar and intricately embroidered bodice. 'Why Mrs Elwood, how can you say such a thing?' she demanded in mock amazement. 'I'm covered right up from chin to ankle.'

She giggled at the other woman's indignant expression,

129

and after a few moments, her infectious gaiety transmitted itself to the cook, who could not restrain a grin of wry amusement.

'You'm a caution, you am, my wench. You'm a real caution,' she said, shaking her head.

'I am, aren't I,' Emma agreed, and her laughter pealed out to fill the room.

'Why am you all dressed up like lady muck then?' Mrs Elwood asked jovially, her good humour restored.

'Because I've got a gentleman coming to visit me,' Emma informed.

'Who'se that then?' the older woman was instantly avid with curiosity.

'Nobody you knows.'

'How can you know whether I knows him or not, if you doon't tell me who he is?'

The logic of this seemed irrefutable, so Emma capitulated and told her: 'It's that chap from Ernie Field's shop. His new salesman. The good-looking chap. I'm going to buy a Talking Machine and he's going to bring a selection up for me to try out.'

The older woman chuckled salaciously, and staring meaningfully at Emma's dress, told her: 'When he sees you looking like that, he'll start wondering if that's all you wants to try out, my wench.'

Emma only smiled ambiguously.

Mrs Elwood's fat face became intent. 'Is he the one who looks like a foreigner? Struts around the town all dressed up like a jack dandy?'

The young woman's black eyes became guarded. 'It could be. Why? What have you heard about him?'

The cook shrugged her meaty shoulders. 'Well, nuthin' really.' She grinned knowingly, and baited: 'Does you want me to find out for you? Has you took a fancy for him? Is that why you'm all dressed up?'

Emma's first impulse was to deny any such interest, but then she hesitated and thought for a few seconds. Eventually she nodded slowly. 'Yes, Mrs Elwood. I do want you to find out whatever you can about him. His name is Vivaldi. Harry Vivaldi.'

'Harry Vivaldi? What sort of a name is that?' Mrs Elwood frowned. 'He's got to be a bloody foreigner with a name like that.' Her large head shook dismissively. 'I can't abear foreigners. Why can't you take an interest in one of your own? Any Englishman is worth ten bloody foreigners any day o' the week.'

Emma betrayed a flash of irritation. 'Just find out what you can about him.'

Before the cook could answer, the front door bell jangled noisily.

'That's most likely him.' Emma instructed: 'Go and show him into here.'

Mrs Elwood tossed her mob-capped head with indignation. 'If it is him then he's got a bloody cheek to come ringing at the front door. He'd oughter use the trade entrance, because that's all he bloody well is, a bloody tradesman.' Her breath hissed derisively: 'He aren't even that. He's nought but a bloody counter-jumper.'

'Just bugger off and answer the door, will you,' Emma instructed irritably.

'I shouldn't be answering the door anyway,' the cook grumbled as she shuffled away. 'If you hadn't give the girls the same day off so they could goo off gallivanting together, I 'udden't have to lower meself so. I'm a cook-housekeeper, I am. Not a bloody parlourmaid.'

She was back within seconds, her face betraying her concern.

Emma stared in alarm. 'What's the matter?'

'It's one of your Mam's neighbours, my duck,' the cook told her. 'She says can you get down to Silver Street straightaway. Your Mam's been took badly. Real badly!'

Instantly all thought of Harry Vivaldi fled from Emma's mind, and fearful dread invaded her. Without a word she jumped up from her languid posture, and hatless and coatless went running from the house and down the road towards Silver Street.

Mrs Elwood stood at the front gate staring after the flying figure of the young woman, uncertain whether she should remain behind or follow after her. As she still hesitated Harry Vivaldi came up to the brow of Prospect

Hill strolling elegantly in front of the handcart which was being pushed by a ragged elderly man, who coughed and wheezed continuously under the strain of his heavy load.

Vivaldi reached the gate where the fat woman stood and spoke to her, 'I'm Mr Harry Vivaldi. I've got an appointment with the lady of the house.'

The fat woman ignored him, keeping her anxious eyes fixed along the line of Church Green.

Piqued he spoke more loudly: 'I'm Harry Vivaldi. I've got an appointment with the lady of the house.'

She turned on him angrily. ' 'Ull you give over werritin' me, young man. I heard you the first time.'

He stared at her in shock, and then she waved her meaty arms as if she were shooing away an importunate stray dog.

'Goo on! Gerrof! Theer's nobody here to see you now. You'll have to come back some other time.'

She hurried back into the house, only to reappear some moments later wrapping a shawl around her shoulders. She slammed the door closed and came brushing past the young man and went hurrying breathlessly along the Church Green, leaving Harry Vivaldi gaping disbelievingly after her.

'Is she bloody mad, or what?' he muttered to himself.

Shaking his head bemusedly he went up to the closed front door and rang the bell. He could hear the janglings reverberating through the house, but no one came to answer the summons. Again and again he tugged on the bell pull, and the realisation dawned that the house was empty.

A sensation of acute dismay struck through him. 'Oh my god!' he moaned softly. 'Where the bloody hell is she?'

' 'Ere Mister, wheer does you want this bloody cart left. I aren't agooing to hang about here all bloody day,' the ragged man wheezed.

Vivaldi turned and barked irritably: 'Hold your bloody rattle, will you. I'm trying to think.'

The elderly man's rat-like face glowered resentfully, and he snarled, 'I aren't being spoke to like that by you, my bucko! It's a fucking threepenny bit you'se give me. Not a gold sovereign. You can shove this lot up your bloody arse.'

He let the handles of the cart drop, and the expensive talking machines rattled metallically from the impact. He spat on the ground, hitched his ragged trousers up high on his skinny body, and stalked away.

'Oh my God!' Harry Vivaldi's olive skin became sheened with a clammy sweat of apprehension. 'If she doesn't come back and buy one of these from me, then what the bloody hell am I going to do?' He thought of the money he had already spent. He thought of Ernie Field's reaction when he should find that money missing. He thought of Caleb Louch's massive fists, and felt like bursting into tears.

'Where's she gone? Where's the bloody cow gone? What am I going to do if she doesn't come back and buy one of these bloody things? What am I going to do?'

Even while he fought to think clearly, a tiny voice kept on repeating in his mind. 'What about Caleb Louch and Ernie Field? What'll they do? What'll they do? What'll they do?'

Chapter Sixteen

'More tea, Miss Josceleyne?' Lady Isobel Margesson invited, and Miriam shook her head.

'No thank you, My Lady.'

'Another slice of cake?'

'No thank you, I've had more than sufficient.'

'You'll take another slice won't you, Mrs Osier?' The long aquiline nose of Lady Isobel twitched as if to encourage acceptance, and the short plump Mrs Osier twittered.

'Well, you'll no doubt think me terribly greedy, My Lady, but I really cannot resist just one tiny portion more. It's so delicious.'

The aristocratic features assumed an expression of gratification. 'I'm so happy that you enjoy it, Mrs Osier.'

The neat maidservant came forward with a slice of the rich dark cake resting on a delicate porcelain plate, which she handed to Lady Margesson, who handed it on to Mrs Osier. A personal attention which caused the short, plump woman to simper in delight.

'And now, Miss Josceleyne,' Lady Margesson turned her attention to her invited visitor once more, 'let us talk of the Women's Suffrage Society.'

Miriam unconsciously leaned slightly towards her hostess in interested expectation, and the narrow-featured, elegantly clad woman began a fluent exposition upon the aims and achievements of the society of which she was the local branch president.

Miriam listened intently as the beautifully modulated voice went on. And on. And on. And on.

Her first eager expectation began to pall under the

barrage of constantly reiterated phrases. 'Women's sacred duty to mankind . . . Women's sacred duty to instruct . . . Women's sacred duty to set an example to the lower orders . . . Women's sacred duty to maintain the morals and mores of society . . . Women's sacred duty to act charitably to those of the respectable lower orders of mankind . . . Women's sacred duty to uphold the Monarchy . . . Women's sacred duty to uphold the rule of Parliament . . . Women's sacred duty to protect property . . . Women's sacred duty to support their menfolk. . . '

Miriam's natural shy diffidence and lack of self-confidence began to be slowly overborne by a growing sense of impatience. She had not come here to be subjected to this type of meaningless verbiage. She had come as a seeker after new, daring, radical ideas. As a seeker for leadership and example. As a seeker for revolutionary fervour, and inspiration.

There came a brief pause in the lecture, as Lady Margesson took breath, and timidly Miriam ventured, 'The question of women gaining the right to vote, My Lady?'

A brief frown of rebuke crossed the aristocratic features, and the blue eyes became momentarily glacial, but Miriam summoned all her courage, and persisted, 'What does your Society intend to do to help women gain the vote?'

The modulated tones now held more than a hint of acerbity. 'Our Society is bringing moral pressure to bear upon Parliament to grant the right to vote to those ladies who are worthy to receive that right.'

Doubt shivered through Miriam's mind. 'Worthy to receive, My Lady?' she queried.

Lady Margesson's expression denoted surprise at her listener's apparent lack of understanding. 'Well, my dear Miss Josceleyne, you would not really expect that the women of the lower orders should receive such a right, I'm sure.'

A mental vision of the women she had met in Silver Street passed through Miriam's mind, and then she thought of Emma, and Emma's courage, and intelligence, and quickness of mind. 'There must be thousands of Emmas in the slums of our towns and cities,' she thought warmly. 'Thousands who are being crushed by this present system. Of course the Emmas deserve the vote. They have more right to it than useless do-nothings like myself.' An unaccustomed feeling of strength and confidence surged through her.

'Why should not the women of the lower orders receive the right to vote, My Lady?' she challenged.

Lady Margesson's manner became distinctly frosty. 'Why, because they are not fit to receive such a right, Miss Josceleyne. They are not made of the same clay as you, or I, or Mrs Osier. They have neither birth nor breeding. Neither manners nor sensitivity. Neither education nor intelligence. They are like so many brute beasts. The vast majority of them are filthy in habit, gross in behaviour, completely undisciplined and unprincipled, and lacking any respect whatsoever for those whom God has set above them. The right to vote must be reserved for those classes of society who are fit to receive it.'

'The Women's Social and Political Union do not share your views on this matter, Lady Margesson.' Miriam was trembling with a mingling of nervousness and outrage. 'They believe that all women, no matter what their social class may be, have the right to vote.'

'The women of the Social and Political Union are a rebellious rabble, and are a disgrace to their own sex,' Lady Isobel retorted sharply. 'And I am shocked that as a gently bred lady you should so lower yourself as to repeat their pernicious doctrines. They are nothing more than Socialists!' The noun was an epithet in her mouth. 'Traitors to their King and to their country!'

Now it was the image of Emma's battered and brutalised mother that rose up in Miriam's mind, and a sudden dislike for this aristocratic lady burgeoned within her.

'I fear that you and I are not in agreement, Lady Margesson,' she said quietly. 'In all honesty I must tell you, that although I respect your viewpoint I myself intend to join the Women's Social and Political Union. I believe that all women, irrespective of the social class they belong to, have the right to vote. How else can the women of the poor ever improve their pitiful lot in life, unless they have some political voice in our country.'

Lady Margesson scowled for long long moments at her guest, then with arrogant disdain radiating from her she spoke sharply to the maidservant. 'Sanders, show this, this . . .' she hesitated deliberately '. . . this person, to the door.'

Miriam's sallow cheeks flared bright with embarrassment at the cutting rudeness, but her green eyes were steady and uncowed as she politely half-bowed towards her hostess and her fellow guest. 'May I say thank you for your hospitality, Lady Margesson, and I truly regret that we are in disagreement over this matter. I bid you good day, Lady Margesson, Mrs Osier.'

The short plump woman sniffed in affront, and with a great show of scorn deliberately turned away.

Miriam walked along the wide rutted roadway towards Redditch and found that her embarrassment over her cavalier dismissal was of very short duration. Her spirits rose and a sense of happy expectancy enveloped her.

'I'm going in search of Laura Hughes tomorrow, and I'm going to tell her that I am joining forces with her.'

The decision infused her with a joyful energy, and she lifted her long skirts from the dust of the road and strode out humming gaily to herself.

Chapter Seventeen

The woman on the blood-soaked mattress had bitten her lips until they were ragged flesh, and her screams of agony filled the cramped, fetid room and echoed down the narrow alleyway. Her dirty grey features were hideously contorted and Emma had to bite her own full lips to keep back the cry of horror that threatened to erupt from her as she first glimpsed her mother through the clustering women who were fighting desperately to bring forth the child from the grotesquely swollen belly, that resembled a huge blue-streaked, pallid white balloon above the splayed, bloodied thighs.

Emma pushed further forward, then her eyes widened in terror and nausea overpowered her senses as she saw the tiny bloodied arm protruding from her mother's vagina. Now she did cry out and the tall raw-boned woman standing between her mother's legs, turned and cursed roughly: 'Shut your noise, you stupid little bitch. If you can't help then doon't bloody hinder.'

Another woman took Emma by the arm and half pushed, half pulled her back from the bed, urging with rough kindliness. 'Come on out of it, you silly little cow. Theer's nothing you can do to help your Mam. Leave it to them that knows what they'm adoing.'

Faint and nauseated by the shock of what she had seen, Emma initially made no resistance, but then when the woman began to urge her down the narrow staircase, Emma fought to master her reeling senses, and stubbornly resisted. 'No, Bessie, I'll not goo. I'll be all right. Let me see my Mam. Let me help her.'

As if she had heard her daughter's pleas, Amy Farr

suddenly screamed out: 'Emmyyyy? I want my Emmyyy!'
Then her eyes rolled up and she writhed and moaned in
mindless agony.

Bessie Clements released Emma's arms, and with
troubled eyes told her, 'Look, if I lets you back to your Mam,
promise you wun't start interfering. Aggie Walton is the
best midwife theer is in this town, and if anyone can save
your Mam and the kid then it's her.'

'I can send for a doctor,' Emma stated wildly. 'I can send
for Doctor Pierce.'

'Phoo!' Bessie Clements puffed contemptuously. 'You
can send for any bloody doctor you likes, my wench, but
theer aren't one on 'um who can do better than Aggie
Walton. Her brought you into this world safe and sound,
didn't her?'

By now Emma had regained some degree of self control,
and she was struggling to think clearly. 'Let me have a word
with Aggie Walton first.' She again struggled through the
clustering women and saw the raw-boned woman pushing
one hand deep inside her mother's body, while with the
other she pressed and kneaded against the great mounded
belly, while all the time screams tore from Amy Farr's
throat, screams which died away into bubbling moans only
to erupt again and again and again.

Emma tried to cut off the sight of blood and body waste
and torn bleeding lips, and disregard the awful howling
shrieks from the creature whom she knew as a loving
mother, but who now resembled some mindless suffering
animal.

'Aggie? Aggie? Does you want me to fetch Doctor Pierce?'
She had her mouth close to the raw-boned woman's ear.

The woman's face was streaming with sweat, and her foul
breath gusted against Emma's nostrils. Her brown-stained
teeth gnawed upon her lower lip, and she seemed undecided. Then she withdrew her fingers from the pregnant
woman, and clutched the tiny protruding arm.

Emma swallowed hard as she stared down at that
perfectly formed arm and hand, and could not help but
think it an obscenity which was mercilessly destroying her
mother.

Aggie Walton's expression was regretful, and she stroked the baby's arm and hand with a tender gesture. Then she sighed heavily, and told Emma, 'Theer's no chance o' saving the babby, Emma. It's already dead I'm sure. And if it aren't brought out double quick, then it'll kill your Mam. Run for Doctor Pierce. Tell him from me that he's going to need his hook. Tell him that the babby is a shoulder presentation, and that the yed's well jammed. But run quick, girl, because if you aren't back here with him in half an hour, then I'll have to try and do the business meself if your Mam's to have a chance of living.'

Emma ran as she had never run before. She was unseeing and uncaring of the curious faces that turned to stare at her and mad career through the streets, and the excited dogs that barked and jumped at her wildly fluttering skirts. Her heart welled with thankfulness as Doctor Pierce himself answered her frantic knocking on his surgery door. He saw her face and had the sense to ask nothing, only listen intently as she breathlessly gabbled the message Aggie Walton had entrusted to her.

Grim featured, the doctor snatched up his bag and taking from a drawer a peculiar long-handled tool with an almost circular saw-toothed hook at its end, he led Emma to his horse and trap, and whipped the beast into a fast canter. They arrived outside the arched entrance to Silver Street in a clattering of hooves and jingling of harness, and the doctor pitched the horse's reins to a lounger.

'Hold it here until I return. I'll pay you,' he shouted, and followed Emma up the alley and into the tenement.

He scowled furiously when he saw the clustering women around the bed, and bellowed: 'Get out! Get out, all of you. Except for you Mrs Walton. I'll need your help. The rest of you get away from here immediately.'

Loath to leave the scene of such drama and excitement, the women went reluctantly down the narrow stairs. The doctor spoke sharply to Emma, who was cradling her mother's sweat-soaked head in her arms, crooning softly to her.

'You'll be all right now, Mam. I'se fetched the Doctor. You'll be all right now, Mam.'

140

'Mrs Josceleyne, you'd best leave as well. What I am about to do is not pleasant to witness.'

Emma shook her head stubbornly. 'I'm staying, Doctor Pierce. I'm staying with my Mam.'

Aggie Walton intervened: 'Theer aren't much time left, Doctor. Her's in a bad way.'

'I can see that for myself,' the man snapped pettishly, then nodded brusquely at Emma. 'So be it, Mrs Josceleyne. Stay if you wish, but it's on your own head.'

Then his professionalism reasserted itself, and he made quick examination of the suffering woman, then nodded at Aggie Walton. 'Well done, Mrs Walton. You were quite correct. It is an impacted shoulder presentation.'

She received the compliment with ill-grace. 'I bin bringing babbies into this world for more years nor you, Doctor. I knows my own business by now, I should think.'

He nodded brusquely. 'Just so, Mrs Walton. Just so.'

He took some twine from his bag and tied a noose around the baby's wrist, then handed the ends of the thread to Aggie Walton, who took station at his side. He lifted the hooked tool in his right hand, and nodded to the woman, who began to pull steadily on the tiny arm, keeping it stretched and extended. The doctor shielded the circular hook with his left hand, and carefully inserted hook and hand together into the pregnant woman, and now for the first time Emma suddenly realised what was to be done.

'Sweet Jesus Christ!' She cradled her mother's face against her breasts, but could not drag her own horrified gaze away from what was happening so close to her eyes.

The hook and hand disappeared, and the doctor's expression was rapt with concentration as he man-oeuvered the long handle of the tool with his right hand.

Amy Farr was comatose, dragging stertorous ragged breaths, and Emma blessed that merciful unconsciousness. The doctor held his breath, and slowly rocked the handle of the tool up and down, all the while exerting a sustained pull. Then he sighed thankfully, withdrew the hook head, and took the tiny arm and gently pulled the decapitated body free from the imprisoning flesh.

141

Amy Farr jerked and moaned as the head was next delivered, but her eyes remained closed and she gave no sign of awareness. Emma, to her own amazement, was able to look at the dead infant dispassionately. Her only emotion was thankfulness that now her mother had a chance of life.

Aggie Walton wrapped the tiny remains in a thick swathe of rag, and put the bundle into a wicker basket. Then she called down the stairs to the waiting women, 'Bring us some water. I wants to get Amy cleaned up a bit.'

The doctor was wiping his soiled hands and arms on a towel he took from his bag, and Emma asked him: 'Was the babby alive, Doctor?'

Pierce shook his head. 'No, Mrs Josceleyne. In my opinion it had been dead for some considerable time.' He bent over the comatose woman and made a brief examination. 'Your mother will survive, Mrs Josceleyne. But will need careful nursing.' He glanced meaningfully around the cramped and rancid room. 'If she could be placed in other surroundings it would greatly aid her recovery.'

'She shall be,' Emma declared forcefully; and beneath her breath vowed, 'If my Dad objects, I'll bloody well swing for the bugger. He'll not stop me shifting me Mam out of here this time.'

When the doctor had left, the woman crowded back into the room and helped Aggie Walton to wash Amy Farr and make her more comfortable. Afterwards some of the women unwrapped the tiny decapitated corpse and examined it curiously.

There were few regrets or expressions of sadness voiced, and Emma knew why. Every woman in this room had been subjected to almost continuous impregnation since their teenage marriages. They had borne children who had lived, and children who had died, and those latter were in the majority. For these women, worn out by childbearing, constant drudgery and bitter poverty, children eventually became a curse rather than a blessing. The overwhelming reaction to a stillborn child after so many pregnancies was a sense of relief that there would not be yet another mouth to try and feed, when already they found it well nigh impossible to feed the mouths already living. Emma knew that when too many children existed in too much poverty, then parental love could become a finite rather than an infinite emotion.

She sighed, then shrugged mentally. This was the way of her world, and as far as she could see, it would be the way forever. She bent and gently kissed her mother's worn, flaccid cheek. 'I'm fetching you out o' this now though, Mam. I swear on my own grave to that.'

She said to the other women, 'Listen, I want to move me Mam up to my house. Will you give me a hand to carry her out?'

They stared at her in an uneasy silence, and Emma questioned: 'Well? What's the matter? Can't you give me an answer?'

It was Aggie Walton who eventually acted as the spokeswoman for the group. 'What 'ull your Dad say about moving her, Emma?'

'It's not up to me Dad. You heard the doctor say that she should be moved into better surroundings to help her get better.'

The tired, grimy faces exchanged looks, and there were one or two who gave warning shakes of their frowsty heads.

Emma's lips twitched angrily. 'What's up? Are you afraid to help me move me Mam?' she demanded.

Hetty Green, the next door neighbour of Amy Farr, scolded the young woman heatedly, 'You'se got no rights to becall any on us, young Emmy. You knows what your Dad's like when he loses his temper. He's likely to kill anybody who crosses him. And if he comes home and finds Amy's bin shifted elsewhere without him saying so, then there'll be bloody murder done. And you knows that's a fact, young Emmy.'

Aggie Walton tried a more placatory course. 'Listen, Emmy, why don't you wait until your Dad comes home, and then ask him about it. I'm sure that when he sees how badly the poor cratur is, then he'll say it's all right for you to take her into your house and look arter her.'

'And bloody pigs 'ull fly!' Emma jeered bitterly. 'You know that the old bastard won't let me Mam goo out of this house unless he's forced into it.' She stared pityingly down at the unconscious woman, who appeared half dead from her ordeal.

'Well, her's no good to him like this, is her?' Hetty Green pointed out reasonably. 'He'll see that himself, wun't he.'

Emma turned on the neighbour in quick fury. 'It aren't a question of her being any good to him, you stupid cow! As he sees it, me Mam's his property, and no matter what state she's in he won't let her goo out from this house. He won't set her free until she's in her coffin, and that's a fact.'

Hetty Green's tallowy features were sullen. 'Well, you can do what you wants, the rest on you. But I aren't gooing to come between a man and his lawful wedded wife. I'm getting out on it now, and if you'se got any sense the rest on you 'ull get out on it afore Winston Farr gets back here.' She paused and glared balefully around her. 'Because he aren't gooing to be in any sweet mood when he finds out what's happened, is he? The bugger 'ull be fit to be tied.'

Suiting action to words she shuffled down the narrow staircase, and after a few moments of uneasy silence the other women followed her, leaving only Aggie Walton.

The midwife shook her head sadly. 'I'm sorry, Emmy, truly I am. But I can't afford to help you move your Mam without your Dad's say so. If once I did summat like that, then all my trade 'ud be gone. No man 'ud have me brought in to birth his kids any more.'

Emma recognised the futility of further argument, but her own determination was if anything even stronger.

'All right, Mrs Walton, that's fair enough. Will you just do me the favour of staying with me Mam for a bit. Until I can get back.'

'O' course I 'ull. That's part o' me job anyway, my duck. To stay until your Mam's all right to be left.'

Emma hurried downstairs, to find Mrs Elwood hovering anxiously. She stared in surprise, and the woman said: 'I'm ever so sorry to hear what's happened.'

Emma shrugged, and then asked quietly, 'Will you help me to shift me Mam up to my house, Mrs Elwood?'

144

The fat woman agreed without any hesitation. 'O' course I will. Does you want me to give you a hand to carry her downstairs?'

'Not yet.' Emma's mind was racing. 'We'll need a carriage. We won't be able to carry her the whole way back to my house. Where's Mr Elwood? Is he in the yard today?'

The broad face opposite her became doubtful. 'I don't know. He took Miss Miriam to Foxlydiate, didn't he. I don't know where he might have gone arter that.'

'Look, we'll go back up towards my house, and see if we can find a carriage. Then we'll come straight back here with it and move me Mam. We'll needs look sharp about it though, else me Dad might come home first.'

She blessed the fact that none of her younger brothers or sisters were around the house. Following custom, various neighbours had taken them into their own houses to keep them there until their mother was recovered enough to be able to speak to them.

The two women hurried up towards the town centre calling at a place that hired carriages, but there were none available.

Emma even approached the drivers of carts, but none of these could leave off from their tasks to help her.

'Come on, let's go round to Cresswell's yard and see if your husband's got back there?' Emma was becoming desperate.

To reach the yard, the women had to pass Cotswold House, and as they neared its porticoed front, Emma squinted curiously at what she saw.

'Look there, Mrs Elwood. What's he doing?'

The figure of a man was seated on the front steps of Cotswold House, slumped in what appeared to be abject despair, his head buried in his hands. Emma saw the handcart, still loaded with Talking Machines, standing against the pavement, and could not help but chuckle mirthlessly.

'It's that bloody salesman of Ernie Field. Well he's got no chance of selling me a Talking Machine at this bloody time, has he?'

Then as the two women neared the handcart, an idea

145

suddenly occurred to Emma. She visually measured the length and breadth of the handcart, and realised that it would do to carry her mother.

Sitting on the steps, Harry Vivaldi had indeed given himself up to abject despair. His vivid imagination had been picturing all the dire consequences that were hovering over him. Caleb Louch. Ernie Field. A terrible beating. Loss of his job. Homelessness. Prosecution for theft. The young man had lost all track of time, and all awareness of his immediate surroundings. Then abruptly there came the staccato clicking of hurrying feet, hands grasped his shoulder and shook hard, and an excited female voice shouted: 'Come on, I want you.' And then went on talking rapidly.

Bemused, he allowed himself to be badgered into unloading the handcart and placing its load inside the hallway of Cotswold House. It was only as he was pushing the handcart behind the hurrying women that the full import of his miraculous rescue from despair struck fully home to him, and he felt like crowing aloud with delighted relief.

'She said she'll give me a sovereign if I help her.' He savoured that glorious fact. 'All I have to do is to help her move her mother to Cotswold House, and I'll have a sovereign.'

He smiled at the lithe figure of Emma Josceleyne, who together with Mrs Elwood had now outdistanced him by many yards. He tried to quicken his pace, but the cumbersome handcart was heavy, and so he contented himself with a slow steady trudge. He did wonder why the pay was so good for such a simple task, and why Emma Josceleyne and her companion had seemed so tense and panicky in their manner. But decided that he had probably been misjudging their mood.

When he reached Silver Street however, the first doubts came into his mind. The narrow alleyway was buzzing with excitement; there was a small crowd of people in front of the Farr's front door, and from every other door and window, eager faces watched him manoeuvering the handcart through the entrance arch.

'You wun't take so long gooing back through theer if Winston Farr catches you,' a man shouted, and his gibe was greeted with roars of laughter from the onlookers.

'No, you'll most probably goo over it.'

'I'll bet he'll wish he hadn't worn his Sunday best to come down here in, when Winston gets hold on him.'

'Winston 'ull take that bloody titfer and shove it right up his arse.'

Sweat was running down from beneath the band of Harry Vivaldi's Homburg hat, and he was panting from the effort of heaving the iron-rimmed wheels over the potholed, rutted surface of the alley.

Emma came to the door of her family home to urge him. 'Be quick, for Christ's sake.' Her face was tense with strain. Now the doubts were clamouring in Harry Vivaldi's mind. There was definitely something more to this job than he had expected.

When he reached the anxious girl he panted out: 'Why are there so many people watching us? And who'se this chap Winston?'

'Never mind that now, I haven't time to explain.' She brushed aside his anxious questions, and snatched a blanket from the heap of pillows and blankets which she had loaded on the cart at Cotswold House.

'Come on in here.'

With considerable trepidation the young man followed Emma into the house. He stared about him in shock, unable to comprehend why the mother of such a wealthy young widow should be living in such squalid poverty.

Upstairs he helped Emma and Mrs Elwood to bundle the apparently senseless woman in the blanket and between them they managed to carry her down the narrow staircase. In the tight squeeze of the staircase Harry Vivaldi's body kept scraping along the greasy, sooty walls and he groaned inwardly as he thought of all that dirt impregnating his suit.

Once outside in the alley, they settled Amy Farr as comfortably as they could upon the heap of blankets and pillows. Then Mrs Elwood and Harry Vivaldi got between the shafts like human draught animals, and with Emma pushing at the rear, made the return journey to Cotswold House followed all the way by a crowd of ragged, hooting street urchins.

Harry Vivaldi was in agonies of embarrassment as they traversed the streets where he had gloried in parading his elegance, and he kept his head bent and his eyes fixed on the ground to avoid meeting the curious stares of those they passed. But Emma was unheeding and uncaring of what anyone might think or say. She was completely dominated by the need to get her mother into the safe haven of Cotswold House and she hounded her helpers continuously, driving them to move faster and faster, until the sweat poured from their bodies and their lungs whooped and strained for air.

Only when the house was reached and her mother settled into bed in Emma's own room, did the young woman relax. She smiled with relief as she wiped away the sweat streaming down her flushed face.

'We've done it!' she announced triumphantly. 'We've got her back safe and sound.'

Leaning over the bed, gasping hoarsely for breath, Mrs Elwood seemed oblivious to the words, while Harry Vivaldi, panting heavily, could only stare ruefully at his expensive suit now smeared and soiled by soot and grease, and the filth of the alleyway caked over his boots.

'What if your Dad comes up here after her?' Mrs Elwood choked out.

'Phooo, even that mad bugger's got more sense than to try breaking his way into this house.' Emma was dismissive. 'He knows well enough that I'd have the police on him, and lay charges. He's had enough o' prison cells now. He aren't a young buck any longer is he? She paused a moment to smile fondly at her mother. 'Anyway, I'll send him some money down shortly. That'll sweeten his temper.'

Harry Vivaldi was absorbing all that she said, and was also rapidly re-evaluating all his previous notions about this young woman. His feral instincts were now in ascendance, and his confidence soared.

'She's nothing but a slumrat,' he told himself gleefully.

148

'I'd already guessed that she'd married above herself, but I hadn't known just how much she had married above her station. She comes from the lowest of the low, this one.' Inwardly he preened himself. 'Now I've got the full picture of her, she'll be easy meat.' He gloated on that assumption. 'Easy meat.'

The cook had by now recovered sufficiently to examine the comatose woman. 'She's lying peaceful enough, the poor soul. I reckon we should leave her quiet. That's what she needs now more nor anything, just to be let rest. That birthing has took everything out on her.'

Amy Farr did appear to be sleeping peacefully, and although Emma was loath to leave her, she knew that there was nothing she could do to aid her mother's recovery at this moment, other than leave her to rest.

'Come on then, we'll go and have a cup of tea.' She smiled warmly at Harry Vivaldi, and then noticed his dirtied clothing.

'I'm sorry about your clothes, Mr Vivaldi. You put them in for cleaning, and I'll pay whatever it costs.' She suddenly remembered her previous promise. 'Oh, and I've got to pay you haven't I.'

Vivaldi's thoughts were moving with a lightning rapidity, as he compared present small gain with possible heady future prospects. 'If I make the right moves here, then I could hit the jackpot! I could really get myself well in with Emma Josceleyne. She already fancies me I can tell. If I make the right moves now, I could have her eating out of my hand in no time at all.' The fearful knowledge of the risks he ran almost unnerved him. 'But if I've read her wrong, then what'll happen? I'll get the sack. There'll be a bloody kicking from Caleb Louch. I'll be thrown out on the streets. Ernie Field might prosecute me for thieving.'

Then, thrusting everything from his mind he drew a deep breath and summoning up all his nerve, decided to take the gamble. He smiled and shook his head. 'You most certainly have not got to pay me, Mrs Josceleyne. I wouldn't dream of taking money for helping you. It was an honour to do so.'

For a moment or two Emma stared at the man, and the

doubt was clear to see in her black eyes. But he met her searching stare with such a dignified manliness, that her doubts dissolved. 'He's a real gentleman!' she thought with a shock of pleasure.

'Well, at least let me pay for having your suit cleaned,' she persisted, but again he smilingly demurred.

'You will offend me grievously, Mrs Josceleyne. I was honoured to be able to be of help to you. And I hope that if in the future there should occur any opportunity of my being of service to you, then you'll not hesitate to call on me for it.'

Emma was charmed. 'Well, at least you'll not refuse a cup of tea, will you, Mr Vivaldi? Or perhaps something stronger?'

He accepted with alacrity. 'Tea will be most welcome, Mrs Josceleyne.' He smiled with a hint of roguishness. 'I never take anything stronger until after sunset.'

The three of them went down to the kitchen and sat companionably around the great table, drinking tea and talking easily. Harry Vivaldi could be an amusing companion, and now he exerted his utmost efforts to charm and entertain the two women.

When he judged that he had fully succeeded in his object, he suggested brightly, 'How would you like to hear some music, or if you like cut a record yourself so that you can hear yourself talk and sing?'

The women, now refreshed and completely at ease, were eager for this further entertainment. While Emma slipped upstairs to check on her mother Harry Vivaldi brought into the kitchen the most expensive Talking Machine – the Improved Edison Phonograph fitted with the Bettini diaphragm and topped by an elongated shiny horn, together with an assortment of records.

When Emma Josceleyne returned contented that her mother was resting peacefully, Harry Vivaldi greeted her entrance with a graceful bow, and announced as if he was a Master of Ceremonies: 'And now ladies, at great expense, I bring for your entertainment this evening, the immortal, the one and only, Miss Ella Shields!'

> *'I'm Burlington Bertie,*
> *I rise at ten thirty and saunter along like a toff.*
> *I walk down the Strand with my gloves on my hand,*
> *then I walk down again with them off.'*

As the languid drawling accents filled the air Emma clapped her hands delightedly, but Mrs Elwood sniffed disparagingly. 'I'se heard Vesta Tilley sing this 'un up at Brummagem. She sounds like a proper toff she does, not like this 'un. Her sounds like a foreigner!'

Harry Vivaldi smiled easily. 'Ella Shields is from Baltimore, Mrs Elwood. She's an American. And this is a different song from the one Vesta Tilley sings.'

'Shhh!' Emma hissed for silence, her eyes shining, her face rapt with pleasure. 'Let's listen. This machine's wonderful, aren't it. You'd swear she was here in this very room singing to us.'

> *'I'm all airs and graces, correct easy paces,*
> *Without food so long, I've forgot where my face is.*
> *I'm Bert, Bert, I haven't a shirt,*
> *But my people are well off, you know!*
> *Nearly ev'ry one knows me, from Smith to Lord Roseberry,*
> *I'm Burlington Bertie from Bowwww. . . .'*

It was early evening when Ernie Field came stumping down Prospect Hill. He was in a foul humour. The business that had taken him to Birmingham was of a very intimate nature. Ernie Field was a man of perverse sexual tastes, and although Mrs Field was in many ways a dutiful and submissive wife, she found her husband's sexual practices abhorrent, and had retreated into chronic, bad-smelling invalidity to avoid any intimate congress with him.

Ernie Field was quite prepared to exert, by force if necessary, his conjugal rights over his wife's body, and during the early years of their marriage had done just that on frequent occasions. But now the awful smell his wife exuded had destroyed any sexual desire he had for her, and so he had accepted defeat and sought elsewhere for his physical satisfaction. At least once a week, sometimes

151

twice, he would travel to Birmingham and seek out one of the prostitutes who frequented certain public houses in the city centre. Because of the nature of his sexual appetites he was forced to pay high prices, and this fact always soured his mood, once he had assuaged his appetites.

His watery eyes peered curiously as he crossed the roadway towards his shop. He could see no sign of movement within, and his puzzlement became tinged with anger when he saw the closed sign. 'Where's that flash bastard got to? It's not half-past eight even, and the shop's closed. If he's gone to the pub I'll bloody hand him his sack.'

Unlocking the front door, he entered the premises and came to an abrupt standstill. 'The stock? Where's my bloody stock?'

In consternation he wandered from stand to stand, running his hands through the empty spaces where all the most expensive Talking Machines had been. He reached the counter and opened the cash drawer, cursing loudly when he found it empty. Then began to pace wildly around the empty stands once again.

'He's robbed me! The flash bastard has robbed me!' he said aloud. Then he remembered that he had not paid the insurance premiums that had fallen due the previous month, and sheer terror caused him to throw both arms up in the air. 'What am I gooing to do? What am I gooing to do? The police. I'll goo to the police! The thievin' bastard can't have got far. Not with a load like that.'

'Wait 'til the sun shines Nellie'. The handcart clattered to a halt outside the open doorway and Harry Vivaldi came in humming the big hit song of the previous year. When he saw his employer's wild eyes, and pale strained features, he became instantly wary. But almost in the same moment realised that he had nothing to worry about, and grinned jauntily.

'What's the matter, Boss?' Indicating the loaded handcart he went on, 'Doon't worry about that lot. It's all right and I'll have it unloaded in a jiffy.'

'Wheer's you bin with my stock? And wheer's the float

152

money?' Ernie Field gritted out, hardly able to restrain his fury.

The young man's jauntiness was not diminished by his realisation of his employer's mood. 'I've been out making you a lot of money, Boss. And earning myself a nice commission as well.'

At the mention of money Ernie Field's anger became instantly overlaid by greed. 'How much? How much have you earned me?'

'I've just sold the Improved Edison machine. Three boxes of the sapphire tipped needles, two Marie Lloyds, two Ella Shields, one Harry Bongo's "Nigger Minstrels", one Hetty King, two Carusos, and four blank cylinders.' He rattled the coins weighing heavily in his jacket pocket.

'A grand total of sixty-three pounds, eighteen shilling and sixpence. Paid cash on the nail.' He paused and assessed the impact of his words, then went on airily. 'Oh, by the way, I took the cash from the drawer with me because I wasn't sure how long I'd be gone, and I didn't like leaving it here unguarded. Well, what do you think, Boss? It hasn't been a bad day's business, has it?' Vivaldi sought for congratulation, which his employer only gave grudgingly.

'Not too bad, I suppose. But I'm wondering how much business you'se missed by being out of the shop?'

'Miserable old bleeder,' Harry Vivaldi thought resentfully, but his own spirits were so high that the momentary resentment passed almost instantly, and he grinned happily. 'Not as much as I've done by being out of it, that's for sure. Anyway, I'll get the stuff unloaded, and then sort the money out.'

As he watched his employee's well-manicured hands stacking up the gold coins Ernie Field could not help but begin to feel somewhat more cheerful. This was a good day's sales by any standards, and his profits from it would more than cover his day's expenses. In fact, the profits would be enough to pay for his next two trips to Birmingham, and still leave change.

The younger man again started to feel resentful as he counted out the coins, and mentally computed what his commission might amount to. 'It's not bloody fair, is it,' he told himself. 'I've done all the work, and this old bastard is getting all the gravy.'

But then he thought of the delightful Emma Josceleyne, and he smiled gleefully to himself. 'I've got really well in there,' he exulted inwardly, 'and made a couple of quid on the side as well as this commission.' He could have laughed aloud with sheer pleasure, as he thought of how his troubles of the morning had so suddenly all evaporated. 'I can pay Caleb Louch, and clear all my slates at the pubs and shops, and still have enough left to go on the spree.'

He visualised Emma Josceleyne's beautiful face and succulent body, and his elation increased even more. 'Things are looking up, Harry boy,' he congratulated himself with immense satisfaction. 'Things are most definitely looking up, and no mistake.'

Chapter Eighteen

It was very hot on this last Saturday in July and there was no cooling breeze to temper the turgid air in the red-brick streets of the town. In Whites restaurant the venetian blinds shading the big plate glass windows did little to lower the overheated temperatures of the large dining-rooms. Each time the service doors to the kitchens opened, more gas-heated air and the fumes of roasting meats and boiling vegetables belched out to thicken the stuffy atmosphere.

Laura Hughes's thin face was glowing fierily and beneath her high-collared black dress, stiffly-starched and high-bibbed apron, her body was damp and sticky with sweat.

'Waitress? Waitress, more iced water here!'

'Waitress, wheer's our main course?'

'Waitress, I've been waiting ten minutes!'

'Come on, Missy! Come onnn! I aren't got all day to waste. Let's have some service here!'

From all sides the impatient voices assailed her, and her head throbbed painfully as she scurried from one table to another doing her best to keep up with the demands.

From his position by the main entrance Reginald White beamed with satisfaction as he surveyed the packed tables.

'You're busy today, White.' One of his regular customers had entered, and frowned as he saw the thronged restaurant. 'Where am I going to sit?'

'I'll find you somewhere, Mr Terry, don't you worry,' the big-paunched proprietor assured, and spread his soft plump hands apologetically. 'It's this Trades Federation rally that's taking place today, Mr Terry. That's what's bringing so many into the town. They've come to hear Keir Hardie speak. Mind you, I've no time for this Independent Labour nonsense meself, but I must admit it's been good for business today.'

'That's about the only thing the Labour Party has ever been good for then,' the other man observed sourly, and scowled at a table of men wearing big red rosettes pinned to the lapels of their coats.

'Damned socialists! I don't know what this country's coming to, White. These days Jack thinks he's as good as his master.'

Reginald White forbore to comment. Only nodded and then suggested, 'Listen, Mr Terry, I'll seat you in my own private room. You'll be more comfortable there.'

He beckoned to Laura as he moved across the crowded floor, and when she came to him told her, 'I'm putting Mr Terry in my private room. You'll see to him, and mind you make a good job on it. He's a very important man in this town.'

Laura glanced anxiously at her other clamorous tables. 'But I'm very busy at this moment, Mr White.'

'You should be thankful that you am busy, my girl – that's what pays your wages,' White snapped brusquely.

Two customers simultaneously shouted for her, and Laura became flustered. 'Can't one of the other girls serve Mr Terry? Only I've got three extra tables as it is.'

'I've told you to serve him, girl.' Reginald White's plump smooth features became irate. 'If you won't do as I tell you, then perhaps I'd best find a wench who will.'

For a moment Laura was tempted to argue further, but knew that if she did she was risking being sacked from her job.

From behind her came another impatient shout for service, and her employer growled, 'Get on with your work, girl. There's customers waiting. And as soon as you've dealt with that 'un, then get upstairs to my private room and serve Mr Terry.'

Perched upon a high stool behind the cash desk, Mrs Ethel White, wife of the proprietor, had noted the exchange. Known to the restaurant's staff as the 'fat vulture' she gave the impression of a hovering bird of prey, with her hooked nose and bulging eyes which seemed able to discern instantly even the slightest infringement of the establishment's rigid work rules. Her massive rear overflowed and hung down around the stool seat, and unkind wags among the staff stated their conviction that the highstool was hopelessly trapped between her huge buttocks, and that this was the reason for her permanently aggrieved expression.

Now she waved imperiously to her husband, and when he hurried to her snapped irritably, 'Is that suffragette giving you lip again, Mister?'

Her husband, secretly nervous of his formidable spouse, shook his head. At heart he was not an unkind man, and he knew that his wife was itching for the opportunity to dismiss Laura from his employment.

'You ought never to have given her a job in the first place. No matter that Ivor Brunton recommended her. Any woman who says that she's a suffragette is nothing more than a shameless trollop!' The long hooked nose quivered indignantly. 'And she thinks herself to be lady muck, that 'un does. If it was up to me, I'd sack her.'

He nodded glumly. 'I know you would, my dear. But she's not a bad worker, you know. She tries hard.' Then he seized the advent of newly entered customers as excuse to bustle away.

The throbbing pain in Laura's head worsened as she hurried backwards and forwards from kitchen to tables. She climbed the stairs to the private room again and again because Mr Terry was a very difficult customer, who instantly sent back any dish which he considered was not up to the high standards of culinary excellence that he demanded. She had desperately wanted to attend the rally and demonstration that was to take place that afternoon. James Keir Hardie M.P., leader of the newly formed Independent Labour Party, was one of her heroes. Against opposition even from within his own party he still dared to speak out for female enfranchisement, and was in the process of introducing a Bill in the House of Commons providing for female emancipation.

157

Slowly the rush of the midday meal eased, and people began to leave. Laura cleared the used crockery and the remnants of food from the tables, and relaid the surfaces with fresh white cloths and clean cutlery. She toyed with the idea of asking Reginald White for some time off so that she could attend the public meeting which was to be held at the Easemore Lane Recreation Ground, some hundred yards to the east of the Church Green. But even as the thought occured to her, she saw the long hooked nose of Mrs White point in her direction, and knew that the woman would veto any request for temporary absence.

'I'm sick of being poor.' Laura experienced a surge of angry resentment. 'I'm trapped by my own poverty. I've no freedom at all.'

Then she thought of Rosie Spiers, who so uncomplainingly endured ill-health and grinding poverty, and still supported and cared for her brother. 'I'm beginning to whine like a spoilt child,' she grimaced in momentary self-disgust. 'Anyway, Miriam Josceleyne says that she intends to go with Rosie to listen to Keir Hardie. They'll be able to tell me all about it.'

Her lips parted in a smile as she thought of how in the past weeks Miriam Josceleyne had become an enthusiastic supporter of the cause of women's suffrage, and how during frequent meetings and long conversations with herself and Rose Spiers the three women had become good friends.

'Hughes, if you spends any more time at that table, you'll get rooted to the spot and start to grow.' Mrs White's shrill nasal voice assaulted Laura's ears.

Without answering Laura quickly finished laying that table and moved to clear away the crockery on the one next to it.

From the direction of the central crossroads there came the sound of a brass band, faintly at first, then becoming steadily louder and louder until Laura could clearly distinguish the tune being played. It was 'La Marseillaise'. She sang the rousing call to revolution beneath her breath.

'Allons enfants de la Patrie, le jour du gloire et arrivée.

158

Contre nous de la tyrannie, l'étendard sanglant a levée. . . .'

She could not help smiling as she peeped at Mrs White's
sour expression. 'She would have looked perfectly at home
knitting beneath the guillotine,' thought Laura. The music
swelled.

> *'Aux armes citoyens, formez vos battailons,*
> *Marchons, marchons, un sang impur,*
> *Abreuve nos sillons. . . .'*

Among the crowds of onlookers ranged along Church
Green Miriam Josceleyne was standing beside Rosie and
Tommy Spiers. Miriam smiled in delight as the Redditch
Town Band resplendent in red-frogged tunics, peaked
caps and white crossbelts came past her. Rosie Spiers's
worn grey face was excited as she exclaimed to the youth
whose hand she held: 'See the band, Tommy. Aren't it
fine!'

His vacuous eyes stared blankly and a thin trickle of
saliva dribbled from his slack mouth.

Rosie's own lips trembled, as pity for his condition
threatened to bring tears to her eyes. 'Carn't you tell me,
Tommy?' There was pleading in her voice. 'Carn't you tell
me if you likes the band?'

Miriam's green eyes were warm with sympathy as she
heard the other woman's words, and on impulse she
tucked Rosie Spiers's painfully thin arm beneath her own.
'I'm sure that your brother is enjoying it hugely, Rosie,'
she told her. Then in an effort to divert her companion
said, 'Oh look there, at that banner. Isn't it splendid!'

The different Trades Federations were now passing,
each detachment behind their own large, colourful
banner, held aloft by proudly marching, heavily sweating
men, dressed in bowler hats and heavy serge suits. Their
dark clothing was badged with big garishly ribboned
rosettes. As the group of workmen and artisans passed,
some marched smartly like the ex-soldiers and sailors that
they were, others shambled uncertainly from the effects of
too much beer, yet others doggedly strode out of step with

the rousing tune and drumbeat. Scattered elements of the onlookers applauded, clapping hands and cheering raggedly. But Miriam noticed that most of the crowds lining the streets stayed silent, and she wondered at their apparent lack of support for their fellow workers and townsmen.

When the last section of the procession had passed, and the spectators were beginning to disperse, some to follow the procession down to the Recreation Ground, others to go about their own personal affairs, Miriam voiced her wonderment to Rosie Spiers. 'I would have thought that the people would have demonstrated more enthusiasm, Rosie.'

Her companion shook her head. 'It doon't do to show your colours in this town, unless you can afford to do it, Miss Miriam. Theer's a lot who'd have liked to cheer, but they doon't know who might be watching 'um.'

Miriam Josceleyne frowned in puzzlement. 'I don't understand you, Rosie.'

'You can't be expected to understand, Miss Miriam.' There was no criticism in the woman's voice, only a sad acceptance.

'Then explain what you mean, and perhaps I will then be able to understand?' Miriam Josceleyne said and smiled.

'Well, I'm not educated, Miss Miriam. But I can manage to read, and to think for meself. But I'se probably got it all wrong, and if I was to tell you what I thinks, I'd most likely only make meself look a fool.'

Rosie Spiers's manner was uncertain and diffident, and Miriam squeezed her thin arm encouragingly, and urged sincerely. 'You could never appear foolish to me, Rosie. I have developed a great respect for your intelligence since I've come to know you. You must act as my teacher in these matters, for I know nothing of them. It is I who am foolish when I pass opinions that are not grounded in experience.'

The other woman's worn face became pensive. 'Well . . .' she spoke hesitantly at first, but then with rapidly increasing fluency. . . 'You see most o' them that was watching the procession works at the big factories, like Abel Morrals, and Allcocks, Terrys, Eadies, Milwards and BSA and suchlike. Their bosses am very anti-union, and supposing a chap was to be seen cheering the socialists and the federations, and his foreman happened to see him doing it, well he might find his job was gone when he went back to his work on Monday.'

The worn face was very thoughtful. 'You see, it aren't only us women who're put upon and kept under. Most o' the working chaps are in the same boat. I suppose that's why a lot of 'um treats their women so harsh – because everybody has to have somebody that they thinks is beneath 'um – and their womenfolk and their kids are all that most working chaps has got who they can boss about.'

Miriam reflected upon Rosie Spiers's words, and found herself accepting wholeheartedly the inherent truth contained in them. She knew well that here, in the richest and most powerful country the world had ever known, the seat of the mightiest empire in recorded history, there were ten million working men and their dependents living in conditions of virtual destitution. That behind the opulent facades of wealth there festered huge slums. Not only in the great industrial and commercial cities, but also in the market towns and the villages of rural Britain. That pullalating in the very shadows of every rich and imposing house and respectable law-abiding street, there were a myriad courts and alleys of rancid squalor, hopeless poverty and vicious propensity. She knew also from her own reading of newspapers that there was severe social unrest and bitter class resentment seething throughout the country. An unrest and bitterness that many in authority feared might well culminate in actual open rebellion and even civil war. And this culmination was not expected to explode primarily in perennially troubled Ireland, but in the cities and coalfields and industrial districts of the British mainland.

The compulsion to hear what James Keir Hardie might have to say, became suddenly all-powerful in Miriam Josceleyne's mind, and she told Rosie Spiers: 'I think you're right in what you say, Rosie. Come on, let's follow the others and go and listen to this Mr Hardie.'

Rosie eagerly agreed, but Tommy Spiers began to mouth guttural and unintelligible protests and pulled back when his sister tried to lead him forwards.

Miriam Josceleyne, to her own amazement, found that she was imbued with a confidence she had never thought herself capable of possessing. Moving to Tommy's side she took his arm and spoke firmly to him: 'You must come with us, Tommy. Now be a good boy, and do as Rosie tells you.'

He gaped at her, and she took her handkerchief from her coat pocket and wiped away the saliva which dribbled from his slack mouth and down his chin.

'Come now, we don't want to miss the speeches.' Miriam pulled him with her, and after a moment he came docilely.

She suddenly found herself experiencing a sensation of pure happiness, and told herself in a marvelling exultation, 'I'm changed! I really am changed! Since meeting Laura and Rosie, I've become the person I've always wanted to be. I've grown strong, where I was once so weak.'

A flat-decked wagon had been pulled on to the Recreation Ground to serve as a temporary platform and a man was already addressing the crowd from it. His voice was high-pitched and had a broad Birmingham accent.

'Brothers, the purpose of this demonstration today is to show the existence of the Labour movement in this district . . . In North Worcestershire Labour is a strong force, and I'm looking forward to the day when Redditch 'ull be strong enough to field a Labour candidate for East Worcestershire. . . '

Miriam Josceleyne made a mental estimate of the numbers clustering before the wagon.

'Maybe two hundred?' She examined the crowd curiously. A cross-section of all ages, from old men with full white beards to youths barely in their teens. She was surprised to note that most were respectably dressed. Clean white collars, neat ties, decent suits, bowler hats, wideawakes, and straw boaters, largely outnumbered the

162

shabby jackets, grimy shirts, knotted mufflers and flat caps. There were several women among the crowd, and a superintendent and inspector of police standing directly in front of the wagon, while several other policemen of lower rank hovered around the crowd's edges.

As Miriam and her companions merged with the rear grouping of spectators she heard the speaker declare: 'We've got with us today a great leader of a great party, Mr Keir Hardie.'

This announcement was greeted with wild cheering, and the policemen stared hard at the most vociferous demonstrators. Other men now clambered up on to the wagon, and after further resolutions had been moved and seconded, Keir Hardie himself came to the front to speak to the crowd, who greeted him with loud and enthusiastic cheering.

Miriam stared with interest at this famous politician. He was stocky with a full white beard and moustache. His dark suit was creased and travel-stained and across his ample paunch there dangled a long watch chain. His narrow-brimmed, light-coloured hat was pushed well back on his broad head, and his expression was one of grim intent. He clasped his lapels in his big toil-thickened hands, and rocked backward and fowards on his heels, then stilled, and stood erect radiating an aura of strength and dour purpose.

He spoke for a long time, his broad Scottish accents making him at times difficult to understand, but the essence of his message was clear and loud. The masses must unite, and fight for justice and equality of opportunity. They must no longer supinely accept the cruel exploitation of their labour. They must unite and fight for the sake of their children and their children's children to create a better life for the working man. And this struggle for the just rights of the working man must be spread throughout the length and breadth of the British Empire. No longer must the fruits of their labour to be enjoyed by a small privileged minority, while the great mass of the people lived and suffered in abject want and poverty. There must be a fair distribution of the wealth that their toil created.

Miriam waited with growing impatience for some mention of the rights of women, but none came, and when the speech came to an end amidst long drawn out applause and shouts of acclamation, she experienced a sharp sense of disappointment.

She said as much to Rosie Spiers, and the young woman smiled bleakly saying, 'Well Miss Miriam, I suppose Mr Hardie has got his hands full with getting the Labour Party on its feet. There's not more than thirty seats in Parliament held by them, is there?'

'Maybe so,' Miriam protested. 'But he could at least have mentioned votes for women.'

Rosie's smile was still bleak. 'I reckon us women 'ull just have to rely on ourselves when push comes to shove. I think that Mr Hardie is a friend to us, but we'em going to have to fight our own battles. He's got enough on his plate already fighting the Tories and the Liberals.'

Miriam nodded reflectively. 'I'm sure you're right, Rosie. I think it's high time that we began to take our own message to the working women in this district. It appears that the Labour Party is really only a party for men after all.'

She was silent as they left the Recreation Ground, and appeared to be deep in thought.

Later that evening there was a further Labour meeting held in the Public Hall, and this time Laura accompanied Miriam. Rosie Spiers had stayed at home to watch over her brother and to work at her trade of seamstress. The hall was well-filled, and now there were more of the poorly-paid semi-skilled and unskilled working men present. The two women sat surrounded by roughly spoken men, in an atmosphere thick with the smells of foul breath, unwashed flesh, work-soiled clothing and rank tobacco. There were groans of disappointment when it was announced that Keir Hardie was not to be present – he had been forced to travel to Sheffield on urgent political business. Other speakers addressed the crowd for considerable periods, and once again Miriam waited in vain for any mention of women's emancipation, but none came.

When the meeting ended and the two women were

outside in Church Road, walking arm in arm among the noisy crowds of men, Miriam asked, 'Were you as disappointed as I was, Laura, by their failure to even give a mention to our cause?'

Laura nodded. 'Of course I was. In fact I felt quite angry about it. Women are workers as well as men. They also help to create wealth and are denied justice.'

Miriam was silent for a few moments. Then she nodded sharply as if she had come to a decision, and asked, 'Can I come back to Rosie's house with you? I've something that I want to talk about with both of you.'

In the tiny room, lit only by a small oil lamp, Miriam faced the other two women across the battered table top, now laden with the shirts which Rosie was stitching. In the poor light the two faces before her were grey and drawn with fatigue, and Rosie's eyes were deeply sunk in her painfully wasted features.

Before Miriam could speak the young woman said apologetically, 'I carn't spend a deal of time talking, Miss Miriam. I'se got to get this lot finished for Monday morning.' She indicated the piles of shirt sections.

Miriam felt a sense of outrage as her own eyes rested on the heaped material. 'This is nothing less than slave labour,' she told herself angrily, knowing well that Rosie Spiers earned only a pathetic pittance for toiling up to 18 hours a day at this work which was damaging her sight, and destroying her health. She glanced at the lines of fatigue furrowing Laura's brows, and thought of the grinding work and long hours, of the insults and harassment that the young woman was subjected to each day by her employers and their customers, and her resolution became granite hard.

Aloud she said quietly, but firmly, 'You've no need to finish these at all, Rosie. And you Laura, need not ever return to that restaurant.'

Both pairs of weary, dark-ringed eyes stared in astonishment.

'Just hear me out.' With uncharacteristic forcefulness Miriam forestalled their attempts to speak.

'I have more than sufficient money for my needs. More

165

than sufficient in fact for the needs of all of us. What I propose is this, that we use that money to live on while we serve our cause. If you no longer have to spend your time stitching shirts, Rosie, and you in waiting on tables and washing dishes, Laura, then the three of us can devote ourselves to the Women's Social and Political Union. We can use all our time to recruit and establish a strong branch of the Union here in this district. We can also travel to the demonstrations and meetings our sisters are holding in other parts of the country. We can serve in the front line, so to speak, instead of only dreaming of doing so. And what is more, if we form our own branch of the movement, then we can regulate outselves, and act independently as and when we see fit to do so. We will be our own mistresses.'

As Miriam continued cajoling, hectoring, demanding and persuading the two women to fall in with her own wishes, a sense of burgeoning fanaticism began to pervade her being. All traces of the diffident, timid and nervous woman her two friends had known were disappearing and being replaced by a strong and confident creature whom they regarded with shock and some degree of apprehension. At times one or other of them would attempt to voice doubt or protest, but Miriam Josceleyne, this new Miriam Josceleyne, refused to be gainsaid, and slowly and inexorably she won them over to her own desires, and infused them with her own fervour. And so finally, after several hours, Laura Hughes and Rosie Spiers agreed to fall in with Miriam Josceleyne's plans, and there and then, in that cramped mean room, the autonomous Redditch branch of the Women's Social and Political Union came into being.

Chapter Nineteen

Clouds of steam billowed up from the long cast-iron trough filling the air with the pungent reek of soda and harsh soap and wet cloth. As Bella Thomas bent over the trough, punching and kneading the thick blanket with hands that were puffy and wrinkled from constant immersion in water and made sore and chapped by contact with soda and soap, she longed for the day's back-breaking toil to be done, so that she could straighten her aching back and rest her weary body.

Spaced along the trough on each side of her, other women were bent low, their arms immersed to the elbows in the scummed water, their faces dripping with sweat and condensed steam and their clothing saturated despite the long rubber aprons they wore to shield themselves.

From the adjoining room there sounded the constant loud rumbling of the wringers' big perforated tubs spinning rapidly to expel water from the washed and rinsed clothing and bedding. From a further room came the echoes of voices singing, and Bella Thomas envied those fortunate women who worked in that room, operating the automatic mangles, hand-ironing the fine linens, folding and packing the cleaned and pressed articles for delivery. Those women went home dry and warm at the end of their long shifts; not shivering as they met the cold night air with its chill tentacles penetrating saturated clothing, and striking at skin made over-tender by constant damp.

But it was not the gruelling, unpleasant work that was now causing Bella Thomas to alternate between savage scowls of anger and pitiful whimpers of despair. 'You bastard! You rotten bastard!' The woman's Cupid-bowed mouth twisted as she spat out the epithets. 'I wish I'd never ever met you, you bastard! You dirty whoring bastard!'

Then tears stung her eyes and a wave of absolute despair caused her stomach to heave sickeningly. 'Oh Harry, darlin'. Doon't leave me! Doon't leave me!' The heartsick pleas reverberated through her being, and the tears fell freely to mingle with the swirling dirty-grey water.

Her immediate neighbour glanced sideways and saw the grief on Bella Thomas's fat face, and nudged the woman on her further side with a sud-streaked elbow, urging in a low-pitched voice. 'Just look at her. Her's bloody skriking again. I'm buggered if I'd let any man get me into that state. I'd swing for the bugger afore I'd let him get me down like that.'

The second woman leaned forwards, stretching out across the trough so that she could obtain a clearer view of Bella Thomas, whose hunched body was now visibly shuddering with heart-rending sobbing. She clucked her tongue sympathetically as she studied the black swollen eye, and the livid abrasions that covered the side of Bella Thomas's jaw. 'The poor cow's bin served real bad by the looks on her. Who is her bloke, anyway? Does I know him?'

'You might do. I'se only seen him with her the once. He's a real jack-dandy. Only about half her age by the looks on him. To tell you the truth, I can't for the life o' me see what he can see in her. I mean to say, her paints her face like a prostitute, but it 'ud take a sight thicker covering than a coating o' paint to hide her bloody wrinkles, 'udden't it.'

Both women grinned broadly, showing gapped, decayed teeth, and the second woman quipped, 'Well they says that theer's many a good tune played on an old fiddle, my duck.'

'Ahr, maybe they does say that, but the fiddle still needs all its strings, doon't it, and I reckon poor old Bella's lost more nor a few of hers.'

They both laughed uproariously, and again set to punching and kneading the soaked blankets.

Submerged in her own misery, Bella Thomas was oblivious to her companions. Like an automaton she laboured on unseeingly. Her mind's eyes filled with the image of

Harry Vivaldi's swarthy handsome face, and she silently pleaded with that image over and over again.

'Doon't leave me, Harry. Doon't leave me, darlin'. Please, please doon't leave me. . . .'

'If you please, Ma'm, it's Mr Vivaldi called again to see you. Shall I tell him you'm at home this time?' The maidservant's pert little face was avid with anticipation.

Emma Josceleyne stretched her lithe body languorously upon the brocaded *chaise-longue*, and her black eyes danced with mischievous satisfaction. She came gracefully to a sitting position and spread her arms, white teeth gleaming as she yawned widely. The little maidservant was suddenly reminded of a picture she had once seen portraying a very beautiful cat, that had just trapped an unfortunate mouse. That remembrance came even more sharply as her mistress smiled lazily, and asked teasingly, 'I don't know, Ivy. What would you do if you were in my place?'

The maidservant giggled delightedly. She adored her daringly unconventional mistress, who treated her and her fellow maidservant with a casual, yet genuine kindness, almost as if they were pets rather than hired servants.

'Well?' Emma smilingly encouraged.

The young girl blushed and threw her hands up before her face, unable to control her fit of giggles.

'Come on now. Tell me. I want you to advise me,' Emma pressed.

Blushing brightly, the young girl told her between smothered fits of laughter, 'Well Ma'm he's ever so good looking, aren't he. If he was my beau I 'udden't treat him like you treats him. Turning him away from the door all the time. I'd be too feared that some other girl might steal him off me.'

Emma chuckled amusedly. 'So then, what you're saying is that I should see him now. Is that it?'

The girl giggled, and nodded furiously, her blush became even more fiery, and once more she hid her glowing face in her hands.

Emma nodded agreeably. 'All right then, Ivy. If you can

stop giggling for long enough, you'd best show the gentleman in.'

The girl bobbed a curtsey and hurried away still trying to smother her giggles.

While this exchange had been taking place, Harry Vivaldi had been standing on the porch outside the front door. His mood oscillated wildly between resentment at being kept waiting, and anxiety that he might yet again be turned away with the message that Mrs Emma Josceleyne was not 'at home'.

His earlier confidence that the young widow would prove to be 'easy meat', had been remorselessly abraded during the past weeks, during which he had called frequently at Cotswold House, only to be turned away from the door without even glimpsing Emma Josceleyne. Paradoxically, the abrasion of his easy confidence had only fuelled his determination to succeed in his conquest of the young widow. Harry Vivaldi was not accustomed to defeat in the warfare of love, and he had no intention of conceding the victory to her. In fact, as he admitted to himself, she was fast becoming an obsession with him. So much so, that his irritation at being still tied to Bella Thomas had begun to explode into violence when he had been drinking. At first he had experienced a degree of shame after he had beaten and ill-treated Bella Thomas. But with each succeeding outburst that shame had lessened, and now he was beginning to derive a perverse satisfaction from inflicting violence upon Bella Thomas to vent his own angry frustation at his lack of success in his pursuit of Emma Josceleyne.

He stared in puzzlement at the little maidservant when she invited him into the hallway and took from him his Homburg hat, gloves and Malacca cane. He could not understand why her face was so red, and why she appeared to have difficulty in breathing.

When he saw Emma Josceleyne however, his own breath caught in his throat. She looked so very beautiful, sitting upon the *chaise-longue*, her mass of high-piled chestnut hair shimmering in the rays of sunlight lancing through the big window, her black eyes dancing, her full shapely lips so moistly inviting, and the thrust of her firm breasts beneath the silken bodice of her dress so sensually exciting.

Despite the involuntary thudding of his heartbeat caused by the physical effect this woman had on him, Harry Vivaldi's shrewd brain was working with its customary efficiency. He had ruthlessly castigated himself for the crassness of his initial confidence that Emma Josceleyne would prove an easy conquest. He now fully appreciated that she was a worthy opponent, and so had planned accordingly. He intended to approach his objective from oblique angles. To keep her guessing, and slightly off balance if possible. For Harry Vivaldi, the conquest of a woman was something akin to a military campaign, and he was now mentally prepared for a long and perhaps arduous route towards that final victory.

For her part, Emma was ready enough to accept that she found this man very attractive, and that in due course she might well invite him into her bed. But before there could be any consummation of the flesh, she must be very very sure that she held him in emotional enslavement. Emma had not spent almost four years satisfying the satyr-like appetites of Hector Josceleyne in order to become any other man's sexual plaything. Neither had she any intention of being inveigled into marriage. She found her present freedom and financial independence too much to her taste to surrender it for the sake of physical passion.

'Good afternoon Mr Vivaldi.' She smiled charmingly. 'What is it you want to see me about?'

He smiled and bowed. 'Making our fortunes, Mrs Josceleyne. I've called to see you about making our fortunes. . . .'

Chapter Twenty

As Cleopatra Dolton read and re-read the dog-eared sheets of notepaper, hungrily devouring every word, her luminous dark eyes shimmered with brimming tears and her heart ached with longing for her sons – Simon, now fourteen years old, and his brothers James and Andrew, twelve and eight years respectively.

When the words before her wavered and blurred so that she could no longer distinguish them she sat back in her chair and let the tears fall freely down her cheeks.

'Simon, Andy, Jamie.' She murmured their names over and over again as if by sheer volume of repetition she could invoke their presence in the flesh. She became so immersed in her sad yearnings that she was unaware of the woman who came into the room.

It was her cook, Mrs Danks, a gaunt-featured, middle-aged woman whose loyalty to her mistress had been forged and proven over many years. She grimaced sympathetically, but when she spoke it was with almost a scolding tone, 'Now what's all this nonsense? You'll be visiting with them in less than two months.'

Cleopatra Dolton stiffened, and quickly blew her nose and wiped her eyes and wet cheeks. Within scant seconds only the faint reddened puffiness around her lustrous eyes bore witness to her weeping. She forced a smile and asked the older woman. 'Did you want me for anything?'

The gaunt features were tender. Ignoring the question the cook said, 'Listen to me, my duck. You was right to send the boys away from this town. Their lives 'ud have bin made a misery here arter what happened to their Dad.' A suggestion of hectoring entered her voice. 'And you should have moved away as well. Gone somewhere that you could all have been together. I'd have come and gladly, you knows that. We'd have bin all right once we'd settled somewhere.'

Stubbornness firmed the beautiful woman's tremulous lips. 'No, Mrs Danks. I should not have moved away. That would have seemed proof to the people in this town that all the lies that were told about John Purvis and me were true after all.'

'Folks 'ull think what they wants to think anyway. No matter if you went or stayed. You'm only making yourself miserable by living so far away from the boys.'

The younger woman shook her head firmly. 'No, Mrs Danks, I'll never run away. I'll never give those who are against me the satisfaction of believing that they've succeeded in driving me away from this town.'

'Yes, but. . . .'

Mrs Danks began to protest, but Cleopatra Dolton cut her short, snapping irritably, 'There's nothing more to be said about it. So please let it rest now, will you. Here I am, and here I stay.'

The other woman shook her head but made no further argument, only informed in an aggrieved tone, 'Ozzie Clarke's downstairs, and he wants to spake wi' you.'

A slight frown of puzzlement momentarily creased Cleopatra Dolton's smooth brows. 'What about?'

Mrs Danks shrugged sullenly.

Cleopatra Dolton's eyes began to gleam with a fond amusement as she looked at the other woman's expression, and rising from her chair she went to her and enfolded the bony shoulders with her arms.

'Now don't be cross with me. I didn't mean to snap at you. But you know that I'm determined to stay here no matter how much it hurts to be separated from my boys. It's just that when you keep going on at me about it, it makes it that much harder to bear. That's why I spoke sharply.'

After a few moments the elder woman capitulated and smiled, disclosing toothless gums. 'That's all right, my duck. It's because I cares so much for you and the boys

173

that I keeps on about it. It grieves me to see you grieving for 'um.'

Satisfied that she had mollified her servant, who was a true friend rather than a paid employee, Cleopatra Dolton's own mood lightened, and she became brisk and businesslike. 'I'll come down now and see Clarke. It's probably about that land he wants to rent for fat stock.'

The butcher was waiting in the hallway. His eyes feasted hungrily upon his employer's lush body as she came down the broad staircase. As always when they met there was a mutual sexual tension radiating between them.

Although she was 10 years older than he, yet Ozzie Clarke freely admitted to himself that he found Cleopatra Dolton more desirable than any of the many women he had made love to, and his desire for her had if anything increased rather than decreased during the years he had known her. Now, as his own maturity stole upon him, he found himself beginning to question whether his feelings for her were not in fact becoming an obsession. Although initially this idea had disturbed him greatly, lately it had ceased to do so, and in his imagination he had begun to picture how life might be if he were married to her. He had in fact, although he would have contemptuously rejected the suggestion, fallen in love with her.

Because Ozzie Clarke had the power to disturb her sexually, and to evoke physical desire in her, Cleopatra Dolton had very ambiguous feelings about him. She resented the attraction he held for her, yet at the same time she needed to know that he was bound to her, even if only in the relationship of employer and employee. Like many in the town she had heard the gossip concerning his sexual conquests of various women, both single and married, and she had no intention of ever putting herself in the position whereby she would be numbered by gossip amongst those conquests. Nevertheless, there were frequent occasions when she could not resist exerting her own power to tantalise and provoke him – because she sensed that he was sexually obsessed with her. She knew from her past experience of men that this was a dangerous game she played at these times, but it had by now become

174

an addiction that she found impossible to break free from.

'Well Clarke?' She raised her well-shaped eyebrows in question, then smiled invitingly.

His strong fingers tightened on the brim of the straw boater he held between them. 'Oh no lady, you'll not trap me into making a fool o' meself by smiling at me like a tanner whore,' he thought angrily, remembering all those other times when she had smiled invitingly and he had taken that apparent invitation as genuine, and advanced, only to be coldly rebuffed. 'I've had the offer of 10 acres from Alf Green at Bridley Moor farm, Mrs Dolton. It's prime land.'

As always when it was a matter of business, her mind closed to any distractions other than the matter at hand.

'What rent does he want, and what length of lease is it?'

'He's prepared to sell, Mrs Dolton, if he can get his price.'

Her dark eyes widened in surprise. It was not often that any of the local farmers were prepared to sell parcels of their land.

'Why?'

Ozzie Clarke grinned with a trace of scorn. 'Alf's very fond of the bottle, and he likes to play cards. The two doon't mix very well.'

She nodded her understanding. 'He's in debt then.' It was a statement, not a question.

'Heavy,' Clarke confirmed.

'So I can get it cheap?' She sought confirmation.

The man's handsome features frowned, and he shrugged his broad shoulders. 'Well, you could most probably beat his price down, but that 'udden't be good business as I see it.'

'Why not?' She was genuinely mystified.

'Because Alf Green is a fair bloke, Mrs Dolton. He might be over fond of the bottle and a bad gambler, but he's as straight as a die, and he's never done anybody any harm that I knows of.'

Her full lips tightened in a hard line. 'I'm sure there are a good many men in this town that description would fit, Clarke. But it's not a reason to pay more than I need.'

175

Ozzie Clarke shook his head, and said disparagingly, 'You'm not thinking ahead, Mrs Dolton. You'm only seeing what's directly in front of your nose.'

Her anger flared instantly. 'Don't you try telling me my business, Clarke. You just remember that I pay your wages. I don't need a hired hand's advice.'

The man's pride finally rebelled. For years now he had forced himself to swallow her arrogant treatment, and now, in this moment, he decided that enough was enough. He was not prepared to accept any more put downs from this woman. 'All right then,' he growled the words. 'You suit yourself what you do, because I've had more than a bellyful of being spoke to like a piece o' dirt by you. Your husband, for all his faults, treated me and the rest of his men better than you treat us. At least he showed us some respect for the way we did our jobs.' He paused and drew a long harsh breath, then told her: 'And if you ever stopped to think about it, you'd realise that it's only thanks to me that your business is doing well. If I didn't do all the buying, and keep a close eye on your other shops, as well as run Evesham Street, you'd have been down the Swanee long since. You thinks you knows it all, just because you runs an eye over the books, and signs the bank drafts, and parades round the bloody shops like lady muck blaggardin' the blokes who works for you. Well I'll tell you straight, Missis. You knows bugger all! You thinks yourself a woman of business, but if it warn't for me, you'd have lost your bloody business when your husband was croaked by Johnny Purvis.'

As she heard his tirade Cleopatra Dolton's olive complexion first paled, then darkened with fury, and as he spat out the final sentence her temper exploded beyond her control. 'You bastard! You rotten fuckin' bastard!' she hissed, and lifting her hand she slashed it across his face.

For an instant his hands bunched into fists, and he seemed ready to hit her. Then he turned away with a contemptuous sneer. 'The breeding 'ull always out, won't it, Cleo Dolton. You might be wearing fine silks and living in a fancy house, but you'm still a bloody slummy from Silver Street, aren't you.' He gusted out a snort of disgust.

176

'You can put on all the airs and graces you likes, Cleo Dolton, but underneath you'll always stay as common as muck.'

He walked to the front door and opened it, then turned to tell her: 'I'll bring the books up to date and fetch 'um down to you after I've closed the shop. I'd leave 'um as they stands but that 'udden't be fair on old Walter. But today's my last day. You can shove this job up your arse and get yourself some other hired hand. I'll find other work.'

He slammed the door behind him, the impact shuddering through the building, and Cleopatra Dolton stood staring at the blank panels, clenching and unclenching her fists in impotent rage.

Attracted by the raised voices Mrs Danks had come to the top of the stairs and had heard and seen all that had transpired. Now she hurried down to her mistress.

'Am you all right, my wench?'

Cleopatra Dolton swung to face the other woman, her expressive features working with her anger. 'Did you hear him insulting me? Did you hear that cheeky bastard?' she demanded furiously. 'And he's told me to shove his job!' She gulped down air, her breasts heaving with her agitation. 'Well, I'll show the bugger. I'll make sure he never works again in this town.'

'Doon't talk so sarft, girl!' Mrs Danks scoffed openly. 'You'm talking like a fool! Ozzie Clarke could walk into any butcher's shop in the Midlands and get a welcome. He's turned down offers that I knows of meself, to stay working for you.'

At first the full import of what the woman was saying did not penetrate Cleopatra Dolton's brain, and she flared at her.

'Whose side are you on? Why are you taking his part against me?'

'I'm on your side o' course, you silly cow!' It was Mrs Danks's turn to flare. 'And I'm not taking Ozzie Clarke's part. He doon't need me to fight his battles for him. But if you'd only stop and think for a minute, you'd understand how lucky you'se bin to have him working for you. Am you

177

forgetting how he caught Jimmy Morris fiddling the books. And am you forgetting how he give a good hiding to that bloke from Brummagem who was trying to cheat you over them sheep.'

The cook waited a moment to see what effect her words were having, and then plunged on. 'And has you forgot that it was him who saved your life when Arthur Dolton was choking the breath out of you that time. Because I hadn't got the strength to pull the bugger off you, and there aren't many men who'd have tackled your husband like Ozzie Clarke did.'

By now Cleopatra's rage was beginning to recede, and she was honest enough with herself to accept the truth in what Mrs Danks was saying. But unable to surrender easily, she rounded on the cook.

'That's as maybe, but I can't have him talking to me, and becalling me the way he's just done, can I? He's got no right or reason to speak to me in that manner, and to call me names.'

Sensing the change in her mistress's mood, the swing from unreasoning fury to dawning doubts, the elder woman smiled wryly. 'Well, he might not have the right to spake to you like he did, my wench, but he's certain sure got plenty of reason. You spakes to him like he's a dog sometimes. And you torments him until he doon't know whether he's here or in the middle of next week.'

'How so?' Cleopatra Dolton demanded indignantly, but her anger was by now almost fully spent.

'Well, it's plain to see, for them who knows how to look for it, aren't it,' the cook declared confidently. 'The poor chap's in love wi' you. Only whether he knows that himself yet, is another story. But I can see it plain enough. He's in love with you, and has bin for years. And you knows he is, that's why you smiles at him one minute, then turns on him the next. You torments him half to death.'

Cleopatra drew a long shuddering breath in an effort to calm the remaining flurries of her disturbed feelings, then exclaimed impatiently: 'It's too close in here, I can't breathe.' She began to go upstairs, telling her cook: 'I'll need a hat, I'm going out for a walk.'

When she returned, dressed to go out in hat, overgown, gloves and carrying a parasol, Mrs Danks hid a sly smile and asked: 'If you'm still out, what does you want me to tell Ozzie Clarke when he brings the books down?'

Her mistress frowned suspiciously and stared hard at her, but Mrs Danks only looked innocently back, and with a brusque shake of her head, Cleopatra Dolton swept out of the front door.

She turned in the direction of the town, walking with hurried footsteps that gradually slowed as her agitation lessened. Just before the Railway Station bridge she turned to her right and went along Cemetery Lane towards the town graveyard, its pathways shaded by many trees promising a cool haven from the heat of the day. For almost an hour, deep in thought, she paced those quiet deserted pathways that threaded between the tombstones and monuments of the rich, and the anonymous mounds of the poor. Then the stamping of horses' hooves and the jingling of harness carried through the still air to announce the arrival of a funeral cortege, and Cleopatra Dolton made her decision.

Walter Spiers was serving a customer when Cleopatra Dolton walked into the shop, and his rheumy eyes fixed with an avid curiosity on his employer's features, but found nothing there to indicate her mood.

'Where's Mr Clarke?' she asked, and he jerked his head towards the rear of the shop, his surprise at her use of the courtesy title showing clearly.

'Attend to the lady, Spiers – don't stand there gawping at me,' Cleopatra snapped, then nodded politely to the customer and walked through to the rear room. She found Ozzie Clarke seated at an old battered desk, his head bent low over the big leatherbound ledgers.

He turned to face her, and she placed her gloved forefinger across her lips in a signal for silence. Then closed the door behind her, and moved to his side.

'I've come to apologise to you, Mr Clarke,' she said in a low voice. 'I've come to realise that I've not shown you the respect that you deserve.'

He stared hard at her, his expression showing mingled

surprise and suspicion.

She drew a long breath, as for a moment her own fierce pride rebelled at what she was doing, but instinct told her that she was only acting justly, and that to make true atonement she would have to accept this hurt to her pride.

'I'd like you to remain in my employment, Mr Clarke.' Again she drew a long breath. 'But, if you feel that you cannot do so, then I am ready to give you the very highest recommendation to anyone that you might want me to. I'm hoping however, that you'll agree to stay with me. If you do, then I promise that I shall in the future treat you with the respect you are owed.'

Again she halted, and regarded him keenly, knowing that despite her good intentions, if she detected in him any sign of triumphant exultation, or contempt for her surrender, she would undoubtedly explode with anger once again. She found the abasement of her pride a very hard pill to swallow.

For long moments he remained silent, staring intently into her eyes, his face expressionless. Inwardly his emotions were in turmoil. Then he drew a deep breath and exhaled gustily. He laid down the pen he had been using, and stood to his feet. For a further long moment he remained silent, still staring intently at her. Then he nodded abruptly.

'I'd like you to come and have a look at this land of Alf Green's, Mrs Dolton. And I'd advise that we pay the price he's asking, because in the long term it's a good investment for your business. And, when he gets himself into debt again, he'll be prepared to sell more land to us, because he'll know that we'll pay him a bit above the current market price. What I'm aiming for eventually, is to have enough land so that we can keep most of our own stock, and be independent of the dealers. In the long run it'll raise your profits.'

It was Cleopatra Dolton's turn to remain silent while she ingested what he had told her. Then she nodded acceptance.

'Very well, Mr Clarke. I'll come and have a look at the land, and then we can settle with Alf Green. I'll leave the price bargaining to you.'

It was as if some invisible boundary had been crossed, and the tension between them dissolved by its crossing.

The grimness fled from Ozzie Clarke's handsome features, and he smiled wryly. 'If we take the dray I can drop off a couple of sides of beef at Bredon, then we can cut back to Bridley Moor. That's if you don't object to sitting on the dray?' The dray was a big open sided wagon used to transport the heavier meat carcasses.

Cleopatra Dolton's wicked humour flashed, as she returned his smile, and told him: 'When I lived in Silver Street, I thought that to ride on any sort of cart was a great treat, Mr Clarke. I haven't changed all that much.'

A sense of ease in each other's company had replaced the earlier tensions, and together they left the shop oblivious to the curious stare of Walter Spiers. He scratched his grizzled head and wondered aloud.

'How come you'm all comfortable together, Ozzie Clarke, when only a couple o' minutes ago you was jackin' the job in?'

Chapter Twenty-One

In between the railway goods yard and the opulent houses of Red Lane and separated from the main body of the town by a broad network of railway shunting and marshalling lines was a grimy enclave of factories, tenements and courts where some of the poorest inhabitants of the town dwelt. It was here that the newly formed Redditch branch of the Women's Social and Political Union decided to launch their initial recruiting campaign, because the factories in this area were engaged in the manufacture of fishing tackle and needles and employed large numbers of women and girls.

During the fine weather it was the custom for women to spend their brief midday respite from work on an open stretch of waste ground known as Holyoaksfield. This was directly opposite the great square red-brick building which was the factory of William Woodfield.

The three women arrived on the open ground shortly before the midday release of the workers, but during their passage along the shabby street which led to the ground from Red Lane they had attracted considerable attention. A curious mob of the workless – the loungers and truanting urchins – were already beginning to collect around them. The reason for this attention was that the three were wearing broad sashes striped in the purple, white and green colours of the Union, and each of them carried a white banner bordered with the same colours and bearing in huge black letters the slogan 'VOTES FOR WOMEN'.

Miriam Josceleyne was filled with a nervous elation, Laura Hughes was quietly determined, but Rosie Spiers was timid and embarrassed by the good natured gibes being flung at them by some of the onlookers.

'What's this then? Sister Anna carry the banner, is it?'

'If you was advertising free beer you'd not need them bloody big flags, Missis!'

'My old 'ooman doon't need a vote. Her needs a gob stopper!'

The women tried to ignore the gibes, as they sought for a suitable speaking platform.

'There, that will do nicely.' Laura pointed to a long low heap of broken bricks. 'Whichever one of us is speaking can stand on those.'

They moved to the heap and then stood uncertainly, glancing at each other, then at the people around them, then back at each other. The shrilling of the steam whistles signalling the midday break for various factories came both as relief and cause for increased nervousness for all three of them. Then they saw the streams of workers issuing out of the big gates and exchanged tense smiles.

'Well then?' Laura looked enquiringly at Rosie, who in her turn stared beseechingly at Miriam.

Miriam's heart was pounding, and her throat seemed so tight that it was difficult to draw breath. Now that the moment for action had arrived, all her old fears rushed in upon her with renewed strength. She shook her head helplessly, unable to give any direction.

It was Laura who broke the tension which for a brief while had held them motionless. She suddenly mounted upon the heap of bricks and waving her banner above her head, called loudly: 'Gather over here, ladies! Gather over here! We've a message for you!'

The younger girls who moved the swiftest were the first to arrive and cluster before the brick heap. Still not of an age to put up their hair they wore it long and flowing down their backs; their skirts, shorter than those of their adult sisters, displayed high-buttoned boots. Many of them wore straw hats perched saucily on their heads and long white aprons. Miriam was struck by their youthful prettiness, as with excited shining eyes they laughed and chattered together; an eager audience for this unexpected novel entertainment. Then their elder colleagues began to swell the gathering crowd, and it was in their faces that Miriam saw the necessity for the cause she now served. All the prettiness of youth had gone to be replaced by the harsh masks of ceaseless drudgery, ill-health, hardship and poverty. Suddenly the old fears that had once more beset her fell away, and her new found strength and confidence flooded back.

The excited chattering and laughter slowly quietened and an expectant silence ensued. Laura glanced down at Miriam and raised her eyebrows in query. Miriam nodded encouragement and the thin face of her friend became serious and determined. She turned back to the upturned faces before her and spoke out in high clear tones.

'Part of the message that I've got for you is that we women are all sisters, and so that is what I shall call you . . . sisters.'

'Am you my sister as well?' a youth jeered, and his covey of friends laughed raucously.

Laura flushed, but her voice did not waver as she looked hard at the youth and told him: 'Yes, I am your sister, just as we are all brothers and sisters of the human race. And because we are all brothers and sisters, then it is not just that some of us should be exploited and cruelly misused . . . That we the women of this country should be denied common justice . . . and denied the right to vote! Without that right to vote we women will never be treated fairly by those who rule us . . . We will always be paid only half what a man receives for doing in many cases almost identical work. This is not fair. If a woman does the same work as a man, then she should receive the same wages!'

This struck a chord among the females in the crowd, and there came shouts of agreement from among them.

A man started to bellow angrily but a score of women shrieked at him to be silent, and overborne by the sheer volume of noise he sullenly subsided.

Laura was by now exulting in the support she was invoking, and she went on with a ringing scorn.

'We have a Liberal government now. Our new Prime Minister, Sir Henry Campbell-Bannerman, has publicly stated that he approves of we women's demand to have the right to vote. He has also stated his belief that if that right were granted it would be to the benefit of the whole country. Mr Balfour, the leader of the Unionist Party, says that he supports our demand for the vote. Mr Keir Hardie, the leader of the Independent Labour Party not only supports our right to the vote, but is even now attempting to introduce a Bill in Parliament which will give us that right.'

She paused for a moment, breasts heaving with emotion, eyes glowing with fervour.

'So, sisters, the leaders of the three political parties in our country all state that they are on our side. Many other Members of Parliament also state that they are on our side. But if this is the case then why do they not give us the vote?'

'Because you'm not fit to bloody well have it! You bloody suffragettes aren't even fit to live wi' pigs,' a male voice shouted.

Laura smiled sweetly at the man who had shouted, a big, florid-featured, heavily-paunched foreman from William Woodfields, who had been intimidating those women nearest to him with his threatening glares.

'Judging from the size of your belly, sir, you are most certainly fit to live with those animals. Whether they would accept you as an equal is quite another matter.'

Her riposte brought howls of laughter from the crowd. The foreman's jowls purpled with fury, and he seemed ready to storm towards the heap of bricks, but the man standing with him tugged at his sleeve and whispered urgently into his ear, and the foreman stayed where he was, glowering murderously at the suffragettes. Then he beckoned a couple of youths to him, and gave them rapid instructions which sent them hurrying away in different directions.

Laura's confidence was now invincible. She spoke almost in a conversational tone. 'The American Revolution began because the demand, "no taxation without representation!" was not heeded by those then in power in this country. If that call had been heeded in time, then

America would still today be a part of the British Empire. . . .

'Mr Herbert Henry Asquith, our present Chancellor of the Exchequer, has obviously taken the lesson of the American Revolution to heart. He signed an autograph book for one of his admirers recently, and in that book he inscribed his favourite maxim, which is, "that taxation and representation must go together". . . .

'Sisters, the honourable Mr Asquith is a liar and a hypocrite, condemned out of his own mouth. Because Mr Asquith is perhaps the bitterest opponent of votes for women in the entire House of Commons, but at the same time he shows no reluctance to tax we women, and we are the unrepresented half of the people of this country. And only last month, when a deputation of working women from the East End of London attempted to speak to Mr Asquith concerning this matter of taxation without representation, why the honourable gentleman set the police upon them, and after being violently treated, three of those women were arrested and sent to jail.'

The crowd emitted audible groans and shouts of outrage.

At the same time, the horse and dray carrying Cleopatra Dolton and Ozzie Clarke back from Bridley Moor farm, came along the road parallel to Holyoaksfield. Cleopatra Dolton stared curiously at the gathering, then recognising Laura, told Ozzie Clarke: 'Pull off the road, and take me nearer, so I can hear what she's saying.'

As the horse and dray swung on to the open ground and bumped over the hummocky turf, a group of men spilled from the doorways of the public house on the street corner across from Holyoaksfield. They moved directly towards the crowd of women, and the burly man in their lead suddenly roared out: 'Gerrout from 'ere, Missis!'

In the forefront of the crowd, a haggard-featured woman turned to the shouting man, and her face blanched as she saw her husband's irate features. Instantly she turned and pulling her shawl tight around her shoulders scurried back towards the Woodfield factory. Other women and girls swung to face the oncoming men, and as they recognised their own husbands and fathers among them, followed the example of the first woman and hurried away. A group of youths came running up from the direction of the railway lines, carrying armfuls of rotten vegetables which they had pilfered from the railway goods yard.

The crowd of women and girls eddied and some cried out in alarm, while others cackled with excited laughter. In front of the heap of bricks Miriam and Rosie stared with dismay and mounting fear at the oncoming men and youths, while Laura, in angry impotence, cried out to her listeners to stand their ground.

'Don't let them drive you away! You have the right to listen to the truth! Don't let them stop you doing so! Stand your ground! Stand your ground!' Her eyes went to where the big-bellied foreman was standing, thumbs tucked into his thick leather belt, his florid face glistening with greasy sweat as he bellowed with triumphant laughter.

By now the men had reached the women and were jostling and hectoring them into dispersal. One woman, bolder than the rest, attempted to dispute with her own husband. He grabbed her by her hair and dragged her with him, ignoring her shrieks of pain, and continued to drag her by her hair, even when she tripped and fell to her knees.

'Laura, come down! Come down from there!' Rosie begged, her thin face showing her burgeoning terror.

But Laura continued to stand aloft, alternately beseeching and challenging the women to stand their ground.

Gleeful, howling youths began to volley the rotted vegetables at the three suffragettes, and some of the missiles found their target, smashing their stinking pulp across the women's heads and bodies.

Cleopatra Dolton instantly realised the real danger the three women were in. 'We must get them from here!' she told Ozzie Clarke urgently.

He chuckled and shook his head. 'They'll not come to any harm. The lads are only having a bit o' sport with 'um.'

Laura was still shouting from the top of the brick heap,

187

but Miriam and Rosie were now cowering before the rain of missiles, trying to shield their heads with their arms.

'It won't stay as a bit of sport!' Cleopatra Dolton spat angrily. 'Those men could turn nasty, and you know well they could. Now, will you help me to get those women away from here, or must I do it by myself?'

'But they're nothing to do with you!' Ozzie Clarke protested heatedly. 'If they gets a few lumps then it's not your concern, is it?'

Through Cleopatra Dolton's mind there raced memories of the brutality and vile abuse that she had been subjected to at the hands of men, and she hissed savagely: 'Oh yes it is! It is my concern!' She went to snatch the reins from the man's hands and he realised the intensity of her feelings. Sudden admiration for her spirited courage coursed through him.

He fought off her snatching hands. 'I'll get them away,' he told her. 'But you get down and keep well distant. I don't want anything happening to you.'

She stared curiously as she detected the note of genuine concern in his voice, but then a concerted shout of acclamation jolted her from her momentary reverie. An accurately flung missile had struck Miriam Josceleyne squarely on her head, causing her to crouch low to the ground with her arms wrapped about her head, whimpering in terror and pain.

'I'm staying with you,' she said grimly. 'We'll get them away together.'

Ozzie Clarke saw the iron determination in his employer's dark eyes and accepted.

'Hold tight then!' he grinned, as the elation of impending action brought a rush of adrenalin surging through his body. And he lashed the horse forwards. The iron-rimmed wheels bounced and jarred over the uneven surface, as he swung the dray through a wide arc and brought the horse to a juddering halt between the swirling crowd and the heap of bricks. Even as it halted Cleopatra Dolton came down from the seat in a billowing of petticoats. With voice and hands she urged the three women up and on to the dray, following them herself, and shouting to Ozzie Clarke.

'Let's go! Let's go!'

The dramatic advent of the rescuers initially shocked the crowd into momentary silence. Then the women and girls started cheering. The men and youths either burst out into laughing plaudits at the action, or as in the case of Woodfield's foreman, cursed and shook their fists at the prey that had so suddenly eluded them.

Miriam Josceleyne stared dazedly at her rescuer, as if disbelieving the evidence of her own eyes. 'It's you! Why have you helped us?' She gasped the words, and there was both astonishment and loathing in her face. Then she pushed herself to her knees, her body jerking from the bouncing of the dray over the pot-holed road, and shouted at Ozzie Clarke: 'Stop! I must get down! Stop will you!'

By now they had almost reached the junction with Red Lane and Ozzie Clarke hauled on the reins.

'Come up! Come uuuppp, blast you! Commmme uuupppp!'

With heaving flanks and snorts of breath the excited horse skidded to a standstill, and Miriam scrambled off the dray. Her eyes angry and outraged, she stared wildly at her two friends, shaking her head as if in bewilderment.

'I'm sorry!' she jerked out. 'I'm sorry!' Then turned and hurried away around the corner into Red Lane, leaving Laura gaping with astonishment.

Rosie Spiers however, had heard all the rumours and gossip of four years previously, and she knew why Miriam had run away. Her wan face flamed with embarrassment as she met Cleopatra Dolton's dark eyes, but the other woman only smiled kindly at her, and shook her head as if to tell Rosie that what had just occurred did not matter.

Laura Hughes began to feel angry at what she thought to be her friend's inexplicable rudeness, and she began to apologise profusely, but Cleopatra Dolton refused to allow her to do so.

'No, there's no need for apologies, Miss Hughes! Your friend has good cause to act as she did.' She paused for an instant, and then qualified, 'At least, she believes she has good cause for acting like that.' Then deliberately changing the subject she said, 'I'm walking home from here. Would you like Mr Clarke to take you to your home?'

Both young women refused with thanks, and Cleopatra Dolton was quick to take her leave of them, waving aside their heartfelt words of gratitude for saving them from the mob.

Ozzie Clarke drove the dray away, and the two young women slowly walked in the direction of the town centre.

'What on earth caused Miriam to behave so badly?' Laura pondered aloud. 'Even if she believed she had good cause it was still unforgiveable to behave so rudely after Mrs Dolton had risked injury to help us! It really was!'

Rosie bit her lip uncertainly, then said quietly, 'I think I know why Miss Miriam acted that way, Laura. . . .'

She waited until her friend told her, 'Perhaps you had better explain it to me then, my dear. Because the more I think about it, the angrier I'm becoming with Miriam.'

Reluctantly Rosie said, 'Well, the talk was in the town that Miss Miriam and Johnny Purvis were lovers.'

'What?' Laura came to an abrupt halt, and gazed with wide eyes at her friend. 'Lovers? Miriam and this Johnny Purvis were lovers? But wasn't the man who killed Mrs Dolton's husband? Wasn't he Mrs Dolton's lover?'

'Well, he killed Arthur Dolton all right.' Rosie was suddenly pensive. 'But Mrs Dolton and him always denied that they was lovers. And as for Miss Miriam, well, although the talk was that her and him were lovers, well, it was only gossip, that's all.'

Laura took Rosie's arm and began to walk slowly on, still shaking her head as if she could not fully comprehend what she had been told.

After a time she remarked reflectively, 'Do you know, Rosie, I can't help but think that this Johnny Purvis was an evil curse upon both their lives.'

'Oh no, doon't you goo thinking that, Laura. From what I knows of it Johnny Purvis warn't an evil man at all. Most people who knows him always speaks well of him. And theer's nobody except Mrs Dolton, and Miss Miriam, and Johnny Purvis himself who really knows the truth about what went on between the three on 'um.'

Laura nodded pensively and stayed silent. But in her mind there was a burning curiosity concerning the man.

'I'd like to meet you,' she admitted silently. 'I really would like to meet you, Johnny Purvis.'

Cleopatra Dolton walked slowly towards her house, a wry smile hovering around her lips.

'What an eventful day I've had,' she told herself ironically. 'I've eaten humble pie. I've surrendered a degree of control over my business. I've made a spectacle of myself rescuing suffragettes. And I've met Johnny Purvis's lover for the first time.' Real regret coursed through her as she thought of Johnny Purvis. 'I wish that helping me had not cost you so dear.' Her mind travelled back towards that day when she had gone to Johnny Purvis's lodgings seeking his help, and her husband had come storming after her, and in the fight that followed her husband had met his death. At the subsequent trial Johnny Purvis had been convicted of manslaughter and sent to prison.

She had written to him several times, to tell him how bitterly she regretted involving him in her troubled personal life, but he had only replied once. In his letter he had told her that she had nothing to reproach herself with, and that he did not in any way blame her for what had happened between himself and Arthur Dolton. He stated his belief in fate, and assured her that he regarded his present situation as having been predestined and unavoidable. But he also said that it was best that they did not have any further contact. She was to go on with her own life, and not think any more about him, just as he would someday resume his own life without thought of her.

Now the memory of the loathing in Miriam Josceleyne's eyes came to trouble Cleopatra. She had of course long known of the gossip concerning Miriam Josceleyne and Johnny Purvis, and today's reaction of the woman when she had seen who her rescuer had been, had served to confirm the truth of that gossip in her mind.

'She must have been in love with him, for her to have reacted to me as she did just now. But I wish she didn't hate me so. I can understand that she holds me

191

responsible for him being sent to jail. But I hope that she knows that there was no physical relationship between me and Johnny Purvis. That we were not lovers.'

Cleopatra had certainly found Johnny Purvis a very attractive man, and was honest enough to admit that had circumstances been different, she could have fallen in love with him herself. 'But it wasn't to be, and it did not happen.'

Yet still the memory of the loathing in Miriam Josceleyne's eyes disturbed her, and she began to wonder if there was anything that she could do which might alter the way in which the other woman regarded her. With a touch of bitterness she was forced to accept that there was probably nothing that she could do. 'I shall just have to live with it, as I have to live with so much more that I do not like about my life.'

Upon her return to Cotswold House Miriam Josceleyne told Mrs Elwood that she had a bad headache and did not wish to be disturbed. Then she went up to her bedroom and after drawing the curtains lay down on her bed. The darkness of her thoughts matched the darkness of the room, and her mind was peopled with images that tormented her almost beyond bearing. Try as she might to dismiss those vivid visual pictures, still they persisted. In them Johnny Purvis was entwined in passion with Cleopatra Dolton, their naked bodies writhing in the act of love.

'How could you lie to me so?' she cried out to Johnny Purvis in her mind. 'How could you tell me that you loved me, and then leave my arms and go to the arms of that woman?' She sobbed helplessly, grief and chagrin enmeshed in the outburst. She had begun to believe that she had recovered from the worst of her grief at losing Johnny Purvis, but now it came surging back with all its poignancy and bitterness, and she found herself yearning for the man with an overwhelming intensity.

'I could have forgiven you,' she told him in her mind. 'I know that she is very beautiful, and could tempt any man. I could have forgiven you, Johnny, if you had only told me about her.'

The hours passed, and with their passing, her distraught

emotions slowly calmed. At times she heard the voices of Emma and the servants, and their shared laughter acted as a healing balm to her wounded spirit.

'Just think of what troubles Emma has known in her life, and yet she can still laugh, and still be kind to others. I should be ashamed of myself, allowing an unhappy love affair to bring me to this state. Four years have passed since I gave myself to Johnny Purvis, and what happened to me has happened to countless thousands of women. I can't believe that all those other women break down like I have done.'

This increasing sense of shame at what she perceived to be her own weakness goaded Miriam to fresh resolve that she would not give in to her own feelings again. 'I must be strong,' she told herself, and with that resolve a feeling of new strength did begin to burgeon within her. She thought of the cause she was now committed to, and realised: 'This can be my salvation. If I throw myself wholeheartedly into the fight, then I'll not have time or inclination to brood on what is passed.' A bleak smile twitched her lips as with maudlin humour she thought, 'At least, I'll try not to have time to brood.'

The resolution fortified her, and not wishing for any further company, she undressed and returned to her bed to sleep.

Chapter Twenty-Two

It was the third Monday in August, and when he awoke that morning Harry Vivaldi felt extremely cheerful and optimistic, despite the throbbing ache in his head engendered by the previous night's debauch. For a time he lay still while the painful throbbing eased, listening to the sounds of Bella Thomas moving in the room beneath, and he smiled cruelly. 'If all goes as I'm expecting it to, then I'll not be listening to you thundering around like a bloody elephant for much longer, you fat slag.'

Then he shouted: 'Bella, bring me my tea.'

'All right, darlin', I'll be up directly.'

Her hoarse reply was instant, as if she had been eagerly awaiting his summons, and he grinned with satisfaction. 'I've got you tamed, aren't I,' he congratulated himself. 'I should have took me fists to you from the first. It would have saved me a deal of earache.'

His bladder felt uncomfortably full, and grunting wearily he swung his feet out from under the stale-smelling bedclothes. Pulling the encrusted half-filled chamberpot from under the bed he ejected a stream of urine into its foul contents, then laid the pot down and once more stretched out at his ease.

Wheezing with effort, Bella Thomas clambered up the narrow staircase and brought a tin mug of tea to him.

He took it from her and with a lordly air instructed, 'Empty that bloody pot, and bring it back up here. Then you can fry me a bit o' bacon.'

With wordless submission she obeyed.

Soon the fragrant scents of the frying bacon wafted up to Harry Vivaldi's nostrils, and he sighed in contentment.

Life was looking decidedly rosy from his vantage point.

Bella Thomas brought him a plate of bacon sandwiches, and a fresh mug of tea, then asked humbly, 'Is there anything special you wants me to get for your supper, darlin'?'

He considered for a moment or two. 'You can get a bit of brawn and some pickles, and a jug of ale, and make sure that Billy Kibler draws the ale from his fresh barrel. That you got me last night tasted like piss.'

'Yes, darlin'. Now I've laid your clothes out, and put a clean collar ready, and your boots is polished. There's a kettle of hot water on the hob. Is there anything else you wants, only I'se got to get to work.'

He shook his head, not even deigning to look at her, but conscious of her tension, as she stood gazing at him with an anxious expectation. Her abject submissiveness gave him an immense sense of power, and with that heady feeling came sexual excitement. He felt his manhood engorging and stiffening, and abruptly he laid aside the plate and mug of tea, and beckoned her.

'Come here.'

Eagerly she stepped to him, her arms outstretched, her lips seeking his mouth, but he told her roughly, 'No kisses! I want you to suck me!' Clamping her head between his hands, he forced her face down to his manhood, and made her take its throbbing length deep into her mouth, then groaned with pleasure and lay back while she brought him to swift climax with the hot wet envelopment of her tongue and lips.

Afterwards he rewarded her with a peck on the cheek, and she beamed happily. He then had another thought. 'Have you got any money?'

She shook her head. 'No darlin'. I'm going to get the stuff for your supper on the slate.'

He scowled, and her heart fell.

'What am I going to eat at dinner time? Bloody fresh air?' he demanded aggrieved.

A spark of rebellion flared within her, briefly overlaying the physical fear of him that his recent brutal treatment of her had given birth to. 'You'se already took what money

I'd got left from me wages haven't you,' she complained sullenly.

He scowled warningly. 'Are you forgetting that it was me who paid off all the back-rent and cleared slates? That took all of my money, didn't it? But you didn't hear me whining and moaning about that, did you.' He appeared to lose his temper, and shouted at her: 'I reckon it's time that you and me parted. All I get from you these days is nagging and whining, and I've had about enough of it, I'll tell you.'

Torn by the dual fears of his violence, and of losing him, she surrendered. 'I'll have to try and pawn something. If I can I'll bring whatever I gets to you at the shop when I has me dinnerbreak.'

'And what time will that be?' he wanted to know.

'About twelve o'clock time.'

He forced himself to smile at her. 'All right then, that will have to do. I'll pay the pawn ticket for you when I get my commission money from Field.'

He gave her another peck on the cheek, and patted her broad rump in dismissal. 'You'd best be going, sweetheart, else you'll be late for work.'

After she had gone he ate the rest of his sandwiches and drained the mug of tea, then rose to begin his toilet. He hummed happily as he shaved and powdered and pomaded. His high spirits were engendered by the expectation that this week he and Emma Josceleyne would finalise the details of the business proposition that he had been laying before her during the previous weeks. He had visited Cotswold House several times in the furtherance of a business scheme that he was trying to get the young widow to invest in. He had exerted all his considerable charm to ingratiate himself with Mrs Elwood and the two maids, and to be an amusing and lively companion to Emma and her convalescent mother.

As he put the final touches to his appearance, he allowed himself congratulation on the way he was conducting his campaign to seduce the young widow. Despite his fierce hungering for her body, he had not made any romantic overtures or sexual advances towards her. He judged accurately that he was now considered a friend by Emma, and was a welcome visitor to Cotswold House. There was only one small matter to mar his satisfaction. He had not succeeded in insinuating himself into Miriam Josceleyne's good opinions. Although she was always polite to him, and had not as far as he knew raised any objections to him visiting Cotswold House, nevertheless he was aware of the constraint in her manner, and sensed the covert disapproval that she nurtured for him. Now he frowned, and shrugged as he tilted his Homburg hat rakishly upon his thick black hair.

'Bollocks to her! She's just a frustrated old maid. If she'd ever known what it was to feel a man between her legs, then she'd appreciate me. I reckon it's just jealousy of me and Emma that makes her look down her nose at me.' Soothed by this explanation, he went out of the house whistling jauntily.

Although it was only half-past seven, the three public houses in George Street, and the four public houses around the corner in Red Lion Street and the other twenty-six public houses within a 600 yard radius were all open for the early morning trade. Many men, and women also, were in the habit of taking a 'livener' on their way to work. Harry Vivaldi was sorely tempted to call in and take a glass of gin, but he knew that if Ernie Field smelt the drink on his breath then he would have money docked from his wages for 'coming to work drunk'.

'Never mind,' the young man comforted himself. 'Soon I'll be able to tell him what he can do with his bloody job.'

He neared the Golden Lion, a public house which stood nearly opposite the Silver Street arch, and noticed two roughly-dressed men standing leaning against its grimy wall. Harry Vivaldi experienced a tremor of foreboding when he saw the men, but found it unaccountable that he should do so. After all, he reassured himself, it was late at night when the pubs turned out that passers-by were subjected to aggressive behaviour by drunks, not at this early hour of the morning. Nevertheless when he passed the two loungers he stepped to the outside edge of the pavement to give them a wide berth, and deliberately kept his gaze fixed straight ahead, to avoid catching their eyes.

Winston Farr, still half-drunk from the previous night, glared sourly at the well-dressed dandy as he passed, and hawked and spat contemptuously at his feet. His companion, Alfred Payne, was glumly contemplating his own cracked boots, and the emptiness of his pockets, and paid no attention to the man passing by, until Winston Farr jabbed him with his elbow and growled.

'Look at that lardy-da bastard! He's got a bob on hisself, aren't he?'

Alfred Payne peered with bleary uninterest as the dandified figure furthered the distance from them. Then he stared harder, and declared: 'That's him!'

Sick and weary with his hangover, Winston Farr shook his head in disgust. 'What does you mean, Alf, that's him? Who, for fuck's sake? Who's him?'

'That's the bugger who helped your Emma take your Missis away. It was him who was pushing the barrow.'

'What!' Winston Farr pushed himself away from the wall, swearing vilely as the sudden movement sent agonising pains lancing through his skull. 'Am you sure that's him?'

His friend nodded wearily. 'I'm sure. I never forgets a face, does I? You knows that. You knows I never forgets a face once I'se sin it. I never does.'

''Ull you shurrup, for Christ's sake,' Winston Farr grumbled, and screwed up his eyes to stare after the retreating figure. 'Now am you sure, Alf? Am you certain sure that it's him?'

'O' course I'm bloody sure. I swears on my babbie's grave, I'm sure!' Alf answered irascibly.

Farr's brutal features lowered with sullen rage, and his meaty hands clenched as if he were crushing a man's throat between them. 'I'll have that bastard! I'll have him right now!'

He started to lumber down the road, bawling at the top of his voice: 'Hey you, come 'ere! I wants a word wi' you, you bastard!'

Harry Vivaldi heard the shouts, and turned his head.

'Come 'ere you bastard!' The hulking figure broke into a shambling run.

198

'Oh my God!' Vivaldi's throat and mouth went dry as terror clutched at his heart. 'Oh my God, that's got to be Emma's father!'

Casting all dignity to the winds he took to his heels and ran. He crossed the roadway at the junction with the Alcester Street and hurled himself into a narrow alleyway that lead to a network of streets behind the main roads.

Badly hungover as he was, Winston Farr could not keep up any pursuit, and he shambled to a halt, dragging strangled breaths into his ruined lungs. Mouthing futile curses, he turned back towards his friend, and when he reached him vowed ferociously: 'I'm going to have that flash bleeder, Alf. You mark my words, I'm going to stamp that bugger into the ground like a piece of shit! That's no promise, it's a solemn fact.'

Knowing his crony's capacity for savage violence, Alfred Payne grinned with avid anticipation. 'I hopes I'm theer when you catches up with him, Winston. I 'udden't want to miss it for the world!'

By detouring through alleyways and entries and climbing over fences and walls, Harry Vivaldi was able to approach his workplace without using a main road. But in the process his highly-polished boots became sadly scuffed and dirtied, and as he entered the shop his employer's eyes immediately fixed on the footwear.

'Them boots are a disgrace, Vivaldi. You'd best get 'um clean before any of the customers sees 'um.' Ernie Field was feeling irritable this morning. An irritation engendered by his sexual frustrations, which he feared he would not be able to satisfy this coming week. Several overdue bills had been presented which would take all his ready money to settle.

Harry Vivaldi scowled, but kept his mouth closed and used some rag to clean his boots.

The morning passed slowly for the young man. Trade was slack, and his employer made him spend the time cleaning and polishing the stock.

Then, just before noon, Ernie Field instructed: 'Take the handcart up to my house. Mrs Field wants a bit of furniture shifting to her sister's. It's only a table and a couple of chairs, so you'll be able to manage it by yourself.'

Harry Vivaldi's resentment at being given this menial labouring task showed in his sullen expression. 'I'm likely to mess my clothes up shifting furniture,' he protested.

His employer only snarled, 'Then put a bloody apron on. There's one hanging on the back of the door there.'

Harry Vivaldi could not bring himself to endure that final indignity, so left the apron hanging, and cursing furiously under his breath, trundled the handcart away.

Some few minutes after the noon hour Bella Thomas came hurrying breathlessly down Prospect Hill and entered the shop.

'Is Mr Vivaldi here? I'm his wife.'

Ernie Field knew that his employee was living with a woman, but he had never seen her until now, and he stared at her curiously. As always her face was painted, a practice only indulged in by 'theatricals', 'fast women' and prostitutes, but this fact only added to her attraction in Ernie Field's eyes. His expression was guarded, but as he took in her blowzy big-breasted, broad-hipped figure, and noted the traces of youthful prettiness that remained in her ravaged features, a gleam of lust entered his eyes.

'His wife, did you say?' He deliberately emphasised the doubt in his tone. 'I didn't know he was married.'

She had the grace to flush, and stuttered in agitation. 'Oh, d. . .didn't you?'

The man slowly shook his head. 'No. Harry told me that he was sharing his house with a lady, but he never told me he was married. In fact he's always led me to believe that he's a single chap.'

Bella Thomas's fat cheeks quivered as she in her turn shook her head, causing the long feathers on her wide-brimmed hat to wave violently. 'Well, I n. . .never!' She attempted to make a joke of it, and trilled with forced laughter: 'He's s. . .s. . .such a card, Harry is. Such a card!' But the flush deepened so that it glowed through the rouge and powder on her face and throat.

Although he was deriving great pleasure from tormenting her like this, Ernie Field decided that it might

200

be to his advantage to stop doing so. His lust was now pulsing strongly, and his brain was working quickly. He smiled, and agreed. 'Yes, he's a card all right is Harry. He's a proper card–' he paused for a long long moment – 'Mrs Vivaldi.'

Relieved that the man had apparently accepted her lie Bella Thomas returned his smile. Although her teeth were dingy and stained, they were not badly decayed, as were the teeth of so many of the women from whom Ernie Field bought the use of their bodies.

'She's a bit of all right, this 'un is,' he told himself, and thinking of his employee's perennial financial problems, as indicated by the young man's constant requests for advances on his wages, the shopkeeper suddenly perceived that he might well have found the solution to his own sexual problems.

'Harry's just gone out on an errand for me, Mrs Vivaldi. I'm not sure how long he'll be away for. Do you want to wait for him to come back, or can I give him a message for you?'

'No, I aren't got time to wait. Could you give him this for me, he'll know what it is.'

She handed Ernie Field some coins wrapped in a scrap of paper.

'I'll do that for you, and gladly, Mrs Vivaldi.' He set himself to be as charming to her as he possibly could, and with a crude gallantry added: 'I didn't know until now just how lucky Harry is. Having a wife as beautiful as you am.'

She fluttered her eyes, and preened. Flattery from any source was like a drug to her, and no matter how blatantly contrived or false it might be, still she hungered to receive it.

Ernie Field accompanied her to the front door, and stood watching her walk heavily back up the steep hill. He watched the wobbling of her large buttocks beneath her skirts, and his tongue snaked out along his thin lips as his imagination pictured those buttocks naked and defenceless beneath him. When she had finally disappeared from view he went back inside, and waited impatiently for his employee to return.

Harry Vivaldi was dishevelled and disgruntled when he came back to the shop in the early afternoon. The couple of chairs and a table had been increased to several other articles of furniture by Mrs Field, and had necessitated three separate journeys to and from her sister's house.

Ernie Field greeted him with a smile, telling him jovially: 'Your lady friend's bin to see you, Harry. She left this for you. She said that you'd know what it was.' He passed over the coins wrapped in paper, which the young man eagerly uncovered and counted. He frowned when he totalled the meagre amount.

'She's calls herself Mrs Vivaldi.' Ernie Field assumed an air of puzzlement. 'But I thought you said that you warn't married, Harry?'

The young man looked warily at his employer. 'I'm not,' he answered shortly.

'Why does she say that you am married to her then?' Ernie Field persisted.

Harry Vivaldi shrugged, and Ernie Field smiled ferally. 'She's a very handsome woman, Harry. A man could do a lot worse than have her in his bed as his wife.'

A customer came into the shop preventing Ernie Field from continuing in that vein.

As Harry Vivaldi played a selection of orchestral records for the customer, his eyes kept flickering to his employer's face. In the early days of their acquaintance, when they had spent a convivial evening in the local public houses, Ernie Field had got drunk, and had let slip the fact that he sometimes went to Birmingham in search of women. It was the only time that Ernie Field had ever talked of his sexual life, and the next time they met he seemed unaware that he had committed such an indiscretion. But Harry Vivaldi had stored that drunken confession in his memory. Now he retrieved it, and mulled it over, and when the customer had gone he said casually, 'You liked the look of Bella then, Mr Field?'

The man ran a hand over his thinning ginger hair, and his tongue snaked along his thin lips. 'That's her name is it, Bella?'

Harry nodded. 'Yes, it's Bella Thomas.' He had

recognised the lust in his employer's eyes, and decided to explore possibilities. 'She is married.' He paused deliberately. 'But not to me. Her husband keeps a grocery shop up in Brummagem. He's only in a very small way of business though.'

To tease the other man, he then fell silent, and busied himself in polishing one of the Talking Machines. Ernie Field paced restlessly up and down the shop, and several times ran his hand over his hair. Then came to stand close to the young man, and in a low voice asked: 'She's your mistress, is she?'

Harry grinned and answered offhandedly: 'You could say that. But if you said it in company, I'd have to deny it, wouldn't I.' He winked conspiratorially. 'Discretion, Mr Field. I'm a great believer in discretion. So is Bella. She thinks the same way as me, that what goes on between a man and a woman in private, should stay private.'

Again he turned away and busied himself with polishing the elongated horn of the Talking Machine, smiling secretly to himself as he listened to the rasping breathing of his companion. Then he went on reminiscently: 'She used to be on the stage, of course. That's where she got in the practice of painting her face like she does. Called herself Bella de Mornay the Dancing Nightingale. That was when I first met her. She used to look gorgeous in her stage costume.' He again looked Ernie Field full in the face and winked lewdly. 'It didn't leave a lot to the imagination, I'll tell you, Mr Field. There was times when the footlights would catch her and make it look as if she was stark naked. The blokes used to cheer like mad when that happened, I'll tell you.' He spread his hands as if seeking confirmation. 'Well, you've just seen her in the flesh, haven't you, Mr Field, and you have to agree that she's still a fine figure of a woman, aren't she?'

Ernie Field's eyes were greedy as he nodded, and breathed out sibilantly: 'She is that, Harry. She certainly is that.'

The young man's eyes gleamed with satisfaction. 'Got you!' he thought happily, sure now in the knowledge of Ernie Field's desire for Bella Thomas.

Casually he asked, 'Could I go and get a bit of dinner now, Mr Field? While it's quiet like this.'

His employer nodded reluctant assent. He would have liked to talk further about Bella Thomas. 'Yes, all right. But doon't take too long.'

'I won't,' Harry Vivaldi assured.

Sauntering up the hill his face was wreathed in a broad smile as he thought of Ernie Field's feral expression when talking about Bella Thomas. Then he sobered and a calculating gleam entered his eyes. 'If Emma Josceleyne don't come across with the business arrangements this week, I reckon I could screw a few quid out of Field.' The smile curved his lips once more. 'Or should I say that it'll be Bella who'll screw a few quid out of the old bastard for me.'

'But what if she don't agree to go with him?' Sudden doubt questioned, but he thrust it from him angrily. 'She'll agree to do whatever I want her to do. Make no mistake about that. She'll do as I tell her, or take the bloody consequences.'

Chapter Twenty-Three

The evening was fine and warm. As on every other Monday evening during the summer months, weather and training commitments permitting, the band of the No 4, Redditch Battery of the First Worcestershire Royal Garrison Volunteer Artillery paraded at their drill ground in Easemore Lane, then marched to the Recreation Garden in Church Green to play a selection of music in the kiosk there under the baton of their Bandmaster, Sergeant Harold Bates. The programme tonight was to include the marches, 'The King's Guard', 'The Sea King', the overture, 'Crown of Mercy', the waltz, 'Flora Dora', selections from *Bohemian Girl* and *The Mikado*, a cornet solo, 'Triplet' and the euphonium solo, 'The Dear Homeland'.

The artillery concerts were immensely popular, matched only in their appeal by the Wednesday evening concerts of their bitter rivals, the Redditch Town Band. Each band had its devoted followers, who often engaged in acrimonious dispute as to their respective merits.

It was Emma Josceleyne's practice to open her bedroom windows, which were almost opposite the band kiosk, and sit looking out, enjoying the music and watching the crowds that congregated. Sometimes Miriam Josceleyne or Mrs Elwood would join her there, at other times she would be alone. She invariably gave her two maids the concert evenings off so that they could join the other young people promenading and flirting around the Green. This evening as the band tuned their instruments and the spectators gathered, Emma Josceleyne opened her bedroom window, then turned to face her mother who was standing with a bundle of spare clothing under one arm, and her shawl around her shoulders.

'You'm not well enough to go back to Silver Street,' she stated forcefully.

Her mother's painfully gaunt, pallid face was set in a stubborn mask. 'I am well enough, our Emmy. Besides, I carn't stop away from home any longer. Your Dad and the kids needs me.'

'Me Dad needs you?' Emma exclaimed in scornful challenges. 'What does he need you for, Mam? Carn't he find anybody else to boot around the bloody room when he comes back from the pub at nights?'

Amy Farr could find no immediate answer to that, so she switched to another tack. 'The kids needs me. They wants looking arter by their Mam. Your Dad aren't able to care for 'um like I does. Men aren't able to do that, even though they tries their best. It aren't the same for the kids having their Dad looking arter 'um, instead of their Mam.'

Emma lifted her black eyes to the heavens as if seeking witness to this statement. Then she told her mother, 'The old bugger aren't done anything at all for the kids while you'se been here, Mam. He aren't had to try and do anything for 'um. Not that he 'ud anyway. You knows that I've been paying Mrs Walton and Mrs Simpson to look arter 'um.' As always when she was talking with her mother, Emma's speech reverted back to the patterns of Silver Street.

Still the older woman's expression remained stubbornly determined. 'Well, even if the kids am being looked arter, what about your Dad? Who'se looking arter him?'

Emma gusted out a noisy breath of exasperation. 'What is theer to look arter, Mam? I sends him money every week, and he spends all his bloody time drinking it away in the pubs. From what I hears he's never in the bloody house, only to sleep. I expect he buys his grub in the pubs, when he's sober enough to remember to ate. But I doubt the bugger has bin sober for a single solitary minute while you'se bin here.'

'Yes, that's just what makes it needful for me to get back home, our Emmy. If I aren't theer then he wun't goo to his work. And if he doon't goo to his work, then he'll lose all his customers, wun't he. And what 'ull become on us all then, if he aren't able to earn his bread?' The woman presented this argument with an air of satisfied certitude, as if it were incontrovertible.

Emma's black eyes flashed with anger. 'Doon't talk so sarft, Mam. You knows very well that it doon't really matter a bugger whether the old sod works or not. You and the kids 'ull always have sufficient to live on. I'll make sure o' that.'

Amy Farr's voice became shrill with indignation. 'Does you really think that I wants that, our Emmy? Does you really think that I'd be content to live on me own daughter's charity for the rest o' me days? Does you really think that?'

Highlights glinted in the glossy chestnut hair as her daughter shook her head helplessly. 'It aren't charity, our Mam! Not if it comes from me! I'm your daughter, not the bloody Workhouse Board!'

Amy Farr was scenting victory, and she refused to be deflected. 'It doon't matter whether the money comes from you, or the Workhouse Board, or the bloody King of England, our Emmy. It's still charity, and I'd sooner be laying dead in me grave before I'd take charity from anybody. I'se always worked for whatever bit o' money I'se had, and your Dad was always a good worker as well.'

Amy Farr halted and drew a shuddering breath, and then hurled the words at Emma like an accusation. 'He was a good worker until you started giving him money. It's your fault that he's on the bloody drink night and day. If you hadn't o' give him money he'd have had to goo out and work to get it. It's your fault that he's gooing on like he is now, spending all his time in the bloody pubs.'

Emma was shocked to silence by the blatant injustice of this accusation, and her mother allowed her no time to collect her thoughts.

'I'm gooing home directly, our Emmy. And theer's nothing you can do or say to stop me.' She transferred the bundle of clothing from one arm to the other, and softened enough to tell her stunned daughter. 'I'll be all right, my duck. And I'se ever so grateful for what you'se done for me. But I'se got to goo back home now, and that's that.'

She moved forwards and kissed her daughter tenderly, then pushed away Emma's arms as the younger woman tried to hold her back.

'Tarra, my duck.'

'Tarra Mam,' Emma glumly accepted defeat, and allowed her mother to leave the house without any further attempt to detain her.

When Amy Farr had gone, Emma returned upstairs and seated herself at the open window, gazing out unseeingly, hearing the opening overture of the band without cognizance of the music. Behind her the house was still and silent. Miriam Josceleyne was out on some business concerning the suffragettes, and Mrs Elwood had gone home. Emma experienced an acute sense of loneliness, and for a moment wished that she had not given the two maidservants the evening off because she felt the need for company. She leaned forwards, resting her elbows upon the window sill and cupping her face between her hands, and stared disconsolately at the scene beneath her.

The older and more staid folk were seated and standing around the kiosk listening to the lilting strains of 'Flora Dora', while the younger elements of the crowd promenaded around the pavements bounding the triangular Recreation Gardens, the girls and young women with linked arms, the boys and young men in noisy groups bantering and trying to flirt with the females, who reacted with demure smiles, or bold glances, or mock indignation, some of the younger girls giggling in loud excitement and slapping the more daring youths who tried to snatch a ribbon from them.

As she watched, Emma's thoughts slipped back to a dusky evening four years previously, when she had been sitting at the window of the servants' attic above her present vantage point, and had seen the figure of a soldier passing through the pools of lamplight, dashing in his plumed slouch hat, spurred riding boots, and tight-cut khaki tunic and breeches.

'That was the first time I ever clapped eyes on Johnny Purvis,' she realised, and inevitably her thoughts went to Miriam Josceleyne.

Emma had been told by Mrs Elwood about the incident that had occurred down in Holyoaksfield when Cleopatra Dolton had intervened to save the suffragettes from injury. She had seen Miriam Josceleyne's drawn face and troubled expression the next day and by gentle coaxing had elicited her friend's own account of what had happened. Miriam Josceleyne had not been able to fully conceal her bitterness against Cleopatra Dolton, and despite her guarded speech had, by her unconscious gestures and tone, betrayed the depths of her loathing for that woman.

Now a familiar guilt assailed Emma as she became enveloped in memory. 'I should have told Miriam,' she regretted sadly. 'I should have given her his letter. It's not fair that Cleopatra Dolton should be blamed for something she did not do. It wasn't her that tried to take Johnny Purvis away from Miriam. It was me, wasn't it, if the truth be told. It was me. And it's my fault that poor Miriam is still suffering from it now.'

Bitter remorse engulfed her as the painful memories assailed her relentlessly. When she had been Miriam Josceleyne's maidservant, Emma had discovered that her mistress and Johnny Purvis were lovers. She herself had been to some degree infatuated with the handsome soldier, and had been intensely jealous of he and Miriam's affair. On the day that Arthur Dolton had met his death, Miriam had been awaiting her lover at Cotswold House. She had been prostrated by the shock of hearing what had happened, and had shut herself away in her darkened room, half-insane with grief and torment.

Then some time later, Saul Shibco, a friend of John Purvis, had brought a letter for Miriam from Purvis, a letter professing his great love for her, and explaining exactly what had happened between himself and Cleopatra Dolton and their mutual innocence of any illicit relationship. Emma had taken the letter from the friend, but instead of giving it to Miriam, she had opened and

209

read it, then in a ferment of jealousy had torn it up and returned it to Shibco. She then told him that Miriam had adamantly refused to read it, and did not wish ever to see, to speak with, or to hear from Johnny Purvis again. As Emma had judged, Johnny Purvis's pride had ensured that he would comply with what he believed to be Miriam's wishes, and the love he bore for her would guarantee that he would not visit further shame and grief upon her by making any further attempts to contact her.

Emma sighed deeply. Her youthful infatuation for Johnny Purvis had long since disappeared, although she readily admitted that she would like to see him again. If only out of curiosity to discover if he still possessed the power to affect her.

'But it looks as if I've sentenced poor Miriam to a lifetime of grieving and pining for Johnny Purvis. I should tell her what I did with that letter. It might help to ease her pain.'

But even as she thought this, Emma realised that in all probability she would never be able to bring herself to make that confession. She would not be able to bear the hatred and disgust that she was sure would be Miriam's reaction upon hearing how the girl she had so absolutely trusted, had so cruelly betrayed her.

The sudden resounding blast of trumpets as the band struck up the 'King's Guard' shocked Emma from her bleak reverie, and she blinked several times and jerked her head sharply as if to expel the painful recollections. Her gaze moved along the roadway and suddenly encountered the smiling face of Harry Vivaldi, cutting a debonair figure in his striped blazer, white trousers and rakishly tilted straw boater. Now that he had caught her attention, he raised his cane in salutation, and Emma, in sore need of escape from her tormenting thoughts, acted on impulse, and beckoned to him to come to the front door.

As he crossed the road she hurried downstairs to let him in.

'What a masher you look tonight, Harry,' she told him teasingly, but at the same time admitted privately that he was a very handsome figure.

His white teeth gleamed and he lifted his straw boater and bowed. 'And how beautiful you look tonight, Emma.' His dark eyes moved admiringly down her shapely figure clad in a dark green silken gown, the emerald pendant nestling between her firm breasts glinting as she moved. 'That colour really becomes you.'

Smiling with satisfaction at his compliment, she led him into the drawing room. 'Would you like a drink?'

'Please. Scotch if you have it.'

They were outwardly relaxed, displaying an easy familiarity in each other's company, but behind that façade both were acutely conscious of the other's physical attractions.

She handed him a glass tumbler half-filled with whisky, and poured herself a generous measure of gin.

He sat down on one of the armchairs, and Emma took her seat on the *chaise-longue* facing him across the big fireplace, which was shielded by a lacquered Chinese screen.

'Smoke if you want to,' she told him. 'I'll have one myself.'

He took out a packet of Turkish cigarettes and extracted two of the long slender tubes. He lit her cigarette with a lucifer match, then his own, and told her jokingly, 'You know that ladies aren't supposed to smoke, don't you?'

She laughed. 'Since when have I been a lady, Harry.'

'Have you decided about the proposition I made to you, Emma? About starting up our own Talking Machine shop?'

She shook her head. 'I haven't made my mind up yet. I'm not sure that this town is big enough to support another shop selling Talking Machines. You say yourself that Ernie Field's trade is slack just lately.'

'Only because Field's an old fool who doesn't know how a business should be run in this day and age. I could double his takings in a month if he'd give me a free hand,' he answered confidently. 'You have to go out and find customers these days. They won't come to you.' He paused for a moment, then went on enthusiastically, 'I'm sure that my ideas would work, Emma. If we fitted up a van and

211

took the Talking Machines around the country areas we could make a fortune. Just you think how many isolated farms there are around this district, and little hamlets tucked away where nobody hardly ever goes. We'd be a tremendous novelty for them. I reckon we could make money just by charging the yokels a tanner to hear their own voices. And there's another thing that I've been considering as well.'

'What's that?' Emma smiled indulgently. She enjoyed his enthusiasm and his wild ideas about money-making.

'Moving Pictures,' he announced portentously. 'There's a fortune to be made in Moving Pictures.'

'But they're nothing new now,' she protested. 'Nearly everybody has seen them. And they're only a novelty that's passing. People are getting fed up with them. Just look at the Public Hall. A few years since Willie Treadgold could fill it if he was showing the Moving Pictures, but now he just uses a couple of them to fill in the bill. People want live acts, not Moving Pictures any more. They're just a novelty that's losing their interest for folks now.'

'Well, I don't agree with you, Emma,' he stated forcefully. 'Oh, I'll accept what you say about people getting tired of them. But you're missing the point I'm trying to make. Moving Pictures are going to be the entertainment of the future. When I last lived in London I used to go to all the Penny Gaffs, and I met quite a few chaps who were involved in making Moving Pictures. They reckoned that some day they'd be able to make Moving Pictures that would last as long as a stage play. They reckoned that they'd be able to tell real stories with them. One chap even told me that someday the Moving Pictures would have talk and sound, and even colour.'

Emma laughed amusedly. 'That'll be the day that pigs can fly, Harry. How can a chap like you, that's travelled a lot and seen life be taken in by such tall stories?'

For a moment he frowned in resentment, but almost instantly forced himself to laugh. He knew that he must not lose his temper with this young woman, not while he was still hopeful of achieving his aims concerning her. 'You might well be right, Emma,' he agreed with a rueful smile. 'I suppose I do let my imagination run away with me sometimes. But I don't think that my ideas about the Talking Machines are all pie in the sky.'

Emma looked thoughtful, and eventually conceded, 'No, perhaps they're not, Harry. But you're asking me to risk a lot of money, what with renting premises and buying stock and getting a horse and van.'

'But you'll get all of that money back and a damn sight more to go with it,' he asserted with conviction radiating from him.

'Maybe!' She nodded. 'But I'll have to give it some more thought.'

'Well don't go thinking about it too long, or the opportunity might be lost.' He hid his acute disappointment behind a light-hearted mask.

The sounds of the band music were muffled by the window glass, and she asked, 'Will you open the window, so that we can hear the band properly?'

For a while they sat without speaking, sipping their drinks, blowing out clouds of fragrant tobacco smoke, and enjoying the music wafting in through the open window behind the net curtains.

'Where's everybody else tonight then?' he wanted to know, after their third generous measure of spirits.

'They're all out.'

'It won't do your reputation any good being alone in the house with a man. What will people say?'

'I've never cared what people say.' She smiled lazily. 'Do you care what people say, Harry?'

He shook his head.

Emma swung her legs up on to the *chaise-longue* and relaxed leaning back against its raised end.

The young man's pulse rate quickened as he thought how desirable she looked, and he hungered to taste her full moist lips.

The large amounts of gin that she had drunk had gone to Emma's head, and a pleasurable sensation of sensual languor was permeating through her body. She let her gaze rest on Harry Vivaldi's well-manicured hands, and allowed herself to imagine how they would feel exploring

213

her body. Recollection of her husband's withered flesh came to disturb her, and with instant repulsion she thrust that memory away, replacing it with imaginings of a young man's smooth firm chest and belly and muscular thighs. She closed her eyes, her lips parted slightly, and her breathing shortened as her vivid imagination took hold of her senses.

Then she gasped and her eyes opened wide as Harry Vivaldi's lips clamped on hers. The scent of his cologne filled her nostrils, and she could taste the whisky upon his tongue as it invaded her mouth. She tried to jerk back her head, but could only move a fraction before the back of her skull impacted upon the raised arm of the *chaise-longue*. His lips crushed harder upon hers, and his tongue raped the soft inner recesses of her mouth. His hands cupped her cheeks with a strangely gentle violence, not hurting, yet imprisoning her head so that she could not escape. She could feel his chest pressing against her breasts, and felt the powerful thudding of his heart as a pulsing sensation through her flesh.

Conflicting emotions surged through her; anger that he should have assaulted her like this, hunger for his body to invade her own. She lifted her hands and clutched his shoulders, trying to push him away, yet at the same time lacking the volition to struggle violently against him. Suddenly he moved, twisting his body, holding her tightly against him, so that she was lifted helplessly and brought down on to the thick carpeting. He moved on top of her, his chest and belly pressing down on her breasts and belly, his thighs clamping her thighs together between them, his hands still cupping her face, his lips still crushed on hers, his tongue still raping her mouth.

Beyond the net curtains the brass blared and the drums beat and as if driven by that pounding rhythm, the man's hips moved in rapid thrusts. Through the layering of clothing Emma could feel the thick hard length of his erection rubbing upon her lower belly and mound of Venus and her own desires flamed unbearably, and she began to moan in wanting. All track of time left her and now her clutching hands moved to his waist and gripped

214

tight and pulled his surging body harder and harder against her own. Her excitement mounted unbearably, and her need became an uncontrollable force. She writhed beneath him as he moved faster and faster and faster, and then like a torrent bursting its banks ecstasy exploded through her and she arched upwards, crying out, squeezing her thighs together, digging her nails deep into the slender muscularity of his waist.

Panting heavily they lay locked tight while their senses calmed, and then she pushed his body off her, and lay gazing upwards at the white ceiling.

He raised himself up on his elbow and smiled down into her face, then bent to kiss her, but she pushed him forcefully away. 'What's the matter, honey?' he frowned in puzzlement.

She furrowed her smooth brows as if deep in thought, then answered slowly, 'Nothing. Nothing's the matter. And I'm not your honey.'

'But you know I love you, don't you,' he told her urgently.

She smiled bleakly, and said in an ambiguous tone, 'No, Harry. No, I don't know that at all.'

Without looking at him, she waved her arm in a gesture of dismissal. 'I want you to go now, Harry.'

He shook his head in bewilderment. 'Why? Are you angry with me?'

She shook her head in denial. 'No, I'm not angry with you. I just want you to go, that's all.'

He would have argued, but she shook her head again and told him sharply, 'Just go, will you, Harry. Just go.'

Slowly, he clambered to his feet, and stood staring uncertainly down at her.

'The maids will be here shortly.' Her voice was expressionless, as if she were talking to a stranger. 'I want you to go before they come back.'

Irritation sparked in his dark eyes, but he made an effort to sound calm. 'When will I see you again?'

'Soon,' she told him quietly, and rolled on to her side, and pillowing her head upon her hands like a child, she closed her eyes as if asleep.

He grimaced in disbelief, then turned and left her.

The artillery band had completed their programme of music and were forming up in the roadway preparatory to returning to their drill hall, and the crowd were standing on both sides of the roadway to watch them march away. Harry Vivaldi pushed his way through the spectators, his mind full of the bizarre finale to his intimate encounter with Emma Josceleyne.

'She's bloody weird, that one,' he told himself disgruntledly. Then he remembered how sweet her mouth had tasted, and the soft moistness of her lips, and the feel of her firm lithe body beneath him, and his imagination took wing as he envisaged how that body would feel in nakedness, rounded thighs wrapped around him, his manhood buried deep in its succulent depths, and his spirits soared dizzyingly.

'It'll be bloody tremendous,' he told himself exultantly. 'It'll be the best thing that has ever happened to me.' And he tilted his hat rakishly upon his thick black hair and went swaggering onwards.

The drawing room in Cotswold House slowly darkened as the dusk of night fell upon the land, and Emma Josceleyne still lay with her head pillowed upon her hands, eyes closed as if asleep. But she did not sleep. Instead her mind was contemplating the way in which her physical needs had so overwhelmed her.

'I really had lost control, hadn't I,' she admitted dispassionately. 'I'm going to have to watch myself very carefully in the future. If Harry Vivaldi can make me lose control when we've both still got all our clothes on, what else can he do? I'm going to have to tread careful with him, and no mistake. I don't want to end up by falling in love with the bugger. He's too much of a fly one.'

Then she smiled slyly. 'But it really did feel good, didn't it. Just think of how it will feel when we're doing it properly. When we're naked together in bed and going the whole way.'

Emma's smile broadened, and if her maidservant could have seen her mistress at this moment, she would have readily recognised the expression of the beautiful cat who had swallowed the cream.

216

Chapter Twenty-Four

The first week in September brought rain and gusting winds and dark clouded skies. As Miriam Josceleyne walked with head bent against the flurrying stinging raindrops, her umbrella handle tugging against her grip as the wind buffeted its black canopy, her mood matched the sombre colour of the sky above her. She turned into Hill Street and walked up its slope and the thick-layered filthy mud sucked at her high-buttoned boots and soddened and soiled the bottoms of her skirts.

From one of the broken, rag-stuffed windows in the court where Rosie Spiers lived there came the sounds of a fierce altercation, then a high-pitched scream of pain and fear and a harsh voice bawling a stream of oaths. Fear clutched Miriam Josceleyne and she hammered on Rosie Spiers's door then gasped in relief when it was opened to her and Laura Hughes beckoned her to enter the cramped, murky room.

'I don't know how you can bear to stay in this vile place, Laura.' Miriam Josceleyne's face was pale from her fright. 'You could be murdered in your bed.'

Laura smiled ruefully as the sound of the shrieking penetrated into the room through the closed door.

'One gets used to it, Miriam.'

The older woman's green eyes blinked anxiously as the shrieking seemed to double in volume. 'Should not we send for a policeman, Laura? It sounds as if that poor woman is being murdered.'

Laura's smile broadened. 'That's not a woman screaming, Miriam. It's Scotch Annie's husband. He was supposed to be at work, but she went down to the Lamb and Flag and found him in there drunk.'

She chuckled at the bemused expression on her friend's face. 'He's a good six feet high, and she's like a dwarf beside him, but she's a holy terror when her temper's roused. Most folk around here steer clear of her then.'

Miriam's face was regaining some colour, and she smiled nervously. She then placed the canvas bag she was carrying on to the well-scrubbed table.

'Here are the leaflets we ordered from the printers, Laura. They've just arrived. Where are Rosie and Tommy?'

The younger woman's thin face became troubled, and she explained in a low voice, 'They're upstairs. Tommy had a fit this morning. A very bad one. Rosie is having to sit with him in case his condition suddenly worsens.'

'Has the doctor seen him?' Miriam questioned without thinking, and immediately realised what she had said, and added apologetically, 'That was a very silly question, wasn't it.'

Laura didn't bother to acknowledge the truth of that statement. Medical doctors were a rare sight in Hill Street. Its residents only sporadically had sufficient money for necessities, never mind luxuries such as professional medical care.

'But you could have sent for a doctor, Laura. You know that I would have gladly paid his fee.'

'You know very well how Rosie feels about accepting your money, Miriam.' Laura's voice held a hint of asperity. 'It sorely troubled her to have you paying for her living expenses, never mind putting you to further expense on her behalf. That's why she took up her needle again, because unlike myself, she couldn't bear having her living expenses paid for by you. Even though she regards you as a friend.'

'But why should she feel like that, Laura?' Miriam truly could not understand, and staring into the puzzled green eyes, Laura could empathise with Miriam's lack of comprehension.

'How could you be expected to understand how Rosie feels, Miriam,' she thought, then wryly accepted: 'I didn't

218

understand until these last weeks when I've come to know her better.'

It was only since she had come to live in the mean fetid court, and to share the daily life of its inhabitants, and come to know some of them well, that Laura herself had discovered the fierce pride that animated many of the poor. A pride that gave them the strength to endure their harsh, hopeless lives. Born into and brought up as a member of the middle classes, Laura had always been taught to believe that the ragged, odorous, teeming masses of the poor could be sharply divided into two groupings. On the one hand there were the immoral, the drunken, the criminal, the rebellious, the idle, vicious, Godless, ungrateful poor, who were completely worthless and undeserving of aid or pity. On the other hand there were the 'Deserving Poor', who were humble, industrious, sober, moral, frugal, God fearing, worshipful of, and grateful to their 'Betters', who so kindly showed them charity in their times of trouble. But! And this was a very important but. She had been taught that there was one cardinal fact that she must always remember. That was that the 'Lower Orders', with extremely rare exception, were lacking the highly developed sensitivity and intelligence of their 'Betters', and were undoubtedly fashioned from a cruder clay incapable of any higher aspirations other than the satisfaction of their physical needs and pleasures.

Laura could accept that there were elements of truth in what she had been taught. That there were indeed numbers of the poor who could be safely slotted into the conceived divisions. But she had discovered that there were greater numbers who could not be so easily categorised. Since living among the poor in the slums of this town she had met men and women who possessed intelligence and sensitivity in abundance. Men and women whose moral standards were of the very highest. Men and women who possessed both pride and self-respect. Men and women whose only crime was to have been born into and raised in dire poverty, and who had every right to feel rebellious, and contemptuous of, and ungrateful to their self-styled 'Betters'.

Now, facing Miriam Josceleyne, knowing the essential

goodness of the woman, Laura forbore from putting her angry thoughts into words. Instead she simply said, 'Rosie has a great deal of pride, Miriam. She has been raised to abhor having to receive charity, no matter how well meant and kindly that charity might be.'

'But I don't offer her charity, Laura. I offer her help from a friend,' Miriam stated quietly.

Laura was moved by the words, and swallowed hard to dispel the lump that suddenly leapt into her throat. Then she smiled sadly. 'I'm sure that Rosie appreciates that, Miriam. And because I know that you are her true friend, then let me ask you to allow Rosie to cling on to her pride. She's had little enough in her life to cherish apart from that.'

Miriam could still not understand such reasoning, but did not press the matter any further.

'Now then, let's have a look at our leaflets.' Laura busied herself in emptying the small bundles from the canvas bag.

'Oh they look very fine, Miriam!' she exclaimed with genuine enthusiasm, and holding one of the black-printed sheets of paper up to the light of the small window she read aloud:

'Women of Great Britain, fight for your right to vote. Without that right you are slaves. With that right you become free. Join the Women's Social and Political Union. Alone you are weak! United you are strong. Join with your sisters in the struggle for freedom. Join the Women's Social and Political Union. Votes for Women!'

She laughed in delight. 'I think that sounds splendid, Miriam!'

Her friend's enthusiastic reaction to the leaflets lightened Miriam's depressed mood, and rekindled her own enthusiasm. 'We must begin the distribution straightaway, Laura. We'll stand outside the factory gates when the women go home and pass them out then.'

Laura had turned the leaflet over and was reading the words printed on the rear of it. 'All enquiries concerning the Women's Social and Political Union can be made to

Miss Miriam Josceleyne, Cotswold House, Church Green East Redditch.'

'Does the lady of the house know that you have given this address, Miriam?' Laura was uncertain of how to refer to Emma Josceleyne. Rosie Spiers had told her all of the lurid stories concerning the marriage of Hector Josceleyne and his maidservant, and Laura regarded the subject as a delicate one, and had never talked about it with Miriam.

Miriam's lips twitched with amusement. 'If you are referring to my stepmother, Laura, then you may call her that if you so wish. Emma and I are very good friends. There is no awkwardness between us concerning her marriage to my father.'

Laura flushed slightly, and would have offered apology, but the older woman motioned in dismissal. 'It doesn't matter, Laura, you weren't to know the situation between myself and Emma. I know that the gossip in the town would have us at each other's throats, but in reality we are as I've already said, close friends. She is very dear to me, and I'm happy that she has gained some advantage from her marriage.' She paused for a moment, lips still twitching amusedly, then went on, 'No, she doesn't yet know what I've given Cotswold House as the address for enquiries. But Emma won't mind. She's a free spirit.'

'Good!' Laura nodded, then asked, 'Well then, where do we start?' She hesitated and her glance went upwards to the ceiling, above which Rosie Spiers was sitting with her sick brother. 'Rosie won't be able to accompany us, Miriam. She'll have to stay here with Tommy.'

'Of course. And before we go I want to have a quick word with her.' Miriam smiled with a touch of irony. 'I must ask her if there is anything at all I can do to help Tommy?'

'*Touché!*' Laura accepted wryly.

'I suggest we begin at Allcocks, down in Badger Lane. That's a good place for us.'

Laura nodded. The firm of Samuel Allcock and Co. was the biggest manufacturer of fishing tackle in the entire world and its massive factory drew in hundreds of women and girls.

From the bottom of the canvas bag, Miriam drew out a long rubberised coat. 'I've brought this mackintosh for Rosie. I know she hasn't got one. I think that whatever the weather it might be a good idea for us all to wear mackintoshes when we go out recruiting. They're easier to wash the dirt off than our other coats, aren't they.'

Laura chuckled grimly. 'That's true. My wardrobe is practically empty I've had to throw so many clothes away. I think it's the rotten eggs and the bad fish that ruin clothes more than anything else. It doesn't matter how much I wash them, the smell still seems to hang on.'

During the week following their attempt to recruit at Holyoaksfield the three of them had tried to hold another meeting outside a factory in a barrage of filth and rotting vegetables from a gang of rowdies.

Before the two women left the house Miriam went upstairs to speak with Rosie. The seamstress looked worn out, her eyes sunken and shadowed, her thin face grey and haggard. The man lying in the bed could have been a corpse, so lifeless did he appear. Only the faint flutterings of breath showed that he still lived.

Miriam asked if she should bring a doctor, telling Rosie that she would be happy to pay his fee. But the young woman was adamant in her refusal. 'There's nothing a doctor can do for Tommy that I can't do meself, Miss Miriam.'

'But perhaps he could prescribe a treatment which might diminish the severity of Tommy's fits?' Miriam argued gently.

Rosie shook her head. 'There's no treatment that can help this poor cratur.' She used a piece of rag to wipe away the saliva trickling from the man's slack lips. 'All that can be done for him, is to make him as comfortable as I can, until the day comes when a fit kills him.' She looked up at Miriam with tragic eyes. 'And God forgive me for saying it, but the more I sees him suffer, then I can't help but wish that that day might come sooner, rather than later.'

Miriam could only pat Rosie's thin shoulder, and leave her to her sad vigil.

Outside the wind still gusted erratically, hurling flurries

222

of raindrops against the bowed figures of the two women as they hurried down Prospect Hill towards the factory of Samuel Allcock and Co. Although it was only approaching the hour of seven o'clock, the lowering skies cast a gloom that forced the early lighting of the lamps in the shops and business premises. As they passed Ernie Field's shop, Miriam lifted her umbrella canopy higher and stared beneath its rim through the plate glass windows to see the tall elegant figure of Harry Vivaldi moving within. Miriam instinctively disliked and distrusted the man, and was concerned about Emma's apparently close friendship with him. But knowing the young woman's fiery temperament Miriam feared that if she were to voice her feelings concerning Harry Vivaldi, then she would only provoke a clash with Emma. So reluctantly she kept her own counsel.

They reached the big arched entrance to the factory just as the steam whistle was shrilling the signal for work to end. Unable to manage both leaflets and umbrellas, Laura and Miriam furled the latter, and took up stations on each side of the entrance. Voices and hurrying footsteps echoed from beneath the vaulted roof of the tunnelled arch and the workers spilled out into the road from its dark confines.

'Votes for women! Votes for women!' Laura and Miriam repeated over and over again as they offered leaflets to those who came hurrying past them.

The strong wind and heavy rain made their task difficult, because with shawls pulled right over their heads, many of the women and girls were not even aware of their presence, while others pushed irritably past them.

'Doon't hinder me, I wants to get home out o' this rain!'

'Gerrout o' the way, carn't you.'

One woman stopped and briefly scanned the leaflet, then stared hard at Miriam, who was by now a sadly bedraggled figure, with rainwater dripping from the brim of her hat and running down her face.

'Show us your 'ands?' the woman ordered brusquely. When Miriam complied she jeered harshly, 'Ne'er had to do a day's work in your life, has you. No wonder you'se got the time to stand out in this bloody weather giving out these arsepapers.'

A few people took the proffered leaflets promising hastily, 'I'll have a look at it when I gets home.'

Others took the leaflets then screwed them up to hurl to the ground. 'Doon't moither me wi' this bloody rubbish!'

The flimsy paper quickly became sodden and the cheap ink started to spread and blur until the printed words were almost illegible.

Then the last stragglers had passed from out of the archway and Miriam and Laura were standing alone, staring at each other across ground thickly strewn with tattered, sodden leaflets. Laura looked utterly dispirited, and even as she examined the last leaflets that she was holding, the flimsy sheets came apart in her hands. In a spurt of annoyance she hurled the remnants from her and they landed in the streaming gutter peeling apart in the rushing torrent of water to be carried away. Miriam let her own soddened, ruined leaflets fall into the gutter also.

In a miserable shared silence the two women slowly walked away, seeking whatever shelter from the wind and rain that they could find beneath their umbrellas. At the top of Prospect Hill they halted and faced each other glumly.

It was Laura who broke the silence. 'Well, at least we won't have to wash our hair and clothes tonight. No one threw rotten eggs at us, did they? That's something to the good.'

Miriam looked down at her long mackintosh coat, glistening with water, pale and pristine in its cleanliness, and suddenly the gallows humour of the situation struck her sharply, and she began to laugh.

Laura stared at her friend in concern, wondering if she had become hysterical. The expression on her face caused Miriam to laugh even louder.

Then, between her peals of laughters Miriam gasped out, 'This is the first time that we've been prepared for a bombardment, and nobody bothers to throw anything at us. Is it our planning that's at fault, I wonder?'

Again she dissolved into helpless laughter, and after a moment Laura began to laugh also, and they fell into each other's arms, and laughed and laughed until their stomachs ached and tears ran down to mingle with the rain upon their faces, and a man walking on the opposite side of the roadway wondered anxiously if they were madwomen running loose about the town.

Chapter Twenty-Five

'Well now, Harry, what with your subs, and less the shilling for that record you broke, you aren't got a lot to come tonight, has you?' Ernie Field declared genially.

The younger man's swarthy features mirrored his sullen mood, but he kept his back turned to his employer and continued sweeping the floor.

Stooping over the opened cash drawer Ernie Field lifted the scrap of paper from it and peered short-sightedly at the scribbled figures.

'I makes it four and a tanner that you'se had in advance this week. Add a shilling for the record, that's five and a tanner you owes me.' He squinted at the open ledger on the counter, and ran his dirty fingernail down the neatly printed columns. 'You'se got a bit o' commission from the Parlaphone sale. And there's a few oddments o' needles, and a couple o' records from last week that I carried over to add to this week's sales.' He pursed his thin lips and whistled tunelessly as he mentally computed the amounts.

Harry Vivaldi stabbed viciously at a matchstalk that stubbornly refused to be shifted by the broom bristles. Saturday night, pay night, always made him disgruntled as he considered the difference in wages between what he considered himself to be worth, and what his employer actually paid him. But it was not only this fact that was souring his mood tonight. Things were not going well for him in other areas of his life either. He scowled ferociously as he thought about it.

Emma Josceleyne was still keeping him dangling on her strings like a puppet. Since their encounter in the drawing-room he had called upon her several times, and she had received him with every sign of pleasure. But she had not permitted him to be alone with her for a single moment. Always she had kept Miriam or Mrs Elwood, or even one of the maidservants with her on some pretext or other. All the time smiling slyly at Harry, as if gloating in the frustrations he was suffering. She had not finalised the business proposition either, putting him off by telling him that she was still thinking about it.

There was also, of course, the perennial problem of lack of funds. He had gone heavily into debt to buy new clothes with which to bedazzle Emma. Also, whenever he called upon her, he brought her flowers and bottles of expensive wine, and had paid for these with the rent money.

He rammed the bristles so hard against the floor that some of them broke, and still the matchstalk remained firmly stuck to the worn linoleum.

Caleb Louch had called at the house two nights ago, and unfortunately Harry had been there and the debt collector had seen him through the window, thus preventing him hiding upstairs until the man had left. The subsequent conversation between the two men had been brief and very much to the point. Pay up all arrears by tomorrow, Sunday, or Caleb Louch would take extreme measures to recover what was owing.

Again he rammed the broomhead at the matchstalk, and again it defied him.

'Here you are, then, Harry. Come and get your wages,' Ernie Field invited, and glumly the young man turned and approached the counter.

'Three shillings and nine pence,' the shopkeeper pronounced sneeringly. 'That wun't buy Bella many luxuries, 'ull it?' He shook his head in assumed bewilderment. 'I carn't understand why a good-looking 'ooman like her is content to live from hand to mouth the way she has to. You'd think that she'd have found herself a chap who could treat her the way she deserves. Buy her what she wants, and show her a good time. A pretty 'ooman like her ought to have the best, not be slaving away in that bloody laundry and living in a bloody hole like George Street.'

A glimmering of light suddenly shone faintly in the dark tunnel of Harry Vivaldi's thoughts. He forced a smile and said casually, 'Well, as a matter of fact, Mr Field, I was intended to show Bella a good time tonight. I was going to take her out for a drink, or maybe to see the second house at the Public Hall.'

Interest gleamed in the older man's eyes. 'Oh yes, you was, was you. Well the bill at the Public Hall is a load of rubbish this week. Not worth going to see, take it from me. And where was you thinking of taking her for a drink? You carn't take a lady like Bella to any of the rough pubs, can you?'

Harry shrugged offhandedly. 'Oh I don't know about that. The select rooms are mostly all right in all of the pubs.'

'Which ones?' Ernie Fields challenged disparagingly. 'They'm all bloody rough, if you asks me. You knows yourself that a woman can get insulted in any of the pubs around here.'

'Maybe, but I'll be with her, won't I?' Harry seemed unconcerned.

'Even if a chap is with a wench it doon't stop some of the hooligans from being saucy to her.' Ernie Field appeared to be very concerned about the danger to Bella Thomas's sensitive feelings of propriety. 'I should think it would be very upsetting to Bella if some drunk got saucy with her, and made improper remarks.'

Harry hid a grin, and remarked diffidently, 'It's a pity that you won't be around tonight, Mr Field. I shouldn't think any of the local hooligans would chance making improper remarks to Bella if a well-known businessman like you was with us.'

The shopkeeper puffed out his narrow chest and tried to look fierce. 'It aren't only the fact that I'm a well-known businessman that makes the hooligans think twice afore they crosses me, Harry. I've left my mark on more nor a few on 'um when I was younger. They knows well that I'm not a chap it pays to come the wrong side of.'

Again Harry was forced to hide a smile as he assumed an expression of respectful admiration. 'I know that, Mr

Field. Even though I've not been long in the town, I've heard people say that you're a tough customer when you've cause to be.'

The shopkeeper visibly preened, then offered magnanimously, 'I'll tell you what, Harry. I warn't intending to goo out tonight, but seeing as how it's a bit of a special treat for Bella, how about if I meets you for a drink. She'll be safe if I'm there, no matter what pub we drinks in.'

The light blazed through the tunnel of Harry Vivaldi's thoughts, banishing every lingering dark shadow. 'Well, I take that most kindly, Mr Field. Shall we say nine o'clock, in the saloon bar at the Plough and Harrow.'

Ernie Field ran his hand across his thinning ginger hair and his tongue snaked out along his lips. 'Nine o'clock it shall be, Harry. Now look sharp and get the shop closed. We'll be late else.'

On Saturday nights Caleb Louch followed a set routine. Beginning at six o'clock he would make the rounds of his current clients and receive from them their lists of debtors. By half-past seven he would invariably have completed those rounds and would be at his home, where his wife would have his supper waiting. This meal was always a thick beefsteak with lashings of onions and fried potatoes, washed down with a flagon of ale. He would then sit at his ease smoking his pipe while his numerous brood of children would take it in turns to tell him of their week's progress at school. Caleb Louch was a fond husband and father, who despite his readiness to use his fists on debtors, never raised a hand against his own family.

Then at nine o'clock Caleb Louch would put his bulky notebook in his pocket, kiss his wife and children good-night, and go out once more. The rest of the night would be spent in wandering from one public house to another. In each he would take a glass of ale, and invariably treat the publican. Many of whom were at various times his clients. His shrewd eyes would study the other drinkers present, and if any of them were named in his bulky notebook he would try to find out from the publican how much the debtor had been spending lately on drink. The vast majority were ready enough to give him the information because every publican in the town kept a 'Slate', whereon they marked the amount of drink given on credit, and it was in their own interest to know which of their customers were good credit risks on any particular week. Caleb Louch was the man they could rely on to tell them if someone they had allowed to run up a large tally on their Slate, was now drinking the money he owed them in some other public house.

This Saturday night the debt collector was following his normal routine, wandering from one crowded noisy, smoke-filled room to another. At intervals he found people on his current list of debtors carousing in the bars, and he discreetly made a note in his notebook. But he did not speak to them, or show any open interest in their doings. From long experience he knew that the worst time to beard a certain type of man with his debts was when that man was drinking in the company of his cronies. Alcohol imparted Dutch courage and the support of cronies engendered confidence and a readiness to fight. Caleb Louch preferred to knock on that type of debtor's door in the cold grey light of early dawn, when an aching head, sick stomach and trembling hands all combined to metamorphose the bold, reckless fighting man of the previous night into a shivering, fearful wreck.

The debt collector worked his way through the town and eventually arrived at the Plough and Harrow Hotel which stood at the junction of Front and Back Hills with Mount Pleasant, the long, gently-sloping roadway leading to the satellite villages of Headless Cross and Crabbs Cross. The ground floor of the hotel was divided between the public bar, the large saloon, and the select room. Caleb Louch stood in the passageway that interconnected with all three rooms and gave his order through the serving hatch to a heavily perspiring barmaid. Above the hubbub of talk and laughter emanating from the surrounding rooms, he heard the sound of a woman singing to the jangly accompaniment of an out of tune piano.

230

'My eye! Here's a lady bicyclist!
Look at her! Look at her! Look at her! Look at her!
She's put her petticoats up the spout,
And now she has to go without . . .'

The landlord, Albert Smith, saw Caleb Louch through the hatchway and came to speak to him.

'How bist, Caleb?'

'How bist, Albert?' The debt collector jerked his head towards the saloon from where the singing was coming. 'Got a variety turn on tonight then, have you?'

The landlord's drink bleared eyes rolled upwards in disparagement, then he scoffed, 'She ought to be on the Halls to look at her. Painted up like a whore, she is.'

The singer's tinny voice carried clearly above the general noise.

'. . . She hopes her mother won't find out,
And thinks they won't be missed.
Ohhh! My! Hi! Hi!
Keep your eye on the lady bi-
The lady bicyclisssssttt.'

The song finished to scattered applause, and after a pause the piano jangled once more and a man's voice bellowed hoarsely:

'On the road to Mandalaaaaayyyyy,
Where the flying fishes plaaayyyy. . . .'

'Jesus Christ! He's a sight worse than her!' Caleb Louch exclaimed jovially. 'You wants to watch out whom you'm letting sing in theer, Albert. They could end up by driving your drinking customers away.'

Albert Smith laid his forefinger along the side of his big plum-coloured nose and winked broadly. 'That wench who was singing is drinking more gin than any three other women in here tonight, my friend. And the blokes with her am sinking down brandy like it was Mafeking Night all over again. If I had a few more customers like them I could close the public and select and just live off the saloon.'

231

At the mention of heavy spending Caleb Louch's professional interest was aroused. 'I hope that none on 'um are in my little book here, Albert.'

The landlord instantly dismissed the idea. 'No, not them, I'd take me oath on it. It's Ernie Field who'se doing the spending. Him as sells Talking Machines down Prospect Hill theer. I don't know who the others am really. The bloke's a real Jack-a-Dandy, and the woman's painted up like an whore. Mind you, she looks as if she's bin a tasty piece o' meat in her time.' He laughed wheezily and quipped, 'Probably that was in the time o' the last Zulu War.'

As he listened Caleb Louch's acute brain was evaluating the information and coming to conclusions. 'Whereabouts am they sitting, Albert?' He grinned conspiratorially. 'I'd like to take a peep at the wench. She sounds like a very interesting cratur.'

'Over in the corner by the window,' the landlord told him, and was then called away by another customer shouting impatiently for service. He bustled off complaining loudly.

'All right, Tod, I'm acoming, hold your bloody horses 'ull you, I'se only got the one pair of hands, aren't I.'

Caleb Louch finished his drink and moved to the saloon door. He cracked it open just wide enough to peer through, and sought for and found the trio in the far corner. He studied them for a brief instant, then grinned savagely and went back to the serving hatch. By positioning himself correctly he could see the door in the saloon which led out on to the street, and so could keep track of anyone coming or going. Also there was a large mirror hanging on the saloon wall and by slightly moving his position he discovered that he could watch the trio in its reflection.

'I reckon I might just hang on and see what's what with them three,' he decided. He had a feeling that any information he could garner about what might be happening between Ernie Field, Harry Vivaldi, and Bella Thomas might some day come in useful to him. He called for another glass of ale, and stood sipping it slowly, content to wait and to watch.

Bella Thomas was by now drunk and becoming a trifle maudlin. Ernie Field was also half-drunk, and his lust for

Bella Thomas's fat white body was pulsing fiercely through him. He was sitting side by side with her on the corner bench, and under cover of the table top he was pressing his thigh against hers, and fighting against the urge to run his hand up that plump soft roundness.

At Bella's other side, sitting in the opposite angle of the corner, Harry Vivaldi was covertly watching his employer's face and smiling to himself with satisfaction as he recognised the hungry need in Field's eyes. Bella was telling the other man the story of her life. Harry Vivaldi's full lips curled in contempt as he listened to the farrago of half-truth, exaggeration and downright lies, but was forced to give Bella credit for the fact that despite her drunkenness she was still editing her tale very skilfully. Now as she told the eager Ernie Field about her triumphs on the stage, and the way she had given up her glittering career to marry her husband, Vivaldi had to fight down the rage to tell the other man: 'She was never a bloody star. Only a cheap slag, who had to drop her drawers to the management even to get bottom billing.' Instead he told himself warningly, 'No, Harry boy. Just keep your mouth shut, and don't ruin everything just for the sake of showing the old cow up. But just look at the stupid bugger!' He snarled in silent contempt at the rapt expression on his employer's drink-reddened face. 'He's eating her up. He's swallowing every soddin' word of what she's telling him. Bloody fool!'

He drained his glass, and offered, 'Another drink, Mr Field? How about you, Bella, my love?'

The woman instantly gulped her own large gin down, and Ernie Field was instantly on his feet, his hands taking the empty glasses. 'No Harry, I'll see to these. I know you can't afford it. What will you have this time, my dear? Same again, is it?'

He leered at Bella, who pouted her Cupid-bowed mouth in grotesque seductiveness at him. 'Oh but you're a real naughty boy, you are, Mr Field. You're going to get me drunk, aren't you?'

'Don't you worry about that, my dear,' he assured her gallantly. 'I'll look after you if you do get a bit tiddly.'

233

'I'll bet you will.' She winked lewdly at him, and with a last hungry look at her big breasts bulged up high by her corset Ernie Field went to the bar.

Bella smiled blearily at Harry Vivaldi. 'Are you having a good time, darlin'?' she asked, and preened herself coquettishly. 'Your boss has taken a real fancy to me, I reckon. Don't it make you jealous?'

The young man leaned closer to her across the table, and beneath its round top his hand fondled her thighs. 'Of course I'm jealous, sweetheart.' He smiled tenderly at her. 'But that don't matter. You've got to be nice to Mr Field for my sake.'

She peered owlishly at him. Then hiccupped loudly, and giggled. 'Oh, 'scuse me, won't you, darlin'. I reckon the gin's going to me head.'

He increased the pressure of his fondling fingers, forcing them deeper and pushing hard against the intimate triangle where her thighs met. 'You will be nice to Mr Field, won't you sweetheart?' he urged. 'Because if you are it will do me a lot of good in my job.'

A frown of suspicion creased her forehead, and she blinked several times in rapid succession as if she found it difficult to focus clearly on his features.

'What does you mean, be nice to him?' she questioned. 'What do you mean exactly?'

He laughed and hastened to reassure her. 'Just be nice to him, that's all, sweetheart. Just like you're being nice to him now. Talk to him, and give him a few smiles, that's all. He's very lonely, you see, sweetheart, and he enjoys having you to talk to. I can see that.'

After a moment's drunken gravity, she appeared satisfied with that explanation, and she smiled radiantly. 'O' course I'll be nice to the old bugger, darlin'. I'll even let him cop a feel, if he wants.'

'There's no need to go that far.' Vivaldi frowned in stern reproof, and she chortled happily.

'I knew that 'ud get you going, darlin'. I knew that 'ud make you jealous.'

'Shush now, he's coming back,' Vivaldi whispered urgently, and leaned back away from her, bringing his hands up and letting them rest on the table top.

By closing time Bella was staggering drunk, but the two men had stronger heads and were steadier. Ernie Field's lust for the woman was by now tormenting him unbearably, and his expression betrayed how he was feeling. Seeing this Vivaldi grinned with satisfaction.

Earlier, upon leaving work, he had called in to a licensed victualler's shop and bought a bottle of brandy and a bottle of gin, which he had secreted in the house without Bella's knowledge. Now, as they left the public house and made their way down Front Hill, with Vivaldi supporting the reeling, unsteady Bella, the young man invited, 'Why don't you come back to my place for a nightcap, Mr Field? It's a shame to spoil a good night by gooing home too early, isn't it?'

The shopkeeper stared hard at Bella's wobbling buttocks as she walked arm in arm with Vivaldi in front of him, and his tongue snaked out along his lips. 'Yes, I'll come back with you Harry,' he assented eagerly.

Bella tripped and staggered and it took all of Harry Vivaldi's strength to keep her from falling headlong.

'Can you take her other arm, Mr Field?' he beseeched.

Field was quick to comply, and his mouth dried suddenly as he felt Bella's body moulding to his side. He could not resist dropping one hand surreptitiously to squeeze her large soft buttocks as the three of them moved unsteadily down the hill.

Many of the customers lingered on the pavement outside the closed doors of the public house, talking and laughing in loud voices, and Caleb Louch lingered amongst them, his eyes fixed on the trio moving downhill. 'I reckon I might just see where you lot go,' he decided, and allowing a sufficient distance to avoid being easily seen, followed discreetly behind.

The trio made their unsteady way to George Street and disappeared down the black opening of the entry. Caleb Louch followed into the blackness then stopped and waited, allowing the men time to empty their bladders in the communal privy. Then as he heard them go into Vivaldi's house he moved quietly to stand close to the

235

door, and listened intently to them talking, their voices carrying easily through the thin warped panelling.

Harry Vivaldi poured a tumbler full of gin and pressed it upon Bella Thomas, but only poured small measures of brandy for himself and Ernie Field.

'Cheers!' The woman raised her glass and gulped greedily at the spirit.

'Here's to your very good health, my dear! And may you always look as beautiful as you do tonight,' Ernie Field toasted her gallantly.

'Pheww! It's hot, aren't it!' Bella slurred, and unbuttoned the neck of her blouse, pulling the garment open until the tops of her breasts were disclosed.

Ernie Field stared greedily at the rounded white flesh and the deep dark cleavage, and his tongue snaked out along his thin lips.

The woman drained her glass, and Vivaldi instantly refilled it, encouraging jovially, 'That's it, my sweetheart, get it down you. There's plenty more where that came from.'

She drank deeply, and then the glass fell from her hand and smashed against the stone floor. Her upper body slowly sagged forwards until her head came to rest upon the table and she snored into unconsciousness.

Vivaldi laughed and told Ernie Field: 'She always passes out like this when she's drinking. She'll not stir now before morning. It won't matter what's done to her, she won't stir.' He stared at his employer, whose features were registering disappointment.

'Will you give me a hand to get her upstairs, Mr Field? She's too heavy for me to manage by myself.'

Between them they manhandled the senseless woman up the narrow staircase and toppled her on to the bed. She lay on her back snoring stertorously.

'Hold on a minute.' Vivaldi fumbled in his pocket for a box of matches and struck one to light the stub of candle which stood on the battered chest of drawers.

'Can I ask you a big favour, Mr Field?'

The other man was feeling somehow cheated. He had thought that he was succeeding in charming this woman, and now she had passed out and all his expense and efforts had come to nothing.

'You can ask, but I aren't saying that you'll get it,' he replied sullenly.

Vivaldi gloated silently at his employer's attitude: 'You're really hungry for this fat cow, aren't you, you bloody lecher?' Aloud he went on, 'I need to undress her, and get her corsets off, Mr Field. She'll be sick in the night else, and she's too heavy for me to maul about by myself. I know you to be a man of discretion, and I know that I can trust you to say nothing about this to anyone else.'

'Nothin' about what?' Field questioned irritably.

'Well, I want you to help me undress her.'

The older man's eyes bulged in shock. 'But I'll see her naked, wun't I?'

Vivaldi shrugged and spread out his arms. 'We're both men o' the world, Mr Field, and you'll only see her in her underclothes after all. Once I've got her corset off then she'll be all right.'

Field was still incredulous. 'I'se never heard the like of this. You'm asking me to help you take her clothes off.' He stared down at the unconscious woman and mentally pictured the white flesh hidden by her clothing, and heat spread in his groin as lust pulsed fiercely through him.

Vivaldi bent and with practised hands undid buttons and loosened straps. Suddenly the big white breasts were almost naked and long underdrawers tight around plump rounded thighs were revealed to the older man's hungry stare.

'Help me turn her over so that I can get to her corset strings,' Vivaldi asked. By now Ernie Field was desperate to feel that soft white flesh and he needed no further urgings to help the other man. As they struggled with the woman's inert body, the shopkeeper's fingers dug deep into the mounds of her buttocks, and clutched greedily at the rounded thighs, feeling the heat of her body through the thin silken underclothes.

Vivaldi dextrously freed the stiff corsets, and as he did so, the great mound of her belly spilled out from the imprisoning whalebones. He felt repulsed by the sight of those folds of flesh, but Field's desire was rampaging, and he lusted to feel that fat belly against his own. Freed from the corset, Bella Thomas was rolled on to her back once more, wearing only long underdrawers and a flimsy bodice top which revealed more of her breasts than it covered.

Ernie Field was breathing hard, his eyes locked on to the defenceless body, and Harry Vivaldi's full lips twisted contemptuously. Then he whispered invitingly, 'You can have her if you want, Mr Field.'

'What?' The man gaped disbelievingly at his companion.

'I said, you can have her if you want.'

Field, still gaping, slowly shook his head as if he could not comprehend what he was hearing.

'She's laying there ready for you, Mr Field. You can do whatever you want to her now. And tomorrow she'll be none the wiser,' Vivaldi whispered huskily.

'But she's your woman!' the older man ejaculated jerkily.

'But I'm your friend, Mr Field. And a friend is ready to share things, aren't he?'

Vivaldi let his hand drop and pulled the flimsy bodice top down to display her big dark nipples. 'There now, that's a lovely pair of tits. Just imagine how they'll feel in your mouth, Mr Field.'

Lust, doubt, suspicion all flashed across Field's face, and the younger man smiled and urged sibilantly, 'Go on, Mr Field, have her now. There's only you and me will ever know about this, and like I told you, I'm a very discreet man.'

'But ... But ...' Ernie Field shook his head in confusion. 'But she's your woman,' he finished weakly.

'And I'm letting you have her tonight. Take all the time you want, Mr Field. Take all night if you want. I'll be downstairs, you won't be interrupted.'

Leaving the woman's big breasts uncovered, Vivaldi turned away and went back downstairs. There he poured himself another drink of brandy and stood toying with the glass between his fingers, his head cocked in a listening attitude, his body tensed nervously. For what seemed a long long time he waited, and then there came the faint sound of the bedframe creaking and hoarse panting and gasping. Vivaldi gusted out a sigh of satisfaction, and took a long swallow of brandy.

Outside in the darkness, Caleb Louch moved to peer surreptitiously through the dirty, cracked window pane. He saw that the young man was alone in the room, and he watched while Vivaldi settled himself comfortably at the table, the bottle of brandy before him, a cigarette between his lips.

'So that's it, is it.' Caleb Louch nodded in understanding. 'Ernie Field is tupping your woman upstairs. You're a bloody pimp, Vivaldi.'

The debt collector moved away and went silently back into George Street and homewards. He could not help but smile grimly. 'At least I'll be able to collect what's owing from you tomorrow, Vivaldi. Never mind that your woman's earning it on her back, it's still money, aren't it.'

The hours slowly passed, and the level in the brandy bottle crept steadily downwards. The sounds from above Vivaldi's head increased and subsided at irregular intervals, and he grinned in sardonic surprise. 'Jesus Christ, you've got a sight more stamina than I ever gave you credit for having, Field, you randy old bastard you!'

Eventually the brandy took effect and his head lowered on to his arms and he slipped into drunken slumber.

He was jolted into wakefulness by the jarring impact of Ernie Field's body stumbling against his chair. It was still dark outside and Vivaldi rubbed his eyes and full recollection of the night's happenings rushed in upon him.

In the glow of the oil lamp Ernie Field's face was sheened with sweat, and he appeared nervous and ill at ease, as he fumbled to button his clothes. Vivaldi grinned savagely. 'How was she, Mr Field? Had a good time, have you?'

'I've got to goo,' the shopkeeper grunted.

The young man nodded understandingly. 'Of course you have, Mr Field. We wouldn't want your lady wife to get worried about you staying out all night, would we.'

Apprehension and suspicion battled for supremacy in the older man's features.

Vivaldi winked broadly, and grinned. 'You've nothing to worry about, Mr Field. Like I told you, I'm a man of discretion, and Bella's very discreet as well. I make sure of that. Nobody but us three need ever know what's happened here tonight.'

Ernie Field stared unhappily at his employee. Then muttered, 'I must be off.'

Harry Vivaldi allowed the other man to reach the door, and then said, 'Oh, by the way, Mr Field. I wonder if you could do me a favour?'

Again suspicion and apprehension battled for dominance in Field's expression.

'You couldn't advance me a couple o' quid on my wages, could you? Only I've a very pressing bill to settle today.'

There was a silence which seemed to go on and on. Then Field gave a sickly grimace and nodded reluctantly. He rummaged in his pocket and extracted two gold sovereigns which he handed to the young man, who smiled brilliantly. 'This is really very kind of you, Mr Field.'

The other man frowned miserably, and left without speaking another word.

Vivaldi held the two gold coins close to the lamp globe, admiring their shimmering lustre and smiling happily. Then he pocketed the coins and took a long gulp from the brandy bottle, exhaling a noisy gasp of satisfaction as the fiery liquid exploded down his throat. Then he laid his head down on his arms once more and went back to sleep.

It was daylight when he was next awoken by Bella shaking him violently and shrieking hysterically. 'Look at the state of me! What happened last night? Was it you who done this? Was it? Was it?'

Fuddled by the brandy and half asleep, Harry Vivaldi rubbed his bleared eyes and squinted at the woman; then his eyes widened and shocked wakefulness rushed in upon him. Bella Thomas was standing naked and her thighs, breasts, belly and buttocks were smeared with blood and patterned with long raw scratches and deep serried indentations as if she had been savaged by the claws and fangs of a wild beast.

'You'se served me real bad you bastard! What did you want to do this to me for? And my arse is hurting me something awful as well. You bloody Turked me didn't you, you dirty swine!'

Vivaldi fought to think clearly despite his sick stomach, pounding headache and foul-tasting mouth. He was truly shocked and disturbed by the woman's injuries. A few bruises, and the occasional bite or scratch mark he could accept as just a bit of rough loving, but these red-weeping lacerations and deep indentations left by Ernie Field's nails and teeth caused him to wonder about the mental stability of the man.

'My arse feels raw, and I'm sore all over, you dirty bastard! You're a fucking animal to do this to me.' Bella Thomas was sobbing now, and the tears ran down her fat cheeks leaving runnels of mascara in the powder and rouge.

The young man decided to counter-attack. 'It wasn't me who did this to you, you bloody whore! It was your new fancy man. I've been sleeping down here all night, while you was upstairs in our bed with the bastard.'

Her grotesquely smeared face was a mask of horrified shock, and he pressed the onslaught.

'I don't know what got into you last night, you was acting so bloody shameless. You was all over Ernie Field, and no matter what I said, you just laughed in my face.'

She seemed utterly bewildered, shaking her head furiously until her great mass of frizzed hair fell around her quivering cheeks and jowls. 'I never! I couldn't have done it! I never!'

'Well there's the proof on it,' he declaimed pointing his forefinger theatrically at her wounds. Then he rose to his feet and shouted in simulated fury: 'You dirty cow! You bloody prostitute! I'll teach you to fix horns on my head!'

He punched her in the mouth and she screamed and stumbled backwards, trying to shield her head and face with her arms, but he followed relentlessly, his fists thudding into her, and she went down on to her knees howling in agony and fear. He kicked her viciously, his toe-cap burying itself in the big soft breasts, and she

241

toppled on to her side cowering into a foetal position, and all the time howling and shrieking.

A sensation of intense pleasure surged through him, and he felt an exultant strength powering his body. Again and again he kicked her, his boots punching deep into the folds of helpless flesh, and then there came a hammering against the thin wall and the bellowings of his next door neighbour. Sudden fear brought his savage onslaught to an abrupt halt, and he dropped to his knees using his hands to smother Bella Thomas's shrieks.

'Be quiet now! Be quiet will you. It's over. I won't hit you again! Be quiet, will you! Be quiet!'

Her muffled howls diminished into moaning sobs, and he listened fearfully as the hammering on the wall ceased and the angry bellowings of his neighbour died away.

'Will you stay quiet now?' he hissed at the woman, and she nodded. He took his hands from her mouth and rose to his feet. 'I'm going to bed,' he told her roughly. 'Wake me up if Caleb Louch comes.'

He left her whimpering on the floor and climbed the narrow staircase. He threw himself still fully clothed on to the bed and sucked a raw patch on his knuckles where the skin had been torn by Bella Thomas's teeth. 'Bloody cow!' he breathed angrily, and settled himself to sleep.

Chapter Twenty-Six

The offices of Harold C Browning were situated in a terrace of Regency style houses leading off the summit of Prospect Hill. He was one of a family of solicitors and the appointed Perpetual Commissioner for taking the acknowledgement of deeds of married women. Normally he would deputise one of his clerks to deal with the more mundane duties that his practice entailed, but today he had made an exception to this general rule. Seated at his desk he regarded the woman opposite him with an appreciative eye.

'So, Mrs Dolton, under the terms of the late Mrs Wilkinson's will all her assets now come to you, as the widow of Mr Arthur Dolton.'

Cleopatra Dolton drew in a long deep breath. The sight of her full firm breasts pushing out against the black silk bodice of her gown momentarily distracted the solicitor and he missed the import of her soft-voiced reply. 'I'm sorry, Mrs Dolton, could you repeat that please?'

Her dark eyes were ambiguous. She had noted where his attention had been directed. But she merely repeated, 'I wanted to know if my husband's relatives are thinking of contesting Mrs Wilkinson's will?'

'They have no grounds upon which to base any challenge to the will as it stands, Mrs Dolton. Mrs Wilkinson was of sound mind when she drew up the document. No court in the land would accept that the family of your late husband has any valid claim on the lady's estate. She had no living relatives, and had always regarded your late husband as a surrogate son.'

Cleopatra Dolton could not help but smile sardonically

as she wondered how any woman could have willingly so regarded her brutal, drunken husband.

As if he had divined her thoughts, Harold Browning's lips twitched briefly in a bleak smile. 'So, Mrs Dolton, when the necessary formalities have been completed, and you have signed various papers for me, you will inherit a very considerable amount of property, money and varied assets. Allow me to offer you my congratulations upon your good fortune, Mrs Dolton.'

An hour later Cleopatra Dolton left the offices and came out into the warm morning sunshine carrying in her reticule the papers detailing her inheritance. An inheritance which had made her a very wealthy woman.

As she walked past the gabled facade of Smallwood Hospital she suddenly thought of her own mother's wretched death and her mood became bitter. 'You died in agony, Mam, because there wasn't a penny piece in our house to buy medicine or a doctor's time. And look at me now. I could afford to buy the whole hospital ten times over.'

At the centre crossroads, instead of turning westwards in the direction of her home, she was irresistibly drawn to the opposite direction. To her birthplace. To Silver Street.

She walked purposefully down Market Place and many pairs of eyes turned towards her sensuous figure. Some people greeted her and she nodded politely in return, but did not deviate from her path. Red Lion Street was grimy in the sunlight, the factories and workshops it contained emitting the noisy clattering of machinery and the hissing, rumbling slappings of steam-driven, multi-variegated pulley wheels and belting. A few rough-looking, shabby men lounged outside the doors of the public house, and they stared hard at her as she passed, but made no attempt to speak or to impede her.

At the archway she halted and stood gazing up the narrow rancid length of her birthplace. Ragged, half-naked, scald-headed, rickety-legged toddlers played listlessly in the long alley, and several mangy half-starved dogs and cats rooted among the rotting, thickly strewn refuse in search of food. Bitter memories flooded back to torment her. Memories of hardship and want. Memories of her mother's harsh life and agonising death. Memories of her brothers and sisters dying one by one. Memories of her father raucously drunk as her mother lay dying. Memories of her father violating her own immature body when she was still only a small child. Venting his lust upon her night after night after night, until he had made her pregnant.

'Thank God the baby was stillborn,' Cleopatra thought bleakly. 'At least I did not have to live with the shame of seeing what my father had given to me growing up before my eyes.'

Unconscious volition caused her to pass under the archway and walk slowly between the fetid hovels, and her nostrils filled with the stench of poverty. Tousled headed women came to stare hostilely at her, thrusting their grimed, haggard faces out of broken-paned casements and crack-panelled doors. The children halted from play and clustered in nervous uncertainty, their eyes wide as they regarded this creature from another world, while the stick-ribbed dogs sniffed at her skirts and growled in challenge.

She reached the mean tumbledown hovel in which she had been born and raised, and halted. Now memory became all enveloping and she lost all sense of time as she heard dead voices clamouring in her ears, and in her mind's eye saw dead faces jostling to confront her.

'What's you want? Why am you staring at me house like this?' The aggressive voice belonged to a young woman, huge-bellied with pregnancy, a tiny baby in her arms and other snot-nosed, barefoot infants clinging whining to her dirty skirts.

'Here you, I'm talkin' to you! What does you want here?'

The strident nasal tones penetrated Cleopatra Dolton's consciousness, and she blinked hard and started as if suddenly roused from sleep. She stared blankly at the young woman, whose resentment was by now goading her into temper.

'Who the fuck does you think you am, lady muck? Coming 'ere and staring at me like I'm summat in a fuckin' cage?'

Cleopatra shook her head. 'I was lost in thought, that's all. I didn't mean to be rude to you.'

The young woman was not prepared to be so easily mollified. 'Who am you? That's what I wants to know!'

Cleopatra remembered parts of the documents the solicitor had read out to her that morning, and which she now carried copies of in her reticule. She smiled mirthlessly. 'My name is Mrs Dolton,' she informed quietly. 'And I'm the new owner of your house.' She turned her gaze from side to side briefly studying the adjoining tenements, then turned back to her questioner. 'In fact, I own most of these other houses as well.'

A shocked silence greeted her announcement, and her lips twisted again with a brief mirthless smile. She nodded in farewell to the young woman and turned and walked back down the long alleyway and under the arch into Red Lion Street.

As she retraced her steps towards the centre crossroads she thrust all memories of the past from her mind, and instead concentrated on the present. The recently deceased Mrs Wilkinson had owned considerable tracts of real estate including shop and factory premises, and houses, many sections of the latter being slum properties.

'I must now be one of the major landladies in the district,' Cleopatra Dolton thought to herself. She also realised that she would need help to administer her newly acquired holdings.

At the crossroads she turned northwards and made her way along Evesham Street to the shop of The Redditch Meat Company near the base of Front Hill. There were several customers in the shop when she arrived there and she went through and into the rear room telling Ozzie Clarke: 'I'll wait in the back until you've finished with these customers, Mr Clarke.'

He nodded, and smiled at her. Since their confrontation, their relationship, although still formal and that of employer and employee, had become much more relaxed and friendly in nature.

When Ozzie Clarke entered the rear room he radiated an air of excitement. 'I'm glad you've called in, Mrs

246

Dolton. I've got some important news for you.'

She smiled encouragingly at him. 'What is it, Mr Clarke?'

'Bridley Moor Farm – Alf Green wants to sell it,' he announced, and his white teeth gleamed in his sun-ruddied features. 'And he'll give us the first offer. He told me so last night. I was going to come down and see you this evening after I'd closed up here.'

She frowned doubtfully. 'The entire farm? The house as well? That would cost a great deal, wouldn't it?'

'Well, it wouldn't be cheap,' he admitted, then went on confidently, 'but it would be a very sound investment for you, Mrs Dolton. We could raise all our own stock, and what we didn't want ourselves we could sell at the marts.'

'But who would run the farm?' she wanted to know.

'Well, I know a young chap who'd jump at the chance. He's hoping to get married, and we could let him live at the house as part of his wages. I'd keep a close eye on it meself o' course.'

Still she hesitated, and a note of impatience entered his voice. 'Trust me, Mrs Dolton,' he urged. 'Buying the farm is a good investment, and a good business move as well.'

'I don't doubt what you tell me, Mr Clarke,' she hastened to assure him, 'the only thing is that today I've had some other news, and that news meant that I had a proposition to make to you . . .' She went on to explain about her inheritance then finished '. . . and what I was hoping for Mr Clarke, was that you would agree to help me to administer the rented properties. Naturally I'd increase your wages to match the added responsibility.'

He remained deep in thought for some time, then told her, 'Yes, I would have agreed to do that for you, Mrs Dolton. But there's no reason why between us we can't run the whole lot. How about if we make old Walter the manager in here and bring in a chap as his assistant; that will free me to oversee everything then, won't it? The shops, the rentals, and the farm.'

She found that this proposal needed only a very brief consideration. 'I think that that will do very well, Mr Clarke. I'll appoint you as my General Manager.'

Enthusiasm for the future burgeoned headily within her.

'I intend to come into this new venture in a full time capacity, Mr Clarke. I intend to become a woman of business.' She smiled warmly at him. 'And I also intend that you shall be fully rewarded for your part in it. You will share in all that the business gains.'

He grinned in happy acceptance. 'That's a bargain, Mrs Dolton. Shall we seal it?'

In the age old custom of the marketplace he spat on his horny palm and held it out towards her. She laughed delightedly, pulled off her glove, spat on her own palm and they slapped hands to seal the bargain.

Chapter Twenty-Seven

The October wind blustered across Church Green bullying the fallen leaves, allowing them no chance to rest, sending them tumbling and skittering in all directions. Emma Josceleyne stood looking out of the drawing-room window, and her thoughts matched the restless vagaries of the wind, veering wildly, changing direction unaccountably. For many nights now she had lain in her bed unable to sleep soundly, dominated by an ever-increasing tormenting need, a need whch consumed her even when she rose from her bed and tried to busy herself in the affairs of the day. Now she moved away from the window and paced haphazardly about the large room, her fingers trailing across polished surfaces, toying with ornaments, twisting the tassels of fabrics. Finally she hissed in exasperation and berated herself angrily, 'Be honest with yourself, girl. What you really wants and needs is a man between your legs. And that man is Harry Vivaldi.'

The vivid memory of his mouth crushed upon hers, his hard muscular body clamped about her, his tongue raping her mouth, caused her heart to pound and her breath to quicken with excitement and desire. She had not let him so much as touch her hand since that day, because she knew the effect he could have upon her, and she was determined that no man would ever dominate her sexually or mentally. But now, racked by her mental frustrations, and tortured by her sexual hungers, she decided that she was going to surrender her body to Harry Vivaldi at the earliest opportunity and find relief from her hungering. Yet even as she accepted this fact, still her native shrewdness gave her pause for caution.

'It'll have to be kept a secret. I don't want anyone else to know about it. Especially not Miriam or Mrs Elwood or the maids. But how am I going to make sure that none of them can find out?' Her brain sought feverishly for answers to that quandary. 'I could give the girls a holiday and get them out of the house for a couple of nights. And Mrs Elwood never sleeps in anyway. But there's still Miriam, aren't there. How do I get shut of Miriam for a night or two?'

Unknown to her the solution to her problem was even then opening the front gate and coming up to the front door.

The bell jangled loudly and Emma heard the hurrying footsteps of one of the maids. She cocked her head and listened hard, and heard the maid flirting. 'My, you looks ever so smart today, Reggie. Is that a new uniform you'm wearing?' For a brief instant the image of John Purvis came sharply into Emma's mind. He had stood at that same front door, dashing in plumed slouch hat, khaki uniform, lustrous leather and bright brasses, and Emma had answered to his ringing, and flirted with him just as her pert maidservant was even now flirting with the postman.

Then another voice sounded and footsteps descended the staircase and tapped across the polished floorboards of the hallway.

'Is there anything for me, Becca?'

'Yes, Miss Miriam. There's a letter, and it's from London.'

The front door slammed shut and the double-peaked shako of the blue-uniformed postman moved back through the gate and went from Emma's view.

'Ahh, here you are, my dear.' Miriam Josceleyne came into the drawing room, the already opened letter in her hands. Flushed with excitement, her green eyes shining, the frail-bodied woman held the sheets of notepaper towards Emma. 'It's from the Union offices in Clement's Inn, Emma, and it's signed by Christabel Pankhurst herself. That's a great honour, isn't it?'

'Is it?' Emma smiled teasingly. 'I thought that it was her

Mam who's the queen of the suffragettes? Seems to me that getting a letter from the daughter aren't quite the same honour as getting one from the old lady.'

Miriam had been subjected to her young friend's teasing over her membership of the suffrage movement for many weeks now, and she refused to rise to the bait. 'I would regard a letter from any of our national leaders to be a signal honour. So it's of no use your trying to tease me about it, Emma. I'll not bite. You would be wise to join yourself, rather than mock those who are members.' Her smile took any sting from the gentle rebuke.

Emma smiled fondly. 'So then, Miriam, what's happening at headquarters to make the generals write to you?'

'Parliament is to reassemble for the autumn session on the twenty-third.' Miriam paused, to think for a moment then said, 'Yes, that's only three days from now, isn't it? And the Movement is to demonstrate at the House of Commons on that day, and make our demand for the right to vote to the Prime Minister himself. The Redditch branch is invited to send a delegation to join in the demonstration.'

Emma could not help but chuckle in wry amusement. 'Send a delegation? But there aren't enough of you in the Redditch branch to make up a delegation, are there? I thought that there had to be at least half a dozen in a delegation? So what are you going to do? Cut yourselves in halves?'

Miriam Josceleyne was too excited to pay heed to her friend's teasing. She was already planning aloud. 'I shall pay the neighbours to care for Tommy, and then Rosie, Laura and myself can travel down to London tomorrow.' She laughed delightedly. 'What fun it will be. I've never been to London, and I doubt that Rosie or Laura have either. Would you like to come with us, Emma? Please say that you will.'

Normally Emma would have been only too ready to take such a trip, but today her mind was engrossed with Harry Vivaldi. She silently blessed this turn of fortune which would enable her to have the house to herself, and aloud said with apparent regret: 'I'm sorry Miriam, but I really can't come with you, much as I'd like to. I have to attend to some matters for my Mam.' She improvised fluently. 'I've arranged for a specialist doctor to examine her, and I want to be there when he does.'

Miriam frowned with concern. 'I didn't know why. Why didn't you tell me about it? I won't go to London. I'll stay here and help you with your mother.'

A faint sense of guilt assailed Emma as she saw the genuine concern in her friend's expression. 'No, you must go down to London,' she insisted forcefully. 'It's very important to you to go, I know that, Miriam. Even though I tease you, I do appreciate the worth in what you and your friends are trying to do. My Mam's not ill or anything now, so there's no call for you to worry about it. I'm having the doctor to her just as a precaution.'

The older woman still hesitated uncertainly. 'Are you sure that you don't need me, Emma. I couldn't bear to go, if I thought that that was the case.'

'Listen, you get on off and see Laura Hughes and Rosie Spiers right this minute. You'll not have enough time to make all your arrangements else.' She physically propelled the other woman from the room. 'Go on now, be off with you!'

Miriam surrendered, and went off happily to arrange matters, and Emma returned to the drawing-room, a satisfied smile curling her full lips in pleasurable anticipation of the coming nights that she intended to spend with Harry Vivaldi.

Chapter Twenty-Eight

Ernie Field had no appetite for the breakfast which his wife placed before him. He stared at the bacon, black pudding and fried eggs swimming in grease, and scowled as he pushed the food away from him.

'What's up with it?' his wife demanded aggressively.

'It's too bloody greasy!' he growled.

'But you always says you likes the fat poured over it?' she protested.

'Not a bloody gallon of it.'

'There's no pleasing you, is there! You'm just contrary!' she grumbled.

He flared back, shouting angrily. 'If you doon't like the way I am, then you knows what you can do, doon't you. The bloody door's always open for you to goo through.'

'And I'll goo through it one o' these days, Ernie Field, and then see how you'll like it.'

'The sooner the better for my liking,' he bawled, and jumping to his feet, he lifted the platter of offending food in his hand and threw it against the wall. The plate shattered and the grease and food added to the stains across the wallpaper of previous meals so disposed of.

Mrs Field howled like a wounded animal and burst into loud sobs, burying her face in her apron, and the man stormed out of the room.

As he left his front door his neighbour exited simultaneously and grinned slyly.

'Good morning, Mr Field, lovely day aren't it?'

'Is it?' Field grunted sourly, and the man's grin broadened.

'I hope everything's all right with Mrs Field. My Missus

thought she heard her crying out just now, like she was taken badly or something. You know how my Missus likes to keep an eye on your wife; Mrs Field being so poorly these days.'

'My Missus is just fine, thank you,' Field grunted and walked away.

His house was one of a row of three-storeyed houses standing on the Millsborough Road which sloped down to the valley of the River Arrow on the south eastern edges of the town. Normally Ernie's Field's sour moods were soothed and his ego massaged by contemplating the road he dwelt in. The houses were fairly new, and solidly built, and inhabited by a very respectable class of people. Householders in Millsborough Road possessed worth and standing in the town. They might lack the same social cachet as the dwellers on the lower slopes of Red Lane, or the recently developed Salop Road, but nevertheless Millsborough Roadians could hold their heads high and walk proudly in the sure knowledge of their established position in the middle ranks of town society.

This morning however, Ernie Field's progress did not mellow his sour mood. The reason for this was the behaviour of his assistant, Harry Vivaldi. It was now several weeks since that Saturday night when Ernie Field had satiated himself on the body of Bella Thomas, and concerning the night the shopkeeper was trapped in a dichotomy of feeling. On the one hand he lusted to repeat it, and on the other hand he still feared possible repercussions from it. On the Monday following that night he had gone to his shop in a fever of apprehension, dreading possible attempts at blackmail from his assistant. But Harry Vivaldi had not by word or gesture even hinted at what had occurred, and neither had he done so in the days following. Of course, he had also not mentioned the two pounds he had borrowed on that night, and even though it irritated him immensely, Ernie Field had not been able to bring himself to mention that money either. Both men had acted as though the events of that night had never happened.

It was this fact that was now daily exacerbating the

sourness of Ernie Field's moods. He could not understand why Vivaldi did not mention what had happened. Naturally, in the early days, Ernie Field had been grateful for Vivaldi's silence on the matter. He had feared that he had gone too far in assuaging his perverted desires, and that if Bella Thomas so choose, she could make life virtually impossible for him. But then, perversely, as the days passed and nothing was said, the very lack of any mention began to trouble the shopkeeper, and he feared that perhaps his assistant was playing a very deep game that might eventually end in his, Ernie Field's, disadvantage. Added to this was the uncomfortable fact that his lust to once more possess the body of Bella Thomas was torturing him almost beyond endurance.

'I'm going to tackle Vivaldi about it,' he decided now as he reached the top of Millsborough Road and crossed over to Alcester Street which would lead him to Church Green. 'I can't goo on like this any longer. It's driving me bloody mad!'

While Ernie Field was walking up Millsborough Road, Harry Vivaldi was opening the shop on Prospect Hill. Like his employer he had his own reasons for making no mention of that Saturday night's events. But those reasons were not as Field feared. Vivaldi was not playing some deep game. Instead he had quite simply been afraid. When he had sobered up from his debauch he had found Bella Thomas lying semi-conscious where he had left her. In his brutal drunken assault he had hurt her more seriously than he had realised, cracking several of her ribs and concussing her badly. In his initial panic, his first impulse had been to run out in search of help, but even as his hand had grasped the doorknob he had suddenly recalled her other injuries – those inflicted on her by Ernie Field, and he had abandoned all ideas of seeking outside help. Although a man might beat his wife or mistress with impunity, it was quite a different matter to subject her to an unnatural sexual assault, which included sodomising her. A sizeable proportion of men, and even some women, would be prepared to condone, even to applaud, a physical beating, but very few would condone perverted sexual practices. It would be assumed that it was himself who had abused Bella in that way, and gossip would spread the news like wildfire. And if that gossip reached the ears of Emma Josceleyne, then he could abandon all hope of ever having her. The worst possible scenario, which he would not allow himself even to think about, was if Bella Thomas herself was to tell the world that he had aided and abetted Ernie Field's assault upon her helpless body.

Vivaldi had therefore cared for Bella alone. Forcing himself to treat her gently, and to nurse her wounds. Bella had mistaken his fear of retribution for genuine remorse, and had forgiven him. She had not been able to go to her work, sending the excuse that she had fallen down the stairs. An excuse which was greeted with knowing guffaws by her employers and fellow workers. So, bereft of Bella's wages, Vivaldi had not been able to afford to drink or to go out in search of enjoyment, and had even been forced to limit his pursuit of Emma Josceleyne to very brief and irregular social calls.

As he carried the shutters into the rear of the shop he glumly cursed his bad luck. 'If it hadn't have been for that bloody night, I'll bet I could have had Emma by now. I wish I'd never took that bastard back home with me. But then, how was I to know that he's a bloody pervert.' Another thought gave him some cause to cheer up a little however. 'At least Bella's gone back to work now, so she'll have a few bob to give me come Saturday. God, I'm dying for a drink.' He grinned wryly. 'Or two, or three, or four.'

He carried the last shutter into the rear, then came to stand outside the front door, enjoying the freshness of the morning.

'Good morning, Mrs Trout.' He smiled charmingly and half bowed to a stout-bodied matron passing.

'Good morning, Mr Vivaldi.' The woman fluttered and preened at being smiled at by such a handsome young man.

Vivaldi's smile stayed in place until he glanced up the hill and saw his employer approaching. 'God save us, here he comes, "Death at the Feast"!'

256

He stepped back into the shop and picking up a duster, began to polish the horns of the Talking Machines. As he worked he thought briefly of how his initial plans to use Bella as a tool against his employer had so badly gone awry. 'I suppose in one way I can only blame myself,' he admitted ruefully. 'If I hadn't of set about her like I did, then she'd have had only the marks of what he'd done to her to show. I could have stuck to the original plan then, couldn't I?'

'Morning Mr Field. Fine day, aren't it?' he greeted, as Ernie Field came scowling into the shop.

The other man made no reply. Instead he shut the door and bolted it, then turned the window sign to 'Closed'. Staring hard at Vivaldi he jerked his head towards the rear of the premises.

Mystified, Vivaldi followed as Field led the way into the back room.

'I've made me mind up to have it out with you, Vivaldi,' he announced grimly. 'This has bin let to drag on long enough. What's your game? Come on now, out with it! What's your game?'

The young man's mouth gaped with shock, and he was so taken aback that he could not answer.

'You heard me. What's your game?' the shopkeeper demanded, his anger fuelled by the other man's reaction.

Now Vivaldi's finely honed instincts galvanised into action, and to gain time to think he shrugged elaborately. Although he was a physical coward, he did not fear the puny-bodied shopkeeper, confident that Field was not a man who would use violence despite his braggadocio.

'Am you gooing to give me an answer?' Field was trembling with tension. 'I wants to know what your game is?'

By now Vivaldi's quick wits had presented him with the probable explanation of what was driving the other man to act so aggressively. But, shrewdly he decided to goad him a little further and gain confirmation. So once more he shrugged his shoulders and assumed an expression of bafflement.

'I don't know what you mean, Mr Field. I haven't got any game.'

257

The last instinct of caution disappeared from Field's mind and he blurted out. 'It's about me and your missus I'm talking, Vivaldi. And what happened between us that night.'

Satisfaction flooded through the young man's being, and he inwardly exulted. 'I thought that it was, you dirty old bastard. I thought that was what was in your mind.' He feigned an expression of deep regret, and said in a tone of quiet reproach. 'I was prepared to forget all about that, Mr Field. It's a pity you've seen your way to bring it all up again.'

It was the shopkeeper's turn to look surprised, and he stared hard at the younger man, as if seeking for hidden motives. Then he blustered, 'Well I'm a straight sort of man, Vivaldi, and I likes to have things out in the open.'

'Not the things like you did to Bella, I'll bet,' Harry Vivaldi sneered inwardly, but he made no answer, only shook his head in apparent regret.

There was an uneasy silence for some moments, then Field asked uncertainly, 'How is her?'

Vivaldi nodded solemnly. 'She's well enough, Mr Field.' He did not elaborate, only lapsed once more into silence.

The shopkeeper's hands clenched and unclenched nervously, while his features twitched visibly. At least he said hesitantly, 'I've bin a bit concerned about her, Vivaldi. Only there's times when I gets a bit rough in loving, if you knows what I mean.'

Harry Vivaldi's handsome features wore a pensive expression, but his thoughts were racing. He instinctively realised that if he made the right moves he could not only retrieve what he had thought to be a lost cause, but could also gain all that he had previously hoped to achieve, and more besides. Careful to keep any calculating expression from his face, he looked levelly at the other man and told him. 'You've been straight with me, Mr Field, and now I'll be straight with you. I acted as a friend towards you that night by giving you Bella. And you repaid my friendship badly. You went too far with her.'

He held up his hands to silence the other man's attempted reply.

'No! You've had your say, now let me have mine.' He softened his hard tone. 'Now I can understand how you might have got a bit carried away with yourself, Mr Field. After all, Bella is a fine woman, and when she's in bed with you, then I know myself that a man can get really excited so that he forgets himself, and goes a bit farther than he might have meant to go. I can understand that. And I know very well that a lot of women like a bit of rough loving more than they like the soft touch.'

He fell silent, evaluating the effect of his words, and Field made no reply, only remained staring intently at him.

'Yes, I've got you now haven't I, you perverted bastard!' Vivaldi jeered in his mind. Then he went on in a friendly way, 'The only thing that was wrong with what you did to Bella, was that you did it too soon. You should have spent a few more nights with her, and brought her to it slowly, Mr Field. She wouldn' have objected then, I can vouch for that. But the way you went at her . . . well, it was like a bull at a gate, wasn't it. No wonder she was so upset. Do you know, it was all I could do to stop her running to the bloody police about it. To listen to her, you'd tried to bloody murder her.'

The shopkeeper's face blanched to a sickly grey pallor. 'I never meant no harm to her,' he flustered. 'I was drunk, that was the trouble. If I'd have been sober I never would have done anything to her.' He paused, then said accusingly, 'Anyway, it was as much your fault as it was mine, Vivaldi. You encouraged me. You put me up to it.'

'But it was you who did it,' the younger man snapped curtly.

Field's grey pallor was that of a corpse. 'I never meant to harm her,' he said weakly. 'I never meant her no harm. It was only a bit of rough loving.'

'I know that.' Vivaldi's tone was reassuring. 'And that's why I've tried so hard to keep Bella quiet about it. She was all for going to see your Missus about it at one time you know.' He paused to let the words sink fully home. 'But I've managed to stop her so far. And it's cost me a pretty penny as well, I'll tell you. What with paying for her medicines, and her having to lay off working, and the presents I've had to buy her to keep her from whingeing and whining to her friends about what happened. You know what women are like for telling each other all their secrets, Mr Field. I've been on tenterhooks, I have.'

Field was by now beginning to regard Vivaldi as his ally. 'Will she carry on keeping her mouth shut, do you think, Harry?'

'I'll do my best to see that she does, Mr Field,' Vivaldi assured. 'But it might help if you was to make some amends to her yourself, you know.'

'Make amends?' Field asked warily, and Harry Vivaldi noted the gleam of doubtful suspicion in his employer's eyes, and trod circumspectly.

'Well, I was thinking that if you was to come home with me sometime, and make her some sort of apology, it might soothe her feelings,' he suggested diffidently.

Ernie Field pondered the idea for some time, then questioned doubtfully, 'Do you really think it will do the business, me apologising to her?'

Vivaldi nodded confidently. 'Oh yes, I'm sure of it. She was very taken with you, you know. She thought you were a real charmer. I'm sure you could both be friends again in due course.'

'Friends?' A calculating look passed across Field's features, and as his imagination began to stir, his tongue snaked out along his thin lips. 'She'd be friends with me again?'

'No doubt of it,' Vivaldi assured heartily. Then he lowered his voice to a confidential whisper, 'Just between you, me and the gatepost, Mr Field, Bella is going to be in need of a good friend shortly.' He winked lewdly. 'Only I've got other irons in the fire, if you get my meaning, and I shan't be staying with Bella for much longer. She'll be all alone in the world then, and she'll be in need of a friend.'

Ernie Field drew in a long breath, and lust rose hotly within him as he pictured himself being Bella Thomas's good friend when she found herself alone in the world.

'Anyway, just leave it with me, Mr Field,' Vivaldi smilingly invited. 'And I'll see to it that everything turns

260

out all right for all of us.'

For the first time for weeks Ernie Field's spirits lifted, and he smiled back at his assistant. 'All right then, I'll leave it to you . . . Harry.'

Later that morning the railway delivery van dropped off a box of records at the shop and Harry Vivaldi happily busied himself in sorting and cataloguing them. He put four aside as he came to them.

'What are these?' Field noticed.

'That's that special order for Mrs Josceleyne. Two Harry Champions, a Phylliss Dare and the new one of Daisy Dormer's. Mrs Josceleyne wanted them delivered to her as soon as they came. I'll drop them off at lunchtime if you like.'

Field grinned salaciously. 'You'm becoming very thick with Mrs Josceleyne aren't you, Harry.'

The young man shrugged non-committally, his swarthy features ambiguous.

'Comes from Silver Street, you know. She's one of Winston Farr – the chimney-sweep's – kids. Did herself a power o' good when she got wed to old Hector Josceleyne. Caused a few ructions that wedding did.' Ernie Field chuckled at the memory. 'Bit skinny for my taste is young Emma, but she's a pretty wench for all that.' He stared questioningly at his assistant. 'Is she one of the irons you'se got in the fire, Harry?'

'Of course not,' Vivaldi denied, but kept his head down and continued sorting the records.

At midday he took the four records directly to Cotswold House, and the young maid, Becca, answered the door.

'My word Becca, you're looking pretty today.' He smiled at the girl, unable to keep from trying to charm every female that he met. 'Is your mistress at home?'

She blushed and giggled and scampered off, to return within moments. 'You'm to come into the drawing room, Mr Vivaldi.'

Emma Josceleyne was wearing outdoor clothes, a wide-brimmed feathered hat was perched on her high-piled chestnut hair.

'Oh, were you going out?' Vivaldi asked.

She shook her head. 'I've just come back in. I've been down to the station to see Miriam off. She's gone to London for a couple of days.'

The young man felt a distinct sense of relief. Although Miriam Josceleyne was always polite to him, he sensed her acute dislike, and always felt constrained and uneasy when she was present, as she frequently had been since the day he had grabbed Emma.

'Well now, Harry. We haven't seen much of you lately, have we? I was starting to wonder if you'd found other amusements?' Emma's tone held challenge.

Normally he would have gladly accepted that challenge, and entered into a flirtatious bout of verbal fencing. But a sudden overwhelming impatience with all the veiled hints and half-concealed meanings of their conversations irresistibly impelled him to blurt out: 'I haven't been calling as often because I'm too much in love with you to play these games any longer, Emma.'

Even as he mouthed the words he was appalled, and cursed himself for having dropped his guard and allowed her the opportunity to deliver a killing stroke. 'What the fuck is the matter with me?' he screamed in his mind. 'I must have gone stark raving mad!'

She remained standing very still, staring at him with a strange intensity, then a smile quirked her lips.

He took that smile to be her sneer of triumph at having finally forced him into abject admission, and furious with himself said angrily: 'There, I've told you now, and made a bloody fool of myself, haven't it? Well I'll not trouble you any further.' He pitched the parcel of records on to one of the armchairs and turned to leave.

'Harry, don't go.' She stepped towards him, and he swung back, suspicion battling with hope in his heart.

Her face was very serious. 'Tell me again,' she ordered.

He scowled resentfully, then swallowed back his impulse to make an angry refusal, and gritted out, 'I'm too much in love with you to play these games any longer.'

Still she stared with that strange intensity, her lips still quirked in that ambiguous smile. Then she nodded slowly, and whispered, 'Very well, Harry. I think that I believe

262

you. Go now . . .'

His spirits fell.

'. . . and come back here tonight. I'll be alone then.'

His spirits soared, and he hardly dared to believe that he had heard her say the words. He moved towards her, his arms oustretched, but she stepped back and held her own hands up in rebuff.

'No, not now, Harry. Come tonight, at ten o'clock. Come the back way, and make sure that no one sees you, and that no one knows you're coming. Go on now.'

Feeling weirdly light-headed, and still hardly daring to believe that he had heard her say what she had said, he went from the house.

'Sent him packing again, have you?' Mrs Elwood came into the drawing-room. 'Just as well really, my duck. I've bin hearing a few tales about him.'

'What sort of tales?' Emma asked curiously.

'About him and that 'ooman he lives with.' The cook's fat face mirrored her unease. 'I know that he tells us that he only lets her share the house as a favour to his Mam. I was told the other day that he lives with her as man and wife. And I was told that he knocks her around as well.'

Emma made no immediate reply; instead she mulled over this information in silence. She found that it made no difference in her feelings towards him. Those feelings, she readily admitted, were compounded mainly of lust, interspersed with a liking for his company.

'Well?' Mrs Elwood pressed.

'Well what?' Emma riposted.

'Well how does that make you feel about him? Knowing that he's sleeping wi' that 'ooman, and he's serving her badly?'

Emma shrugged. 'It's only gossip. You've no proof.'

The fat woman shook her head regretfully. 'You wun't be told, 'ull you, my wench. If you'se got any sense you'll send him packing for good and always. I know he's pretty looking, and he's smooth-tongued with it, but from what I'se found out, he's a bad 'un.'

'You've always said how much you liked him,' Emma accused.

'Oh yes he's likeable, I'll grant you that. And he's good company as well. But he's arter you for his own ends, and not for your own good, my duck.'

The young woman tossed her head impatiently. 'I can take care of myself, Mrs Elwood, I know what's what.'

'That's as maybe, but sometimes a bloke can worm his way into your heart without you realising it. And by the time you has realised it, why then it's too late, and he's got you wheer he wants you.'

Emma recognised the wisdom in the other woman's words, but contemptuously rejected the idea that she could be entrapped in that manner by any man, and she voiced the same. 'I'm not some green young girl, Mrs Elwood. I learned my lessons years since. You've no need to worry your head about me and Harry Vivaldi. He'll jump through my hoop, I won't be jumping through his.'

Mrs Elwood hissed impatiently, and her eyes were troubled as she said, 'I wish you'd be told, girl. You should get shut of Harry Vivaldi. He's no good. And if you wun't believe me, then goo and ask Bella Thomas about him.'

Emma frowned and waved her arms in a gesture of dismissal. 'Just leave it, will you. The last thing in the world that concerns me is what Bella Thomas might be thinking. I know what I'm doing, Mrs Elwood, so there's no call for you to moither your head about me and Harry Vivaldi.'

Chapter Twenty-Nine

Because she was still showing the effects of her savage beating, and her ribs were very painful, the foreman had given Bella Thomas lighter work in the ironing and folding department of the laundry, a kindness which created considerable resentment among some of her fellow employees.

'They didn't shift me the last time my bloke give me a hammering.'

'I reckon her and the boss am having a bit on the bloody side.'

'Just goes to show girls, paint your face like a trollop, and you gets an easy job give you.'

Others were more charitable.

'Now fair play, you lot. Her's showed me the strapping round her ribs. They'm broke near to pieces.'

'She's bin served real bad, the poor cow.'

But the charitable few were heavily outnumbered by the hostile many.

'Must have bin a bloody big flight o' stairs her fell down then.'

'I didn't know they had any bloody stairs in George Street.'

'It's all bleedin' rope ladders theer, aren't it.'

'You know what, girls, her chap must have the biggest pair o' boots in Redditch, to do that amount o' damage.'

'I doon't know about boots, I reckon he must have the biggest cock to be able to satisfy the fat cow.'

'Ahhrr, if her cunt's as big as her belly his cock must be as big as a bloody stallion's.'

'He most probably calls in the Rifle Volunteers when her

wants a bit. Their drill hall's only just round the corner from George Street, aren't it.'

'I dunno, I reckon it 'ud take more than the "Old and Bold" to give her the needful. My bloke was in it for ten years and he's never bin able to satisfy me.'

The comments and the raucous laughter were directed at Bella Thomas day after day. At times she was driven to fury, and would have rounded on her tormentors, but she knew that if she did so, then they would present a united front, and she would only end up getting another beating. So she tried to ignore them, but their unremitting hostility and the cruel gibes wore her down, and sometimes she shed self-pitying tears in her private moments.

She was able to draw comfort from one fact however, and that was that Harry's violence towards her had halted since the night of the beating. Since then he had treated her very kindly, nursing her and dressing her wounds with considerable gentleness, and telling her of his remorse for what he had done. He had even forgiven her for what had happened between herself and Ernie Field. She totally accepted the blame for that particular happening. During her past there had been many other occasions when drink had overcome her senses, and she had awoken in strangers' beds, found herself looking into strangers' faces, and had had no clear recollection of how she had come to be there. So, despite her hard times at work, she was feeling happier on the whole than she had felt for some considerable period.

On this morning she worked contentedly. The most hostile among her tormentors appeared to have tired of their sport, and were leaving her alone, and she savoured the memory of the previous night, when for the first time since the beating she and Harry had made love. She would have let him use her body as he chose, despite the pain it would have inflicted upon her damaged ribs, but he had shown her consideration. He had refused to risk hurting her by having full intercourse, but instead had allowed her to caress and kiss him and bring him to satisfaction with her mouth and tongue. Immersed in the memory she murmured, 'I love you, Harry. I'd do anything for you.

266

Anything at all.'

Her reverie was shattered by the shrilling of the steam whistle signalling the midday break. There was a ripple of ironic cheering as the women applauded their brief respite from the gruelling toil, and they hurried to gather in their coteries and eat their meagre lunches.

Bella Thomas sat alone and stolidly munched her slab of bread and dripping, and drank from her bottle of cold tea. While she was eating the foreman came in search of her.

'You'se got a visitor,' he grinned teasingly. 'You must be giving him cause to check on you, Bella. Coming here like this.'

Flustered she put down her half-eaten bread and dripping and hurried out of the steam-filled building to the gate where the elegant figure of Harry Vivaldi stood waiting.

'Are my clothes done?' he demanded.

The laundry workers were allowed to do their own washing and ironing during their breaks or before the start of the work hours, subject to a deduction from their wages for using the firm's soap, water and equipment, and Bella had taken a bundle of clothing with her that morning.

'I haven't ironed them yet, darlin'. I was just having a bite to eat first.'

He snorted impatiently. 'I need a change of vest and drawers, and a fresh shirt and collar. I've got to do a music party tonight.'

She was instantly curious. 'Where are you going, darlin'? Is it somewhere posh? Do you want me to help you push the cart there?'

Sometimes, when Vivaldi took the Talking Machines and records to an evening 'music party', he had allowed her to push the handcart and its load to the venue so that his own clothing would not become soiled or rumpled with the manual labour.

He frowned angrily, and she flinched in dread that she had upset him. Then he forced a smile. 'No, sweetheart, I'm not having you strain your ribs. I can manage.'

'Where is it then?' She could not help persisting.

'Somewhere up Webheath way, I think,' he answered vaguely. 'Ernie Field knows where. He's going with me tonight.'

'I can iron your clothes now, darlin'. And I'll bring them back home when I finish work.'

'No, that'll be too late. I've got to go to Webheath before you'll be done here. Look, just iron me a shirt and collar and bring me a change of vest and drawers. I'll wait here.'

'All right darlin'. I'll be as quick as I can.' She was pathetically eager to please him.

'Have you got any money?' he wanted to know. 'I'll need a bob or so in my pocket, won't I?'

She looked crestfallen. 'No, I aren't got a penny piece 'til pay day.'

'Well, see if you can sub a couple of bob for me.'

'All right, darlin'.'

She hurried away and Vivaldi watched her go with a strange and uncomfortable *mélange* of feelings stirring inside him. Her pathetic eagerness to please him and her slavish obedience touched a softer chord in his nature invoking a feeling akin to pity for her. But that feeling in its turn provoked inner resentment that he was able to be moved so. He did not want to feel any sort of pity for her. He wanted to be able to finally discard her from his life with as little emotion as he would feel when tossing away a smoked cigarette stub.

By the time she returned to the gate carrying the bundle of clothes and a florin coin she had subbed for him clutched in her hand, the momentary softness had been crushed in Harry Vivaldi's heart, and he told her brusquely: 'Don't wait up for me, it'll be really late by the time I'm finished. From what Ernie Field's told me I'll probably get offered a bed there, so if that's the case I'll not bother coming back home until tomorrow sometime.'

'All right darlin'.'

She stood watching him walk away, and her mascaraed eyes suddenly brimmed with tears.

'Don't ever leave me, will you darlin',' she cried out in her mind. 'Please don't ever leave me.'

Chapter Thirty

The streets were dark and deserted when Harry Vivaldi made his way towards Cotswold House. He took care to avoid the pools of lamplight, and stared cautiously around him making sure that he was not being seen entering the gate and going down the side entry of the building.

The back door was unfastened and he entered the big kitchen, its long space dimly lit by a single gaslight turned very low. Puzzled by the fact that Emma Josceleyne was not there to greet him, he moved on into the house. The central hall was again only illuminated by a single hissing gaslight. The drawing-room was empty and in darkness, as were the other rooms on the ground floor, and only the ticking of clocks broke the silence. He went to the foot of the broad staircase and listened hard, wondering if Emma was playing some perverse game of her own; wondering if in fact she was actually here in the house.

At last he called softly up the stairs, and when there was no reply, called again louder. This time he heard her voice, but it was muffled by distance, and he could not distinguish what she said. Quickly he went up the stairs and moved along the passageway between the bedrooms and saw that the door of the master bedroom was ajar. His breathing quickened, and his excited anticipation caused his throat to feel thick and his mouth to dry. He lifted his hand and slowly pushed the door wider. His sharply in-drawn breath was an audible hiss as by the soft light of an oil-lamp he saw Emma lying on top of the bed, wearing a silken nightgown which moulded itself to the curves of her body. Her waist-length hair was unbound and fell in a soft lustrous cloud about her neck and shoulders, and spread across the pillows in shimmering waves. She looked at him and smiled, and lifted her arms in invitation, and as he moved towards her he began to tear his clothes from his body.

Emma's lips opened moistly as he threw aside his upper clothing and she saw his muscular torso, his skin smooth and pale in the lamplight. He sat on the side of the bed and leaned down to kiss her, his hands clutching her upper arms. Just before his mouth closed upon hers she whispered, 'Slow and gentle, Harry. Take it slow and gentle.'

Their mouths met and opened and their tongues probed and mingled. She could taste the harsh sweetness of brandy on his breath and feel his hands caressing her arms and shoulders. After long long moments he pulled back from her, and deftly took off his lower clothing. Her breath caught in her throat as she saw his long and thick manhood throbbing powerfully, jutting out from its forest of black hair. Then he delicately lifted the long nightdress up and over her head, and as she once more lay back against the pillows, he feasted his eyes on her naked body. She felt a delightful languor and sighed with pleasure as his fingers moved in slow, gentle, lingering exploration of her thighs and belly and breasts, and his lips and tongue followed, suckling, nibbling, tasting, seeking out her intimate body, savouring the silky softness of her private flesh. Then his mouth captured her own mouth once again, and now his hands moved with more urgency, penetrating the hot moistness between her legs, cupping and squeezing the swelling globes of her breasts, and the firm roundness of her buttocks. Her need for him burgeoned uncontrollably, and her hunger to enfold his body pulsed through her, and she moaned with wanting and moved urgently against him. She felt his warm, hard thighs come down between her own and she spread herself wider. Her hands moved across his broad muscular back and shoulders, fingers digging deep into the flesh, her thighs crushing around his slender hips.

'Now Harry, now,' she urged huskily, and tensed her buttocks and lifted her hips so that he could enter her. She

270

cried out in pleasure as his manhood filled the aching void between her legs; and as he thrust and thrust and thrust ever harder, ever quicker, ever deeper, waves of need exploded through her body and she surrendered to her long frustrated hungers and allowed herself to dissolve into wriggling, clutching, mindless greed, submerged and lost in ecstasies of the flesh.

Chapter Thirty-One

For Miriam Josceleyne, Laura Hughes and Rosie Spiers their first impression of London was a confusion of noise, bodies, traffic and smutted, sulphurous air. The streaming, rumbling traffic jamming its streets and the people swarming through its confined thoroughfares, filling the air with a babble of tongues and cries, made them feel as if they had been ingested into a human anthill. Carrying their small valises, buffeted and jostled by hurrying strangers and black-grimed towering buildings frowning down upon them, they made their nervous progress towards their goal – the office of the Women's Social and Political Union, in Clement's Inn, adjacent to Fleet Street.

Dusk fell before they reached their destination, but the loss of daylight was hardly discernible as the globed gaslamps flared, and the huge plate glass windows of the shops shone brilliantly on to crowded pavements. In Fleet Street itself the three women gazed with awe at the various signs denoting the offices and print shops of the great national newspapers.

'If just one of these gave us their full backing, it would make our task so much easier,' Laura stated, with aggrievement in her tone. Miriam was quick to acknowledge the truth of the statement. In the harsh glare of the street lights Rosie Spiers's thin face was grey and haggard, and there were huge black circles shadowing her eyes.

'Are you all right, Rosie?' Laura asked anxiously, and the other girl forced a smile.

'I'm just a bit tired, Laura, that's all. I'll be fine when we can sit down and have a rest.'

'We must be very near by now,' Miriam encouraged, and stopped a passer-by to ask directions.

'Clement's Inn?' The man appeared to stare suspiciously at the three women. 'Clement's Inn, did you say?'

'Yes, Clement's Inn,' Miriam repeated.

'Just over there, Madam.' The man pointed.

'Thank God for that,' Laura breathed thankfully.

In the ancient cluster of buildings that comprised Clement's Inn they were further directed up flights of stairs and down crooked passageways. They found the door finally with a neat plaque proclaiming: WOMEN'S SOCIAL AND POLITICAL UNION.

A middle-aged, bespectacled woman answered to their knocking, and her gaze was stern and unwelcoming.

'Yes, what can I do for you?'

Laura took the spokeswoman's role. 'We're the delegation from the Redditch branch.'

The grim features in the doorway scowled. 'What branch?'

'The Redditch branch.' Laura was a little disconcerted by the woman's hostile attitude. 'That's in Worcestershire.' She tried to smile. 'In the Midlands, the West Midlands.'

'I am not in need of a geography lesson, young woman.' The light glinted on the thick, round lenses of the spectacles. 'I know very well that Worcestershire is in the West Midlands.'

A silence ensued, and the bespectacled woman made no effort to speak, and only remained blocking the doorway with her considerable bulk. Her thick lenses glinted as she switched her gaze from one to the other of the three visitors.

Miriam was feeling very disconcerted: this was not the reception she had envisaged, and all her romantic notions of a devoted sisterhood bonded together in close comradeship were being rapidly replaced by a feeling of disillusionment. She felt driven to break the uncomfortable silence. 'I have a letter from Miss Christabel Pankhurst. In it she invites this delegation to join in the demonstration at the Houses of Parliament tomorrow.'

The almost opaque lenses swung to glint at her. 'This is

273

not the Houses of Parliament. This is Clement's Inn. Surely you can see the difference between the two establishments?' The sneering question was voiced in the tone of someone talking to an idiot child.

'Now just a minute.' It was Rosie Spiers who stepped forwards to confront the woman angrily. 'We'se travelled a long way to get here, and theer's no call for you to treat us like we'em beggars looking for charity.' Laura and Miriam stared at their normally submissive and timid mannered friend with open amazement. Rosie's voice was strained, and her hands trembled visibly, but her eyes were fixed levelly on the glinting spectacles, and her manner was determined. 'What Miss Miriam here has just told you is the truth. We'se got an invitation from Christabel Pankhurst to come down here and demonstrate. And that's exactly what we intends doing. Now I doon't know who you might be, and truth to tell, I doon't much care. But I'm not gooing to stand by and let you spake to my friends like they'm beggars, or fools, or worse.'

She drew a long ragged breath, and stared briefly at her companions before turning once more to the woman in the doorway. 'Like I'se already told you, I doon't know who you am, and I doon't know what work you does for the Movement. But what I does know is what these two ladies has done for it, and that's more than anybody else could have done in the town that we lives in. They'se sacrificed their own comforts and money and position, to fight for the rights of women, so you just show 'um the respect that they'm deserving of. And I'll tell you summat else as well. No matter how you treats us, we'll all three on us be at the Houses o' Parliament tomorow, and we'll be a part of that demonstration, because that's what we'se come all the way down here to do. And when we goes back to Redditch, we'll be keeping up the fight for the vote, no matter how sour you might be towards us.'

'Bravo!' a soft voice called, and there was a clapping of hands from along the ill-lit corridor. A young woman came towards them, her hands still clapping lightly.

'I'm Christabel Pankhurst,' she introduced herself and

held out her hand to shake the hands of the three women in turn.

Miriam couldn't help but stare curiously at the notorious suffragette, and what she saw contrasted oddly with the images drawn by the enemies of the suffrage movement. Short in stature, with a round face, wide-spaced eyes and soft brown hair piled loosely on her hatless head, the young woman was hardly the epitome of a bloodthirsty revolutionary.

'You say that you've travelled from Redditch. I've heard of the town. It manufactures needles, does it not? Do please come into the office and have a cup of tea.' She smiled at the glinting spectacles. 'Be a dear, Bronwen and fill the kettle will you.'

When the woman had disappeared down the corridor carrying a large iron kettle Christabel Pankhurst smiled at her visitors.

'You must not mind Bronwen Pugh's manner. She's a dear woman, and devoted to the cause. But we get quite a lot of visitors to this office who are unwelcome to us, and Bronwen sees herself in the role of our sentinel. Please sit down.' She indicated the chairs lining the walls, and seated herself at one of the small tables which served as desks.

'Now Miss Josceleyne, I do remember writing to you, please do tell me all about the Redditch branch.'

She listened intently to the account of hostile audiences, apathetic women, and lack of progress, and when it was done smiled sympathetically. 'You must not allow yourselves to become discouraged, ladies. I have spent most of my formative years serving the cause, and I know that the way towards our eventual victory will be long and hard, and that we shall meet with many setbacks.' Her wide spaced eyes gleamed fanatically, and fervour throbbed in her voice.

'But we shall win. Of that there can be no doubt. We shall triumph in the end.'

Bronwen Pugh re-entered the room and placed the kettle on the hearth fire to boil. Soon tea was brewed and the five women sat drinking and chatting. During the course of the next hour other women came and went, and the three friends were introduced to some who were fast becoming almost legendary figures in the struggle for the vote: Sylvia Pankhurst, Christabel's younger sister, beautiful and artistic; Emmeline Pethwick-Lawrence, the elegant wife of an eminent barrister, and honorary treasurer of the Union; Mrs Edith How-Martyn, a science graduate of London University; Theresa Billington, strong and upstanding, her bare head crowned with an abundance of glossy brown coils of hair; the elderly Mrs Wolstenholme-Elmy, tiny, fragile, her face like a delicate porcelain image, her shining dark brown eyes framed by coils of grey curls; lastly a young woman who impressed them more than any of the others – the Lancashire factory girl, Annie Kenny, her long, soft hair hanging down her back in a single plait and a grey shawl covering her plain white blouse. Peeping out from under her dark blue serge skirt were the steel tips of a pair clogs.

In the accents of the Oldham backstreets, Annie Kenny told them of her work in the East End of London, and her struggles to recruit and organise the poor and wretched women of the East End slums. As she spoke her natural simplicity and goodness shone through. All three of the Redditch women felt inspired by her example, and slightly ashamed that they had not succeeded as she had in organising cadres of working class women to carry the message of women's suffrage to their sisters.

When the night grew late it was the dour, forbidding sentinel, Bronwen Pugh, who insisted that the three Redditch women should come with her to her own cramped rooms to share her meagre supper, and spend the night there on makeshift mattresses of old clothes and cushions.

Miriam found it impossible to sleep, and she lay for seemingly endless hours listening to the soft snorings of Laura, and the wheezing breath of Rosie's damaged lungs. But it was not the unfamiliar quarters, or the close proximity of her companions, or the discomfort of her makeshift bed that kept her awake. It was her own excited thoughts that would not permit her to rest. The evening spent in meeting and talking with the suffragettes had completely expelled any feelings of doubt or disillusion that the initial reception had engendered. Now she truly felt that she was indeed a member of a sisterhood. A sisterhood bonded to each other in a great cause, and she for one now felt ready to fight on for the rest of her days in the service of that cause. Ready to make any sacrifice that the cause demanded of her. Ready even to lay down her own life . . .

Chapter Thirty-Two

There were large numbers of suffragettes already collected in the street outside the Houses of Parliament when Miriam and her friends arrived with Bronwen Pugh. Miriam stared about her eagerly, noting the wide diversities of dress and appearance among the assembled suffragettes. Rags and riches, want and plenitude, high and low born, had all gathered to make common cause. Silken banners waved beside crudely lettered cardboard placards and West End mansion stood side by side with East End garret and cellar.

'Wait by here while I'll find out what is happening,' Bronwen Pugh instructed and threaded her way through the throng towards the ornate entrance, guarded by an elderly uniformed door-keeper.

Within moments she was back to tell the three friends, 'They're only allowing twenty women at a time into the House of Commons Lobby. Mrs Pankhurst and Mrs Pethwick-Lawrence and some others are in there now. Come on, we'll go into the Central Lobby at any rate.'

They went through the entrance and into the long high-vaulted hallway which led into the great Central Lobby. As they passed along its length Miriam saw several groups of shabby women with pallid, haggard features sitting on the stone benches which lined the hallway.

'Some of Annie Kenny's recruits, they are.' Bronwen Pugh's spectacles glinted from side to side. 'Poor souls are worn out. Marched all the way from the East End, they have, and I expect that most of them have had to slave all through the night to make up for the earnings they're losing from their work by coming here today.'

Even as she spoke policemen were approaching the resting women, brusquely ordering them to leave the benches and go outside into the street.

Laura's thin face mirrored her indignation, and she accosted one young constable: 'Why are you sending these poor women away?'

He stared at her, his fresh countrified features showing his surprise. 'It's orders, Ma'am. No roughs and scruffs are to be allowed into the building. They shouldn't have been let in in the first place.'

'But they're not roughs and scruffs!' she protested heatedly.

'You'd best take that up wi' my sergeant, Ma'am. I'm only doing what I bin told to do,' the constable answered stolidly, and walked away from Laura to challenge another ill-clad woman.

'I am going to speak to his sergeant about this,' Laura declared forcefully.

'Leave it for now,' Bronwen Pugh pointed ahead into the Central Lobby. 'Look, there's Mrs Pankhurst.'

The three friends stared eagerly at the famed leader of the suffragettes who had not appeared at Clement's Inn the previous night. They saw a small, slight-bodied, very pretty woman with large eyes and a gentle mouth.

'But she's so tiny and frail looking!' Laura blurted out.

Bronwen Pugh smiled grimly. 'Don't you worry about her size, young woman. They put good stuff in little bottles, you know.'

Led by Bronwen Pugh they pushed through the crowded Central Lobby, where many people were waiting to meet their Members of Parliament, and joined the group of women clustering around Emmeline Pankhurst, who had Emmeline Pethwick-Lawrence standing by her side.

'We have spoken with the Chief Liberal Whip . . .' Emmeline Pankhurst was explaining in her soft clear voice 'and we requested him to ask the Prime Minister whether he proposed to do anything to enfranchise the women of this country during the session, either by including the registration of qualified women in the provisions of the

279

Plural Voting Bill, or by any other means. The Prime Minister sent word back to us of his government's refusal to hold out the very faintest hope that the vote will be given to women at any time during the Liberals' term of office.'

A concerted exclamation of outrage and indignation greeted her words.

'What shall we do, Mrs Pankhurst?' one young woman wanted to know, and her leader smiled.

'We shall hold a protest meeting, my dear.'

A chorus of agreement sounded, and some of the women began to turn as if to leave, but Emmeline Pankhurst stopped them.

'No, not outside! We shall hold our protest down there.' She pointed along the corridor to the Lobby of the House of Commons. For a moment there was complete silence, as if the audacity of her proposal had stunned them. Then Bronwen Pugh cheered, and in a rushing swirling of skirts the group of suffragettes swept down into the lobby of the House of Commons. Before the startled eyes of Members of Parliament and their visitors, the diminutive figure of a suffragette named Mary Gawthorpe stepped up on to one of the settees that lined the walls.

With a twinkle in her eyes, she first of all addressed the statue of Sir Stafford Northcote which adjoined her perch: 'You will excuse me, sir, if I make my speech before yours.'

The suffragettes laughed and applauded wildly, and then, before Mary Gawthorpe could continue, several policeman materialised as if from an ambush and burst through the crowd of suffragettes clustering around the speaker. Despite the efforts of the women to impede them the policemen grabbed Mary Gawthorpe and hustled her from the lobby.

Instantly another famous leader of the movement, Mrs Despard, took Mary Gawthorpe's place, but she also was instantly torn down. Woman after woman attempted to climb up on the settees and speak but the police roughly hustled each of them away, and then began to clear the lobbies and hallways of all the suffragettes.

The women resisted spiritedly and caught up in the

jostling, heaving struggle, Miriam, Laura and Rosie were gradually forced back through the Central Lobby and into the long entrance hallway. Miriam saw the tiny figure of Emmeline Pankhurst hurled bodily to the floor, and a violent escalation of scuffling ensued as her supporters rallied to shield her fallen body.

Outside in the roadway crowds had begun to gather, drawn by the noisy uproar, and as the suffragettes were physically ejected from the building some of the women attempted to address the spectators. The crowd's mood suddenly became hostile, and one or two of those suffragettes who had attemped to address them were subjected to rough handling, punches and kicks. To her own amazement, Miriam found that she was not afraid, instead she was filled with a mad elation as she pushed and shoved and struggled against the burly bodies of the police. In the swirling, scuffling melee she became separated from her two friends, and was finally forced out of the building and into the roadway. Gasping for breath she moved further away from the crush of people around the entrance, finding herself overcome by physical weakness. Her violent efforts had taxed her frail physique beyond its capability. She stared around her searching for sight of her friends, and then heard a despairing wail.

'Miss Miriam? Miss Miriam? Help me! Help me, Miss Miriam!'

A horse-drawn Black Maria had been brought up close to the entrance and struggling, shrieking women were being forced into it by sweating, cursing policemen. As Miriam stared wildly about her she glimpsed Rosie being roughly dragged towards the large van by two burly constables.

'No!' she shouted. 'No! Leave her alone.'

She hurled herself through the intervening bodies towards the screaming Rosie and reached the van door, just as the two constables physically threw her friend into its dark confines.

'No, let her go! Let her go!' Miriam shrieked, and tried to grab Rosie's arms to pull her out of the van.

'You wants to gerrin there wi' your mate, do you?' the

biggest of the constables bellowed, and grinned at his colleague. 'Here's a fuckin' volunteer, Jem!'

He grabbed Miriam around her waist, lifted her bodily and thrust her into the van, then slammed and bolted the door. He mounted the rear step and shouted to the driver, 'That's the lot, let's go!' And the driver's whip cracked out upon the heaving flanks of the horse, and the Black Maria rattled off to the jeering plaudits of the massed spectators.

As the large van lurched and swayed the women packed inside its low-roofed interior were thrown against one another, and Miriam, still on hands and knees, cried out in pain and shock as a foot came down heavily on to her hand. She dragged herself upright, and found herself face to face with Rosie. The younger woman's face was grey and drawn, and she looked as if she would faint. Miriam threw her arms around Rosie's wasted body and held her protectively. 'I've got you, Rosie. I've got you,' she repeated comfortingly. 'I've got you.'

She stared curiously about her at these novel surroundings. The van was long and very gloomy, lined with narrow cubicles like cramped cells, and each cubicle was occupied by a seated suffragette, while the central passageway was crammed tightly with standing women.

The uncomfortable journey was mercifully short, and the van juddered to a halt. The rear doors were flung open and a tall police sergeant bellowed.

'Come on you lot. Let's be having you.'

The women scrambled out on to the cobbles of the Police Station yard and were hustled into the station building. Then they were lined up before a tall desk behind which an elderly grey-haired sergeant, who sniffed continuously, entered their names and particulars into a large ledger on the desk before him. As each woman was done with she was taken and locked up in the holding cells – large bleak dungeons with only a wooden pallet and a urinal bucket for furnishings.

As the cell filled up Miriam recognised some of the women she had been introduced to at Clement's Inn, and felt proud that she was in such fine company. Emmeline Pethwick-Lawrence smiled at her encouragingly, and the

282

diminutive Mary Gawthorpe waved and nodded from across the cell. The beautiful Sylvia Pankhurst was thrust in with them, and the elderly Mrs Despard. Also another woman named Mrs Cobden-Sanderson, daughter of the famous politician Richard Cobden, one of the founders of the Liberal Party, whose name, although he had been long dead, was still revered by the elder statesmen in the Houses of Parliament.

After an hour had passed all the women were brought back into the charge room, where a ferociously moustached chief superintendent, resplendent in a frogged uniform frock coat, released them on bail to appear before the magistrate at the Rochester Row Police Court the following morning.

Outside the Police Station a large crowd of suffragettes had gathered, and as the released women came down the flight of stone steps into the street, cheers went up and banners were waved. Miriam was elated with excitement. 'This is really living,' she told herself delightedly. 'I've never had such adventures! This is really living.'

Christabel Pankhurst came alongside and told Miriam: 'You've behaved marvellously, Miriam. You're a real fighter, aren't you. Many of the ladies are remarking on it. I think that you will become one of the leaders of our movement. I'll see you tomorrow in court.' She moved away to greet friends.

The compliment had a strange effect upon Miriam. It pleased her immensely, and at the same time it seemed as if the praise had unlocked a hidden force within her mind. A sense of power and confidence surged through her. She felt absolutely fearless, and ready to face any foe, make any sacrifice, let nothing or no one stand in her way to gain victory for the cause that she was now committed to. Then she looked sideways at Rosie, and concern lanced through her. The young woman looked to be really ill, her colour was a deathly livid pallor, and she clung on to Miriam's arm as if without its support she would fall to the ground.

'Miriam? Rosie?' Laura came running to them, hatless, her hair flying loose and tangled.

'What happened to your hat?' Miriam demanded, and

the younger woman laughed excitedly.

'I think it's still inside the House of Commons, together with my umbrella.'

Then her laughter died away as she stared closely at Rosie Spiers. 'Are you all right, Rosie?'

Rosie Spiers shook her head. 'I feel bad. I'm all dizzy and sick.'

By now the released suffragettes were surrounded by groups of their friends, and the crowd was rapidly dispersing as each group moved away to its separate destination.

'We must find a room where Rosie can lie down,' Laura said, and her anxiety for her friend increased as the young woman swayed and closed her sunken eyes.

'There you are.' Bronwen Pugh came up to them, and when she saw Rosie exclaimed: 'Duw Duw, Cariad! We'd best get you home straightaway. You don't look at all well.'

She hailed a hansom cab and bundled Rosie into it, telling Miriam and Laura: 'You follow on to my rooms. I'll get Rosie settled comfortably.'

As the two-wheeled cab moved away Laura stared doubtfully at Miriam. 'I wonder if we did the right thing to bring Rosie down here with us? It looks as if it is all too much for her health to bear.'

Miriam was staring after the receding hansom cab, and her pale features held a hard expression which was at variance with her normal gentle demeanour. 'We are fighting a war here, Laura,' she said, and her voice was so harsh and determined that Laura stared at her in surprise. 'And in every war there are inevitably casualties to be suffered. If we are to win this struggle, then we must all be prepared to sacrifice our health, and even our lives if needs be.'

Laura's thin face became troubled, and she murmured as if to herself, 'I've never seen you like this before, Miriam. It doesn't sound like you at all.'

Miriam frowned slightly, keeping her gaze fixed on the cab which by now was almost lost to view in the streaming traffic. 'That's because I've never been like this before, Laura.' She spoke with a quiet force. 'Becoming a suffragette has changed me. I can feel it. I am changing fast from what I used to be.'

Chapter Thirty-Three

Mr Horace Smith, Stipendiary Magistrate at Rochester Row Police Court, had listened intently to the evidence offered by the police, and now he looked sternly at the ten women ranged in the dock, and told them sonorously, 'Each of you must enter into your own recognisance to keep the peace for six months, and must find a surety for your good behaviour in the sum of ten pounds. If you fail to do this, then you will be sent to prison for two months in the second division.'

'Well of all the cheek!' Adela, the youngest of the Pankhurst sisters, whispered indignantly to Miriam Josceleyne who was standing next to her in the dock. 'We should be imprisoned in the first division, because that denotes political prisoner status and carries certain privileges. The second and third divisions are meant for the criminal classes, and if he sends us there then they can require us to do menial work, even hard labour, and the treatment is much harsher for the prisoners.'

Further along the dock there was a sudden flurry of movement as Emmeline Pethwick-Lawrence and another woman unfurled a banner and held it high above their heads. Miriam craned forwards and twisted her head to read the words lettered on it. 'Women should vote for the laws they obey, and the taxes they pay.'

One woman shouted defiantly: 'We refuse to leave this dock until we are allowed the rights to which all prisoners are entitled, namely that of calling witnesses, and making statements in our own defence.'

Mr Horace Smith merely appeared contemptuous and ignored her outburst, then one by one asked each woman directly: 'Do you give your recognisance that you will keep the peace for six months, and have you a surety for your good behaviour in the sum of ten pounds?'

As each woman in turn refused to give their recognisance, the magistrate snapped curtly: 'The sentence of this court is that you serve two months' imprisonment in the second division.'

When he had finished with the last woman he ordered the policemen to, 'Take them down.'

The defendants attempted to resist, but the policemen forced them out of the dock and down into the cells, their loud protests going unheeded in the small, nearly empty courtroom from which their supporters had been excluded.

In the witness room, which was on the opposite side of a small lobby from the courtroom, Laura was waiting with other suffragettes, expecting to be called as witnesses. When the police inspector entered the room all the women present looked at him expectantly.

'That's it, ladies. You may all go home now. The case is ended.'

'What has happened?' Sylvia Pankhurst demanded to know, and the man smirked.

'They've all been given two months in the second division. They've already left for Holloway Prison.'

The news was greeted with outcries of incredulous indignation, which the Inspector met with a frown. 'It's their own faults that they've been sent down. The Magistrate offered them to be bound over, and find a surety of ten pounds. But none of them wanted to accept that. Now I suggest that you all leave. There's nothing to be gained by your remaining here any longer.'

'I'll not go without telling that Magistrate exactly what I think about this travesty of justice.' Sylvia Pankhurst's beautiful face was flushed with anger, and she stormed from the room and crossed the lobby to the courtroom. After a momentary exchange with the door-keepers she pushed on into the room and her voice could be heard raised in angry altercation.

Laura allowed herself to be ushered out into the street

with the rest of the suffragettes. She found that at this moment she had no real desire to continue the present confrontation with the law. She was far too worried about her two friends. Particularly Rosie Spiers, who had gone to court that morning despite the fact that she was ill. The street was filled with a mass of curious onlookers, and immersed in her own troubled thoughts, and at a loss as to what she should do now, Laura stood with strangers. She watched Sylvia Pankhurst's ejection into the street by two policemen, her attempt to address the crowd and her almost immediate arrest and disappearance back inside the court building, without making any move to rejoin the other suffragettes. Many of these now started to force their way back into the court building following Sylvia Pankhurst's arrest, but instead of joining them Laura turned to a woman standing by her, and asked, 'How can I get to Holloway Prison?'

'That's easy, lady,' a shabby, down-at-heel man laughed. 'Just 'eave 'alf a brick through that bleedin' winder there.'

His hearers joined in his raucous laughter, but the woman, seeing Laura's obvious distress, quickly gave her the necessary directions as to how to get to the prison, and Laura thanked her and hurried away. Since she had no money Laura was forced to walk the weary miles to the prison, and when she reached it, stood and rested for a while at the wrought-iron gates and posts mounted by gaslamps which fronted its short tree-lined entrance drive. The prison's massive gatehouse resembled a fairy tale castle with its battlemented, arrow-slitted turrets, narrow gothic-arched windows and massive bolt-studded doors.

When she rang the electric bell a hatchway opened in the door and a peak-capped male warder listened to her request to see her friends, and told her gruffly, 'This is a prison, Miss, not a public visiting ward in some hospital. Your friends will have to make application to the Governor for you to visit them. You can write to them and ask them if they wants you to visit. But it'll take a few weeks to be processed through the proper channels. And if they've only bin sentenced to a couple o'months, I can't think it's worth all the trouble you'll have to go to, to get in to see them.'

'Can you get a message through to them for me?' Laura asked desperately, and the man shook his head.

'No, Miss, I can't do that. You must go through the proper channels.'

The hatch closed, and Laura felt near to tears, but fiercely berated herself for her own weakness in giving way to her emotions. And then turned away from the great doors and began the weary trudge back towards Clement's Inn and Bronwen Pugh's rooms.

Chapter Thirty-Four

The wardress was tall and raw-boned, with a grim scarred face and large hands. Her uniform gown was black, and on her bunned hair she wore a small black toque bonnet, tied under her chin with broad black ribbons. Around her waist was a black leather belt from which hung a chained ring of keys. She marched along the landing of the cell block and Miriam Josceleyne followed, her arms laden with bedding, her eyes flickering about her as she examined her new abode. From ground to roof there were three tiers of cells facing each other across the open central space of the gloomy high-vaulted block. Stretched across the space from landing to landing were the nets of strong wire designed to prevent suicidal prisoners from hurling themselves to the stone slabs of the ground floor. The long blank rows of cell doors were recessed slightly into the thick white-washed walls, and each door was shut and barred and no sounds came from within their secret confines.

Miriam was struck by the unnatural oppressive silence, broken only by the echoing footsteps of herself and her escort, and for a moment she had the fanciful notion that perhaps she was the sole prisoner on this block, although she knew well that each locked cell contained its occupant.

As if she divined Miriam's thoughts the wardress turned and grinned, not unkindly, at her. 'One thing about living here, the neighbours are usually nice and quiet.' Her voice had the rustic burr of Suffolk. They reached a cell with its door standing ajar, and the wardress halted outside it, and jerked her head in signal to Miriam to enter.

Its interior resembled the reception cell that Miriam had

been put into on her arrival at Holloway that morning, with a low wooden pallet and headrest, a low four-legged wooden stool, battered metal chamberpot and tiny washbasin and water-jug, and a single wall-fixed shelf. But it was smaller, and instead of a gaslight recessed behind thick glass, it had an electric light high on the wall with a small wire cage protecting it.

The wardress grinned again as she noted Miriam stare upwards at the electric light bulb.

'Oh yes, we lays on every modern convenience for our guests. Most on them aren't got even an oil-lamp back at home, never mind the electric light.' She pointed at a large round badge made of yellow cloth with numbers and a single letter printed upon it which was hanging from a nail on the wall.

'That's your badge, and you're to wear it at all times, and you answer to the number on it. You'll be Twenty-three, while you're in here. That's your cell number, and you're in C Block number Two. That's on the badge as well, as you can see. When you gets given your sewing things you must sew the badge on your dress on the right chest.' Yet again she grinned. 'The colour sets off your uniform just right, don't you agree.'

Miriam had been issued with her prison uniform when she was in the reception cells after being stripped of her own clothing and personal possessions. Now she grimaced ruefully as she stared down at the threadbare brown serge gown and white canvas apron she wore, beneath which the coarse woven prison-issue vest and long-drawers and stockings had already begun to chafe her skin. The knowledge that all of the patched and darned garments had been worn by countless other prisoners made her feel itchy and unclean.

With a proprietorial air the wardress reached out and straightened the small flat white canvas cap perched on Miriam's head, and tugged on the long ribbons which secured it beneath her chin.

'Make sure that you're always neat and tidy, Twenty-three. I likes my section to look tidy at all times, and if any of them don't look tidy, then I takes steps to correct them.'

Her voice had hardened into threat. 'This cell might not look very nice and commodious, Twenty-three, but there's a sight worse cells that you can find yourself in, in this place. Just remember that.'

She reached for the bedding in Miriam's arms. 'Now I'm going to show you how your pallet must be laid out at all times, except when you're meant to be sleeping. Then I'll show you what else you must do every morning just as soon as you've slopped out your chamberpot. Pay attention, because I shan't tell you twice, and if you gets it wrong in future, then you'll find yourself in trouble.'

There were three threadbare grey blankets, two coarse grey-looking sheets and a shabby wafer-thin quilt. The wardress took the first sheet, folded it into four then placed it on the stone-flagged floor and rolled it tightly like a sausage. She then rolled the second sheet around it, followed by each blanket in turn, and lastly the quilt, to form a big wheel of bedding.

'This is placed on your pallet so.' She arranged the big round wheel at one end of the wooden bed.

'Next you must polish your tinware.' These utensils were a metal spoon, a pintpot, a bowl-like platter, and the washing basin, water jug and chamberpot.

The wardress produced three dirty-looking pieces of rag, two of which were scraps of brown serge, and the third of white calico. She also produced a square of reddish-brown bath-brick.

'Give us your soap, Twenty-three,' she ordered, and Miriam dutifully took the cake of coarse yellow washing soap from out of the strip of towelling she had been issued with, and handed it to the other woman.

'You rubs the brick on the floor like this, until you obtains a sufficient quantity of brick dust.' The wardress demonstrated, and her manner was that of a pedantic schoolmarm. 'Next you takes one of the brown rags and soaps it well on the cake of soap. With the soapy rag you rubs hard all over your tins. Next you dips the soapy rag into the brick dust and likewise rubs it hard all over your tins to remove stains and dirt. Then you takes your second brown rag, and likewise rubs it all over your tins to get rid of the brick dust and soap. Lastly you takes your white rag and polishes all your tins. And you must make sure that all of your tins shines like the sun in its heavens. If I don't think that your tins are shiny enough, then you will be in very serious trouble, Twenty-three.

'By the time you've finished your tins you'll have been given a bucket of water, and a brush. You'll scrub your stool, bed table and shelves, and then the floor. If you does it all satisfactory, and to my liking, then you'll be able to eat your breakfast. If the work aren't done to my satisfaction, then you'll be tasting another sort of breakfast, and I can assure you, Twenty-three, that it will not be a breakfast that you will find at all to your liking. Am I making myself clear to you, Twenty-three?'

'Yes Ma'am,' Miriam answered submissively.

'Very well, go on cleaning your tins. I'll come back to you presently.'

The wardress left the cell, slamming the door shut, and Miriam heard the keys rattle and the lock turn, and the bolt shot heavily home, and for the first time since her arrest she felt a sense of desperation and intense loneliness. She hungered to see friendly faces, to hear friendly voices, but all was still and silent and empty. And then, unbidden, the memory of her one-time lover, Johnny Purvis, came sharp in her mind, and she thought of the long weary years he had now spent in a cell like this one, and pity for him swept over her, and a poignant yearning flooded through her. Terrible sadness assailed her, and tears stung her eyes, and she wept helplessly for what might have been.

Chapter Thirty-Five

'Prison? Miriam's bin in prison since last week, and you'se only just bothered to tell me about it? Wheer the bloody hell has you bin since then?' Emma Josceleyne's anger was strident. 'I'se bin worried to death for days wondering wheer she was, and why she hadn't come back home, and here's you coming here as cool as a cowcumber to tell me that she's in bloody prison!'

Laura Hughes stood with bowed head and allowed the storm to break over her. Once or twice she attempted to speak, but the other woman only continued to rant and rave, so Laura gave up her attempt and remained silent waiting for the storm to spend itself.

'I knew summat like this 'ud happen!' Emma stated vehemently. 'I knew from the minute that she got mixed up with the bloody suffragettes that she'd end up in bloody trouble.' As always, when her mood was stressed Emma's speech patterns reverted to those of Silver Street.

'Bloody stupid lardy-yedded buggers, the lot on 'um! Bloody suffragettes! I tried to tell her, but she 'udden't listen. Her's not strong enough to be in prison. Her's bin brought up a lady. Prison 'ull bloody well kill her!' She glared furiously at the other woman. 'And why aren't you in the bloody nick with her? You'm the one who got her into this trouble by filling her yed with your rubbish about votes for women!'

Laura shook her head and shrugged. 'I did not happen to get arrested.'

'No, I can bloody well see that!' Emma retorted scathingly. 'That's why you'm standing here as bold as brass, and poor Miriam is in the bloody nick. What happened? Did you run away when the police come?'

Laura shook her head. 'No, I did not run away.' Then she shrugged in a gesture of helplessness. 'There seems to be no point in my trying to explain what happened in London. You do not appear prepared to give me a hearing.'

'No, I'm bloody well not!' Emma shrieked stridently. 'But I'll tell you what I am prepared to do, my fine lady. And that's to kick your bloody arse if you ever comes near me again. Now just sod off out of my house, and stay right away from me. Goo on! Get out!'

Laura Hughes sighed heavily, and turned away. The pert maidservant showed her out of the front door of Cotswold House and she walked dispiritedly to the front gate. As she lifted its latch Mrs Elwood came hurrying after her.

'Just hold on a minute, Missy.'

Laura turned back to face the oncoming woman, wary at the prospect of more abuse. But the fat face bore only a look of concern.

'Tell me quick, what happened, and how long has Miss Miriam got? Is she hurt in any way? Is she all right?'

Rapidly Laura told the other woman about all that had occurred, and explained.

'. . . I went up to Holloway every day to try and see Miriam and Rosie. But I wasn't even allowed to pass a message to them. I've come back now because of Tommy, Rosie's brother. I have to care for him, and to try and earn enough money for our rent and food.'

Mrs Elwood looked at her suspiciously. 'I thought you had money. You being a lady.'

Laura smiled wryly. 'Miriam has been supporting me these last months. But now she is in prison, I'm going to have to find something very quickly to support myself and Tommy until the others get back home.'

Upon hearing that her beloved Miss Miriam had been financially supporting this young woman, Mrs Elwood's attitude became distinctly frosty towards her. 'Yes well,' she snapped. 'We all has to work for our daily bread, doon't us? I'se had to work all me life, and bloody hard as well. I aren't never had nobody paying for my keep. But then, I aren't never bin a lady, has I?'

With that parting gibe she hurried back into the house, leaving Laura looking ruefully after her.

Inside Emma was still greatly agitated, and when the cook came to her she spat out angrily: 'I could have wrung that lardy-da cow's neck for her. Getting Miriam into trouble like she's done. If it hadn't bin for her Miriam 'ud never have got mixed up with the bloody suffragettes!'

'There there now, 'tis no use you getting all riled up about it, Emma. There's nothing any of us can do to change what's happened, is there?' the cook soothed.

Emma shook her head regretfully. 'No, it's too bloody late now, aren't it.'

The cook quickly related what she had found out from Laura Hughes and Emma reflected briefly, then remarked, 'Oh well, two months isn't too bad, I suppose. I'll write to her and find out if she can get permission for me to visit. But remembering me dad, I doon't think it'll be worth trying really. What I can do is to arrange to be waiting outside the nick for her when she's released.'

By now she had recovered from the shock of hearing the news about Miriam's imprisonment, and her raffish humour was rekindling.

'Who'd ever have thought it, Mrs Elwood, that our Miss Miriam 'ud end up in the bloody nick,' she chuckled wryly. 'There's more to her than meets the eye, aren't there. O' course, I knew that years ago, when I found out about her and Johnny Purvis having it off. She might look to be a timid mouse on top, but underneath there's a bit of a wildcat in our Miriam.'

Mrs Elwood's own mood lightened in response to Emma's change of temper, and she now smirked and said meaningfully, 'At least you knows now that you'se got a clear field to enjoy yourself in for the next few weeks. I expect the girls 'ull be having quite a few more holidays before Miss Miriam gets back, wun't they?'

Emma frowned and demanded heatedly: 'What does you mean by that?'

The older woman was not at all disconcerted by her

296

mistress's aggressive reaction, and replied airily, 'You knows very well what I means, my wench. I took it on myself to change your sheets, instead of leaving the job to the girls. I knows love stains when I sees 'um.'

At first Emma feigned anger, but then she could not help but laugh, and admit: 'Yes, they'd got a bit messy, hadn't they? I'm glad you changed 'um instead of the girls. I wouldn't want them getting all excited and worked up about it.'

'It's Harry Vivaldi, aren't it,' Mrs Elwood stated, rather than queried.

Emma nodded in resigned acceptance that she had been hoping for an impossibility in trying to keep her lover secret from Mrs Elwood.

'Well, you deserves a bit o' pleasure in your bed, arter putting up wi' old Hector all that time, my duck,' the elder woman conceded reluctantly. 'But you take care with that Vivaldi chap. I still reckons that he's a wrong 'un.'

'Doon't you worry about me, Mrs Elwood, I know what I'm doing,' Emma asserted confidently. 'Like I said before, he jumps through my hoop, there's no danger o' me ever jumping through his.'

The cook's eyes slitted shrewdly in their puffballs of fat. 'Just you make sure that it stays that way then,' she warned. 'Because I doon't want to see you weeping like other poor wenches does over some man or other.'

The younger woman chuckled. 'The only woman you'll ever see weeping in this house, Mrs Elwood, 'ull be that soddin' suffragette if she ever shows her nose here again.'

Emma Josceleyne's prediction was most unlikely to come true, since Laura Hughes had no intention of ever entering Cotswold House again, at least while Emma Josceleyne still resided there. Burdened with her own, and both Miriam and Rosie's small reticules, she walked down Unicorn Hill and turned up into the rutted, odorous Hill Street. She had gone directly from the railway station upon her return to Redditch to give Cotswold House the information about Miriam's imprisonment, and was now regretting that politeness.

As she passed the decayed, tumbledown tenements, noisy children trailed after her skirts, and men and women came to the doorways to greet her, and to ask where Rosie was. Laura was forced to halt and tell her story several times before she reached the dark cramped court where she lived.

It was Maudie Emms, Rosie's next door neighbour, who had taken care of Tommy during their absence, and as soon as Laura had dumped her load into Rosie's house, she went next door.

Tommy greeted her with every appearance of joy, grunting happily, and patting her face and stroking her shoulders with his grimy hands.

Maudie Emms, a dumpy-bodied little woman smiled warmly. 'Theer now, Tommy, it's your lady friend come back agen to see you. Bless him, the poor sarft bugger. He's real pleased to see you, aren't he, Laura?'

She stared questioningly. 'Wheer's Rosie then? Aren't her come back with you?'

For what seemed to be the hundredth time, Laura once more told her story. Like the other neighbours who had previously heard it, Maudie Emms accepted the fact of Rosie's imprisonment without undue concern. In the slums to have a neighbour sent to prison, or to be imprisoned oneself, was a not infrequent happening, and for many slum dwellers being sent to prison was not in itself any great disgrace.

The dumpy little woman was concerned however about Tommy Spiers. 'If it's really needful, seeing that Rosie's bin put inside, I can keep him there wi' me for another day or so, Laura. But my chap wun't let me keep the poor sarft bugger any longer than that, even though we'se found the extra money handy. Tommy's bin getting on his nerves, you see. My chap says that it's bin nigh on unbearable having him here for these few days, and he carn't stand much more on it.'

'That's all right, Maudie,' Laurie hastened to reassure her. 'I'm going to look after Tommy until Rosie comes back.' She paused, then said hesitantly, 'There is one thing though. I'm going to have to find some work to support us

298

both, and that means that perhaps I won't be able to be here during the day to look after Tommy. Do you think that you might be able to keep an eye on him for me while I'm at work? I'll pay you for doing so, of course.'

It was the other woman's turn to show hesitance. 'Well, I'se bin promised some hooks to gut to do at home, so I aren't gooing to be able to keep a proper eye on him. You know how the sarft bugger wanders off if he aren't close watched.'

She paused and appeared to be thinking hard, then offered, 'I'll tell you what, Laura, you try the Culls and the others, and see if any o' them can look arter him. If you carn't find anybody, then perhaps we might be able to sort summat out. What we could do if the wust comes to the wust, is to keep him tied to his bed while you'm working, and I'll pop in every so often and see that he's all right.'

Laura nodded grateful acceptance. 'Thank you, Maudie. Well if you can just keep him here with you for another hour, I'll go and get everything arranged next door, and then I'll come and fetch him from you.'

It was while she was busily unpacking her meagre belongings, and finding coal and wood for the fire to dry and air the house which had become damp and musty during her absence, that Laura thought of how much her sojourn in Hill Street had changed her. Scant months previously the thought of tying a mentally retarded man to a bed and leaving him alone for hours would have filled her with horror. She would have regarded such a course of action as barbarous. As a dark medievalism having no place in this modern world. Now, grown used to the harshness of sheer necessity, she could accept the proposal as perfectly sensible and was not in the least disturbed by it.

She grinned wryly as she remembered her earlier idealistic beliefs. 'What an insufferably high-minded prig I was. Dwelling in my ivory tower looking down and condemning others, and not knowing the slightest thing about why they acted as they did. I've learned not to be so ready to take the moral high ground now though.'

When she had finished her tasks she went back next

door to fetch Tommy Spiers, and Maudie Emms told her: 'You know that you was saying you'd got to find work, Laura. Well I reckon you might get a start at the Steam Laundry down St George's Road. My sister's eldest had to leave theer last week because she's near to her time for birthing, and she told me yesterday that so far they hadn't filled her place. Why doon't you pop down theer now? I can keep Tommy here 'till you gets back.'

Laura gratefully accepted the offer and hurried to the Steam Laundry, where after a brief interview with the manager, she was offered and accepted a job in the washing room to start the very next morning.

Chapter Thirty-Six

Dusk had fallen and the air was cold and dank.

'Remember, remember the Fifth of November, Gunpowder, Treason and Plot! Penny for the Guy! Penny for the Guy! Spare a penny for the Guy!' The gang of children chanted loudly as they paraded a guy fashioned from straw-stuffed old clothes, a painted mask and a battered old top hat along Evesham Street. The guy was enthroned on an old chair carried by the tallest and strongest boys.

The mare pulling the smart gig shied nervously as the children noisily passed waving a variety of tattered flags on long sticks, and Ozzie Clarke called: 'Whoaa now, easy, easy.' Then he told the gang sharply: 'Don't go frightening my mare, you little buggers. Stop waving them bloody flags in her face.'

He brought the gig to a halt outside the door of The Redditch Meat Company shop and shouted: 'Walter, send the lad out.'

When the youth appeared, muffled in a voluminous apron far too large for him, Ozzie Clarke got down from the gig and handed the reins to him. 'I want you to lead her down to the yard, and feed and water her, then bed her down in the stable for the night.'

'Yes, Mr Clarke.' The youth led the mare and gig away and Ozzie Clarke entered the shop.

Old Walter Spiers grinned, showing his long blackened gnarls of teeth.

'You'm looking very smart today, Ozzie. Another new suit, is it?'

The younger man glanced at his reflection in the gilt-lettered mirror which hung behind the counter. He

301

smiled with satisfaction as he regarded his curly-brimmed bowler hat, immaculate white collar, silk cravat, smart oatmeal tweed suit and tan waistcoat. 'Yes, Walter, it is. I've got to look the part now that I'm a man of business, haven't I?' His tone was joking. 'I can't goo about looking scruffy, like you, can I?'

'Finished for the day, have you?' the older man enquired. 'It's a bit early aren't it?'

'No.' Clarke shook his head. 'I've got to goo down and see the boss lady later on and sort out a few details.'

'Sooner you than me, Ozzie.' There was a note of commiseration in Walter Spiers's voice. 'The less I sees o' the Queen of Egypt these days, the better I likes it. There aren't any pleasing of her lately, is there?'

'She's all right. It's just that she's got a lot on her mind,' the younger man affirmed. 'There's been a lot of pressure on her since she inherited old Mother Wilkinson's properties you know.'

'Phoo!' the other man snorted in disparagement. 'I can't think how coming into a bloody fortune like her's done, can be called pressure. I wish it 'ud bin me who Mother Wilkinson left her bundle to, I'll tell you. You 'udden't see me walking about with a face like a wet week, snapping and snarling at everybody.'

'The old girl had let everything get into a real mess, Walter. Some of the properties am nearly falling down, and her rent accounts hadn't been kept up to date, and some of the buggers who're renting from us are trying to come the old soldier. Claiming that they'se paid, when I'm bloody sure that they aren't, and trying to get money from the estate for repairs which they aren't had done, and suchlike. No, poor Cleo has got a lot on her plate just now.'

The older man peered shrewdly, and remarked, 'Oh it's Cleo, now, is it? You aren't half changed your tune about her, aren't you, my buck. I can recollect when you couldn't say a good word about her, but now you carn't say a bad 'un, can you?'

'You're right there, Walter,' Ozzie Clarke agreed cheerfully, and tipped his hat. 'It's got dark early aren't it? I'll say tarraa, my old fruit. I'm off down to see Cleo.'

One of the ground floor rooms in Cleopatra Dolton's house had been utilised for an office, and she was sitting at a big roll-top desk in that room when the maid showed Ozzie Clarke in.

'I'm glad you've come now, Mr Clarke,' she greeted. 'I've just had this estimate come from Huxley for the work in Walford Street.' Huxley was one of the local builders.

Ozzie Clarke took the papers and scanned them briefly. Then hissed sibilantly. 'This is a bit of a dear price, aren't it?'

She nodded. 'I thought so too.'

She took back the papers and pored over them, and Ozzie Clarke watched her. Despite all his resolutions to regard her only as his employer, he could still not control his feelings for Cleopatra Dolton. Despite the fact that she was ten years older than him, despite her having three children, despite knowing the unsavoury stories about her earlier life in Silver Street, and the lurid gossip concerning her and Johnny Purvis, Ozzie Clarke still hungered for this woman. His new position which entailed him spending much more time in her company had only served to increase his desire for her, and lately he had been forced to acknowledge to himself that he was hopelessly besotted with her, and that no other woman would do any more. He had actually, and for him almost unbelievably, remained celibate for some time now, distancing himself from those complaisant ladies with whom he had been accustomed to find his sexual pleasures.

'I can have a word with Huxley,' he offered now. 'And see if we can bring the price down a bit. If he won't, then I'll get some more estimates.'

'Very well.' She nodded. 'Now, there's another matter.' She rummaged among the scattered papers on the desk and found the one she sought. 'I've been going through the rent accounts and I think that some of these properties have been let at too low a rate. I've found some, like these houses in Hill Street for example, that have been let at the same rate for the past 30 years or more. Now I'm prepared to do the necessary repairs, and to see if we can modernise them, but I'm going to have to put the rents up first to pay for the work.'

The man frowned doutbfully, and she queried, 'Why do you look like that?'

'Well,' he said hesitantly, 'the thing is, Mrs Dolton, that there's some of the houses that Mrs Wilkinson left you, that by rights should be pulled down, never mind have their rents increased. There's some not fit to keep a dog in, never mind families.'

'But I intend to modernise them, Mr Clarke,' she challenged.

'Even so, the rents that some of the people have been paying are too high for the state of the houses. When the houses have been modernised and made fit to live in, then I think that the rents they're now paying will be just about right and fair.'

She scowled angrily, but made an obvious effort to keep her voice equable. 'Look Mr Clarke. We've both studied the rent accounts haven't we, and we both know that there's outstanding amounts, even though the tenants are denying it, and telling us that they're fully paid up. Because of the state of the accounts we can't prove that they haven't paid, even though we are sure that they haven't. So in effect that money is lost to us.'

His expression was uncomprehending. 'Yes, that may be the case, Mrs Dolton – but we've no proof have we, that they haven't paid?'

She gestured impatiently. 'I've already said such, Mr Clarke.'

'Then what does that have to do with the level of the rents?' He sought clarification.

'It has everything to do with it,' she exclaimed forcefully. 'Because it demonstrates that my tenants will cheat me at every opportunity. Therefore I owe them nothing in the way of consideration.'

'But they're not all cheating you, Mrs Dolton,' he was driven to protest.

'They all would, given the chance to do so,' she insisted vehemently. 'However, I'm determined that they shan't ever get that chance. From now on for every tenant it's going to be a case of pay promptly, or get out.'

The man's pleasant and handsome features were

troubled. 'That's a bit hard, Mrs Dolton,' he said quietly. 'Oh, I know that there's some who don't deserve to be given any chances, but there's others who might fall a bit behind with their rent through no faults of their own, — they might be taken badly, or lose their job, or have a death in the family.'

Her lustrous dark eyes were hard and her expression unyielding. 'Let me tell you something, Mr Clarke,' she told him grimly. 'I've endured a great deal of harship and want in my time. And not one of these people that you seem so concerned about, ever lifted a finger to help me. My only concern now is for my sons' future. I told you that I intended to become a woman of business. Well that is what I have become, and there is no room for sentiment or softness in business, Mr Clarke.' She tapped her fingers on the papers scattered before her. 'I inherited a mess, but I shall clear that mess up. I shall leave my sons an inheritance that will enable them to live their lives like gentlemen. If to achieve that I have to be hard on others, then so be it. After all, others have always been hard on me.'

She paused, as if expecting him to speak, but when he stayed silent, went on, 'Now, Mr Clarke, I want you to remain with me, and you can be sure that as the business grows wealthier, then you also will share in that wealth. I include my other employees in that guarantee. If they give their loyalty to me, and work hard and honestly for me, then I shall pay them well, and give them security. But, if at any time, and for any reason, any of my employees put the interests of others above my interests, then I'll hand them their sacks instantly. That applies to every single one of my employees without exception. So Mr Clarke, if you wish to stay in my employment then you must only give consideration to what is in my interest, and disregard completely the interests of others.'

Again she paused and regarded him intently, before finishing, 'So, Mr Clarke, what is it to be?'

Troubled though he might be about the unfairness and ruthlessness which she was now showing herself to be capable of, Ozzie Clarke knew that he could not bear to be separated from her. After a few seconds' hesitation, he nodded. 'It shall be as you want, Mrs Dolton.'

'Good.' She gusted a sigh of satisfaction. During the past weeks she had come to rely more and more upon the services of Ozzie Clarke, and she wanted to bind him ever closer to her. Now that she had won her point she visibly relaxed, and smiled warmly at him.

'Listen, Mr Clarke, I do not expect you to go round hounding people for their rents, or to go from door to door informing the tenants about the rent increases. You will have more than enough on your hands in watching over the builders, and overseeing the shops and farm. I'm bringing in a man to deal with the rents and the bad payers and those in arrears.'

'That'll be Caleb Louch, will it?' he asked.

She nodded. 'Yes, it will. I've already made the necessary arrangements with him, and he will be directly answerable to me, so you'll not be troubled with him at all.'

Now her smile was seductive. 'You've a good heart, Mr Clarke. And I don't want to make you unhappy by having you do things which you find hard and unpleasant to do. Caleb Louch is accustomed to the type of work that I need him for.'

She rose to her feet, and the black satin of her gown shimmered in the lamplight. The man swallowed hard as she came to him and he caught the scents of her voluptuous body. As on so many many occasions in the past he experienced an almost uncontrollable urging to take her in his arms and crush his lips against the full, moist ripeness of her mouth.

'Goodnight, Mr Clarke. Can you see yourself out,' she bade him softly, and moving past him opened the door of the room in dismissal.

Chapter Thirty-Seven

Harry Vivaldi was not as happy as he had expected to be after his conquest of Emma Josceleyne. When he analysed his feelings he was driven to conclude that the reason for his dissatisfaction was the fact that his conquest of the young woman was not really a conquest at all. In fact, he was beginning to strongly suspect that the young widow was using him merely as a sexual plaything. During the past fortnight he had spent five nights in her bed – nights of passionate, ecstatic pleasure. But always he had been forced to sneak into Cotswold House late at night, and leave early in the morning before the arrival of Mrs Elwood. Also, Emma Josceleyne had only allowed him to visit her twice during daylight hours, and when he had done so, had not allowed him even to touch her hands, and had kept the visit short and almost impersonal. Yet another gnawing worry was his failure to obtain any guarantee of funds from her to enable him to go into business for himself. When he had raised that question she had brusquely brushed it aside.

He lay in his bed waiting for Bella Thomas to bring him up his morning mug of tea, and glumly considered his present situation. Financially it was desperate. The rent was again in arrears. He had run large amounts on the 'slate' at his favourite public houses, and the local grocery shop was refusing to extend Bella any further credit. Also there were other personal loans to be repaid, and some of those creditors were becoming more than a little irate at his failure to repay them.

On the sexual side he had gloried in possessing Emma Josceleyne's sweet, lithe body. They had agreed a system of arranging their night-time assignations. Each morning on his way to work Vivaldi would pass Cotswold House. Emma would watch for him from her bedroom window, and if an assignation was possible that night she would draw aside the net curtains and make a signal. But those curtains had remained closed for the last four mornings, and he was beginning to be troubled by an unpalatable notion. He was beginning to wonder if Emma might be tiring of him sexually. It was a thought that he thrust away, but which returned constantly to torment him.

His job security was another recently arisen worry for him as well. During the last two days Ernie Field had started to grumble and complain even more than usual about the slackness of trade, and hint darkly of economies that must be made. Economies which Field made plain could well include the shedding of his assistant.

'What am I going to do?' the young man thought dispiritedly. 'Perhaps it's time I left this town? But how can I go somewhere else, when I haven't got a penny piece to bless myself with?'

'Here's your tea, darlin'.' Bella Thomas puffed up the steep stairs and came bearing the steaming mug in her pudgy hands.

He took the drink from her without acknowledgement, and sipped it slowly, staring gloomily at the greasy, stained wallpaper opposite him.

'Darlin'?' the woman asked tentatively. 'Darlin', I doon't suppose that you might have a shillin' to spare, has you? Only I aren't got nothing in for your supper, and the shop's stopped my tick.'

His first impulse was to snarl angrily at her, but even as he opened his mouth to do so, he bit back the cruel words. 'Now Harry boy, keep cool,' he warned himself. 'Keep cool and remember that you still need this fat cow. She's going to have to do the business for you, so you'll need to keep her sweet.'

He forced himself to smile sadly at her. 'I'm sorry, sweetheart. I haven't got a bean. I'm flat broke.' He shook his head and the smile was replaced by a despondent grimace. 'I reckon it's all up for me, Bella. It don't seem to matter how hard I work, and how much I try, things just never go right for me. I'm cursed with bad luck.'

Her painted Cupid-bowed lips trembled. 'Now don't you go upsetting yourself, darlin'. Things will get better for us. You see if they won't.'

Again the urge to shout and curse her for her bovine stupidity surged through him, but again he bit it back, and looked at her tenderly. 'Well, I just can't see how things can get back for us. I'm sorry, sweetheart, but I've just about lost all hope,' he told her huskily, and suffered her to clasp him to her big breasts and cover his face with eager, foul-breathed kisses.

'I do love you so, darlin',' she whimpered, over and over again. 'I do love you so! I do love you so!'

He stood it as long as he was able, and then pushed her gently away.

'You're too good for me, Bella,' he whispered brokenly. 'Do you know, I think it would be for the best if I was dead, and you were free from the bad luck I carry with me. It wouldn't take but a minute to finish it all, would it? One slash with my razor and I'd be gone, and you'd be free to find happiness.'

She stared at him with horror-struck eyes and shrieked fearfully, 'No, darlin', no! Don't you ever say such terrible things! You're all I lives for, Harry. If you was to die, then I'd kill meself! I'd kill meself and join you! I couldn't live without you, darlin'! I couldn't bear to live without you!' Again she smothered him in her embrace and his face became wet and stained with her slobbering kisses.

For the next few minutes he continued to proclaim his worthlessness and his desire to kill himself, and by doing so set her free, and she reacted with an ever more strident hysteria. Then, when he judged that he had prepared the ground sufficiently, he told her hoarsely: 'There is a way out of our troubles, you know, sweetheart. You could get us out of them. But it would be asking an awful lot of you to do it. And to tell you the truth, I doon't know if I could stand having you do it.'

'I'll do anything for you, darlin'. You knows that,' she assured fervently.

309

He stared at her ravaged features, and the mascara running down the rouged and powdered cheeks, and thought savagely, 'What a fuckin' mess you are, you raddled old bitch!' He shook his head as if in dismissal and said aloud, 'No! I can't ask you to do it. It would be better to kill myself and end it all, rather than shame myself by letting you do it.'

'Don't say that!' she begged tearfully. 'Don't say that you'll kill yourself. Let me do whatever I needs to do, darlin'. Please let me do it! Please!'

For a brief while further he continued to refuse and she to insist and to beg, and finally he reluctantly surrendered to her pleas, and told her what she must do. She stared at him with shock and disbelief, and he forced himself to take her in his arms and to kiss and caress her soothingly, and to coax her gently until at last she agreed.

Later, when quiet and subdued she had gone off to her work at the laundry, Vivaldi washed and dressed himself with great care, then whistling gaily, he let himself out of the house and made his way towards Prospect Hill.

As he passed Cotswold House he stared up at Emma's bedroom window, and his heart leapt as he saw the net curtain drawn aside and the beautiful features of Emma looking down at him. He halted and she smiled and nodded, and held up both hands with her fingers and thumbs spread. Then the net curtain fell into place once more and she was hidden from his view.

'Jesus!' he exclaimed with delight as he went on his way with the assignation for ten o'clock that night having been made. 'Your luck's on the turn again, Harry boy,' he congratulated himself. As Vivaldi came whistling into the shop, Ernie Field peered sourly over the rims of his spectacles.

'What time does you call this, Vivaldi?'

The young man made a show of pulling out his own pocket watch and examining its face. 'Why, it's twenty-eight minutes past eight o'clock to my reckoning, Mr Field.'

'You was supposed to be here at a quarter-past this morning, warn't you,' Field stated severely. 'So you'se lost a bit o' pay for coming late, aren't you?'

The young man's swarthy features beamed radiantly, and the shopkeeper glared suspiciously. 'What's you grinning like a Cheshire cat about?' he demanded to know.

'I've a proposition to make to you, Mr Field,' Vivaldi declared, still grinning. 'And I think that it will even put a smile on your face when you hears what it is.'

Again doubt and suspicion radiated from Ernie Field. 'Well?'

The younger man gestured expansively. 'Let's be straight, and call a spade a spade, Mr Field. You spends more than you can rightly afford on those Brummagem whores, don't you? And you takes a risk of catching the clap, or getting your head kicked in by some ponce or bully boy every time you goes up there. No! Let me finish!'

He held up his hands to halt the other man's indignant reaction.

'I'm speaking as one man of the world to another, Mr Field. And what passes between us now, stays between us. Nobody else will ever know about it. That I can guarantee you.' He paused to evaluate the effect of his words, and saw that he had got the other man's full attention.

'Good.' He nodded with satisfaction. 'I see that we understand each other. Now my proposition is very simple. Instead of you taking the risks you do in going up to Brummagem for your pleasures, why don't you take them the safe way? Why don't you give the money to me instead, and use my woman? I've talked to her, and she's agreeable. You can do anything you like to her, so long as you don't cause any lasting damage, of course.' He paused again, studying the other man with greedy eyes.

'Just think how convenient and easy it will be for you, Mr Field. And how much safer. Cheaper as well, because you'll not have to spend money on fares, and take time off from work, will you. Bella is close, and and ready for you whenever you feels inclined for a bit of fun. Well, what do you say? Is it a deal?'

Ernie Field's shocked and doubtful expression was fast being overlayed with a calculating frown. Then he nodded slowly.

'All right, it's a deal.'

Harry Vivaldi grinned broadly, and in that grin was a hint of contemptuous triumph.

'Right then, you're on, Ernie!' He hesitated a moment, then offered. 'How about tonight? Do you fancy a bit of fun with Bella tonight?'

The shopkeeper's tongue flickered out along his thin lips, and he nodded.

Chapter Thirty-Eight

The bells rang throughout the high-vaulted halls and the electric lights flashed on to drive back the darkness. The tramping of heavy-shod feet echoed along the landings, keys rattled and iron-clad doors crashed open in swift succession.

'Empty your slops, Twelve!'

'Empty your slops, Thirteen!'

'Come on Fourteen, gerrout o' that bed or I'll have you on report!'

'Empty your slops, Fifteen!'

Still half-asleep Miriam Josceleyne rose from her hard bed and hastily washed her face and hands in the tiny basin, then dressed hurriedly. A key turned in the lock, the bolt was withdrawn and the door crashed open.

'Empty your slops, Twenty-three!'

Miriam lifted the half-full chamberpot in one hand, took her small water jug in the other and hurried out to join the procession of women filing towards the latrine recess at the end of the landing. She reached the recess and emptied the foul-smelling contents of the pot into the large iron trough, and she gagged at the stench and sight of swirling urine and excreta as she leaned over the high rim to swill out the pot and refill her jug from the gushing water tap which fed the trough.

'Come on now, move along, move along!' The wardress, wearing a black cape against the cold of the early morning, kept on repeating mechanically. 'Move along, move along. Come on now, move along.'

Back in the cell the door slammed shut behind her, and Miriam began the task of rolling her bedding and cleaning and polishing her tins. Later the door crashed open again and a pail of water and a brush was thrust into her hands. Then the door slammed shut, the lock turned and the bolt shot home.

She was still on her knees scrubbing the stone-flagged floor when the door opened once more.

'You should have finished that by now, Twenty-three,' the wardress scolded. 'Laziness don't pay in here, Twenty-three. If you won't work willingly, then you'll be driven to it.'

Miriam kept her head down and scrubbed even more furiously.

'Leave that now, and give us your pint,' the wardress instructed.

Miriam handed out the pint pot, then spread her strip of coarse tablecloth on the shelf and laid her tin plate and spoon neatly upon it. The pint pot was filled with gruel by a 'trusty' prisoner, who with another 'trusty' was carrying a big iron serving container from cell to cell. A third 'trusty' handed Miriam a six ounce hunk of stale grey bread, then her door was slammed shut yet again, and she was left alone to eat her breakfast.

The gruel was made from plain oatmeal and water without any seasoning, and was more water than meal. On her arrival in prison Miriam had been unable to stomach the food. But by now she had realised that if she did not keep her strength up, her already weakly constitution would fast deteriorate while undergoing this harsh regime, and so she forced herself to eat anything and everything that was issued to her. She broke the stale bread into small pieces and added them to the watery gruel which at least imparted the illusion of chewing something more substantial, and began to eat the unappetising mess.

As soon as she had finished eating, she drank some cold water from her jug, and then recommenced scrubbing the floor. Once that was done she began her cell task. Some women were given work in the laundry, or the kitchens or various other cleaning and labouring tasks within the prison, but the vast majority were made to work in their

314

cells at sewing. Some sewed sacks, others fashioned sheets, some of the more skilled made the uniforms for the prisoners, or shirts and underclothing.

It was sheet sewing that Miriam had been given, and she had to hem top and bottom and mid seam a minimum total of 15 sheets a week. The check of the numbers completed were entered on the prisoners' individual 'labour cards'. If a prisoner regularly completed more than the minimum numbers of her particular cell task, she was rewarded by being allowed to write a letter, or receive a visit. If in any week she completed less, then she was punished by refusal of privileges, or solitary confinement on bread and water. If failure to complete the task was considered by the authorities to be a deliberate defiance or rebellion, then the prisoner stood the risk of being brought before the visiting magistrates and having her sentence extended.

Miriam had never been a particularly dextrous seamstress, and she found it very difficult to complete the necessary numbers, but the wardresses accepted that she was trying her hardest, and so took a lenient view. Although they gave her the rough edges of their tongues, and jeered at her ladylike inability to do any heavy manual work, and her slowness at sewing, they did not place her on 'report'.

As she sat sewing in her cell for hour after hour with bowed head, her eyes straining in the poor light to measure the regulation eight stitches per inch along the mid seam of the sheet, Miriam increasingly found that she was becoming able to work automatically, and allow her thoughts to wander freely. She did not know if it was a conscious decision of the authorities to keep the suffragettes separated from each other, but this is what had happened. They had been widely dispersed throughout the prison and consequently only ever encountered each other on rare occasions and at a distance, and since a silence rule was strictly enforced they had not been able to shout any messages or encouragement to each other.

She had served nearly three weeks of her sentence now,

and during that time had only glimpsed Rosie at a distance once each day, when Miriam was taken to the vast exercise yard for the daily hour of compulsory exercise. This process entailed hundreds of prisoners walking anti-clockwise in single file around several concentric oval concrete rings, widely separated by grass swards. They were forbidden to attempt to talk or to signal to each other, and were closely watched by warders and wardresses.

Despite these strictures Miriam welcomed the daily respite from the bleak, damp-smelling confines of the cell block, and breathed deeply of the fresh air, and feasted her eyes on the lush greenery of the trees which towered up from the gardens of the opulent villas beyond the high yard walls. Any other type of contact with the outside world had been virtually non-existent. Miriam had only been allowed to send one letter, and that was after she had served a fortnight. She had written to Emma at Cotswold House and was anxiously awaiting a reply.

The glimpses she had obtained of Rosie caused Miriam considerable concern however. Rosie's face had appeared pallid and haggard, she had walked with a bowed head and shoulders and a shuffling, uncertain gait as if her body was hardly strong enough to support her weight.

Immersed in her thoughts Miriam sewed steadily on, knowing that at half-past eight there would be a welcome break from this mindless drudgery. Each morning at that time her cell block was unlocked and taken to the chapel for their daily religious service. And now the bells rang to signal that fleeting respite.

'Line up! Line up! Stop talking Seven. Tie your cap-strings Thirteen, you looks like a cinder-picker.'

The tall raw-boned wardress hectored the line of prisoners as she moved down them, her hard eyes seeking and finding faults.

'When was the last time you changed that apron, Sixteen? It's a disgrace!'

'Stop talking, Eighteen!'

'I warn't talkin' Ma'am,' the woman denied, and the wardress shouted angrily.

'If I says you were talking, then you were talking. And if you gives me any more of your sauce, you'll be on report! So keep your big mouth shut.'

She reached the end of the line and then retraced her steps to its centre. Spaced at periodic intervals along the landing her fellow wardresses awaited her commands.

'Turn to your left, left turn!' she shouted, and the prisoners raggedly obeyed.

'By the left, forward march!'

The long line shuffled off, and the wardresses marched beside them hectoring as they moved.

'Keep your head up, Ten!'

'Move smartly there, Twenty-one, you're waddling along like a ruptured duck!'

'Swing those arms! Swing those arms!'

'No talking! No talking!'

'If you looks at me like that again Seventeen, you'll be on report!'

They filed into the chapel and lined out in the pews. Still in this hallowed place the wardresses harried and chivvied like sheepdogs.

'Stop looking about you, Twelve!'

'Keep your eyes to the front! Keep your eyes to the front! Next one I sees looking about will be on report!'

'Silence! Keep silence!'

But despite all the threats and harassment, and the vigilance of the wardresses, there was a continuous sly susurration of voices underlying the outbursts of hacking coughing. Prisoners' eyes met and winked. Hissed messages were passed and received. Notes scribbled on fragments of paper were surreptitiously passed from hand to hand.

Miriam's eyes flickered in search of familiar faces, hoping against hope for some sight of Rosie, but all surrounding her were nameless strangers. Once more she was struck at how many old, grey heads were present among the prisoners, and how many women there were who seemed never to have been young, so cruelly battered had they been by their lives. Here and there she encountered a fresh complexion and bright eyes, but these were rare in the worn, faded mass. There was an almost tangible air of hopelessness and defeat emanating from these women, and their faces were anxious and tense as if they were expecting dread news at any moment.

The clergyman was young and boyish looking, and his eyes were kindly behind his pince-nez. His voice was soft, and he spoke in the mellifluous fluting tones favoured by the Anglican clergy.

The prisoners remained standing all through the short service, which consisted of a lesson read by the clergyman, another read by the chief wardress, three hymns and joint prayers. As on every other morning many of the prisoners wept bitterly as certain words spoken or sung touched the bitter memories they carried within their hearts. It seemed to Miriam that every time there was a mention of children, home, affection, pity for the sinner, hope for the hopeless, rest for the weary, then somewhere among the mass of prisoners some poor soul would break down and give vent to her grief and anguish. Some even sobbed as the first chords of the organ resounded and massed voices began to sing.

The service ended with the clergyman's final blessing and file by file the prisoners were marched out of the lines of pews. Miriam moved in her turn and was walking up the centre aisle when she felt a hand fleetingly clasp her own and a piece of paper was thrust into her fingers. She started with shock, and instantly the sharp eyes of a wardress fixed on her.

'What's the matter with you, Twenty-three?'

'Nothing Ma'am,' Miriam answered submissively, and crushed the scrap of paper into a tiny ball within her clenched fist.

Locked in her cell once more, with the parting admonition of the wardress to be quicker with her sewing task, Miriam smoothed out the scrap of paper and quickly scanned the few words scribbled upon it.

'Rosie Spiers ill. Taken to infirmary.'

Miriam drew a sharp breath of apprehension, and for brief moments did not know whether she wanted to blame or curse the unknown woman who had sent her that information.

'What does she think I can do?' she asked herself with a sensation of utter helplessness. 'What can I do to help poor Rosie?'

She experienced a fleeting sense of angry resentment directed against the hapless Rosie for having allowed herself to fall ill. And then instantly furiously admonished herself for that reaction.

'The poor girl cannot help her own ill-health, can she! Are you becoming so heartless, that you could feel anything other than pity for her?'

Following her own moments of weakness and surrender to self-pity when she had first been locked in this cell, Miriam had found, to her own surprise, that she possessed considerable resources of courage and fortitude in the face of her own adversity. She had discovered that although she was not enjoying her imprisonment, she was able in some strange and perverse fashion to draw satisfaction from this unpleasant and degrading experience, and regard it in much the same way that she imagined a soldier would regard the sufferings he must endure in a campaign of war. At times she would smile to herself at this fancy, amusedly picturing a scenario in which – just as a soldier was awarded a medal for each campaign – the suffragette would be awarded a medal for each prison sentence she served: Holloway 1906, Winson Green 1907, Walton 1909, Warwick and Worcester 1910.

She returned to sewing, the coarse-woven sheets, but found that the visual image of Rosie Spiers's pallid, haggard features, and faltering gait continually imposed itself upon her mental vision. Although Miriam had managed to harden herself against her own sufferings, and accepted fully the necessity for all suffragettes to make sacrifices and take risks in their battle against the authorities, still she could not repress her concern for Rosie, and the sense of burgeoning guilt that in a way it was her, Miriam's, fault, that the young woman had been drawn into this present predicament. As she sewed hour after weary hour she argued with herself.

'I should never have persuaded her to come to London.'

'You didn't persuade her, she came of her own accord!'

'But she didn't know that it would end by her being sent to prison.'

'Neither did any of the others.'

'I should never have influenced her to become a militant suffragette.'

'You didn't. She was a suffragette before you were. Rosie knew what she was about when she joined the movement.'

'But did she though?'

'Of course. She's not a child.'

' But she is a child in her knowledge of the world.'

'Nonsense! She knows more about life than you do!'

'But she is ignorant and uneducated.'

'And so are millions of other women, and that is why we must fight to better their lives.'

'How can being sent to prison better Rosie's life?'

'It can, and it will. Sacrifices have to be made, and some of us have to pay the price. Rosie is a suffragette. She wanted to fight for the rights of women. All you have done is to enable her to achieve her wish to join in the front line of the fight.'

Although the harder side of Miriam's nature appeared to have won the argument, still the softer side continued to torment her. So much so, that when eventually during the afternoon the time came for exercise, Miriam resolved to do whatever she could to find out about Rosie's illness. She knew that she would have to go about this in a devious manner, and not give away the information about the illicit note she had received in the chapel. If that occurrence was discovered by the prison officials then she could well find herself in solitary confinement.

The day was cold and overcast, and Miriam shivered as the chill air struck through her threadbare clothing. Throughout the hour of exercise, as she tramped round and round the great yard she searched constantly for Rosie's thin figure. But although she spotted several of the other suffragettes, there was no sign of her friend.

When she returned to the cell block it was one of the younger wardresses who was locking the prisoners back into their cells. This wardress had the plump, ruddy features of a countrywoman, and had not yet acquired the grim, forbidding mask of her older colleagues.

Miriam waited until the young wardress came to her cell door and asked tentatively: 'May I speak with you, Ma'am?'

The plump, ruddy features were impassive, but the wide-spaced blue eyes were hostile. 'What about, Twenty-three?' The accent was a rustic burr.

'If you please, Ma'am. I'm greatly worried about my friend, Rosie Spiers. I've noticed during the last few days when I've been on exercise that she looking very ill. And today I couldn't see her in the yard at all. I was wondering if she is all right?'

'How should I know that?' the wardress challenged brusquely. 'And how should I know who the devil Rosie Spiers might be? There's hundreds of thieves and worse in this place. Why should you think that I take any interest in knowing who they are, and how they might be feeling?'

Miriam felt angry resentment stirring within her, that she should be in the position of having to beg humbly for such a simple, harmless piece of information. But she maintained her humble, submissive manner. 'I'm sorry to trouble you, Ma'am. But I'm really worried about my friend. It's not as though she's a criminal, or has done anything wrong. She's one of the suffragettes.'

'Oh, she's one of you lot, is she?' The wardress seemed unimpressed by that information.

'Yes, Ma'am, she is.'

The young woman frowned, and gave a disparaging toss of her head. 'One of the rich ladies, is she? Amusing herself by being a suffragette, 'cos she aren't got anything better to do?'

'No Ma'am, she's a working girl.' Miriam found that her indignation was flaring, and now her voice lost some of its humble submissiveness. 'And she's not amusing herself by being a suffragette at all, Ma'am. She's suffered poverty and hardship all her life, and all she is trying to do is to improve the lot of all working women. She's not a thief, but a good-living, honest, hard-working young woman, who would not be in here at all if there was any justice to be found in this world.'

'You watch your tone of voice, Twenty-three!' the wardress barked sharply. 'In here you're all the same. You're convicted prisoners. Now, get away from the door.'

Miriam's impulse was to argue, but she realised the utter futility of doing so. She stepped back as the door slammed shut, the key rattled and the bolt shot home.

Slowly the seething frustration of her own impotence calmed and she seated herself and once more took up the sheet, needle and thread.

It was several hours later when the hunk of bread and margarine which constituted the evening meal was being handed to Miriam by the 'trusty' prisoner, that the young wardress came down the landing and stopped at the open cell door.

As the trusty moved to the next cell the young wardress told Miriam gruffly, 'Your friend, Rosie Spiers, is in the infirmary. She collapsed last night and coughed up a lot of blood. From what's been told me, she's got galloping consumption I should think. Anyway, she's being cared for, but she's very sick at present, and if she keeps coughing up the amount o' blood that she's doing, then it don't look very promising for her.'

Before Miriam could reply, the door was slammed closed and locked and bolted. Miriam slumped down on her stool and put the hunk of bread and margarine aside. If what the wardress had said was true, if Rosie Spiers had got the virulent tubercular illness popularly known as galloping consumption, then the young woman was most certainly under sentence of death! A sentence against which there was no appeal, and that would rapidly and mercilessly claim her life. Miriam gazed unseeing at the thick, white-limed walls closing her in, and pity for Rosie whelmed over her. 'Poor poor Rosie. She doesn't deserve this to happen to her. Not after the hard life she's been forced to lead.'

Now the pity became slowly laced with a smouldering anger and resolve hardened and steeled within Miriam Josceleyne's heart. 'No woman should be forced to lead such a life as poor Rosie has. No woman should have to die such a death, without ever having known what it is to live without want and hardship. If poor Rosie dies, then I'll not let that weaken me. I'll only fight all the harder to achieve what she wanted herself. Justice, and a fair chance for all women everywhere.' Her gaze fell upon the hunk of hard stale bread and greyish greasy margarine, and suddenly she picked it up in both hands and bit at it voraciously. Tearing off chunks with her teeth and chewing and swallowing in rapid succession.

'I've got to be strong and hard, and do whatever I must to keep my own health. Otherwise I'll be of no use in this war.' Her resolve became implacable. 'I won't stop fighting now. No matter what might happen to me. I won't stop fighting.'

Chapter Thirty-Nine

Because of her youth and resilience. Laura Hughes adapted quickly to the hard, back breaking work in the washing room at the laundry. At first the other women there were suspicious of her. Her obvious lack of manual work experience and her educated accent caused them to regard her with a latent hostility. But inevitably in the small gossipy world of the town with its intermingled networks of relationships the other women soon came to know Laura's story. The fact that she was supporting and caring for Rosie Spiers's brother, and was regarded as a good neighbour by her fellow inhabitants of Hill Street, coupled with her willingness to work, and her unfailing good temper, disarmed them and they accepted her and began to include her in their chatter and crude, bawdy humour.

The fact that she was a suffragette also became known to the women, but Laura resisted the temptation to proselytise. She feared that the management would not take kindly to one of their employees pointing out how working women were being exploited and victimised by employers like the Steam Laundry. Some of the more intelligent women however, expressed a great interest in the question of female suffrage, and at times during their brief rest-breaks, Laura would talk quietly to them about the aims and work of the Women's Social and Political Union. The seed she sowed fell on fertile soil in some cases, and there were several of the younger women who expressed their desires to join the movement.

Laura asked them to wait until Miriam Josceleyne should be freed from prison, and then they could re-form the Redditch Branch of the movement, and once more embark on a recruiting drive.

When at odd moments Laura stopped to think about her present life of almost ceaseless work, and hard times, she was amazed to find how cheerful she felt about it, and with what high hopes she faced her future. 'You are being tempered in the fires of adversity, my girl,' she would tell herself jokingly. 'And will soon become pure steel.'

> *'She's only a bird in a gilded cage,*
> *A beautiful sight to see,*
> *You'd think she was happy and free from care,*
> *She's not though she seems to beeee . . .'*

The washing room rang with a cacophony of chorusing voices, ranging from the tuneful to the discordant. Laura smiled as she bent over the steaming trough and mauled the thick, heavy, saturated blankets. One aspect of life in the laundry never failed to excite her wonder, and her admiration. This was the almost constant good humour of her fellow workers. She knew enough about them now, to appreciate the harshness of their lives, and the tragedies and sufferings that some of them had undergone, and indeed were undergoing. Yet they could still laugh and sing, and face life with an undaunted courage. She raised her own pleasant-timbred voice with the others.

> *''Tis sad when you think of her wasted life,*
> *For youth cannot mate with age,*
> *Her beauty was sold for an old man's gold,*
> *She's a bird in a gilded caaaggggeeee.'*

As the last lingering notes died away Laura's neighbour at the trough, a squat, tough-featured Irishwoman named Bridget Gorman, suddenly exclaimed: 'Jasus, Joseph and Mary! Look what the cat's dragged in?'

Another woman, Letty Lewis, snorted disgustedly, 'Gawd Strewth! Has we got to have that lazy cow back in here?'

'Her's still got enough bloody muck plastered on her face to fill a midden, I see,' a third woman sneered.

Laura peered through the steam clouds that filled the big room. She saw that the foreman had entered accompanied by a fat woman with a mass of frizzed hair jutting out around her head, and a thickly powdered and rouged face. Curious about the hostile reaction of her colleagues, Laura asked, 'Who is she?'

'That's Bella Thomas,' the Irishwoman told her. 'She managed to wangle herself an easy job in the folding room, but it looks as if she's being shifted back in here. She's a useless cow!'

'Her's a bloody whore! No decent 'ooman 'ud goo around with her face plastered with paint like her does,' Letty Lewis growled.

'Bella Thomas?' Laura murmured, and wondered why the name seemed familiar to her. She stared curiously at the rouged flabby cheeks and the red-painted Cupid-bowed lips. Although she also had been bred to believe that a decent woman never painted her face, and that those women who did so were little better than common prostitutes, in her secret heart Laura could not really condemn any ageing woman who tried to hide the ravages of time by using powder and other cosmetics. She pitied them rather, because she found the final results to be pathetic and grotesque in appearance.

The foreman brought Bella Thomas to a place at the long wash-trough opposite Laura's, and as Laura stared the newcomer's mascaraed eyes briefly met her own, and pity suddenly lanced through her as she realised, 'The poor thing is frightened.'

Laura glanced from side to side at the glowering features of her neighbours. 'Judging by the looks they're giving her, she might well have good cause to be,' she thought. She felt apprehensive that the women might make some actual physical assault on Bella Thomas, once the foreman had left the washing room. But in the event they merely ignored the newcomer. They isolated her by moving as far away from where she stood as was possible, and even trying to avoid looking at her, and continued with their own chattering along the length of the trough.

Laura was troubled by this cruel ostracism, but could not

help but wonder if the women might have very good reasons for behaving as they did, and so she also made no attempt to talk to Bella Thomas. But she took surreptitious glances at the painted face, and felt pity for the misery she saw mirrored there.

Just before the midday break however something happened that drove all thoughts of Bella Thomas's purgatory from her mind.

'Laura, come to the office 'ull you,' the foreman shouted from the doorway, and Laura wiped her hands on her already damp skirts and removed her long rubber apron. As she hurried through the room her workmates teased her good naturedly.

'You'm gooing to be give the manager's job, I shouldn't wonder, kid.'

'You take care that the foreman doon't get you across the bloody table, my duck. He's a sod for the women!'

'Perhaps the boss wants to join the suffragettes, Laura?'

Inside the foreman's small office a middle-aged constable was waiting.

'Am you Laura Hughes, young 'ooman?'

'I am.' Laura frowned with apprehensive concern. 'Have I done something wrong?'

The man smiled bleakly. 'Not to my knowledge, Missy. Be you living in number 3 court, Hill Street, in the house of a woman named Rose Spiers?'

Sheer dread exploded in Laura's mind, causing her to demand in panic, 'Is it Tommy? Is it Tommy Spiers? Has something happened to him?'

'No Missy, the poor bugger's still where you left him. Tied to his bed.' The constable's tone was ambiguous, then recognising Laura's fear his grim manner softened a trifle. 'No Missy, it aren't about Tommy Spiers I've come. It's his sister, Rose Spiers.'

Premonition of doom swept over Laura, and she suddenly felt weak at the knees.

'There was a phone call come to the Police Station an hour past, from Holloway Prison in London. I have to inform you that Rose Spiers, a prisoner at Holloway, died at approximately twenty minutes past two o'clock this morning. They said she died as a result of an uncontrollable haemorrhage. It seems she'd got galloping consumption. Only they also called it summat else. Pulmon . . . pulmonary tuberculosis, I think it was what they said.'

'Ohh dear God!' Laura ejaculated, and her body swayed visibly as she fought against the wave of nausea that threatened to overwhelm her.

"Ere my duck, you sit down!' the foreman intervened, and taking Laura by her arm guided her on to a stool. He scowled at the policeman, and challenged angrily. 'Couldn't you have broke the news a bit more gently?'

The constable shook his grizzled head. 'I'se never known any way that bad news can be delivered without causing pain.' He stared down at Laura's bowed head and shaking shoulders, as she buried her face in her hands and began to weep, and he gnawed his lower lip uncertainly. Then he told the foreman in a hoarse whisper. 'I doon't want to moither this young 'ooman any further, but the prison has got to be told what the next o'kin wants doing wi' the body.' He paused and spread his arms in a rueful gesture of bafflement. 'The only next o' kin that I'se seen so far is that idiot brother. And I've been informed that her Dad and Mam are in the Workhouse. They'm in the Bromsgrove Union, and has bin for years. So they aren't got any money for a funeral, tha's for certain. They'll be buried in paupers' graves themselves, wun't they?'

The foreman nodded agreement, then said: 'Well, if I recollects correctly, old Walter Spiers, the butcher, is related to 'um. But how close, I don't know. It's a shame about Rosie though. Her used to play with my kids when they were all nippers. Her was a nice little wench.'

He fell silent for a moment or two, looking down at the weeping woman with an expression of sympathy. Then asked, 'What'll happen to Rosie if there's nobody can afford to bury her?'

'She'll be planted in the nearest Potter's Field to the prison,' the constable stated positively. 'That's the usual procedure.'

'Jesus Christ! What a bloody disgrace!' the foreman exclaimed feelingly, and the constable nodded.

'I know, but what else can be done with her? She wunt be the first to have the shame of a pauper's grave, 'ull she? And it's as sure as God made little apples, that she wunt be the last. Not by millions she wunt.'

Even through the depths of her misery Laura had absorbed what the two men had been saying, and now she stared up at them with tears still falling and declared fiercely. 'No she shan't! Rosie shan't be buried in any pauper's grave if I can help it.'

The constable nodded encouragingly. 'That's the spirit, Missy. Does you want us to inform the prison that you'll be paying the expenses for having the body sent back here to Redditch?'

'Yes please, if you will,' Laura choked out between her tears. 'I shall bury Rosie decently. She deserves that. She doesn't deserve the shame of being buried in a pauper's grave. I want her to come back to her home.'

The constable nodded approvingly. 'All right Missy, I'll goo back directly to the station and have the message phoned through to Holloway. You'd best come round to the station yourself, as soon as you feels up to it, and find out how to make the necessary arrangements for having Rose Spiers brought back here.'

Laura gulped back a sob, and nodded. 'I will, Officer.' Then once again grief shuddered through her and she could only weep helplessly.

Chapter Forty

'He was here again last night then,' Mrs Elwood declared disapprovingly, and clucked her tongue loudly against the roof of her mouth.

Emma Josceleyne turned on to her back in the rumpled bed and stretched out her arms, her love-swollen lips parting as she yawned widely.

'You'm a bloody fool, girl!' Mrs Elwood scolded, and this time Emma Josceleyne reacted sharply.

'It's none o' your business!'

'It is my business when I sees somebody I'm fond of making a bloody fool of hersen!' the cook retorted. 'Harry Vivaldi has slept here wi' you every night for the past week, aren't he?'

'So, what if he has?' Emma's beautiful face was sullen. 'Nobody else knows about it!'

'Doon't talk so bloody sarft!' the cook riposted scathingly. 'The girls know about it. You sends 'um to bed early, but they'se got eyes and ears, and they knows who it is that you lets into the back door. And who it is that sneaks out of the house in the early hours. I caught 'um giggling about you and your fancy man this morning when I come to work.'

'They'll be giggling the other side of their bloody faces if you'm telling the truth,' Emma threatened fiercely.

'Oh yes! Oh yes!' The fat woman stood with her massive arms akimbo, hands on her broad hips. 'That's the answer, aren't it? Smack the poor wenches' faces because you'm making a bloody fool of yoursen! That's the answer! I doon't think!'

The younger woman became a little flustered. 'Well, I

'doon't know what you'm getting all roiled up about, Mrs Elwood. I'm doing no harm to anybody by having a bit of fun, am I?'

'Youm going the right way round to doing harm to yourself.' The cook now seemed more distressed than angry. 'Harry Vivaldi is no good, my duck! He's only out for what he can get for himself.'

'Well, he's got precious little out of me, has he?' the young woman protested, and then reddened and grinned wryly. 'Well, I suppose you could say he's had plenty of something from me.' The grin became mischievously salacious, and she chuckled. 'But then, I'm getting an awful lot out of him, aren't I?'

'You'm getting yourself talked about all over the bloody town!' The broad features of the older woman were troubled. 'I'se heard a few things said, and they warn't pleasant to hear, I'll tell you. You'm becoming the mock of the town.'

'Fuck the town!' Emma lifted forked fingers in a gesture of obscene contempt. 'I was the talk of the bloody town when I married old Hector, warn't I? And all their talk did me no harm then, did it? So I'm buggered if it's gooing to worry me now. Whatever the town wants to say about me then let 'um say it. I don't give a bugger for any on 'um!'

Mrs Elwood recognised the obduracy in the young woman's expression, and shrugged in defeat. 'All right then. Have it your way. But doon't you come shrikin' to me when the bugger does you down!'

Emma grinned confidently. 'Doon't you worry about me, Mrs Elwood. There's no man ever gooing to do me down!'

'I'll get your breakfast ready,' the cook grunted, and waddled heavily out of the room.

Beneath the sheets Emma ran her hands slowly over her naked body, and her throat tightened as she mentally relived the wild passion of the past night. She had never in her life known such thrilling pleasure, such exquisite lust, such ecstatic satisfaction as that she was experiencing with Harry Vivaldi in her bed. Even now, satisfied as she had been in the early hours of that morning, she felt the

331

tremors of desire begin to course up from her intimate flesh and spread throughout her body in shivering waves. The man was beginning to affect her like an addictive drug, and memories of his smooth warm muscularity teased and excited her through the hours that they were apart. Until, when he came to her in the darkness of the night, she was so hungry for his thrusting maleness that she could hardly contain herself.

Now she experienced a fleeting disquietude. Although she would never admit it to herself, and would die before speaking of it to anyone else, she was beginning to sense that the dominance in this relationship was gradually passing to Harry Vivaldi. Whereas scant weeks ago she had only toyed with him, and pleasured herself, now she was finding that thoughts of him were starting to fill her mind at all hours of the day and night, and that the desire to see, and to be with him was ever strengthening. A short time ago she had not cared whether or not he shared a house, a bed, an intimacy with Bella Thomas. Lately the imps of jealousy had started to tease and torment her, and their teasing and tormenting were fast becoming more aggravating, and harder to endure. Now lying in the bed, her fingers tantalising her flesh, her thoughts filled with images of her lover, the taste and smell of him still lingering upon her senses, Emma fought to consider rationally what was happening to her.

'Am I falling in love with him?' she asked herself with a stirring of alarm. 'I didn't want that to happen.' Then a tiny voice in her mind queried: 'Well, what does it matter if you're falling in love with him? He's in love with you, isn't he? He tells you he is night after night, doesn't he?'

A smile of satisfaction wreathed her shapely mouth, but that smile was almost instantly wiped away as a more strident unbidden voice invaded her thoughts: 'But does he really mean what he says? How can you be sure that he means it? A handsome chap like him has bound to have had hundreds of women after him. How can you be so sure that he really loves you?'

Made disturbed and uncertain by this fresh voice, the young woman rose from her bed and in effort to dispel her disquieting thoughts, hastened to dress and go downstairs.

By the time that she reached the kitchen, Emma had recovered all her customary confidence in herself, and had succeeded in quelling her doubts about Harry Vivaldi's love for her. Her two pert maidservants kept flicking sly glances towards her, and she smiled inwardly as she seated herself at the big kitchen table, and told Mrs Elwood: 'I'll have two eggs with my bacon this morning, Mrs Elwood. I'm really hungry after last night.'

From the corner of her eye she surreptitiously watched the maidservants winking at each other and smothering their giggles. Emma came to a sudden decision, and acted on impulse. 'Right, you two. Come and stand in front of me, where I can see you.'

Flustered and made instantly apprehensive by the harshness with which their normally good-tempered mistress spoke to them, the two young girls did as she had bidden, and stood side by side before her, their hands nervously fidgeting from their aprons to the long strings of their dainty white lace caps.

Emma deliberately kept them standing there, until Mrs Elwood had finished cooking her breakfast and had laid it before her. Then she said: 'You sit down there, Mrs Elwood, so I can see you as well.'

The fat woman frowned doubtfully but obeyed, and gruntingly settled her great bulk on to a chair across the table from Emma's seat.

Emma cut and ate a few mouthfuls of the crisp bacon, and richly-yoked eggs, chewing and swallowing with gusto.

'These eggs are grand, Mrs Elwood.' She smiled at the cook. Then she abruptly sobered, and went on in a hard firm voice, 'Right then, it's time to clear the air, I reckon. Now, as you all well know, I've had a gentleman friend of mine sleeping with me this last week.' She stared hard at the girls, as if daring them to giggle. But they only blushed to the roots of their frizzed hair, and stared back, wide-eyed in shock.

'Now that gentleman friend is going to continue sleeping in my bed for just as long as I want him to do. But from now on, he's not going to be sneaking into this house like a thief in the bloody night, and sneaking out again before dawn, just because somebody might see him, and bad mouth me around the town.'

'We'se never bad mouthed you, Ma'm!' Becca the maid shook her head frantically, blurting out denials in a tumble of words. 'We'se never! I'se never said. None of us ... We'se never said nothing ... Nothing at all ... It's the truth, Ma'm.'

'Hold your tongue!' Emma whiplashed the command, and the girl fell silent, her hands twisting and wrenching her apron.

Her fellow maid began to sob noisily, rubbing her fists into her eyes, and choking out: 'We both loves you, Ma'm. We aren't never said nothing bad about you. Never, Ma'm. Never ever.'

Emma softened abruptly, and rising from her chair she went to the crying girls and hugged them both in her arms, soothing them. 'There now, there now, hush your crying. I know that you've never said anything bad about me. Hush up now, hush.'

'Am you gooing to send us away, Ma'm?' one girl asked in a frightened tone.

'Doon't send us away, Ma'm. Doon't do that. Please doon't,' her friend begged tearfully.

Emma shook her head, and reassured, 'No, of course I'm not going to send you away. Now dry your eyes and stop this nonsense.'

Slowly their sobs hiccupped to a halt, and they stared up at her with tremulous lips and reddened eyes.

'That's better.' Emma smiled, and released them to return to her seat.

She addressed all three servants: 'Right then, girls. From now on, my gentleman friend, Mr Harry Vivaldi, will be coming to this house at whatever hour might be convenient. And he'll be sharing my bed.' She beamed radiantly at their stunned faces, and added, 'And if anyone in the town wants to know about it, you can tell 'um the truth. And you can also tell 'um from me, that I sleeps with Mr Harry Vivaldi because he's a bloody marvellous shag!'

334

All three mouths gaped, and six eyes stared wide in stupefaction.

Emma threw back her head and laughter pealed from her mouth, and as she laughed the infection of her mirth spread to her companions. Hesitant smiles curved their lips, giggles erupted.

Mrs Elwood shook her head and gasped out: 'Gawd Strewth! You'm a bloody caution, you am, Emma Josceleyne. You'm a bloody caution!' She then burst out laughing and the two maids followed suit, and all four women laughed and laughed until the tears streamed down their cheeks, and their sides ached, and their breath whooped in their throats.

Chapter Forty-One

During the days immediately following on Rosie Spier's death, Laura Hughes learned another bitter lesson about poverty. She learned that for the poor death could be an unaffordable luxury. She was forced to pawn almost everything that was pawnable from the house and her own belongings to pay for the cost of transporting Rosie's corpse back to Hill Street. Now the large oblong box in which the prison had returned Rosie was resting on trestles in the minute back yard, covered with a borrowed tarpaulin sheet.

Laura could draw comfort from one thing however, and that was that Tommy Spiers appeared unaffected by his sister's death. Indeed, Laura sometimes wondered if the poor man even remembered that he had had a sister named Rosie. When the long wooden box containing Rosie's body had been carried through the tiny house and into the back yard, Tommy Spiers had evinced great interest in it, stroking and patting the rough, unplaned wood, and muttered gibberish. Laura had tried to explain gently that Rosie was inside the box, but Tommy had only grunted and chuckled and talked to himself without any sign of understanding.

It was dark when Laura came back this night from her work, and as she let herself into the tenement, she called loudly: 'Hello Tommy, I'm home.'

She lit the oil-lamp and went upstairs to check that Tommy was all right, and found him lying asleep, the rope harness securely tied as she had left it that morning. Tommy's jaw had fallen slackly, and as he snored, saliva snaked from the corners of his mouth. Laura took a piece of clean rag and wiped his mouth and stubbled chin and throat, but he did not wake. She saw the empty bowl by the bedside and knew that Maudie Emms had fed him during the long day, and she took the empty bowl and the almost full chamber-pot back downstairs with her.

Laura went outside and emptied the chamber-pot on to the stinking midden heap which filled the centre of the courtyard. This offensive box no longer turned her stomach as it had done when she had first come to live in the court, and Laura sometimes marvelled at how quickly she had accustomed herself to the less savoury aspects of Hill Street life. As she moved back to the open door one of the neighbours from across the court came to the bedroom window to call to her.

'Is that you, Laura?'

Laura turned back to see the shabby figure of Maria Cull framed against the weakly light of an oil-lamp in a broken-glassed window.

'Yes, it is, Maria.'

'Has you 'eard about the bloody rent?' the woman demanded to know.

Laura shook her head. 'No. I've heard nothing.'

'They'se only bin and gone and raised it!' the other woman cursed aggrievedly. 'The bloody bastards!'

Actual alarm shivered through Laura. She was finding it so difficult to manage financially at this time, that even the slightest increase in her rent could well mean disaster. 'How much extra are they asking, Maria?' she asked fearfully.

'Another bloody one and six!' the other woman spat out disgustedly.

'But how can they possibly justify any increase at all?' Laura exclaimed plaintively.

'We'em under a new owner now, aren't we?' Maria Cull explained. 'This court used to be owned by old Mother Wilkinson. But since her's passed away it's come down to Cleopatra Dolton. Does you know her? Her's the one they calls the "Queen of Egypt". Bloody hard-hearted whore that her is! I knew her when her was a raggedy-arsed morsel in Silver Street! I could spit when I sees her now, parading around the town like her was bloody royalty with her bloody nose in the air. Stuck up cow!'

Laura felt physically sick. A shilling and sixpence on the rent at this time would meant that it would take even longer to raise the money for Rosie's burial. As it was, she was already being forced to face the fact that she might have to let Rosie be buried by the Parish in a pauper's grave after all. A prospect that – knowing how shameful the living Rosie would have found it – Laura could hardly bear to contemplate. The neighbours were taking up a collection among themselves to help Laura to buy Rosie a proper coffin, and to pay for the burial. But with the current high levels of unemployment in Hill Street and consequent lack of money, that collection was mounting with a painful slowness, and as the days passed the smell emanating from Rosie's temporary coffin was giving ever stronger warnings that her burial was overdue.

'Are you sure that it's that much, Maria?' Laura desperately hoped for some mistake to have been made. 'One and sixpence seems an awfully large increase.'

'O' course I'm sure,' the woman asserted irritably. 'It was Caleb Louch who come round to tell us not a bloody hour since. Cleo Dolton's made him her rent man. He says that her's gooing to have the water and gas piped to every one of her houses. And that the rent increase is to help pay for it. He says that her's going to have proper drainage put in, and even new privies built.'

Maria Cull cackled with derisive laughter.

'To lissen to him you'd ha' thought that we'em gooing to be living in a bloody palace, instead o' this shit. Lying bastard that he is.'

'But if it is true, then it will be wonderful, won't it?' Despite her worry, Laura could not help but be impressed by what she had been told.

Drawn by the voices Maudie Emms came to her front door. 'Laura, I'se bin left a message for you from Caleb Louch. Has Maria told you that he's our new rent man?'

'Yes, she has,' Laura confirmed.

'Ahhr,' Maudie Emms nodded, then went on in troubled tones, 'It aren't good news for you, I'm afraid, my wench.

338

Caleb Louch reckons that you and Rosie am behind wi'
your rent. He reckons you owes three weeks. And he says
to tell you that he'll be back for all the rent you owes come
Saturday night.'

'Dear God!' Laura exclaimed softly. 'I never knew we
owed that.'

She had always paid her share of the household
expenses to Rosie at the end of each week, and Rosie had
then dealt with the payment of the rent and so on.

'He's a hard bugger, is Caleb Louch!' Maria Cull stated
feelingly, having had dealings with the man in her own
life. 'If he comes for the rent, you make sure that you'se
got it ready to give him, my duck. Because if you aren't
he'll hoick you and Tommy out into the street as soon as
look at you.'

When she was again in the small front room of the
house, Laura sat staring at the dead ashes in the firegrate,
and depression threatened to overwhelm her. She shivered
as the cold crept into her body, but somehow could not
find the necessary volition to clear out the ashes and light a
fire to warm herself.

Over and over again she made mental reckonings of
income, and outgoings, and over and over again found
that the totals she arrived at brought her only despair. 'I
could only just about manage to survive even if I didn't
have to find the money for Rosie's coffin, and to bury her
in a private grave,' she concluded sadly. She felt near to
tears. 'The neighbours aren't going to be able to collect
enough money in time to bury Rosie, try though they
might. And I can't keep her out in the yard there for much
longer. Poor Rosie is fast becoming a health hazard for all
of us.' She sighed raggedly, rubbed her brimming eyes,
then blew her nose hard on a large piece of rag.

'It looks as if I'm going to have to apply to the Parish to
bury you, Rosie. I'm sorry. I'm so sorry. I know how
shamed you will be by it. But there's nothing else that I can
do. There's no way I can raise the money. I've nothing left
to pawn or to sell.'

She thought of the coming Saturday when the daunting
Caleb Louch would come to demand the rent owing, and

she shook her head defeatedly. 'It's going to take the money I've saved towards Rosie's burial, and nearly all my wages for this week. Tommy and I will be on short rations next week, that's certain.' Another long ragged sigh of despair gusted from her. 'If only Miriam were here. I could have borrowed the money from her. It's no use my going to see Emma Josceleyne though. She's made her views on us suffragettes very clear.'

Then a fresh thought occurred, and with that thought there burgeoned a faint hope. 'I could go and see Cleopatra Dolton, and explain the problems I face to her. She was kind to me before, and she offered to contribute towards the Movement, didn't she? Maybe she would be prepared to let me pay the rent off later, after I've buried Rosie.'

Laura decided to act immediately, knowing that if she continued to ponder this idea, she would find a thousand reasons for not throwing herself on the mercy of Cleopatra Dolton.

It was the gaunt, sour-featured housekeeper, Mrs Danks, who opened the door to Laura.

'My name is Laura Hughes. I'd like to see Mrs Dolton, please,' Laura requested quietly.

The housekeeper's eyes flickered up and down the young woman's figure, and Laura could sense the difficulty the woman was experiencing in placing her, Laura, in the social scale. Mrs Danks was finding it hard to reconcile this visitor's educated accents and self-confident manner, with the worn and work-stained clothing. While she was still trying to decide how to treat the unexpected caller, her mistress came into the gaslit hallway and up to the door.

'What is it, Mrs Danks?'

'It's a young 'ooman – says she wants to see you, Mrs Dolton.'

Cleopatra Dolton peered out of the doorway, and then smiled. 'Why, it's Laura Hughes, isn't it? Do come in.'

She led the way into the drawing-room where a large fire was burning in a highly-polished grate.

'Please sit down, Miss Hughes.'

Now that the meeting had come, Laura found herself

feeling almost ashamed of her reason for making this call. She shook her head. 'I'll remain standing, if you don't mind, Mrs Dolton. This isn't really a social call.'

As always when she saw this woman Laura was struck by the sensuality she exuded. Cleopatra Dolton was dressed in high-collared, close-fitting, hip-hugging black silk, and wore her mass of black hair loosely coiled, with tendrils of curls curling in the Spanish style around her small shapely ears.

Cleopatra Dolton shrugged casually. 'As you prefer, Miss Hughes.' Then sat down herself. 'What did you want to see me about?'

Laura was by now feeling distinctly ill at ease. Her own pride was hurting at having to come here as a supplicant for favours. But she told herself angrily, 'Stop behaving like a damn fool. Rosie must be buried decently.' She drew a deep breath, and steeled herself. 'I've come about the new rent increase, Mrs Dolton . . .'

She saw the surprise in the older woman's dark eyes, and hurriedly explained. 'You are our new landlady, you see. And Caleb Louch has informed us that the rents are to be increased by one and sixpence weekly . . .'

She continued on to tell of Rosie's death, and the difficulty she was experiencing in saving sufficient money to bury her friend decently, and finished: '. . . So I was hoping that you might agree to let me owe the rent until I've paid for Rosie Spiers's burial?'

The olive features of the older woman were inscrutable, but the dark eyes held a curious gleam. 'From what you've told me, Miss Hughes, a large portion of your wages from the laundry are spent in maintaining the idiot brother of Rose Spiers. If you did not have to maintain him, then I take it that you could afford to pay the new rent, and still contribute towards the burial expenses of Rose Spiers?'

'Well, yes, I suppose I could,' Laura agreed, not understanding the reason for this question. 'But that doesn't really have anything to do with this matter does it, Mrs Dolton?'

The other woman frowned sternly. 'On the contrary, Miss Hughes, I think it has a great deal to do with it. This

341

idiot brother of Rose Spiers is no relative of yours, is he? Therefore you are under no legal obligation to spend money that you really cannot afford, in maintaining and supporting him. You could have him put into the Workhouse.'

Laura shook her head in bafflement. 'Legal obligation, no, but I have a moral obligation to support Tommy, Mrs Dolton. I cannot even consider having the poor fellow put into the Workhouse.'

'How so?' the other woman demanded harshly.

'Because Rosie Spiers was my dear friend, Mrs Dolton. And she helped and befriended me in my hour of need. Why, she'd turn in her grave at the thought of poor Tommy being shut away among strangers.'

'And that is also the reason that you are insisting on spending money that you do not possess, in giving her a fine funeral, is it?' Cleopatra Dolton's expression was bordering on the contemptuous. 'And you are asking me to forgo what is rightfully mine, because you wish to spend my money to satisfy your own pretensions as to moral superiority.' Her voice became scathing. 'Frankly, Miss Hughes, it all smacks of hypocritical sanctimoniousness to me. And that sanctimoniousness must be paid for by others such as myself.'

Laura had been listening with an increasing sense of outrage, and now she had heard enough. 'I'll not bother you any longer, Mrs Dolton,' she snapped heatedly. 'There's no need to worry about your money. You'll get it on Saturday, every penny of it. And what is more, I'll still give Rosie a decent burial, and I'll still care for her poor brother for just as long as I am able to do so.'

She swung round and started to leave, but the other woman said sharply: 'Wait!'

Laura halted momentarily, with her hand resting on the shiny brass doorknob. Then shook her head and opened the door to go through it. But before she could take more than a couple of steps, she felt Cleopatra Dolton's hand on her shoulder.

'Please, Miss Hughes! Please wait for just a moment, and hear what I have to say. Please!'

342

Reluctantly Laura turned to face the other woman, and found the dark eyes warm, and the full lips curved in a smile.

'I needed to satisfy myself about the sincerity of your motives, Miss Hughes,' Cleopatra Dolton said huskily. 'Now please wait here for just a few moments. I'll return directly.' She stared hard at Laura's face as if willing the younger woman to accede to her plea.

'I'll be as quick as I possibly can, Miss Hughes. So do please wait.' She hesitated until she saw Laura's reluctant nod of agreement.

'Thank you, Miss Hughes. I shall be as quick as I can,' she affirmed once more, and then disappeared through the doorway across the hall. Despite her promise of speedy return, it was several minutes before she came back carrying two sealed envelopes which she pressed into Laura's hand.

'When Caleb Louch calls on Saturday you are to give him the envelope addressed to him,' she instructed. 'The other envelope is for you. But you are not to open it until you have returned to Hill Street.' She pressed Laura's shoulder warmly with her fingers. 'You're a good woman, Miss Hughes. And now I'll bid you good-night.'

She opened the front door for Laura to pass through.

Laura felt almost dazed with the strangeness of what had occurred, and she mumbled her goodbyes as she went out into the chill of the night, and heard the door close behind her, and the pale shaft of gaslight abruptly vanished leaving her in darkness. Now she felt weariness assail her, and she trudged slowly down Red Lane, and over the railway bridge and up the steep rise of Unicorn Hill.

In the cramped mean tenement she lit the oil-lamp and went first to check that Tommy Spiers was all right. He was still sleeping, but his arms and legs were twitching restlessly, and he was muttering unintelligibly as his head moved from side to side.

For some time Laura remained at his side, and stroked his hot forehead with her cold hands in an attempt to soothe him. When he was quieter she returned downstairs. She felt hungry, but in the tiny cupboard in the back scullery there was only a hunk of stale bread and some hard sour cheese. On her way back home she had passed the fried fish shop at the bottom of Unicorn Hill, and now the memories of the appetising scents of hot fish and chips and saveloys and meat pies that had enveloped her as she passed the shop returned at full strength to torment her, and the juices of raging appetite filled her mouth. She had a shilling in her pocket, and for a few moments was sorely tempted to return to the shop and buy something to eat. But then she remembered that Maudie Emms needed to be paid for feeding and caring for Tommy, and regretfully she thrust the thought of crisp batter, and succulent flakes of fish, and fat golden chips tart with vinegar and salt away from her. Instead she went to the scullery and fetched out the bread and hard cheese, and dipping the bread in a cup of water to soften it, she made a meagre supper.

Deliberately she had fought against the temptation to rip open the envelopes that Cleopatra Dolton had given her. Although even as she did so, she ironically mocked herself for this pointless display of self-discipline. However, she still continued stoically munching her bread and cheese, and drank her cold water, until her hunger was deadened. Only then did she take out the two envelopes, and open the one meant for her.

It contained a sheet of notepaper, and another sealed envelope. Laura scanned the neatly penned note.

Dear Miss Hughes,
Take the enclosed instructions to M. Huntley, the undertaker in Park Road. On receipt he will make all the necessary arrangements to bury your friend, Rose Spiers, in the manner that you wish for. I shall meet all expenses for the funeral and grave plot etc. Knowing your pride, I expect you may raise some objections to this, but please allow me to make this gesture of respect toward Rose Spiers, and towards yourself also.

Sincerely,
Cleopatra Dolton.

P.S. Count it if you will, as my salute for the generosity and self-sacrifice you are displaying in caring for Tommy Spiers.

P.P.S I would also greatly appreciate your allowing my part in this to remain a secret between you and I.

Tears of thankfulness and relief filled Laura's eyes, and it was some seconds before her sight was clear enough for her to carefully open the second envelope. She knew that it was not the act of a lady to read a message addressed to someone else, but in this case she thought that her breaking of the ladylike code of behaviour was forgiveable.

Inside the envelope was a brief note instructing Caleb Louch that until further notice Miss Laura Hughes was to continue paying rent for her tenement at the old rate, and that any arrears owing up to the date of writing were to be written off. Again tears of gratitude brimmed and fell down Laura's cheeks as she carefully replaced the note in the envelope and resealed it.

That night, for the first time since Rosie's death, Laura slept peacefully.

Chapter Forty-Two

It was at breakfast time on the 24th November that the chief wardress came to Miriam Josceleyne's cell to tell her that she was to be released at midday together with the other imprisoned suffragettes. Miriam's faded green eyes stared in disbelief, and the wardress chuckled.

'You lot are becoming very popular, Twenty-three. It seems that there's been a lot of support for you amongst all the political parties. So the Home Secretary's ordered your early release.'

She tapped the side of Miriam's pint pot with her fingers, and instructed: 'Now make sure that you eats every bit of your porridge this morning. It's something you must be sure to do.'

'Why?' Miriam questioned; any appetite she might have had for the watery gruel having disappeared completely in the knowledge that in scant hours she would be free to eat anything that she might fancy.

'Well it's a belief among prisoners that if they leaves their last pot o' porridge uneaten, then they'll have to come back to finish it.' The woman grinned broadly. 'I know it's only superstition, Twenty-three, but strange to say I've seen it happen more than a few times – that when prisoners has left their porridge, they've come back in through the gates again before very long.'

She relocked the cell door, and for some minutes Miriam sat staring at the congealing grey mess in the pint pot. Then she smiled ruefully at her own suggestibility, and forced herself to eat every last spoonful of the gruel.

At midday another wardress came to escort Miriam to the reception block, where she found the other imprisoned suffragettes excitedly preparing for their release. Miriam was greeted like an old and trusted comrade, and she experienced a tremendous sense of bonding and solidarity with these other women, who like her had suffered for their cause. Many of the women expressed their regrets for Rosie Spiers's death, and a fleeting sadness clouded Miriam's mood. Then the excitement in the atmosphere lifted that momentary sadness from her, and she was able to observe philosophically, 'Poor Rosie's health was such that she was doomed to an early death. At least she died happy in the knowledge that she was fighting for our cause.' Her words were greeted with a murmuring of approving agreement.

Mrs Cobden-Sanderson came to Miriam and told her that the reason for the early release was because there was to be a by-election in Huddersfield, and the Liberal Government was anxious to win votes by appearing to be in favour of women's suffrage.

'There is a great deal of sympathy and support for us spreading throughout the country, my dear. The Tories, the Socialists and the Liberals are all anxious to win us over.'

Outside the prison gates a large crowd of suffragettes and supporters were waiting for the released prisoners, and amid scenes of wild enthusiasm, the women were borne off to a dinner given in their honour by Mrs Fawcett and the older non-militant suffragettes at the Savoy Hotel.

After the dinner Christabel Pankhurst addressed the gathering, to tell them that her mother and a band of helpers were already in Huddersfield campaigning against the government, and that she, Christabel, was going to that town tonight to join in the fight. Caught up in the general excitement, Miriam abandoned all thoughts of returning immediately to Redditch, and instead joined those among the released prisoners who had decided to travel to Huddersfield in company with Christabel Pankhurst.

She managed to find time to scribble and post brief letters to Emma Josceleyne and Laura Hughes, and then filled with all the zeal of the convert, hurried with her comrades to catch the train to the north.

Chapter Forty-Three

There were no carriages for the mourners at the funeral of Rosie Spiers. Only the glass-sided hearse drawn by a black-plumed black horse. Laura Hughes and several of her neighbours from Hill Street followed the hearse on foot. Rosie's parents were both ill in the Workhouse, and so did not come to the funeral. None of her other relatives were there, except for Tommy, who walked arm in arm with Laura, chuckling and excited by the sight of the resplendent plumed horse, and seemingly unaware that it was his sister being carried inside the hearse.

After the morning interment Laura had to change and go back to work at the laundry, leaving Tommy in the care of Maudie Emms.

'Well, you had a fine day for it, Laura,' one of her workmates greeted sympathetically. 'How are you feeling? Glad it's all over, I should think?'

Laura nodded, and although her sadness at losing her friend was deep, she found herself taking comfort because the young woman had had a decent burial, and was lying in her own grave plot.

'I'm becoming a regular Hill Streeter, aren't I?' she thought wryly. 'Placing so much importance on a respectable funeral.'

Her thoughts turned to the absent Miriam Josceleyne, and she mentally went back over the brief letter she had received from her explaining Miriam's reasons for going directly up to Huddersfield. The main reason being that Miriam considered the best epitaph she could offer to Rosie Spiers was to continue the fight for women's suffrage, and to lose no opportunity to carry the struggle

348

onwards. In her letter Miriam had made no mention of when she intended to return to Redditch, but had said that she would try to arrange for some financial support for Laura to continue the struggle to form a branch of the Union in Redditch.

'It seems as if the only thing that has any importance for Miriam now, is the movement,' Laura was forced to conclude. 'Perhaps she won't return to this town at all. Not now she is so involved with all the militants on a national level.'

Laura threw herself into her work, mauling, pounding, wringing the heavy, saturated blankets, and found that the hard physical effort acted as a salve for her loss of her friend, Rosie, and the apparent loss of Miriam. As the long hours passed Laura considered her own future, and found that she was firmly committed to continuing to care for Tommy Spiers. 'That shall be my epitaph for you, Rosie.' She smiled sadly. 'The welfare of your poor brother.'

She still intended to continue her efforts for the cause of women's suffrage. But now she found that her views about the methods she would use had undergone considerable alteration. 'I can no longer accept any financial help from Miriam,' she knew with absolute certainty. 'If I am to help these women to organise into a branch, then I have to be one of them in every sense. It would be hypocritical for me to urge them to make sacrifices, if all the time I was cocooned by Miriam's money. If the message I preach to poor working women is to carry any validity, then I must be one of them. Working as hard as they have to, and undergoing the same privations and hardships as they have to.'

The thought that some people might find this attitude to be merely quixotic posturing on her part, she was able to dismiss firmly. 'I know that I'm sincere in what I intend doing. So it doesn't matter what others may say or think.'

Laura became aware that the ostracised Bella Thomas, who was working across the trough from her own position, was weeping soundlessly, the tears running down her thickly-powdered cheeks. Pity for the woman's misery whelmed over her, and she leaned across to ask kindly,

'What is it? What's the matter?'

The woman's reddened eyes stared at her piteously.

'Is there anything I can do to help you?' Laura pressed gently.

Bella Thomas shook her head, then suddenly howled as if in agony and hurried from the washing room, her face buried in her hands.

Laura stared after her with concern. 'What's the matter with her?'

It was Letty Lewis who answered with a snort of derision: 'I expect it's that bloke of hers playing her up again. I'm buggered if I'd let my bloke get me in that state! I'd swing for the bastard first!'

As always in this town, there was someone who had heard gossip. And now another woman spoke up with an air of relish. 'You knows who her chap is doon't you? He's that foreign looking bugger with a funny name. Him who works at Ernie Field's shop down Fish Hill theer. From what I'se heard he's got his boots under young Emma Farr's bed.'

Letty Lewis was instantly intrigued. 'Emma Farr? Her as married old man Josceleyne?'

'That's her,' the woman confirmed with a broad grin. 'My neighbour's girl works as a maid for her. So it's gospel truth, because the young wench told her Mam all about it. Her said that her mistress was as bold as bloody brass about having that chap in her bed. Told the wenches that if anybody wanted to know about it, they was to say that the reason she's got him sharing her bed is because he's a bloody good shag!'

The other women shrieked with delighted laughter.

'Jasus, but she's the bold one, that Emma Josceleyne!' Bridget Gorman exclaimed admiringly. 'And good luck to her for being so!'

Laura heard the news with a sense of shock and concern. She realised that the women were referring to Harry Vivaldi, whom Miriam Josceleyne had told her that she strongly disapproved of. 'Does Miriam know, I wonder? No, she can't know of it. It will come as a terrible shock to her. What will she do when she finds out?' Even as

350

these thoughts raced through Laura's mind, she knew that she was powerless to warn her friend.

'I'll just have to hope that it won't upset her too much when she comes to hear of it,' she accepted, and concentrated once again on her work.

Chapter Forty-Four

Whistling tunefully Harry Vivaldi finished sweeping the shop floor and returned the broom to its cupboard. At the counter Ernie Field was totting up the day's takings, and shaking his head in apparent disgust.

Vivaldi grinned at his employer, and there was contempt in his eyes.

'Right then, Ernie, I'll be off.'

'You'm a bit early, aren't you?' the older man grumbled, and Vivaldi laughed.

'Now then, Ernie, I've got an important appointment, and I mustn't be late.'

Field clucked his tongue disapprovingly. 'That bloody 'ooman has got you running after her like a dog in heat.'

'Not a bad day today, was it?' the young man declared cheerfully. 'I earned a nice bit of commission with that Edison sale.'

His employer grudgingly conceded: 'It warn't too bad. But we needs to do a sight better, my bucko, if I'm to be able to afford to keep you on here.'

The implied threat did not cause Vivaldi any concern. For him at this time life was decidedly good. Although his employer had assumed that his appointment was with Emma Josceleyne, in fact the young man was going elsewhere. He was going to check on the progress made in preparing his new travelling van. Emma had finally agreed to finance him in setting up his business. Which was to be that of a travelling 'Talking Machine and Moving Picture Show'.

Now he smiled at the other man, and inwardly scoffed: 'I'll be taking the bread out of your mouth very soon, you miserable old bastard! So moan and whine at me while you've still got the chance.'

Aloud he asked: 'Are you thinking of visiting Bella tonight? Only you still owe me for the other night, don't you?'

Ernie Field scowled. 'Doon't worry, I aren't forgot I owes you.' Then he grumbled bitterly, 'It's turning out to be a dear game with your 'ooman. It's costing me a bloody fortune.'

Vivaldi's good humour did not falter. 'Now Ernie, I can't be blamed if you're so hungry for her, can I? I don't force you to come round to the house, do I? It's your own choice.'

'Well, I thought that being as I'm so regular, you could bring the price down a bit?' Field suggested.

For the first time in the conversation Vivaldi's swarthy handsome features frowned. 'How can I bring the price down, Ernie? Bella moans at me about you treating her so rough, so I have to buy her all sorts of bloody luxuries to shut her up. If you took your loving in the normal way, then perhaps I could bring the price down. But so long as you want special services from her, then the price has to stay the same.'

The other man only scowled silently, and Vivaldi took his Homburg hat and placed it at a rakish angle on his oiled hair.

'See you in the morning then, Ernie.'

He was walking through the door when the older man called him back. 'All right Harry. Tell Bella I'll be round later.'

Vivaldi grinned, and holding up his hand he rubbed his thumb and fingers together meaningfully.

'All right, all right, you greedy bugger.' Field swore, and reluctantly handed over some coins.

Vivaldi sauntered up Prospect Hill and through the town. Despite his outwardly jaunty air, he was experiencing some misgivings about telling Bella Thomas that Ernie Field would be visiting her later that night. His older mistress was becoming increasingly difficult to control, and on several occasions lately he had been forced to beat her brutally when she had tried to refuse to cater to Ernie Field's sexual needs. Up until now he had managed to keep Emma convinced that his relationship with Bella Thomas was purely philanthropic on his part. Although he was fairly confident that he was becoming the dominant partner in his affair with Emma, he knew the fiery young woman well enough to realise that if she ever found out that he was forcing Bella Thomas to prostitute herself with Field, then that would mean the ending of his relationship with Emma. Of course, the fact that recently he had been spending so many nights with Emma meant that Bella was certain that he was having an affair. But up to this point she had not offered any identification as to who his new lover was. He accepted that in a small town like this it could be only a matter of time before Bella would come to know that his new mistress was Emma Josceleyne. But he was hopeful that by the time Bella did find out, he would be so well entrenched with Emma that he could then leave Bella Thomas. He wanted above all else at this time to rid himself of his ageing mistress, but he still needed the money she earned at work and from Ernie Field to supplement his own inadequate wages.

By now he had reached his destination which was a collection of sheds and workshops behind the Royal Hotel in Market Place. In the largest shed which was like a warehouse with its large floorspace and high roof, a man was busily painting a long pantechnicon using flaring naphtha lamps to give him light to see by. Harry Vivaldi stood in the darkness outside the open double doors of the shed and stared greedily at his new acquisition. Against the dark green sides of the massive van the bright yellow letterings shone in the lamplight: 'Vivaldi's Moving Pictures and Talking Machines'.

Then he frowned and went quickly into the shed.

'Evenin',' the painter greeted.

'I thought I told you to keep this a secret?' Vivaldi challenged angrily.

The man stared at him in surprise, and retorted indignantly, 'I has kept it a bloody secret.'

'How can you say that, when you've got the bloody doors

open so that anybody can look in and see what you're doing?'

'I was just letting in a breath o' fresh air, that's all. The heat from these lamps strikes fumes off the paint and near chokes me. Them doors aren't bin open more nor a couple o' minutes,' the man explained.

'Well get them bloody shut right now!' Vivaldi snarled, and the man scowled surlily, but did as he was told.

'Will you have it done tonight?' Vivaldi wanted to know.

The painter nodded, then questioned in his turn: ' 'Ull you have me money tonight?'

Vivaldi scowled irritably. It was a sore point with him that although Emma Josceleyne was financing his new business, she retained full control of that finance. All bills were settled by her directly, and she did not allow him, Harry Vivaldi, to get his hands on any of the money at any point in the various transactions.

'If the work's been done to my satisfaction, then you'll get your money in the morning. You're to go to Cotswold House, on Church Green East, and ask for Mrs Josceleyne. She'll pay you. But I'll be checking the work first.'

The painter scowled resentfully. 'I'm a craftsman, Mr Vivaldi, not a bloody labourer. The work 'ull be first class like all my jobs.'

'You make sure that it is,' Vivaldi instructed arrogantly. 'Meet me here at seven o'clock tomorrow morning. I'll inspect what you've done then. And keep these bloody doors shut, and don't breathe a word to anybody about this job, or I'll see to it that you won't get any more jobs in this town. Understand?'

Despite his obvious resentment of this hectoring and aggressive manner, the workman nodded agreement.

Vivaldi took a last lingering look at the gleaming pantechnicon, then smiling with satisfaction he left the shed.

Outside the Royal Hotel he paused momentarily, debating whether or not to go into its brightly lit interior for a drink. Then decided against it. 'I'd best get on home first and have a bite to eat, and tell Bella that Ernie Field is coming round to see her tonight.' ·

He grinned happily. Emma Josceleyne was expecting him later, but if he hurried he would still have time for a few drinks before he went to Cotswold House. Although Harry Vivaldi lusted almost constantly for the young widow, still he needed the freedom to visit public houses and drink and talk in convivial company. At this present time he was enjoying the best of both worlds – money enough for his convivial drinking, and nights of sexual ecstasy with his new mistress. He gusted a sigh of utter satisfaction.

'And the cream on the cake is going to be my new business.' He felt like hugging himself with delight. 'Life couldn't be better, could it?'

His euphoria was diminished however when he reached his house in George Street and found it in darkness. He fumbled his way into the room and lit a lucifer match, then emitted a sharp cry and let the burning match fall from his fingers.

'What the bloody hell are you sitting here in the dark for? You gave me a real shock,' he demanded irately, and striking another lucifer turned the wall tap and lit the gasjet. Then he swung to confront Bella Thomas, who was sitting on the broken-backed chair at the side of the fireless grate.

'What in Hell's the matter with you? Why aren't you lit the fire? And where's my supper?'

She made no answer, only stared at him with eyes that were wild and glaring in the grotesquely painted mask of her face.

He began to feel slightly unnerved by her strangeness, and blustered to hide this: 'Get off your arse and get a fire lit. It's cold in here, and Ernie Field is calling later.'

She shook her head and told him jerkily, 'I'm not having anything more to do with him! I've had enough of it! I can't do it any more!'

'Don't talk so bloody stupid!' he told her harshly. 'He's coming here tonight, and you'll be nice to him!'

Again her frizzed mass of hair swung to and fro. 'I can't! I can't stand what he does to me any more!'

Vivaldi's breath hissed impatiently between his clenched

teeth, and he forced himself to speak in a gentler tone. 'Look Bella, just do it tonight. Just do it tonight for my sake!'

She laughed bitterly. 'For your sake? Do it for your fuckin' sake? And where 'ull you be while that bastard is tearing and clawing at me like a bloody mad animal?' Her voice rose shrilly. 'You'll be shaggin' your bloody fancy woman, won't you? While that dirty bastard is ramming himself up my arse, you'll be in bed with your bloody fancy woman. That's where you'll be.'

She was shrieking hysterically now, and fearful of his formidable neighbour's possible reaction to the noise, Vivaldi hissed savagely: 'Shut your bloody rattle, or I'll give you the biggest hiding you've ever had.'

'You can do what you like, but I'm telling you now that I'm not having anything more to do with Ernie Field. And you'd better pack it in with your bloody fancy woman as well.'

Her voice reverberated in his ears, and the next instant came the heavy pounding on the thin partition wall and the furious shouting of his neighbour.

Vivaldi's handsome features became a twisted snarl of mingled fear and fury and he hurled himself at the woman, his hands grabbing her throat, squeezing and tightening as she fought to free herself, choking her shrieks into a gurgling squeal that gradually diminished and died away. He stared into her bulging eyes and saw her tongue protuding from the scarlet gash of her mouth, and in a sudden panic he released her and let her sag to the floor, where she lay coughing and gasping liquidly to draw breath.

He stood panting hoarsely, staring down at her, and kept on repeating in jerky utterance: 'Now just shut up. Now just shut up. Now just shut up.'

Slowly her coughing and gasping eased and she was able to draw sufficient breath to fill her straining lungs.

Vivaldi knelt down and gripped her meaty shoulders, then shook her hard. 'Ernie Field is coming here tonight. And you'll be nice to him. Understand? Do you understand?'

Terrified by the savagery of his assault, she nodded dumbly, and in his turn he nodded.

'Right then, make sure that you are nice to him. Or it'll go hard with you tomorrow. That's a promise that is.'

He rose to his feet and straightened his rumpled clothing. Then combed his hair and replaced his Homburg at its rakish angle.

'I'm going now, but I'll be back tomorrow. Remember what I've told you.'

The woman remained crouching on her knees, wincing with pain as her fingers explored her badly bruised throat, tears falling from her eyes. 'I can't stand it any more!' she moaned brokenly. 'I can't stand it any more! I can't stand it any more!'

Chapter Forty-Five

The big wall-clock whirred noisily and then sonorously chimed the morning hour of six. Emma Josceleyne turned on her side and moved to cuddle the naked body of her lover. As her fingers explored his warm, smooth skin her hunger for him swiftly mounted and her hand moved to stroke his long, hard manhood and to cup and fondle the full, soft pouch beneath it. She felt him stir and heard his throaty chuckle, then he turned to her and crushed her body to him, and his mouth came seeking hers. When he tried to push her on to her back she resisted.

'No, let me do it to you this time.'

He allowed her to move on top of him, his hands caressing the soft silkiness of her thighs and he moaned as she took his manhood and guided it into her body. As she began to move upon him her own excitement burgeoned into a raging lust, and her gasping moaning mingled with his, and she felt his hands squeezing her swollen breasts and taut nipples and she cried out as those hard firm hands moved to clutch her buttocks and ram her ever harder down upon him. The bed creaked and rocked under the fury of their lovemaking and then she climaxed explosively and collapsed upon his body, and their juices mingled, as the thudding of their hearts gradually slowed in concert.

She smiled wryly and lifted herself from his supine body.

'I reckon you'se turned me into a nymphomaniac.'

He chuckled and told her huskily, 'I reckon it's the other way around, honey. I can't get enough of you, can I?' He fumbled in the darkness to find his packet of cigarettes and struck a match to light one for each of them.

Emma stared as the flare of light briefly illuminated his swarthy features, and her throat tightened as she thought how handsome he was. Warily she examined her own feelings, and was drawn to a disquieting conclusion. 'I think I've fallen in love with the bugger!' The thought sent a fleeting wave of angry resentment coursing through her. 'That was the last thing that I wanted to happen to me.' Then, as was occurring increasingly of late, the gnawing of jealousy came to torment her. 'And he's still sharing a house with that old cow, isn't he?'

Although Emma had concluded and accepted the fact that despite his denials Bella Thomas had been in fact his mistress, she would not allow herself to believe that her lover was still living as man and wife with the other woman. She clung fiercely to this self-imposed belief despite the gossip concerning Harry Vivaldi and Bella Thomas which Mrs Elwood had garnered for her from a myriad of sources. It was essential for her own peace of mind that she must believe his story that he was only allowing Bella Thomas to remain at his house out of pity, and that there was now no sexual relationship between them. Nevertheless Emma was beginning to find that the continued presence of Bella Thomas in her lover's life was becoming increasingly intolerable. Now she broached the subject.

'How much longer are you going to keep Bella Thomas in your house?'

Harry Vivaldi grinned in the darkness. Satisfaction surged through him at this sign that the young widow was becoming so possessive of him. Aloud he spoke with a tone of sober concern: 'I just don't know, honey. She's got nowhere to go, and she hardly earns enough money to keep herself with. I can't find the heart to throw her out on to the street. God only knows what would become of her, if I did.'

An idea which had been building in Emma's mind now sprang into full flower. 'You don't have to throw her out on to the street. She could stay there, and you could leave.'

A sensation of pure exultation flooded through Harry

Vivaldi. 'I've done it! I've won! I've got her!' he crowed silently.

He deliberately remained silent, hoping to goad his mistress into committing herself further. The stratagem worked.

'Well, why couldn't you do that? Why couldn't you let her stay there, and leave yourself?' Emma demanded impatiently.

He sighed with apparent regret. 'There's nothing I'd like more, honey. But you know well that at present all my money is going to be needed to get the business established. I just can't afford to take another house and furnish it.'

Now Emma felt driven. It was a major facet of her character that when she had determined to achieve something, any obstacle to that achievement would only increase her determination and cause her to throw all caution to the winds, and she would act without giving any real thought to the eventual consequences.

'You don't have to take another house, do you? There's plenty of spare rooms here. You can move into one of them. You can be a paying guest in this house.'

The man cheered silently in victory. But still his finely honed instincts made him advance cautiously. 'That would be wonderful,' he said fervently. 'But how about what people might say? They'd gossip and bad-mouth us all over the town.'

'Phoo! Let 'um! I couldn't care less!' Emma declared forcefully.

Still Vivaldi obeyed the promptings of instinct. 'Then there's Miss Miriam to think about, honey. She doesn't like me, I can tell. And I'm sure that she wouldn't accept me staying here in her family's old home.'

Now it was Emma's turn to hesitate. Memories raced through her mind. Resentful memories that she unconsciously selected out of their true context. 'Miriam took Johnny Purvis away from me, didn't she?' The thought rankled bitterly. 'He should have been mine, but she took him from me. Well she's not going to stop me from having Harry.'

Aloud Emma gritted out her determination: 'This house is mine now, Harry. I know that it's Miss Miriam's old family home. But now it belongs to me, and I paid a bloody high price for it. It's me who decides who lives here. And if Miss Miriam objects to you, then she'll just have to go and find somewhere else to live.'

'I love you, honey,' he whispered, and kissed her passionately, then moved on top of her, and parted her thighs, and thrust deeply into her hot, welcoming moistness.

Chapter Forty-Six

It was ten minutes to seven when Harry Vivaldi left Cotswold House. But on this morning there was a difference in his departure. Instead of going cautiously out of the back way, he left by the front door and sauntered in full view of any passer-by out of the front gate. Vivaldi's elation soared and he whistled happily as he strolled toward the yard behind the Royal Hotel. He and Emma Josceleyne had agreed that he would move his belongings into Cotswold House during the evening of the following day. Admittedly he experienced misgivings when he thought of Bella Thomas's likely reaction to his news, but he thrust those unpleasant thoughts from his mind, and concentrated on all the good things to come. He decided that he would not return to George Street that morning, but would instead get shaved in one of the early opening barber's shops, and take breakfast in a public house before going to his work. But first he was going to inspect his pantechnicon.

The painter was waiting outside the big shed, and dourly he greeted him.

'It's all done, Mister. And it's a good job. A real craftsman's job.'

Vivaldi smiled brilliantly at the other man. This morning, dull and overcast though it was, the painter's dourness could do nothing to diminish his sense of happiness and well being. He gave the van a cursory inspection, then nodded genially. 'Yes, it looks all right to me. Go over to Cotswold House any time after nine o'clock and collect your money. And mind, keep quiet about what you've done here.'

The man nodded, and walked away.

Later, shaved and freshly pomaded, his belly comfortably replete with ham and eggs, coffee and brandy, Harry Vivaldi came jovially into his employer's shop.

Ernie Field's thin face was thunderous, and the younger man spread his arms apologetically. 'I'm only two minutes past my time, Ernie. There's no call for you to glare at me so.'

'Never mind the bloody time!' the other man snapped curtly. 'Just put your hand in your pocket and fetch out my money!'

Vivaldi's dark eyes widened in surprise. 'What do you mean?'

'Exactly what I said, fetch out my money and hand it over.'

Vivaldi shook his head in bafflement. 'What's up, Ernie?'

'I'll tell you what's up, you fly bastard!' the older man suddenly raged violently. 'I doon't like being made a cunt out on! That's what's up!'

Again the younger man exclaimed in bewilderment: 'I don't know what you mean, Ernie. God's truth, I don't.'

Field realised that his employee's protestations were genuine, and he said in a lower tone, 'Bella warn't there, was she. There was no light in the windows, and I couldn't get any answer.'

'Perhaps she'd fallen asleep,' Vivaldi offered.

'Oh no!' Field was very definite. 'She couldn't have slept through the hammering I give the bloody door. It even fetched that soddin' neighbour o' yours out. He was very nasty about it, as well, I can tell you.' Field's narrow chest puffed out like a poulter pigeon as he blustered. 'It's a good job for him that I didn't want people to know I was theer, or I'd have give him a smack in the gob in double quick time. Cheeky, big-mouthed bugger that he is.'

Harry Vivaldi was genuinely mystified. 'I don't understand it, Ernie. I left her there waiting for you to come. She was going to light the fire and get ready for you. I can't understand where she might have gone.'

'It looks to me as if her's buggered off and left you.

Her's said a couple of times to me that if you didn't start treating her better then she 'ud clear off. That's what her's done, I'll bet. Buggered off!' Field growled, 'So you'd better give me my money back.'

'I can't, Ernie. I've spent it,' Vivaldi told him nervously. Then hastened to assure him. 'But don't worry, I'll see that this gets sorted out in double quick time. I'm really sorry about this, Ernie. Really I am. But it's no fault of mine. Honestly it aren't. If she has gone off in a huff, then she'll soon come back. She always does.'

For some moments the shopkeeper made no reply, only glared angrily. Then eventually he accepted with apparent reluctance. 'All right then, Harry. Perhaps you can't be blamed for it. But it's discommoded me, aren't it. Discommoded me very badly.'

Harry Vivaldi made no reply but inwardly promised Bella Thomas: 'I'll be teaching you a lesson for acting up like this, you fat cow.'

At midday Vivaldi decided to forgo his normal refreshment and instead go to the Steam Laundry and see if Bella Thomas was there. But when he arrived there the foreman told him that she had not come to work that day. Harry Vivaldi heard his news with mixed feelings. Her absence from work might mean that she had indeed left the town to return to her husband in Birmingham. The young man welcomed her departure, but at the same time deplored it, because it meant that he would now have to repay Ernie Field his money. 'I'd better check to see if the cow is at home,' he decided, and made his way to George Street.

The door was locked and the curtains were open. Harry Vivaldi peered through the cracked dirty window pane and saw that the room was empty. He unlocked the door and went in. A cursory check showed that nothing had been taken, and Bella's coat was still hanging on the back of the door. A sense of foreboding swept over the young man, and he called up the stairs.

'Bella? Bella, are you up there?'

There was no reply, and Vivaldi's sense of foreboding intensified. Breathing hard he went up the narrow stairs and as he saw into the bedroom cried out in sudden frightened shock. Bella Thomas was sprawled on her back upon the bed. Her eyes were open and bulging, her face a mask of frozen horror. Dark stains covered her mouth and chin and clutched in her dead hand was a wine bottle from which a dark liquid had leaked to saturate the blanket beneath.

Walking on tiptoe as if he feared to make any noise, his own eyes wide in horror, Vivaldi moved to the side of the bed and bent to sniff the dark liquid. He recognised its familiar odour. It was phenol, carbolic acid. A poison that was widely used for domestic purposes, and which caused many accidental and suicidal deaths.

Panic began to shriek in Vivaldi's brain. 'She's bloody killed herself! Drunk it to do herself in!'

He stumbled back down the stairs, and leaned his sweat-beaded forehead against the greasy stained wall, while he gagged helplessly with nausea.

'I'll get blamed for this!' The thought reverberated through his skull. 'I'll get blamed for this!'

He began to shiver and a wave of giddiness forced him to slump down upon the broken backed chair. 'I'll get blamed for this! I'll get blamed for this!' The thought was a merciless instrument of torture. 'I'll get blamed for this!'

He opened his mouth and a torrent of invective poured from it directed against the dead woman. The outpouring of hate and anger served to dull the sharp edges of the panic that was threatening to overwhelm him, and slowly his dominant instinct for self-preservation began to assert itself once more.

'Now think, Harry!' he exhorted himself desperately. 'Think! Think! Think!'

Gradually his brain became able to concentrate and evaluate. He knew that an inquest and post-mortem examination would undoubtedly reveal the physical abuse that both he and Ernie Field had inflicted on her. He knew that Ernie Field would try to lay all blame for Bella's physical abuse and subsequent suicide on him. He knew that if Emma should come to know of this abuse, then she would sever her relationship with him. He knew also the impossibility of trying to keep that knowledge from Emma if there was an inquest and post-mortem exaination. He concluded therefore that he must keep Bella Thomas's death hidden. The more he pondered this conclusion, the more convinced he became that it was the only course of action that was possible for him.

'Ernie already thinks that Bella might have run off from me. So I'll have no problem in convincing him that she's done that. And Emma will believe it when I tell her that Bella's gone back to her husband after I told her about me moving to live in Cotswold House.' In a bizarre way, Harry Vivaldi began to feel almost light-hearted.

'All I've got to do, is to get rid of her body.'

He grinned mirthlessly. 'Pity she's so bloody fat! I'll not be able to carry her very far, perhaps not even lift her off the bed.'

For a moment his new-found resolution threatened to dissolve into craven panic, but he fought for self-control, and reiterated over and over again. 'I'll manage it! I'll manage it! I'll manage it! I'll manage it!'

He forced himself to plan his immediate actions, and deliberately put the question of disposing of Bella Thomas's body into the background.

'I'll deal with that when I have to. The first thing is to convince Ernie that Bella's run off.'

Now, almost miraculously, Harry Vivaldi found that his confidence had returned in full measure, and he was able to draw on all his reserves of natural cunning to make his plans. He searched for and found a shopping list that Bella Thomas had written out ready for the weekend, and copying her writing style, he carefully composed a note addressed to himself and signed with her name.

He meticulously checked his appearance in the mottled looking-glass, and then left the house, locking the door securely behind him.

By the time he had reached the shop, his vanity had helped to convince him that he could not fail, and he grinned ruefully as he told the waiting Ernie Field: 'You were right, Ernie. The bloody cow has run off. Just read this!'

His employer's thin face looked glum when he heard this news, but as he scanned the note his expression became a mingling of apprehension and anger.

'Her's got a bloody cheek!' he blustered in protest. 'Blaming me for it! I never served her that bad! She liked what I did to her!'

Vivaldi was jeering inwardly as he spread his hands and assured his employer: 'I expect she really does like what you do to her, Ernie. But you know what a loony she can be at times!'

He deftly lifted the note from the other man's grasp, and folded it carefully before placing it in his waistcoat pocket.

'I think I'll keep this as a souvenir.'

Ernie Field glared suspiciously. 'Why? Why bother to keep it?'

Harry Vivaldi returned the glare with a look of wide-eyed innocence. 'Well, it's proof that it wasn't my treatment of her that drove her to run away.'

The older man's suspicious glare became tinged with wariness. Then Vivaldi shrugged. 'Nobody's going to ask why she's buggered off anyway, Ernie. She hadn't got any friends hereabouts, had she? No one will be the least bit interested in where she's gone, or why. Just think how many people run away on any day of the week. There must be thousands of them do it. I'll never show this note to anybody, so don't worry what it says about you.'

Ernie Field's expression gradually relaxed, and eventually he also shrugged and nodded. 'You're right, Harry. Nobody 'ull give a bugger about her.' He sighed regretfully. 'I hopes she comes back sometime though. I really enjoyed shagging her.' Then he scowled and added, 'Don't forget that you owes me that money again, now that she's buggered off, 'ull you?'

Vivaldi nodded wryly. 'I won't forget, Ernie. How could I, when you won't let me?'

Later that day Ernie Field announced that he had urgent business to attend to in Birmingham. 'If I'm not back then close up at half-past eight,' he instructed. 'And doon't try sneaking off any earlier.'

Vivaldi watched his employer leave and sighed with heartfelt relief. He was finding it very difficult to maintain the facade of normality, tormented as he was by the knowledge of Bella Thomas's body lying in the mean bedroom in George Street.

'Once I've got her out of the way, then I'll be all right,' he assured himself. 'I'll be able to relax then.'

In between serving customers he devoted all his attention to the problem of disposing of the corpse. It was the sheer physical bulk of the dead woman that was the major difficulty. 'She's too heavy for me to carry. I reckon I'll have to cut her up.'

The gory vision that sprang into his imagination caused him instant queasiness, and for a brief instant the impulse to just run away coursed through him. But that impulse was fleeting. He knew that such a reaction would only bring ruin on to his head. He summoned all his determination. 'For once in your life, Harry boy, you've got to stick at it. You're on the brink of getting everything you ever wanted in life. All you've got to do is to keep your nerve and stick at it.'

He wandered to the door and opened it, and a chill gust of air sent a shiver through him. He fervently blessed this sudden onset of much colder weather. 'Thank Christ it's turning frosty! It'll keep Bella from stinking the place out.'

He paced restlessly around and around the shop floor, considering and dismissing solutions to his problems of disposal and concealment. A flash of grim gallows humour caused him to smile bleakly. 'Pity there aren't a cellar at home.'

He came to an abrupt standstill. There might not be a cellar, but there was a stone-flagged floor in the cramped downstairs room, and beneath those stone flags there might well be only hard packed earth. He wanted to rush home straightaway and check what lay beneath the stone-flagged floor. But his native cunning warned against doing anything which might be considered unusual, such as closing the shop at this early hour.

With nagging impatience he forced himself to wait until work was over for the day. Then he hurried back to

George Street. His neighbour's slatternly wife was talking to another woman at the door of the communal wash-house, and he lifted his Homburg and smiled charmingly at them.

'Turned cold, hasn't it, ladies?'

They both smiled and simpered back at him. For the women in the neighbouring tenements Harry Vivaldi was a glamorous figure, whose never-failing gallant manner towards them caused their hearts to flutter, and their husbands' fists to clench.

'Mr Vivaldi?' His neighbour's wife came towards him. 'I wanted to have a word wi' your Missus. What time's she coming back from work?'

Vivaldi's heart seemed to stop, and the breath caught in his throat. For a moment he kept his face turned downwards towards the door lock, and fumbled with his key against it. Then, he forced a polite smile to his suddenly parched lips, and told the woman: 'I'm not expecting her back today, Mrs Croxall.'

Her grimy features frowned curiously. 'Why not?'

He grimaced with mock sadness, and shrugged. 'To tell you the truth, I think Bella's left me. We haven't been getting on very well lately. And she's been saying that she wanted to get away for a while and be by herself.'

Both women hissed in gratified acknowledgement at being given such a tasty piece of gossip which they would later retail with many embellishments.

'I expect you heard Bella and me quarrelling the other night, Mrs Croxall. I think that that was the last straw for both of us really,' he informed with an air of regretful sadness. 'Naturally, I'm hoping that she'll come back, but . . .' He shrugged and spread his arms as if beseeching their understanding, and their frowsty heads nodded vigorously.

'Well, I shouldn't let it get you down too much, Mr Vivaldi,' the second woman sympathised. 'Her 'ull more nor likely come back. I mean to say, every couple has their ups and downs, doon't they?' She grimaced displaying broken, blackened teeth. 'I know me and my old man does. You might have heard us gooing at it?'

370

'I should reckon the whole o' bloody George Street has heard you and your old man gooing at it, Ida,' Mrs Croxall chuckled grimly.

Again Harry Vivaldi tipped his hat to the women. 'Now, if you'll excuse me, ladies. I've got something to attend to.'

'That's all right, Mr Vivaldi. You must get on with it.' The second woman looked at him with an inviting expression in her eyes. 'If you finds that you needs a bit of housework doing, then you just tell me, and I'll see to it for you.'

'That's very kind of you.' He smiled gratefully.

'It's nothing, my duck,' she assured fervently. 'Only being a good neighbour, that's all.'

Still thanking her profusely he went into his house and closed the door behind him with a sigh of relief. Then he moved quickly, clearing the sparse articles of furniture, and rolling back the threadbare, dirty matting so as to uncover a section of the stone slabs of the floor. They were uneven, several deeply cracked, and there were spaces between some of them, which enabled him to use a knife to scrape away the rotted mortar and impacted earth, and lever a piece of slab upwards. Feverishly he dug at the exposed ground with his knife, and exclaimed with relief when he found that the blade penetrated the clay and earth with comparative ease.

Then he replaced the matting and furniture, washed his hands in the wooden bucket of water by the side of the firegrate, and crept quietly upstairs. A quick glance showed him that Bella Thomas's body was as he had left it. Her returned downstairs, and again went out of the house, carefully locking the door behind him, thankful to find that his neighbours had disappeared.

As he strolled back towards the town centre he found that he was feeling relatively calm and relaxed, and his confidence burgeoned as he remembered how the two women had received his news of Bella's departure. 'They didn't suspect a damn thing, did they? Just accepted it as if it was the most natural thing in the world. But then so it is a natural thing, isn't it? Men and women run off every day, don't they? Why should anybody think that Bella's running away is suspicious?'

His certainty that he was going to succeed in his plan hardened. 'A bit of digging, that's all that it needs, and then I can relax and enjoy life.' He smiled with satisfaction. 'By this time tomorrow, it'll be all over and done with, and I'll not have a single thing to worry about.'

He started to make a mental inventory of his requirements. 'I'll need a spade, and some sacks for any dirt left over. There's no need for me to cut Bella up now. Just so long as I remember to slit her belly so she'll lie flatter. And I'll need a bag of quicklime to stop her smelling.'

As he walked onwards his confidence soared and his step became noticeably jauntier.

Chapter Forty-Seven

Miriam Josceleyne returned from Huddersfield one cold, raw evening in the second week of December. From the railway station she went directly to Hill Street to find Laura Hughes preparing a sparse supper for herself and Tommy Spiers. The women greeted each other affectionately, and then sat for some considerable time facing each other across the well-scrubbed table, while Miriam related her adventures.

Laura found herself marvelling at the changes she discerned in her friend. There was a new vivacity and confidence exuding from the older woman, and even her frail body seemed somehow to have become stronger. Miriam was bubbling with plans for the coming months. On February 13th of the coming year the Women's Social and Political Union were to convene a 'Women's Parliament' at Caxton Hall in London, to consider the provisions of the King's Speech, which would be read in the national Parliament on the opening day of the session on the 12th of February.

'You and I shall attend as the delegates from the Redditch branch, my dear,' she informed Laura. 'So there's much to be done before then. We must immediately set about and get our Redditch branch fully organised. I'll have leaflets printed tomorrow to advertise a meeting in the Public Hall. Some of our leaders have agreed to come and address the meeting.' She laughed excitedly, her cheeks glowing, and she looked like a young girl in the dull light of the oil-lamp. Then she noticed the constraint in Laura's manner, and questioned: 'What is it,

Laura? Do you no longer have interest in the cause?'

'Oh of course I do.' Laura drew a deep breath. 'But my circumstances have altered now, Miriam.' She went on to explain what she had resolved to do. Which was not to live on Miriam's money any longer. But to support herself and Tommy Spiers by her own efforts. She further explained her reasoning, and Miriam Josceleyne listened without attempting to interrupt, and when the younger woman had finished speaking, remained silent while she pondered on what she had been told.

Eventually she nodded, and said warmly: 'Of course I understand, and accept what you wish to do, my dear. But you must promise me, that if you are in need, then you will not hesitate to let me help you financially.'

Laura agreed gratefully. 'I shall still be at your side in our work in Redditch, Miriam. You may be sure of that.'

'Good. Now I must go home and see Emma and Mrs Elwood,' Miriam announced briskly, and saw Laura frown uncomfortably.

'What is it, Laura? Has something happened at Cotswold House? Emma and Mrs Elwood are all right, aren't they?'

'Oh yes, I'm sure that they are both very well,' Laura hastened to reassure her friend.

'Then what is it?' Miriam insisted on knowing, and reluctantly Laura told her what the gossips at the laundry were saying concerning Emma and Harry Vivaldi.

'Apparently the woman he was living with has left him, and now to all intents and purposes he lives at Cotswold House.'

'And Emma is his mistress?' Miriam looked very troubled as she sought clarification.

Laura nodded unhappily. 'So they are saying, Miriam.'

The older woman shook her head. 'The little fool!'

'But they do say also that Harry Vivaldi is a very charming man,' Laura said trying to give some comfort.

'That's as maybe. Personally I've always disliked and distrusted him. I think he's a rogue!' Miriam's thin features were grim. 'I'll have to go, Laura. I must speak with Emma myself and find out the truth of the matter.'

She took up her small reticule and made her way to Cotswold House.

It was Rebecca, the pert-faced maid who answered to her ringing.

'Why, Miss Miriam, you'm come back,' the girl exclaimed.

'Where's your Mistress?' Miriam asked brusquely, too disturbed in her mind to bother with any pleasantries.

'Her's in the drawing room, Miss Miriam.'

Emma was sitting in one of the large, plush velvet armchairs at the side of the glowing fire. Dressed in a dark green gown, her chestnut hair hanging loose, she was very beautiful. She stared at Miriam Josceleyne's grim face as the older woman entered the room, and her expression became sullenly defiant.

'I see you've heard then, Miriam. I can tell by the sour look.'

'It's true then is it Emma? Harry Vivaldi is living here in this house, and you are his mistress?' It was more statement than question.

The young woman nodded slowly, and the lamplight shimmered on her glossy flowing hair.

'Oh Emma, how foolish you are,' Miriam uttered sadly, and the young woman instantly flared back at her.

'How am I foolish? Harry loves me, and I love him. We're very happy together.'

'The man is a rogue, Emma!' Miriam Josceleyne exclaimed heatedly.

'Don't you becall him,' Emma spat out, and her face became cruel. 'You're just jealous because I've got someone who loves me, and you've got no one. You're just a frustrated old maid!'

'That isn't true, Emma,' Miriam protested. 'I'm not jealous, and I do want you to have someone to love you. But not Harry Vivaldi! He's no good!'

'You doon't even know him,' the younger woman snarled. 'And how can you say that you wants me to have somebody to love me? You wouldn't let me have Johnny Purvis, 'ud you?'

375

Miriam stared in shock. 'I don't know what you mean!' she uttered shakenly. 'What was John Purvis to you?'

'He could have been everything if you hadn't took him from me!' Emma snarled viciously.

Miriam fought to recover from the shock of the accusation. 'John Purvis has got nothing to do with his present situation,' she stated quietly. 'We're talking about Harry Vivaldi. I cannot remain living here in this house with that man under this roof.'

'Then you can just bugger off!' Emma shouted. 'Because here he is, and here he stays.'

'Very well.' Miriam was outwardly icy calm, but inwardly felt grief-stricken. 'I'll leave directly. I shall send for my belongings.'

'Suit yourself!' Emma tossed her head petulantly, and watched Miriam walk out of the room, and out of the house, without saying another word.

It was only when she heard the front door close behind the older woman, that Emma's black eyes suddenly brimmed with tears, and she muttered, 'I'm sorry for what I said, Miss Miriam. But I can't give Harry up now! I can't live without him!'

Outside in the dank cold air Miriam walked back towards Hill Street. A heartache that she had believed had ceased to torment her, had been cruelly resurrected by Emma's words. But she summoned all her new-found strength of purpose to combat her pain. With that pain came the added sorrow of the rift with Emma, but she realised the hopelessness of trying to heal that rift while the younger woman was so deeply infatuated with Harry Vivaldi. 'It will just have to wait until such time as Emma sees for herself what a worthless man he is!'

A sob broke from her lips. 'Why couldn't it have all been different? Why couldn't I have found happiness with Johnny Purvis?'

She steeled herself to think of other matters. 'I'll stay with Laura tonight, and find accommodation for myself tomorrow.'

As she passed in front of the Unicorn Inn she heard the sounds of loud raucous singing coming from the Tap Room.

> *'For we are the boys of the Bulldog Breed.*
> *Who made Old Ennnggllannnd Freeeee . . .'*

Harry Vivaldi roared out the closing words of the song, and then laughed hugely, and invited his drinking cronies: 'Come on, lads. See them up and have another. The night's still young, aren't it?'

He accepted the plaudits of his drunken companions with a bow, and his white teeth glistened in his swarthy, beer-flushed face, as he told the landlord: 'That's it, Gaffer, fill 'um up.'

While he waited for his replenished drink he thought with relish of his good fortune. His beautiful mistress was waiting for him, in his new living quarters. His pantechnicon and horses were waiting in their stables. His stock of talking machines were waiting for him in the house in George Street, which he had persuaded Emma to continue to rent for use as storage space for his new stock in trade.

He grinned blearily and lifted his brimming glass. 'Here lads, I'll give you a toast! To absent friends!'

They cheered while he drained the glass, and he smiled inwardly. 'But you're not really absent, are you Bella? You're waiting for me in George Street as well, aren't you?' His mouth opened slackly and inside himself he roared with laughter. 'I've finally got you planted exactly where I want you, haven't I? You're the quietest woman in the town.'

Away over on the opposite side of the railway bridge in the large house on the lower slopes of Red Lane, Cleopatra Dolton laid aside her pen, used a large sheet of blotting paper to dry the freshly written columns of figures, sighed and rose from her chair.

She went through the house checking that all the doors and windows were secured and then went slowly upstairs to her bedroom. She undressed in the darkness and lay down in her bed, shivering slightly as the cold sheets enfolded her nakedness. Her thoughts ranged haphazardly. Images of her sons came and went in her mind. She was becoming very rich, but feeling an ever-deepening loneliness as time passed. For a brief moment she wondered if she should accept the love that Ozzie Clarke offered her. But then shook her head.

'No, he's not for me. Not as a husband.'

Sleep slowly came, and with it troubled dreams in which she wandered through veiling mists seeking for someone whom she could not in her dream remember.

In the railway station the last train of the night came rumbling and clanking to a standstill, snorting out clouds of black smoke and hissing steam. A few passengers alighted, among them a tall strong-bodied man, who walked with a military erectness. Johnny Purvis had come home again to Redditch.

THE SUMMER OF THE
FANCY MAN

Sara Fraser

In a quiet Worcestershire town in 1902, the return from
the Boer War of dashing, handsome and newly rich
Johnny Purvis has a devastating effect on the lives of
three very different women . . .

CLEOPATRA DOLTON

Beautiful and intelligent, her life is made miserable by the
violence of her drunkard husband.

MIRIAM JOSCELEYNE

At the mercy of her invalid father and penny-pinching
brother, she is reconciling herself to a dull life as a
spinster.

EMMA FARR

A spirited girl from the slums, she has set her sights on
being more than a maid. And if that means manipulating
her employers, then so be it . . .

Into each of their lives comes a man who can help them
achieve their dreams. And at the dawning of the
Edwardian era, the town will be rife with rumours and
scandal, and destinies changed forever.